THE FINAL ACT OF DAPHNE DEVINE

SYD MOORE

MAGPIE
BOOKS

A Magpie Book

First published by Magpie,
an imprint of Oneworld Publications Ltd, 2026

A CIP record for this title is available from the British Library

ISBN 978-0-86154-164-5
eISBN 978-0-86154-165-2

Typeset in Dante by Hewer Text UK Ltd, Edinburgh
Printed and bound in Great Britain by Clays Ltd, Elcograf S.p.A

The authorised representative in the EEA is eucomply OÜ,
Pärnu mnt 139b–14, 11317 Tallinn, Estonia
(email: hello@eucompliancepartner.com / phone: +33757690241)

Oneworld Publications Ltd
10 Bloomsbury Street
London WC1B 3SR
England

This book is dedicated to Andrée de Jongh
and all those who worked on the Comet Line.

I

CHAPTER ONE

Close to midnight, 30th April 1941

A waning moon. Gibbous. Two hours after nautical twilight.

Mist lifts in gauzy veils from the surface of the water.

Oars dip and rise, dip and rise.

So often, the sound has calmed her, made her relax into the gentle rock and tilt of a pleasure boat, give herself over to the warmth of the sunshine. But tonight, Daphne Devine tenses with every single splash.

They are too loud.

Too loud.

Calm now. Come on. Don't dwell on it. Think about something else.

As she looks down, the air coats her cheeks. Her hair is heavy with moisture and chill to the touch. This is no pleasure.

Jack grunts with the effort of rowing.

Also too loud.

She holds her breath steady and fixes her eyes on the approaching shore.

Behind her, the alps tower, hazily black in the night. Past her right shoulder: danger. Austria has embraced the Nazi storm. Beyond her left, Switzerland. Neutrality. Safety. And she is leaving it behind.

There is, within her, a temptation to wave at the receding Santis peak, under whose watchful regard she has made her way to Lake Constance. However, the action – the sight of it decreasing – she knows, might well spark panic. Resisting, she decides she shall not gaze upon it until this is over.

She shall not gaze upon it again.

The idea of turning back is fully there in the front of her mind. Never before has she faced such danger as that which lies ahead. The thought of what she must do is daunting: her most perilous mission yet. Though it sounds so easy – deliver the grimoire to a bookseller in Augsburg, then leave as quickly as possible.

She could have refused the task – God knows the damn thing has almost taken her life already – but there is too much at stake. The war has spread like a cancer across Europe: Greece and Yugoslavia have fallen. And now North Africa. There is no doubt about it – Germany is winning. They are unstoppable, it seems. But Daphne knows appearances can be deceiving. There will always be fractures, fissures, hidden inner conflicts that might be exploited. Even the most towering of regimes can totter with a push. It is her duty to summon her courage, deliver the book that might find a flaw and drive it open. Though behind enemy lines.

God, even the phrase on its own sends a shudder right through her and, for a moment, her conviction falters. Not that it is worth anything – she has no other options. It is impossible to turn back now, even if she wanted. The mesh of routes that has brought her to this place has been covered over. She has left no footprints. The contacts who helped have gone to ground. Her previous identity, as a Swiss business translator, lies in a safe, in the furthest corner of a cellar in a bookbinder's at Amriswil, an arrangement facilitated by one of her old teachers, Madame Renée, at the finishing school. A place she once despised, but now finds herself unexpectedly grateful to. The French she learnt there is not as good as her German or Italian but is about to become more useful than she could have ever imagined. In fourteen days, if she does not return, her papers will be burnt. She does not know yet that she will never see that town again.

Ahead lies Germany. Jeopardy.

She reminds herself once more that there is no going back, that she must just get on with it. And then, as if another part of her brain has come to her aid to soothe her, she is visited by a childhood memory. It is something her trainers told her to do when faced with extreme stress. On the lap of her father she sits, holding his hands while he sings, 'Row row row the boat, gently down the stream, merrily merrily merrily merrily, life is but a dream.'

She breathes in, holds the breath, breathes out and finds that a soft sigh also escapes her lips.

'All right there?' It is Jack, her radio operator. A man with whom she has been paired not only for his French fluency but because, well, because an affinity has been observed. Canadian by birth, he has worked with her on several operations and spent time alongside Daphne in intensive German-language lessons finessing Bavarian accents. She is a quick learner and has capitalised on the foundation taught by her paternal grandfather, Günter, when she was a child. Once, she had supposed her ancestry a handicap in this new world of war, but recently she has seen it for what it is – an advantage for certain operations, *if* one has the fortitude, or folly, to take them on.

With the partially clouded moon and mist, visibility is much diminished, yet Jack's outline is so familiar, she can fill in all details. The firm shoulders have a slight incline in the rise to his neck as he pulls the oars back. Though they too are obscured by a thick coat, she knows that above his strong jaw is a face that is at once both feminine and masculine. The lips are full and generally pink, but probably tinged with purple from the cold. No doubt his cheeks will be flushed from exertion. The nose, slightly too long for his features, is unblemished, though will have little droplets of sweat appearing on the sides. His odour, which is powerful now with the effort of rowing, contains notes of hay that are strangely sweet. He is robust, male, and his presence, though she can't call it comforting, makes her feel more solid.

'Quite fine,' she tells him, gripping the side of the little boat with her free hand. 'The fog has seeped through my clothes.'

'It won't be long now,' he whispers. 'Five minutes at most.'

She knows that: the land is rearing up.

Pinpricks of light indicate the sleeping town they are passing. It is strange to think that German citizens there are tucked up cozily in their beds. What will this enemy look like, she wonders? Part of her imagines them monsters, blackened beasts like the ogres of her nightmares. But she recognises this as childish fancy. Though news from this land does not sit straight with her own notions of what humanity is capable of. The transgressions she has been told of defy decency. This country is full of darkness. And they are making for it.

With one final grunt Jack presses down on the oars so they break free of the water and stay above it, and they glide as soundlessly as is possible, heading for the specified location, part of an inlet that is not patrolled. Intelligence has confirmed an absence of soldiers in this tiny stretch. But there are no guarantees.

Lindau, where her grandfather was born, has a lighthouse which flashes over them every three seconds. They have rowed as far as they can away from the circumference of its beam. Though they are still close to a training base for units of the Wehrmacht. Goodness knows how many soldiers are there, less than a mile away. She dares not think of it and glances down to see the needle of the compass in her hand quiver. She tells herself it is only the movement of the boat that makes it tremble so. 'Due northeast,' she whispers to Jack in a voice that reveals nothing of her trepidation. He adapts his stroke.

They have made it all the way across the lake without attracting attention, stilling when searchlights sweep over the water or ducking and lying flat on the bottom of the boat. Luck is a lady and Daphne is grateful that she has travelled with them this far. So far.

The trees are becoming real now, emerging as single entities from the untidy mass of twigs and leaves. She can see some beginning to bud, softening the gnarly arms of the ancient trunks. Others, with sharp pointy needles, look like they are ready to reach down and grab at them as they float, hunched, under their stoop. For a second, the sight of them makes her think of being snared by the enemy. But then she quashes the thought; Odette, who she trained with, sewed an 'L-pill' underneath her coat buttons should such a situation arise. Daphne has one too, a bead of deadly cyanide, in the hem of her skirt.

But it won't come to that. Every detail of this mission has been rehearsed, time and time again, until they had grown tired of the drill. Both she and Jack have had the notion drummed into them that just one misstep is likely to cost lives and may threaten the entire operation. It is a strain so heavy it would sink the boat if they were to give in to it.

Yet both are now made of tougher stuff. Older, softer skins shed, their new wartime characters have been tempered by their own personal calamities, each one carrying a scar and a secret unknown to the other. Jack does not know, though he senses, that Daphne has loved another. A man of great integrity cut down, in his prime, by a bullet from an enemy's gun. Her heart has not quite grown back to its full size yet. Though she keeps this knowledge under wraps. Grief is weakness. Her intention to serve her country is strengthened by a fervour that runs thick with vengeance.

She will find out Jack's secret soon enough.

'Almost there,' he says, trying hard to muster cheer.

The oars come up and over the sides, dowsing her with very cold water, so surprisingly icy it shocks and snaps her senses to full attention. They ship the paddles inside.

The little boat floats closer to the shore under the lowest overhanging branches, one of which catches her hair.

She ducks, brushes it away, bends to the laces on her shoes, undoes them and stows them in her suitcase.

'Ready?' Jack asks.

She rolls her skirt up by the waistband, exposing her thighs. Though she has shown more leg onstage and is unbothered. The theatre of war, like the Oriental, is no place for shrinking violets. 'Yes. As I'll ever be.'

The boat thuds against the muddy bank.

They have reached the reeds.

Jack's weight rocks the vessel as he transfers from it into the creek.

A couple of small splashes.

He offers a hand to Daphne who takes it and climbs out into the water. A quick gasp at the temperature of the lake, which even in these shallows comes up over her knees. But there is no time to complain or acclimatise.

Her companion wades round to the other side and together they pull the rowing boat up onto the lake's shore.

Daphne steps on a sharp broken reed. 'Damn!' It is sure to have cut her.

'Shh,' warns Jack.

She does not like being told what to do by men, though it is an occupational hazard, but he is right. They must be quiet. She presses her lips together.

The cuddy smell of damp earth fills her nostrils as she slips wet feet back into her shoes, with some difficulty.

The action must have woken a bird, for something nearby shrieks.

While eerie and unsettling, the noise may help obscure the sounds that they make as they conceal the boat behind a clump of reeds. Daphne covers it with fallen branches and loose leaves.

Once Jack has relaced his own boots, they set off towards the tree line, following the black silhouettes into the heart of the enemy and a country that is possessed.

CHAPTER TWO

1st May 1941

Not the whole of the German population has been captured by this new ideology. There are small pockets of resistance: independent thinkers who cannot accept the absurdity and ill logic of the Reich's dogma. Others are horrified by the rumours they hear: reports of despicable behaviour carried out willingly by fellow countrymen. After months of denial some are starting to give credence to these accounts.

One of these is an unassuming middle-aged man, codename: Twenty-Four. And it is to his house, marked by a cross on their map, that Daphne and Jack must hurry.

The mist is thinning now that they are moving inland. As are the clouds; and in between the dark, bristling trees the light of the moon filters through. Thankfully the terrain is just as their briefings detailed. Though every leaf that brushes another and emits a light scratching sound, every scuff of her heel or twig that snaps underfoot, irregulates the compressions of her heart.

They squeeze round the banks of a pond, keeping to the trees, then take a narrow track bordered by hedges. The path beneath their feet is uneven. They stumble often but at least the earth is dew-dampened and softens the sound of their footfalls. Daphne can smell the Christmassy scent of wet pine needles in the forest which looks as if it is sloping upwards and then dropping over to the next valley. Beyond that, she knows, are the alps. They will be snow-capped though she cannot see them. Does not want to see them. The last time she was high on a mountain ridge, she lost her lover, and she worries that, while she has held her feelings at bay, the sight of those white peaks might unleash emotions that she has gulped down and hidden in a small stone chapel in her heart. At least, that is how she imagines the place: a cold and tiny stronghold where she stores her innermost thoughts and desolations, and to where she goes sometimes at night to feel again.

'Oh dear,' says Jack, and Daphne pauses. Odd. They should maintain silence, he has shushed her only an hour ago.

But when she looks straight ahead she doesn't need to ask what has prompted his words. She can see it for herself. The trees are giving way to an expanse of fields and there is a half-timbered farmhouse perhaps six hundred yards away. Underneath the triangular roof, beyond a wooden balcony, lights are flickering within.

This is not what they expected. The route has been chosen to avoid human habitation as much as possible.

It is conceivable that their intelligence is outdated. Or the farmer has cut down this part of forest to grow crops. Whatever has happened is irrelevant: they are now faced with two choices. They can continue along the lane, thereby exposing themselves to any open eyes in the farmstead. Or they go around, through the trees, but lose precious time.

Jack takes a step forward towards the farm.

Daphne reaches out and touches his arm, 'Wait! What are you doing?'

As he turns, she sees his eyes, caught in a shard of moonlight. The irises are bright with tension, but his lids are baggy. He is tired. She is feeling it too.

'We must continue the route,' he says.

'That way we risk detection,' she tells him, nodding to the farm. 'We should keep to the shadows of the trees. It will be circuitous but minimises the danger.'

He blinks then points to the sky in the east, which she has not noticed becoming navy. 'Dawn is not far off. We must get to the safe house before sunrise. Or else we'll be easy pickings for anyone who might want to stop and see our papers.'

He is right. Though the documents have been well forged. Her Ausweis states her to be 'Dora de Vigne', a book dealer. Her legend, her backstory, has based her in a family antiquarian business back in Cologne. She has a ration card in that name and a Certificate of Residence showing her false address in the city. All their clothes have been sewn with German labels; her bags cut from Westphalian leather. Soap, hair milk and face cream are produced by the Nivea factory in Hamburg. But Jack has a large suitcase with him, in which a radio is concealed. If anyone delves too deeply, the hidden compartment may be found.

'We'll be as quiet as we can,' he whispers. 'If we're challenged, we're heading to an early meeting in Memmingen.'

'That's miles away!'

'Our car has broken down.'

It's an acceptable excuse, she thinks. Though what if the farmer offers them a lift? Unlikely, she reasons, he will be busy with his morning routine.

'All right,' she says and swallows hard as they walk out into the moonlight, two dark figures creeping across the horizon.

The fields, she sees now, contain a fresh crop. Green shoots reach up to her knees. It must have been sown recently. The farmers at home are also chopping down woodland to turn over to edible crops. Germany's trade has been blockaded, and these farms must now, no doubt, supply local troops.

While Jack's breaths are audible, she keeps the air inside her lungs as long as she can and lets it out through her nostrils, scared to make any sound at all.

A hundred yards away, they hear a door slam.

Both freeze.

Jack drops to the ground. She follows suit.

Someone coughs.

Blood roars through her ears. What on earth are they doing? Should they be discovered how will they explain their position, face down in the mud! She hopes that the crop in the fields will hide them. Though she can't be sure.

Now there is a trickling sound. Ugh. Whoever has come out of the house is relieving himself in the yard. He farts, coughs, hoiks up phlegm, spits it onto the ground. Then, seconds later, the door slams again.

She momentarily relaxes and lets her forehead sink onto the prickly grass verge. Her skin moistens with drops of dew.

They wait for a long minute like that, then she crawls up and begins to walk as quickly as she can. The farmer is inside now, busying himself with another job. Something clatters into a sink. A tap is turned on. They have a small window of opportunity to get past.

A quick glance: Jack is on his feet catching up with her. The sky behind him is now turning from navy to indigo. They *must* go.

She passes the farmstead and immediately advances towards the trees which border the road. It is only once she has reached their shady darkness she allows herself to slow, but only minutely.

Jack catches up with her and they snake round a curve in the road. Daphne's eyes are on the lane as it bends. Something is not quite right about the way it looks.

Her pace changes to a cautious prowl as they approach. There is a spinning thing dangling from a branch. At eight feet away, it takes her a moment to realise it is human. *Was* human.

Once a man, now a tattered corpse hangs there.

His feet are bloody and pulped, fingernails missing.

Long streaks of rusty stains have dried into his shirt and trousers. Body fluids are dripping onto a dark-green puddle. The stomach is distended, face swollen and unrecognisable, tongue projecting from thick purple lips. Around his neck a sign has been hung – 'Verräter'. Traitor.

Jack pushes her away, and she stumbles forward. *Don't think upon it.*

'Come on,' he says, grimacing and touching the side of his nose. The stench is awful. 'It's getting light.'

'How much further?' she asks, just for the sake of saying something, inserting life into the awful air of this place. Though she knows the answer. About four miles.

'Can you run?' he asks.

Fatigue wants her. She can feel her body jerking as she fights it. The night has been long and arduous. But if they are not careful the day will be far worse. So she nods.

And they set off at a jog, keeping to the shadows, both aware they are not likely to get there before the sun rises.

They make it in forty minutes, as the sky is turning golden. The silhouette of the farm is in view over tall hedgerows, up a mud track, away from the road. With extreme vigilance they approach the back door.

Jack knocks softly, a predetermined sequence of taps, the code that identifies them.

After two minutes the door creaks open.

Twenty-Four stands there, not at all what one might expect from an active dissident, which makes him the perfect choice. For he is a sturdy man in country clothes with an untidy beard and wary eyes. Without a word, he steps aside, allowing them to slip in before closing the door quickly behind them.

'Welcome.' His English is clear, though thickly accented, pronouncing the 'W' as a 'V'. 'You're just in time. I have word that there are patrols nearby.'

Goodness, she thinks, and is glad they did not know that.

Twenty-Four reads her expression and frowns. His own face is bronzed and weatherbeaten. 'It is of too much peril to move you now,' he says clumsily, then switches to German. 'You must stay here. Later we will get you to the city.'

'Danke,' Daphne's voice sounds exhausted even to her own ears, but also grateful, for which she is pleased.

Nodding, Twenty-Four points to a door underneath the stairs. 'I'll take you to the basement.'

They cross the floor as he unlocks a small door which is short and thin like that of a cupboard. There are hats and coats inside. He pushes them aside and unfixes the back panel, and she glimpses stairs going down.

'Rest while you can,' he tells them. 'You'll need all strength, for what is coming, yes.'

They clamber through the cupboard and into the darkness. Behind them Twenty-Four locks the door.

CHAPTER THREE

It is nothing like Narnia over the other side, though the walls down in the cellar look as if they are icy. But it is only mould and damp. There are two makeshift beds and a lamp. A jug of milk sits on a small table, with a half loaf of bread and some cheese.

She had not realised how hungry she was until she sees the food. It is evidently Jack's first thought too. He grabs the bread, tears it apart and stuffs a chunk into his mouth, chewing while he slices the cheese. After a moment he remembers Daphne and cuts a slice for her. She exhibits more decorum as she takes it and rips the hunk of bread open, places the cheese within and folds it over. The cheese is creamy and crumbly. It is delicious, the best thing she has ever tasted. For five minutes they gorge themselves, standing by the table, saying nothing. Then she pours the milk into the two pottery tumblers. It is fresh! And so buttery. Possibly the *nicest milk* she has ever drunk too.

Once their bellies are no longer empty, they sit upon the bunks and Daphne realises that this is the first time in a long while that they have been alone together in a room. Jack stares into space, depleted. There is a crumb of bread on his lower lip. His mouth, she thought less than a year ago, was as pretty and sensual as a peony: pink and full, with the promise of long summer evenings. For all his weariness he still looks handsome. Everyone, all the girls, agree on this. He has many admirers.

They have kissed once. In a dark alley near Piccadilly.

She shudders at the thought if it now. But back then she desperately needed something to relieve, however momentary, the drab and weary tension of blackout London. In fact, as she remembers, it was almost a craving. A compulsion. Her life had not gone well since her return from Iceland.

From the moment she stepped foot on London soil, she saw that her world had spun into an unstable new orbit. Even Bunty, the young woman who introduced her to Section W, was changed. She had met Daphne at Kings Cross station and informed her she was to be escorted home. The irritating cheerfulness, which had characterised the young driver's demeanour, had completely disappeared. She did not chatter nor chirp and Daphne was able to sit in comfortable silence as she was chauffeured through the streets of the damaged city. So unfamiliar was the broken cityscape, she had not really noticed, until they were almost there, that Bunty was taking her to Jonty's house in Mayfair. And so, when challenged, a grim duty fell to the young girl: Daphne's lodgings had been bombed three weeks earlier. Her landlady had survived but her landlord, Mr Thomas, had not been so lucky and perished in the ruins of his corner shop. Nothing remained.

So many casualties, so much grief and horror, Britain was ablaze with it.

Of course, Jonty had done his best to raise her spirits with his own tales of escapades in the south. 'Two years of training,' he'd told her, 'crammed into five months. Some in Oxfordshire too.'

'And have you been back to Wormwood Scrubs?' she'd asked, desiring to hear news of the others she had once met there.

'No,' he told her. 'That's gone too. Our section was bombed to smithereens.'

So it was to a small, cramped building near Baker Street that she reported two days later. From here she was taken to the back room of a shop and given access to the upper floors along with two men, Freddie and John, swelling to three when Jack joined, and two women of the same age, Deirdre and Susan, and began the arduous task of brushing up on her German, practising diction. Over the next weeks they were immersed in a crash course on the enemy's way of life.

The sessions were demanding, intense and often lasted more than fourteen hours. It was after one particularly gruelling day that they had decided to let off some steam. There was a new band leader at Café de Paris, who was the talk of the town. The place had become a bit of a regular haunt since it had lowered its prices. And for a while they were able to lose themselves in the rhythms conducted by the young and gifted Ken 'Snakehips' Johnson, who certainly lived up to his nickname. But, halfway through, Daphne had developed a headache. Gallantly, Jack had escorted her out.

They were five streets away when the bomb tore through the roof of the club and exploded on the balcony above the band. Although they had raced back to help, air wardens and off-duty nurses were already there attending to the casualties.

The night was noisy, their shock all-encompassing, and when they walked into a darkened alley and Jack had taken her in his arms, she had responded with an unexpected surge of vitality of an almost primal nature. When she had pulled away, fearful of going too far, he had understood and acquiesced.

They could not look at each other as they sat and waited for the others at the Baker Street shop. But only Freddie, with his arm in a sling and a bandage round his head, turned up the following day. And the day after. And all the days after that. John, they learned, was alive but had lost his legs, Susan and Deirdre perished instantly in the blast wave. The war was like a beast unleashed: of man's making, but indifferent to its creators and devouring all of them.

Neither Daphne nor Jack had spoken about it again. They couldn't. It seemed too improper, too tasteless, to mention the moment their lips had touched when their friends had been screaming or gasping their last breaths.

Whatever passion they had once felt was overwhelmed by guilt and more pressing concerns. In this painful, self-conscious, self-reproaching manner, their relationship evolved into one characterised by pragmatism.

And then, they had been paired for this mission.

Now Jack is snoring lightly. Still sitting up. Eyes closed, chin on his chest. His hair has flopped forward and sticks out at 45 degrees. Poor thing. Exhaustion, she laments, is a naughty thief that strips out all dignity. She takes a blanket and pillow, places the pillow behind his neck, pushes him back so he is more comfortable and smooths down his hair. Then she tucks him in. It's simply the decent thing to do, she thinks. But there is still fondness there.

When she is sure he is settled, she turns to her suitcase and opens it, takes out the book that is wrapped in paper within to check it is still intact after their journey.

She hates it, she hates it, she hates it.

Jack has been so curious about the package she must deliver. The ancient grimoire with its strange runic symbols has intrigued him. On the flight into Switzerland, he had asked her straight out, 'You must tell me – where is it to go?'

Something in his tone had stilled her. Perhaps it was his use of the imperative – the 'must' in his order. Being told what to do by men of rank was something she simply had to endure. But Jack's standing was equal to her own. She did not 'have' to tell him anything, so decided just then she would keep it to herself for the time being and tapped the page, directing his gaze down to a page. 'This one is used to raise the dead.'

He had bitten his lip as he stared at the strange sigil with a face etched within, and blenched right then, though the turbulence and the bumpy flight had not stirred him once. 'You understand it? The magic?'

And she had nodded, remembering another journey: the voyage back to Scotland on the boat from Reykjavík with nothing to do but listen to the farmer-sorcerer explain the spells, teach her about runes and hieroglyphic marks. It wasn't an entertainment, as such, but it did serve to distract her from grief. Even thinking about that time now sparks a cold burn of anger within her. A debt must be paid. Her mission is personal.

She had talked to Jack about the sorcerer, mentioned the traditions of seiðr. How its practitioners were believed to have the gift to foresee the future, alter destiny, control weather, heal or harm, even shape-shift or send their spirits out travelling through the cold night air.

And he had listened. Rapt.

It is an old book, a magical book. And sewn into its spine is something else: prophecies of the sage, Nostradamus. Rare prophecies. Important prophecies.

Not all of them authentic.

Though she has not mentioned this to Jack.

Section W has worked with a Nostradamus expert to insert one specific new prediction amongst the rest. Cyril, a man of rather flamboyant style and raffish looks, who is surprisingly well versed in witchcraft and occult practices, has explained the significance of it.

She had not known, till then, that German planes, only last year, dropped thousands of the prophet's booklets over France and Belgium when they attacked in May. For many of those in the upper echelons of the Reich believe that their triumphs have been cosmically ordained and that Nostradamus had, in the sixteenth century, foreseen their ultimate victory. The words of the sage carry a weight for some that logic is unable to dislodge.

Though she detests the antique tome, she understands the importance of delivering it to the bookseller in Augsburg. And she will do whatever she can to ensure it reaches its final destination. The book has been paid for with loss, grief and blood.

So much of it.

Spilled at home in the charred ruins of cafés and streets, her own home, on foreign soil, in battlegrounds and arctic mountains.

The damn stuff is everywhere.

And for a moment, she perceives sprays of it colouring the air, soaking everything in a darkening red.

No, she blinks, it is an illusion. She is tired, she must try to sleep.

But it is not illusory.

It is an omen of what she will see, what is yet to come.

CHAPTER FOUR

1st May 1941

There has been a change of plan. Their transportation has not arrived. No one knows why.

Daphne fears the worst – that it has been intercepted by the enemy. That they are about to be discovered. She senses Jack's discomfort, observes the skin on Twenty-Four's leathery forehead tighten and wrinkle.

'I will do it,' he says. 'In my truck. But you cannot travel like this.' He points at their feet then disappears through the wardrobe.

Left alone Jack begins to pace the room. 'This is not what I had hoped for.'

Who would, she thinks? But there is no point stating it.

Flexibility is all. She knows from her time spent at Farnham Castle that adaptation enhances the chances of survival. It is an evolutionary trait that has allowed Homo sapiens to thrive. They must use it now.

'Twenty-Four has come up with a solution though,' she says, 'and we must take it.' She smiles, hoping to reassure him, but he frowns, as if she is trivialising the matter.

For a moment she wonders if he wants her to feel as concerned and alarmed as he does. She does, of course, but will not show it, will not give in to it. It gains nothing to lose one's head. So she reminds him of the words of the poster back home: 'Your Courage, Your Cheerfulness, Your Resolution Will Bring Us Victory.'

He shakes his head and she is not sure if it is another

disparaging gesture or if he is dismissing her words. Do they sound over-used, trite?

There is no time to dwell on it. Both bristle at the knock on the back of the wardrobe door and, without waiting for a response, Twenty-Four emerges at the top of the steps carrying a pile of clothes. 'These . . .' he hands Daphne a skirt, scarf and blouse which smell of mothballs, 'for you.' He gives the rest to Jack. 'Two minutes, then come, come.' The door shuts behind him.

Daphne eyes the clothes. Not what she would prefer to wear in all honesty, but she must blend in, and supposes if they are to be ferried across the country in a farm truck, then they must look like farm workers.

She coughs, 'Turn your back please Jack,' and waits till he obeys before removing her smart skirt, blouse and jacket, and slips into the clothes that must, judging by the size of them, once have belonged to her host's mother. The waist is so big she has to knot it to stop it falling down. The blouse swamps her too, but she tucks it into the skirt and plucks out some of the fabric so it falls over the top and disguises the poor fit. The scarf she ties round her hair.

When she turns back she finds Jack in corduroy trousers and a smock shirt. He looks so odd she wants to laugh but now is not the time.

'Come on,' he says, and they pack their suits, gather their belongings and go through the wardrobe.

The roads twist and turn as they climb hills and descend. She is thrown against the side of the cab several times and silently curses the suspension which bobs her up and down inelegantly. Sitting up front with her case at her feet, she is developing an ache in her back. She yawns. For days now it has been impossible to sleep properly. She wonders if she ever will again.

Around her the countryside stretches to the mountainous horizon. It is quite beautiful really. Though every so often a church spire points up, with a cross on the top like a warning – do not enter. The small villages pass and the view opens onto flat fields. The scarecrows propped up in them look as if they are either rigid with fear or collapsed with dismay. She sees a boy walking across a wheat field with a stick in his hand, swiping vacantly at the crop. His dog runs on ahead. If it were photographed it could easily pass as a scene of pastoral England. But it's not. The boy is German. He and the dog are enemies.

So strange to think like this. Though Twenty-Four is German and he is not an adversary. He is an ally. And of course, the boy must be too. Children and dogs know nothing of their leaders' dark and bitter hearts.

There are few other vehicles on the route, for which she is grateful. The sun is on its way down to the hills in the West.

It is risky for Twenty-Four to be out at this time, rather than about his usual routine on the farm, but he bears it with what she has come to see as his innate stoicism. Or perhaps his face is paralysed with fear.

After two hours Twenty-Four turns down a country lane and pulls into a crossing place, by a densely wooded copse.

Daphne tenses – what is he doing? Why is he stopping?

He lifts one hand off the steering wheel, palm up and shrugs, 'For relief,' he says. Then adds, 'It is also preferable for you that you return to your city clothes now. In Augsburg, not many farm workers.'

She cannot help sighing with relief, a different variety from the one that Twenty-Four is offering. Thank goodness that is all – a rest stop. But she doesn't want their contact to notice her emotions, so camouflages them with her stage smile, a thin and rigid uplift through the cheeks. She has found that, rather like the prophecies of Nostradamus, people see in this grin exactly what they want to see. Usually gentility. Which has its uses.

They get down from the cab while Twenty-Four fetches Jack's bag from underneath haybales in the back.

Daphne takes her case and heads for the darkest part of the trees. There is much bracken and foliage underfoot, so she cannot get far. Swiftly she swaps the peasant garb for her suit and starched blouse.

As she returns to Twenty-Four to give the farm clothes back, the circular motion of turning and handing the clothes over provokes a curious feeling, as if she is pivoting, passing through one stage of life and into another. She is, but right then her mind interprets it as a flush of anxiety. It makes Daphne hesitate and she wonders if, by giving the costume up, she is relinquishing a protection, exposing herself?

No, she thinks. It is a silly, childish thought and she chastises herself for it.

They move on.

Soon the little hamlets give over to villages. The residential buildings grow larger and thicken. The road widens, the sky grows cluttered with rooftops and chimneys.

Twenty-Four takes a final right turn and stops a little way down the road, pulling over to the pavement. He doesn't wish them luck but asks, 'You know where to go?'

They nod. Daphne thanks him 'for everything' and receives the smallest of smiles. On the pavement an urge to wave tugs at her as their contact executes a U-turn and drives away. She keeps it in, picks up her case and watches his truck disappear.

They are on their own.

Though surrounded by a population of approximately one hundred and eighty-five thousand, according to the briefing.

They begin the walk to Jack's guesthouse. Here she will leave him to find her own contact in the Fuggerei, an ancient housing complex for Catholic citizens further into the city.

She keeps her eyes down but soon becomes aware that this is not the behaviour of an everyday townsman, so raises her gaze. The people on the street, about their business, look jarringly normal. It surprises her. Somehow she had imagined them to be swarthy, bullish hulks, depraved and maniacal. Though they appear very similar to the English, at least on the outside – more so than the French, Italian or Icelandic people she has encountered. Anglo-Saxon in appearance, they share the same mannerisms, hair colours and skin tones as many of those back home . . .

The women's hairstyles are not unlike her own and those sported by actresses on the silver screen. She does see a couple of men in lederhosen, carrying briefcases. Though short shorts, long socks and traditional braces are peculiar, she does not look twice. It is only when one shouts to a passing cyclist that she looks over. Her heartbeat quickens as she registers, beyond him, an armoured truck approaching. Two soldiers, in field-grey with helmets, sit behind the steering wheel surveying the street. The uniforms dehumanise them, erase their distinct and differing features – they aren't individuals, but components of a massive military machine. As their eyes sweep over her she cannot help but hold her breath, and darts a glance at Jack.

He has seen them too, she thinks. His eyes have narrowed and his face is hard. She cannot tell what emotion lies behind the skin and bone. Fear, yes, but something else. Resolve, she thinks and takes her cue from him, gritting her teeth but forcing her facial muscles to relax.

It is acceptable to walk briskly with purpose, but they should not appear tightened, nervous, as if they have anything to conceal, so she says to him, in German, 'It's such a nice day, isn't it? Though warm.'

'Fine, fine,' Jack says.

She knows the guesthouse is not far. She has practised the walk with her briefing officers many times: up another two blocks, then a right turn for four hundred yards, then a left up a narrow, cobbled street into one even narrower, the type that she would call an alley at home. The boarding house will be slim and four storeys high with a green-painted door. Jack's room should be on the first floor.

She clears her throat to get his attention. His eyes are still fixed on the soldiers' truck.

But it passes them without stopping.

They walk on and must cross a road. Both of them look left first, rather than right: they drive on a different side here. Their training has impressed upon them the importance of lots of tiny details – don't take your hat off inside, don't put milk in before the tea.

The day is hotter than Britain at this hour. Her suit is cut from more climate-appropriate cloth than the one she wore in Iceland. It is thinner, made of rayon, though not particularly breathable. A few holes have been sewn around the armpits to allow for air. The blades in her lapels and belt are finer, sharper, easier to slice through flesh. The mechanisms in her shoes have been made from a metal that is dense but much lighter than those she had to clunk around in in Reykjavík. It is far easier to walk on these heels. Her feedback to the Security Service, after using her old pair, has ensured that each heel on these new ones has a rubber cushion on the bottom, to muffle the sound it makes, and grooves across the sole for grip. Unlike those she wore last autumn, she could dance in these if she needed to. Or run.

Jack nudges her and she sees they have reached their turning. As planned, she slows a little, puts a few paces between him and herself and follows him to the guesthouse.

Houses rise up either side, blocking the sun. Some have

triangular roofs like the farmhouse, but they are more ornate, with curls fashioned into their design. The place looks like something out of a Grimms' fairytale.

Jack stops and turns. Her eyes have been lifted to a jutting balcony, adorned on either side by quite marvelous murals, so she almost bumps into him and curses. That's another thing she should not do – look upwards at the unusual architectural features. Locals never do. They keep their eyes fixed on the way ahead. They are used to their environment. Only those new to town look around wide-eyed like Daphne.

Her sudden proximity to Jack prompts her to swallow. Though their relationship has certainly changed, not everything completely died. He is a good man, prepared to risk his life for her and for their mission. And she trusts him.

He smiles and cups her elbow, as if steadying her. She feels his fingers, the firm grasp and, though she has not thought about it before, it seems obvious why they were paired. There is some kind of chemistry there that others must have seen. And they are both damn good at their jobs. Jack's fluent French will be invaluable if they need to cross through that country once their objective is achieved. Though the Vichy government is collaborating fully with their occupiers, former President de Gaulle broadcasts regularly on the BBC's French Service, appealing for uprisings and countering the propaganda sent out there. A few operatives suspect that a resistance of some kind might be brewing.

'I will see you then,' he says, and she senses a reluctance to let go of her. His eyes brighten, the peony lips part. There is something in the tilt of his head and the way he leans across, touches her hand, that makes her suddenly think that he wants to take her in his arms, embrace her. Perhaps with passion, perhaps with compassion. Human touch, in this world of peril and isolation, can be so very persuasive.

Though she feels it too, this need for warmth and connection, she says, 'Yes,' then forces herself to take a step back, withdraws from him. Her manner comes across as hard. But there must be eyes on them somewhere. It is vital that their conduct aligns to standards of German decorum. Their papers detail that they are business associates so they should not appear too intimate. There is no room for doubt or else Death will be ready with its scythe, round any street corner or behind any of these wooden doors.

She is not sure whether she has hurt him with her retreat because the skin around his eyes creases. He frowns as he speaks, 'Yes, quite.' The words are coming out slowly. 'All right.' Is he flustered? She can't tell. Conflicted, she decides. Some internal battle is raging within.

At last, he drops his gaze to his watch. 'And you're sure you won't tell me where you're bound?' A bird flies above them casting a shadow over his face. In the fleeting darkness she sees not only something quiet and concerned, but another emotion which she cannot put a name to. He shifts, unsettled. 'I . . . I worry.'

Replying with a quick shake of her head, when she looks back up, she finds his lips are pursed.

'I will radio confirmation that we've arrived.' He is returning to his crisp formal delivery, then softens a touch. 'After that, it's a matter of adhering to the sked.' He always uses this shorthand for schedule, but she knows what he means: Jack has an arranged time to transmit, and a code unique to him, which he will relay to the receiving operator. Other codes are printed on a tiny piece of silk, hidden on his person. The system is unbreakable if sender and receiver keep to the rules. It is a safety net of sorts, albeit a fragile one.

'If plans change,' he says, lines breaking out across his forehead. 'I will leave first thing on the 3rd.'

Her voice becomes softer, though keeps its firmness, as she says, 'I'll be back tomorrow night, Jack.'

There is more distance now in his thin smile. The peony petals have lost some of their lustre. 'And then I'll radio for exit instructions,' he continues.

These words have been practised, rehearsed, repeated so many times, almost vacuously, and yet now hearing them releases a flush of adrenaline within her. The thought of not 'exiting', of being left here alone, is suddenly real and very troubling. She takes a breath. In German, she says, 'Communicate my good wishes to the bookbinders,' and shakes his hand. It is sweaty.

Then she crosses the street and walks away without looking back.

'Ich, Jakob Fugger, Bürger zu Augsburg, bekenne mit diesem Brief, der armen Leute Häuser am Kappenzipfel als Stiftung zu vollenden und die Nachfahren auf ewig mit der Vollstreckung zu verpflichten.'

'I, Jakob Fugger, citizen of Augsburg, hereby with this letter acknowledge the completion of the houses for poor people at Kappenzipfel as a foundation and obligate my descendants forever to its execution.'

Conditions:
Annual rent: one Rhenish
Daily prayers: one Our Father, one Ave Maria, and the Apostles' Creed for the charitable intent of the Fugger family
To accommodate: Augsburg citizenship, Catholic, poor but respectable, striving to earn an income

–Jakob Fugger, 23 August 1521

CHAPTER FIVE

She had not expected it to look so pretty. Surrounded by a wall, the Fuggerei is almost a village of its own within the old city, ancient and untouched by time. The houses are small and narrow, built in rows, all painted a mustard colour with green shutters folded back to allow the sunshine in. The place seems to have been spared the ravages of war. So far. Though nothing here will escape its domain. Lots of the windows are open and Daphne can hear the sounds of metal cutlery and plates being collected or perhaps set out. It is supper time.

Daphne's stomach rumbles and she wonders if there will be food for her when she gets to number 21.

The lanes between the houses are cobbled and bumpy, with just enough room for a cart to pass down. She has entered through the gates and there had been no watchman on duty, though there was a cubby where she guessed he sat at night.

There are no soldiers within the Fuggerei's walls, none that she can see anyway. It is quiet, the exterior walls block out much of the city's bustle and noise. However, she is far too experienced now to be lulled into a false sense of security and watches the shadows, notes which windows have boxes sprouting fresh blooms and which block out the daylight with their red swastika flags. The walls round here no doubt have ears.

A child, a little girl with hair braided into short, caramel plaits, crosses the lane dragging a little wooden horse on a rope. Its wheels click, tick, tick, tick. Daphne dips her head, sends a wink and a smile and receives a chary nod back.

She continues, passing an old woman who is shaking out a tablecloth on her doorstep, till she encounters a gurgling fountain where two lanes meet.

It is surprisingly easy to orientate herself, despite the fact the little roads and houses are virtually identical: the complex has been set out simply and built in an orderly fashion.

Noting the numbers of the houses, she hears the distant bells of the cathedral chime as she counts. Ah, it is later than she thought, so she speeds up and hurries past garden plots full of herbs and vegetables and courtyards with plants in pots, until she reaches the right dwelling. Same as the rest but with a lemon tree growing out front.

The door is opened by a fresh-faced woman in her thirties. Immediately, she clasps Daphne in her arms.

'Cousin!' she exclaims in a Swabian accent, which Daphne has been taught to recognise. 'Come, come. It is good to see you again.' Before the door is even closed, the woman plants a kiss on Daphne's cheek. 'Dear Dora,' she adds.

The enthusiasm and sincerity which she feels in the strength of her embrace causes a little parcel of warmth to unfold inside Daphne. The woman lets go and leads her into a modestly furnished room and shuts the door.

'Sit, sit,' she says, 'Dora,' and points to a table with three chairs arranged around it. 'You must be famished and tired after your journey from Cologne. Let me fetch some milk and bread.'

'Thank you, Greta,' says Daphne, using the woman's name for the first time. It feels natural on her tongue, which she takes as a good omen. When her host disappears into another room, she takes a chair, stows her suitcase underneath and sits down.

She is not at ease but the house is old in a way that is sturdy and solid and protective. It has endured for centuries, she thinks, and will endure for centuries more. Unless, of course – bombs. While Old Blighty suffers regular air raids, the RAF conducts its own bombing campaign over here. Such terrible devastation on both sides. Madness really, what we do to each other. She sighs and looks around.

The room gives off an air of frugality and thrift; however, she notices touches of personality dotted around the place: a flowerpot with a bright-pink geranium on the windowsill, an embroidered Bible verse, a framed image of the Virgin Mary bordered with lace that looks like it has been handmade with bobbins. No surprise that religious paraphernalia decorates the home – the community here is Catholic. It is one of the criteria for entry.

She is rather taken aback when Greta returns with a tray bearing food, a jug of milk and a bottle of wine. Wine indeed! Then she remembers Germany has its own vineyards.

'You're right,' says Greta. 'It is getting chilly.' Though it isn't yet and Daphne has made no comment on the temperature. But her host moves to the window and pulls it shut.

Returning to the table she offers Daphne bread and milk. 'Or perhaps,' she says, now in a hushed voice, 'you would prefer some of this,' and indicates the bottle.

It seems wildly exotic and imprudent, though she does not wish to offend her host and hears herself saying in clipped German, 'Yes, thank you, that would be nice.'

Greta pours out two small glasses, handing one to Daphne. 'Zum Wohlsein.'

She nods and takes a larger gulp than she expected. It is sour and strangely sweet. The second sip is better, as ever.

'Your journey?' asks Greta without smiling. 'Lacking in incidents?' She raises an eyebrow. 'Incidents' can cover a range of difficulties and Daphne glimpses a gravity beneath external bonhomie.

'Fine,' says Daphne. 'Thank you.'

It is her clothes, she thinks, that make Greta appear of a

lighter disposition. She wears a blouse with puffed sleeves and a square neckline which is trimmed with embroidery. Over this, a fitted bodice, laced tightly, and a calf-length green skirt, almost the same colour as the shutters outside. The look reminds her of Heidi, the eponymous little girl she has read about in a childhood book.

Greta urges Daphne to eat and once she starts, she cannot stop. Hunger is upon her like a wolf. She has had nothing since breakfast, or was it dinner? Her hearty appreciation seems to please her host.

When she is finished, Greta tells her she will show her the sleeping quarters, and she follows her upstairs to a small, whitewashed room with a wooden bed covered in a patchwork quilt. Beside it a nightstand with a candlestick, above it, a crucifix. Opposite is a wooden cupboard and a stool.

Daphne thanks her and lays her suitcase on the bed, expecting Greta to leave, but she stands for a moment then sits down on the stool.

'You know where to go, tonight?' she asks. 'Need me?'

'Thank you but I'm quite all right. It's all up here,' Daphne taps her head. 'I've memorised the map.'

Greta mumbles an affirmation.

'But one thing,' Daphne hesitates. 'My accent. Is it acceptable?'

Greta stops and thinks. 'There is more music in the way you speak, a slight lilt that is not quite of Cologne. Have you any other ancestry?'

'My grandfather was German. From Lindau,' she says.

Greta nods her head swiftly. 'Yes, yes I can hear that. And you are more fluent than some who I have . . .' she stops and Daphne understands she cannot say any more. Her host has evidently helped other Brits too. What a fine woman.

'My mother,' Daphne adds, 'is Italian.'

'Our allies,' says Greta, her lips tightening. 'If questioned, you can offer that – your Italian ancestry. It is good that you don't roll your "R"s. They are in your throat. You will suffice.'

Well, she will have to, she thinks. But she will not be speaking to anyone of importance and only has to get through checkpoints. She will suffice indeed.

'When you return,' Greta pipes up. 'I must speak with you.'

This is off plan. Greta was simply to house her for a night. 'Oh?' she asks, alarm beginning to dry her throat.

Greta rubs her eyes. When she removes her hands, her face looks like she has aged ten years. 'There are things which you must report back to your superiors.'

Watching her, Daphne is not sure what to say. But it is Greta who speaks next.

She pulls herself to her feet and says, 'Later.'

Then she goes out the door and closes it, leaving Daphne.

Unease pricks at her shoulders.

CHAPTER SIX

Night has fallen across this alien land. But only just. The light in the west, above the rooftops, still holds a faint trace of indigo.

It is an acceptable time for a young woman to be making her way home after a long day's work or a dinner meeting. Not too late as to arouse suspicion. Not too bright to be seen clearly. No lights shine from any windows. The streetlights are unlit. Blackout exists here as it does back home. Though, she reminds herself, there is no curfew. Not for Augsburg citizens, unless they are Jews. Two years ago, she has read in her notes, this community was evicted from their own homes and forced into a handful of designated 'Jew Houses' or cramped 'barracks' in apartment blocks. The able and affluent mostly fled. Only the infirm, old and poor were left behind. Now they are forbidden to leave their residences for any reason, till six in the morning. It is inhumane, she thinks, the way they treat them. How will they survive the war in these conditions?

Once, she had assumed that the world was tied together by a shared view of morality, a common sense of right and wrong. That good was universally applauded, and what was wrong or bad was condemned with a swiftness and severity that kept it in check. But that view has been shattered. Only a handful are standing up against this emergent and, quite frankly, deranged set of new values. The Allied Powers are such a small group – how can other countries stand by and do nothing?

For Germany is winning. They must not triumph.

Her pace quickens.

The details of the town, compass points, distances and landmarks are already stored in her memory. So when she reaches the side of the town hall, she slows and keeps to the shadows cast by the tall buildings around it. It is called the Rathaus. An apt name, she thinks, occupied as it is by the SA and SS.

Swastika flags hang out of every window here. There is something threatening about all the red and black – blood and darkness – as if visual intimidation is the whole point of the design. Perhaps it is. With so many on display here, at the Rathaus, the effect is overwhelming and her senses trip to full alert.

Though the casual observer might assume she is taking care by angling her eyes to the cobbles and paying attention to the uneven ground, she is actually taking in the detail of the place. That man on the corner – is he pretending not to watch her? She glances into an empty shop window and checks the reflection of the street. He stows a newspaper under his arm and saunters off whistling. She pauses for a second and listens, pretending to catch her breath: has anyone followed her? Are there footsteps behind her? Is there a shadow creeping up on her right? Hard to tell but she thinks not.

As she gets closer to the Rathaus, the street begins to swarm with soldiers. At least it seems this way, though there cannot be more than a dozen. They dominate the view, and of course her own inner landscape: the agent-radar that she has refined which scans continuously for danger.

She had expected them all to be blond, but one approaches who is brown-haired beneath his helmet. His head is up, jaw jutting out, squarish, just like the cartoons on the posters at home, walking confidently with long, self-important strides.

She has not come so close to one before – a fully grown Nazi soldier. This, she thinks, is someone who has truly embraced the Führer's demented logic, affirmed his country's superiority and that of its people. For a moment, he becomes symbolic – a black-hearted giant on a collision course with her – and she cannot help herself gulping down air, pushing out her ribcage. She imagines, as he passes, his nostrils flare. Fee fi fo fum, does he smell the blood of an Englishman?

Stop it! she warns herself. I am a bookseller from Cologne about my business, delivering a package for one of their own. She gets a grip on herself and remembers, if questioned, she must react with indignity. But best not to be questioned at all. Not to be noticed.

She adjusts her gait, inches closer to the walls.

The soldier continues down the road without acknowledging her.

She walks a few more paces before releasing all her pent-up breath and closing her eyes, briefly.

When she moves on, she spots another two in the Schutzstaffel uniform, smoking on the corner. As she passes them, a muscle in her knee weakens with fear and her heel hits a cobble at an awkward angle. She stumbles, throws out her arm for balance and drops the package she is carrying. It flies over and lands at their feet.

One of the men thrusts out an arm, grabs her. His grip is firm.

Oh God, oh God.

He pulls her up. 'All right?' he says and smiles.

'Sorry,' she says. 'Wine.'

Leaning towards her, he sniffs her breath.

Fee fi fo fum.

She waits for his reaction, wondering if this is it: is her accent too Anglicised? Her speech full of prickly nerves?

He laughs, 'Not too much, now,' and then pats her on the bottom.

The other soldier has picked up her package and turns it over in his hands.

Her heart is hammering, sweat begins to bubble out of the pores on her forehead – has he noticed?

But he hands it back with a smile and a nod, then turns back to the other chap and continues his conversation.

She cannot believe it. How could they *not* know? As she walks away at a determinedly steady pace, heartbeat decelerating – though only slightly – a release passes through her, like pressure hissing from a bicycle's tyre valve. That was a test. And she has passed.

So close to the Rathaus now, she can't pause to collect herself, so her steps quicken. Ahead are more corners. More uniforms. More tests. She adjusts the package in her arms and continues up the street.

The buildings here are older, the windows shuttered against eyes in the sky and the bombs that may rain down. As she passes an old, shadowy, unlit house, in a window above, a curtain twitches. There is a flicker of movement in the darkness behind it. Someone watching, she wonders? Or perhaps just a draught? The day has been blustery in the countryside, though in this valley of cobbles between the tall houses, the air does not move much at all. She doesn't look back to check. There are some situations where it is better not to know.

Soon, she sights the bookshop. A sign hangs outside: a picture of an open book upon a stack of others, with an owl at one end, a quill and inkpot at the other. The name 'Keller & Sohn' is followed by 'Antiquarische Bücher' and 'Gegründet 1813'. It is an old business then if it has been trading for over a hundred and twenty years. She wonders how contact was established. What do they know about her?

After the correct number of knocks, the door is opened not by the owner Jakob, as expected, but by a woman with light sandy hair in a style much like her own. Daphne cannot see her features, but her comportment and energy suggest she is about the same age. She steps aside without a word and lets Daphne cross the threshold into the shop.

Three bolts slide across the door behind her.

'Upstairs,' she says without a smile and leads Daphne through the shop. Mahogany shelves line the walls, some so high they have ladders running up them. There are tables full of hardbacks and all those familiar smells – parchment, dust, leather. In other worlds she would loiter, run her fingers over the spines, browse the titles, but not this new one.

The woman walks behind the counter then ducks as she goes through a low door. Daphne does the same and enters a narrow hall with a staircase. The blonde jerks her head up it.

They ascend to a landing with two doors. She opens the one on her left and they go through into a room which is both living quarters and workshop. A lamp on a wide desk illuminates the room with its dim glow. A couple of wooden chairs, a chaise longue with boxes covered by a blanket, an old iron safe in the corner, more shelves and many, many more books. By the boarded windows is a counter, it's top full of tools, bottles of liquid and parchment.

Someone coughs and she sees on the chaise longue it's not boxes that have been covered, but an old man. He pulls back the blanket and struggles to sit up.

'Ah,' he says, 'Fräulein de Vigne.' His voice is weak, breaking as he pronounces her name. This must be Heinrich Keller, the current owner of the family business. Frailer than she imagined, his skin is one shade lighter than the grey of the blanket that covers him, his lips whitish. Soft wispy hair sticks out on one side of his head and is plastered flat against the other. He reaches for a pair of round spectacles and pushes them up his long nose over large milky blue eyes.

An older woman shuffles in from another door at the back and helps lift him by the shoulders, adjusts the blanket over his knees with tenderness. His wife?

Daphne approaches, hand outstretched. 'Guten Abend, Herr Keller.'

He takes it and shakes it, his grip limp and clammy. 'My wife, Klara. Daughter, Hedwig.' The wife smiles but there is uncertainty in it. His daughter grimaces, her face, like grey cement, sets. If the wind changes, you'll stay like that, thinks Daphne.

The dynamic is not right. In here, the air is charged, like the sky before a thunderstorm. What is it? Daphne wonders and pays close attention to the language of their bodies. Her theatrical background as a magician's assistant has taught her it is often louder than words.

'Right,' says Herr Keller. He is fragile, she can see that. But there is no aggression in his gestures. 'First, can I see *it*?' he holds out his hand. 'A seventeenth-century grimoire, I'm told?'

'Yes,' she says. The book trembles as he takes it. 'The Nostradamus prophecies are at the back.'

'My, my,' says Herr Keller.

His wife, Klara, is more robust-looking, though tremors run through her left hand, which she tries to hide. Plump and rosy-cheeked with a double chin, she is rounded from that point down. Her hair has been braided into a 'Gretchen' hairstyle, with two plaits wrapped over the crown and pinned on top, forming a light-grey wreath on her head. As Herr Keller settles the grimoire on his lap, she averts her eyes. She is nervy, Daphne thinks as she watches the mother call to her daughter in a watery voice, 'Hedwig! Fetch a seat for our guest.' Then to Daphne, 'Would you like a drink, Fräulein de Vigne?'

'Water please,' says Daphne and Klara bustles off back through the door at the rear by which she entered.

A chair squeaks on the floor next to Daphne. She turns to thank Hedwig but before she gets the words out, sees her properly, in the lamplight, for the first time. She was right about the age: the same as Daphne, maybe a year or two either side of her twenty-three. She has unfortunately inherited her father's nose and her mother's chin and has an unhappy, shrewish look about her. Daphne smiles as she sits down and thanks Hedwig for finding the seat but gets only a grunt of acknowledgement.

Klara returns with an earthenware tumbler that shakes lightly when she passes it to Daphne. She drinks, tries not to gulp, for her throat is itchy and dry.

'It is good,' says Herr Keller from the couch. He has opened the package carefully, spreading the wrappings over his blanket, and moved his eyes to the book's leather jacket, passing his fingertips over the etched grooves.

Daphne finds herself pleased by his comment, as if she has made the thing herself.

'How did you come by it? I heard Iceland?'

'Yes,' she says. 'It was discovered in an ancient farmhouse in the northwest fjords. Brought into Germany via Switzerland.' All true, though the months it has spent in England have been omitted.

'Ah, yes. That route, I understand, is still open,' he says. Unable to tear his gaze from the jacket, he opens the pages. Slowly his eyebrows rise.

Another test.

She holds her nerve and reminds herself that the trade in antiquities here often requires dealers to turn a blind eye to the question of provenance and legitimacy. There is talk of the requisition of Jewish families' valuable possessions. Many dealers and curators have overlooked the dubious ethics of such stage-managed theft, eager to sort through and acquire interesting items.

Herr Keller does not seem at all conflicted as he pauses to smell the parchment. When he reaches the back, the set of papers – the predictions – sewn into the grimoire, Daphne holds her breath and awaits judgement, plasters her stage grin over her face.

Will his expert eyes detect that one of them is forged?

'It is most strange,' he says.

Don't look at him, she tells herself, *don't you dare betray concern*. Instead, she transfers her gaze to Klara, then Hedwig. Both are fixed on Herr Keller's face. Hedwig's hand twitches.

How long would she have to make her escape, should he denounce the forgery and raise the alarm? Would he even do that? If the deception is discovered, he might merely return the book. Though the rest of the mission will be scuppered, at least she will get out alive. Worst-case scenario, she must retrace her steps, down the stairs, across the bookshop. She has memorised the way – three bolts across the door, then out into the street, as long as Hedwig doesn't . . .

A wheezy exhalation calls her to Herr Keller.

He raises his head, pushes his spectacles back up his nose.

'Ja,' he says, 'I will issue a certificate of authenticity.'

Hallelujah! Weeks have been spent developing this plan. Experts have been summoned, syntax and handwriting laboured over, the pages aged with a concoction which involved amongst other things, according to Cyril, tea. It hadn't sounded very scientific. But if this antiquarian bookdealer approves, then her part of the mission is complete.

She can return to Jack who will radio for exit. The strategy has not yet been supplied – things change, people are compromised – but they will be surely out of the country in a matter of days. Elation floods through her. She wants to clap her hands, but controls herself, and says in a measured manner, as if it was never in doubt, 'That is most satisfactory.'

The aged bookseller raises a shaking hand to the desk. 'Klara,' he says, 'bring me the paperwork.'

His wife bustles to the counter by the blackened windows, takes some paper, a pen, inkpad and stamp, and presses them into her husband's hands.

Herr Keller unfolds it and signs, finishes the certificate with a stamp of authentication.

Though the effort causes him to cough, painfully. Fighting for breath, he holds his ribs.

In order to avoid watching as he suffers, Daphne sips the water.

'Well,' she says, when Herr Keller's paroxysm has passed and he has come to rest, 'I will leave it in your hands now,' and she rises.

The bookseller quickly wipes his mouth and lifts his hand. 'No,' he rasps, but the tone of his voice is firm. 'I will write the certificate, but *you* will need to deliver it tomorrow.'

'Oh,' she says as calmly as possible. 'But I was told that you would be taking it to the buyer?' Her pulse speeds up again.

Herr Keller rewraps the grimoire and offers it over. Her arms remain by her sides. She doesn't take it but looks at him for an explanation.

'My heart,' he says and moves a translucent hand to his chest. 'I had an attack two days past. It has weakened me greatly. The will is strong, as they say, but the body cannot deliver to him.'

Him – the unknown man, a high-ranking Nazi, who wishes to buy this magical book and all its mysteries.

No, no, no, she screams inside her head. But Herr Keller's comment has been delivered as a statement, a full-stop with no room for negotiation.

'He is expecting the grimoire with my stamp of authentication.' Herr Keller reiterates folding the certificate and inserting it into the leaves of the book.

It takes a moment for her to order her thoughts and smooth out the fraught note in her voice. 'I have appointments tomorrow, I'm afraid. Can your daughter do it?'

Herr Keller shakes his head. 'Hedwig and Klara are required in the shop. I am expecting another delivery.'

'But my appointments . . .' she begins.

'Must be cancelled,' Herr Keller finishes for her. 'Fräulein de Vigne, you should understand – one does not disappoint a man like this.'

In her head she sees all the carefully laid plans shatter like a dropped glass. Herr Keller nods, assuming her slack jaw and parted lips are about to request more detail. 'The Deputy Führer will be inspecting a plane at the aircraft factory tomorrow afternoon. Giving a speech to the workers. You will see him afterwards. There is a small window of time for the transaction. He is a busy man. It has been arranged for weeks.' Then, for the first time since she has entered the room, she hears steel in the bookseller's voice. 'He will not take kindly should he hear of your refusal.'

The.

Deputy.

Führer!

Fluttering a veined hand towards her, he wheezes, oblivious to how still she has become. 'I know you are unfamiliar with the city, so my son, Hans, will meet you at the library, not far from here, at three o'clock, and take you there. His superior has permitted him an hour's absence, for such a special duty, but no more. So do not be late.'

Oh God. How can she meet the Deputy Führer? A man of such high standing in the government. And she, a stage magician's assistant turned agent! He will see through her immediately. No, she cannot do it.

'I, I . . .' she hesitates.

Daphne's palms are so moist, she wipes them on her skirt without thinking. The collar of her blouse, with its embedded steel feels too high, too obvious, and scratches her neck. This is not what she has been trained for. Her brief is to deliver innocuous packages, to roam, gather intelligence and send it back. She is a courier, trained only to play a supporting role in this theatre of war. Not take to the main stage and stand face to face with the Deputy Führer himself.

To do so would be folly, surely?

'It is an honour,' says Herr Keller, waving the book at her again.

On reflex, she reaches out both arms and takes it.

The decision has been made.

Her world is spinning.

Desperately she tries to ground herself, summon resolve, manifest an impression of grace, though all she can feel is the hot, volcanic rise of panic.

As she steps back, still rigid, holding the book at arm's length, Herr Keller's nose wrinkles. 'And Fräulein de Vigne, you should ensure that you are well presented.' He gestures to her hair.

The admonition, if it is that, wrenches her from the clutches of dread. She hasn't washed properly for days. The smell of the farmyard, the hidden basement room with its damp walls, the lake water – she is carrying all of them on her. Goodness, yes, she must mend her appearance. He's right.

Reddening with embarrassment, she conceals her face by rewrapping the book in its coverings.

'Thank you,' she says and nods at Herr Keller and his family.

One minute later she is out the front door.

CHAPTER SEVEN

Greta has not been easy with Daphne's requests.

She fetched the bucket and passed over the soap with reluctance. But as Daphne began to wash her hair in the kitchen, spilling water across the counter, knocking utensils and pots over, sending some of them clanging onto the floor, Greta tutted, intervened and then took control.

Now Daphne sits on a low stool as Greta combs a mixture of egg yolks and herbs through her hair with a toothbrush.

The act is restorative, soothing, and helps to reassert cool logic over her frazzled brain. She can do this, she thinks. It is just a delivery.

Downplaying the danger is what helps control her fear.

Though, of course, she understands the magnitude of the risk she will be taking.

'Your hair will shine,' Greta says when all of it is covered. She smiles and Daphne forces her mouth to send one back. The action of doing so makes her feel marginally better.

Wrapping Daphne's head in a towel, the older woman sits her by the stove.

Under the towel her mind is still whirling. Should she get a message to Jack, warn him about the change of plan? He has only the barest outline of her task. He knows about the grimoire and that she must deliver it, nothing more. That is always the rule. Keep your worlds separate so that, if one of you is taken, there is nothing to betray. The thought chills her, a flash of cold anxiety spiders up her spine making her shudder. Tortured into revealing secrets is what that means.

Calm now, she tells herself, think! If she can get to the factory, deliver the grimoire to the Reichsminister and return as quickly as possible to Jack, then there is no need to mention any of it. Though should she tell London? Jack has the radio, so, no.

There are fingers tugging at the towel; Greta is unwrapping a section, checking the texture. 'Yes, we can take it off now,' she says and guides Daphne to the sink, bending her over and using a jug of water to rinse her hair.

'Now stand,' says Greta and hands her a clean towel, which Daphne uses on her hair.

Greta leads her back to the stool, takes up the comb once more and begins to detangle her tresses.

Just like her mother, Carabella, would do when Daphne was a girl.

Again, she notes how comforting it is.

Greta may only be mortal, but the woman is becoming something of an angel in Daphne's eyes.

'Thank you,' she says to her host. 'For helping me. It is *so* good of you.' She is not purely referring to her hair.

Greta nods and points to an embroidered sampler, framed and hung on the wall. 'Withhold not good from those who are due it, when it is in thy power to give.' Underneath it reads, 'Proverbs 3:27'.

Daphne repeats the words in acknowledgement. 'But many wouldn't,' she says, 'give it as freely as you do.'

Greta stands back and admires her handiwork. Daphne's hair is clean and neat.

She blinks and leans against the sink. And, for a moment, the two women sit and stand in companionable silence. Then Greta opens her eyes, breathes in deeply and breaks it.

'It is Aloisia,' she says suddenly, then puts a finger to her lips, goes to the open window and pulls it shut. 'No,' she shakes her head.

Is she talking to me or herself, Daphne wonders?

Then her host points to the partitioned wall that separates the cottages. 'There used to be a girl, well – a woman really. She was unwell.' Greta taps her forehead. 'Her mind was not fully formed. More like a child's. Innocent. Pure. She lived here, happily, with her family. This is a good place. The walls – they keep bad people out, and they hold "the wandering" within: babies, children, old people who are confused, and those like Aloisia. Four houses down, they lived. Until her mother died. A few of us, here in the Fuggerei, neighbours, we helped out with her care. But her father, Alban . . .' She pauses and mimics tipping a glass of liquid down her throat – the universal gesture for drinking. 'He couldn't cope.' Her head drops for a moment, and she presses her lips together. 'The drink got hold of him and would not let him go.'

Daphne's mind roams back to her stage partner, The Grand Mystique, and the dark nights and similar demon that had possessed him after his wife died. 'It is not uncommon,' she says to Greta.

The older woman raises her head. A weak smile indicates gratitude for Daphne's sympathy. The regime here has a strict moral tone: any kind of weakness is viewed as 'asocial'. Daphne has read about it in the papers. The term is used to describe a category of people deemed undesirable, 'unworthy'. But it is broad and includes those like Aloisia's father, prostitutes, beggars and Romani. Anyone who is unable to work or who is different. This German system sharpens its claws on the vulnerable.

'So,' Greta continues, rocking on her heels, hands clasped in front of her, tightening as she speaks. 'Aloisia was entered into Schutzengelheim Deybach in Lautrach. A home for such girls. Alban went into a nursing home just south of here. He died three years ago.'

Daphne nods, wondering where this is going. Judging from the way her chest rises and falls so rapidly, it is important for Greta to communicate this matter. But Daphne cannot really see the relevance. It seems strange to her that she should choose this – her poor neighbour – on which to speak, when so much else far more pressing, more urgent, is swirling around them.

Perceiving Daphne's confusion, Greta sniffs and moves on. 'Last year Aloisia was transferred to Kaufbeuren-Irsee.' Daphne hears her voice quiver as she pronounces the name.

'What is that?' she asks.

'My cousin,' Greta answers, 'she has worked there. It is not a good facility. Despite the fact that there are Catholic sisters working within its walls.' She crosses herself and mutters under her breath.

Daphne's mind tries to reach for a mental picture of the place. 'A convent?'

'A sanatorium, hospital, for the sick and those like Aloisia with a feebleness of the mind or physical handicap, illness. This government, they believe,' she falters, takes a breath, and Daphne can tell that something is fighting its way out with great difficulty. 'They believe that God cannot want the sick and ailing to reproduce.' A hand covers her mouth as if it is a sin to speak such words. Her eyes remain on Daphne, allowing a moment for this to sink in.

But her guest cannot absorb the assertion and is unsure what Greta means. 'They don't let the sexes mix?'

'No,' says Greta firmly. 'They say they are a burden on the national community. Biologically inferior . . .' she pauses. 'Undeserving of life.'

'Oh,' says Daphne and her stomach pitches. An awful feeling of sickness and dread comes over her.

Before she can find words with which to react to Greta's statement, her host adds, 'They have children there too.'

'And what is going on?' Daphne asks, requiring clarity though feeling as if she does not really want to know.

'My cousin says – they are starving them.'

Now her body reacts and she finds herself gasping. Starve children? In a hospital? 'Just a minute – a sanatorium is charged with healing, no?'

Greta does not answer. She talks quickly, as if she must spit the words out of her body before they begin to contaminate. 'Starvation for some. Others they inject with luminal – barbiturate. More than the body can endure. It started last year. Hundreds,' she says, 'hundreds have passed this way.'

Passed? What does that mean: 'Passed this way?' She shakes her head. 'You mean, through the hospital?' Though deep inside she understands she is delaying the need to engage with this news, preferring her suspicions to be a misunderstanding.

Greta swallows. 'No, passed into the arms of the Lord. Perhaps they find a better place there, away from the misery.'

And then it is there, in front of her. 'You don't mean . . .' she says. The thought of it . . . the thought of it is too . . . 'They're not . . . *killing* them?'

Slowly, eyes fixed on Daphne's face, Greta nods.

For a heartbeat, Daphne wonders again if she has misheard something. 'But, but . . .' she stammers. It is at odds with her perception of the world and difficult for her to shape this idea into a reality. Can doctors and nurses really be carrying out such acts?

Greta's head dips again – an affirmative. 'They say they are euthanised.'

It is almost as if all other words have been whipped away, leaving only the vilest in Daphne's throat. 'Murder!'

'Some Catholic sisters are there,' Greta says again, her top lip glistening with sweat.

A frown takes Daphne's forehead and squeezes it hard. 'Surely that is against the doctrine? The commandments? "Thou shall not kill."' The sixth command fills up the small kitchen as Daphne utters it. The words are imperative, holy, sacred.

Greta's arms brush with gooseflesh. 'The Führer has decreed it. It is his dictat and he is the ultimate authority in the land. Not the church.' She begins to run her hands up and down her arms. 'The sisters, they are used to submitting to the male staff. Obedience to the state is deeply enforced, challenging state orders can result in arrest.'

'What about the relatives? The parents?'

'The medical staff lie about how their patients pass.'

A pause now, in which they both flounder. Daphne shakes her head. 'But your cousin knows this? For sure?'

'She has seen it. With her own eyes.' Another nod. Then she lets out a deep breath which is almost a sob. 'And Aloisia is there.'

Daphne cannot help what happens next.

She makes it to the sink before the contents of her stomach come up.

There have been terrible stories circulating about atrocities inflicted by the enemy but that was also true of the Great War, and many of them turned out to be false. Some, whispered in cafés and pubs back home, she has believed too extreme, too horrific, exaggerated, and assumed them propaganda or ill-founded rumour. But to hear this now, from Greta, a German citizen, to listen to her account . . . Daphne's mind briefly stops working. She experiences a numbing blackness as if everything has frozen and nothing will work. Then her body responds once more.

Greta is behind her, rubbing her back as she retches, gathering up her clean hair and holding it back so it is not spattered by vomit.

When Daphne has finally stopped, Greta hands her a glass of water, which she takes gratefully.

It is too dark, too horrific, too awful to be real, she thinks and wipes her mouth and looks back at Greta. It is then that she suddenly notices, really notices, the lines carved into Greta's forehead. Wrinkles that should not be as deep for a woman her age. Her eyes are taut, the bags underneath them heavy. And she knows this is the truth.

'Kaufbeuren-Irsee,' says Greta, 'is a killing factory. When you get back to England you must tell them what is going on.'

CHAPTER EIGHT

2nd May 1941

Cannot be real, Daphne thinks. Though even as her inner voice speaks those words, she knows her gut has absorbed the fact of it.

Abhorrent, disgusting, unconscionable – darker than she ever imagined. Yet, so is this regime. They don't play by the rules of war, the rules of law, or the rules of any civilised society. They are a new incarnation of the very devil, who some say they worship.

She lifts her chin with absolute resolution and scowls at the mirror. A different woman is reflected back. There is something hard in the line of her jaw and toughened in the jade of her eyes. She can do this, she tells herself again. Everything *must* be done to stop the Nazis. Humanity and decency must prevail. And she is bound to help them. She draws a steadying breath – first things first – and grounds herself in the ordinary, running fingers through her clean hair. She is amazed by its softness. Greta's herb garden has created a wonderful tonic that makes her locks gleam.

Her suit is smart, her blouse freshened and pressed.

She lifts the package from the trunk at the foot of her bed, where it has rested all night, and takes the stairs into the kitchen. A vague smell of lavender lingers.

Greta is there washing in the sink. There is no bathroom in the house, they must visit the communal toilets and washing facilities when necessary.

She wipes her face with a towel and smiles. Something passed between them last night. Their relationship has deepened. As well as trust, they share a terrible clarity. There is a bleak darkness here, an insanity that seems contagious, but there are also a few that resist it. Greta, thank God, is one.

Daphne has promised the woman she will alert her superiors to the killings. Though she knows that it will need to be corroborated. And even then, what can they do? Without firm, detailed intelligence, the British government cannot respond formally or publicly. They have no troops here on German soil, so no operational path to intervene militarily in Bavaria, storm the hospital and release the patients. Diplomatic pressure is non-existent. The Nazis do not care about the condemnation of other governments.

Still, to do nothing would be worse.

She *will* speak to those in command. If nothing else, she can carry Greta's words in her head, try to reach someone with power, someone who will listen. Perhaps nothing will happen, but at least she will know that she tried.

Evil spreads through apathy.

'Not all of us are cowards,' Greta told her last night. 'We know here, in the Fuggerei, that all human life is sacred, regardless of physical or mental ability. It is blasphemous to say otherwise. But, I'm afraid to say, many are muzzled by fear or complicity. We have tried to tell our bishop, Dr Joseph Kumpfmüller, but,' she shrugged, 'nothing. Yet, there is a man in the north, Münster, Bishop von Galen, who is the same as you and me.'

She remembers it now, as she prepares to leave. 'I was thinking about what you said – that man you talked about last night,' she tells Greta. 'The bishop in Münster, von Galen. Can you not get word to him?'

Greta hangs the towel around her neck and sighs. 'We fear that post to the bishop is intercepted and monitored. And I cannot travel there. I have no family in Münster, no reason.'

Then she looks at the package in Daphne's hands and brightens. 'After this, you go north, to your home, don't you? His cathedral is not far from you.'

She cannot break her cover, although she has a strong suspicion that Greta does not really believe she is a bookseller from Cologne. 'I will report it, I promise,' she says. Though to her own superiors, when she gets home. After this, she should return back through the south as quickly as possible.

'To Bishop von Galen?' Greta persists.

She does not want to lie so says, 'Let me see. I will try to get word.'

Is this how it changes for her? That words spoken can become reality? Is there magic out there that forks your destiny?

She is not aware yet, but Daphne will play her part.

Oblivious to the wheel of fortune turning, she absently smooths down her hair.

Greta takes her hand. 'All in order?'

'Yes,' she says. 'How do I look? Presentable?'

'Professional and businesslike. The hair helps enormously,' Greta adds. And they both feel better. 'So you will return later for your suitcase?'

'Yes, indeed. Hopefully by six.'

She stows the grimoire in her satchel.

'Right,' says Greta, and straightens Daphne's collar. 'God speed you.'

CHAPTER NINE

Despite the fact she is early, the car is already waiting for her when she arrives at the library. It is a huge building and very grand, with a baroque entrance and pillars either side. Parked just beyond the railings she sees a grey Opel. It is the only car there.

A tram scuttles past, shrieking as the driver applies the brakes to round the curve of the street. A bell rings out to warn pedestrians of its approach.

The Kellers' son steps out as she approaches. He is wearing driving gloves and raises one hand in greeting.

She goes straight over and he receives her with a light handshake.

There is a frankness about him. Dressed in a dark-grey suit which has been tailored to fit and a maroon tie, he is not nearly as dour as his sister. Though his hair, half-hidden under a trilby, is the same straw-coloured shade.

As she gets in beside him, she says. 'Guten Tag Herr Keller. How is your father?'

'Improving,' he says, and starts the engine.

Herr Keller Junior does not invite conversation but that is fine for her. She can use the time to regulate herself, stamp out fear and build her resolve.

After a few minutes, Daphne's internal radar alerts her to a man on the street, a Luftwaffe officer, walking briskly past a bakery. Somewhere behind them a horn blares loudly and does not stop for five whole seconds. She jumps slightly and the hair on the back of her neck prickles to attention.

Whether Hans sees this movement or not, she doesn't know, but he says, 'It won't be long now.'

Silence stretches to fill the car. And despite her best intentions she cannot stop her mind returning to her task. It is not just the Deputy Führer who worries her. For he won't be alone. The Reichsminister will be surrounded by other high-ranking officers, aides with suspicious eyes and soldiers to protect him. Every word she says will be overheard, every facial expression she makes observed and noted.

But it is also an incredible opportunity, she affirms. The things she might learn are innumerable, valuable.

Hans taps the steering wheel with his gloved finger. 'It is up ahead,' he says and nods to a building.

The structure itself is innocuous, utilitarian, comprising vast, grey concrete and brick structures with high windows to let in daylight. But it is also foreboding: surrounded by walls, barbed wire, checkpoints. She recognises anti-aircraft guns pointed at the sky. Though just as the Home Guard are doing in old Blighty, here too they have camouflaged their forms under foliage and netting.

She can also see a watchtower.

It can see her.

Hans Keller pulls in to a sentry post. It is a squat brick building over which hangs a khaki canvas awning. It billows out in the late-afternoon wind. A white-painted barrier stretches across the road. Two soldiers lounge, but their eyes sharpen as the car stops. One nods with lethargy as Herr Keller flashes his papers.

'Name and purpose of visit?' the soldier asks.

'Hans Keller of Keller & Sohn. I am in place of my father, who has suffered a heart attack.'

Both of them look up. One is expressionless. The other raises an eyebrow then looks back down at the list of names.

Neither offer condolences or says 'I'm sorry to hear that,' as one might at home. But here, of course, weakness is worthy of contempt not compassion. Unless, it seems, you live in the Fuggerei or are a bishop in Münster.

'He has issued a certificate of authenticity for the book that Fräulein de Vigne is to deliver.' He gestures to Daphne.

The soldier squints, his eyes running down her suit to her legs, where they linger.

She forces a smile, 'I have an important package,' holds her satchel up, 'for the Deputy Führer.' His eyes widen at the title and he seems to contract inside his uniform.

Has she said it wrong? Is her accent off kilter? Has she used the wrong term? She suddenly worries and adds, 'Herr Hess.'

The last two words snap him to tight attention. And now she has said them for the first time out loud, heard the sting in the tail – the snake-hiss of his name – she too, finds herself momentarily flustered. Words have a power of their own, oh how she knows this. He *may* be just a man, but his name features in newspaper headlines, is spoken on newsreels and known internationally. It carries a force of its own, an authority that inserts itself into the air and makes it heavy.

The other guard shuffles over with a ledger. 'Both of you?' he asks.

Hans shakes his head. 'I am only to drop off Fräulein de Vigne. Is that acceptable?'

The soldier scouring the appointment list mumbles an affirmation and taps the page. The other looks at it and nods. 'All right.' Then he indicates for Daphne to get out of the car and present her satchel. 'Please.'

She glances at Herr Keller to see if he will follow suit but the soldier barks, 'Nein. Fräulein only,' and taps the visitors ledger.

Herr Keller shrugs. 'I leave you here then. Guten Abend Fräulein de Vigne.'

Without any further option, she gets out and watches the Opel reverse out and onto the road.

Once more she is on her own.

'Here . . .' the guard reaches for her bag. She watches as he pulls everything out, including the book, which he shakes, then puts to his ear. Of course, they must check for threats, concealed weapons. He begins to unwrap the grimoire.

'Careful,' says Daphne, and he darts his eyes at her, then juts out his chin with defiance: he isn't going to be told what to do by a woman. His grimy fingers begin untying the string. When he lifts it out and turns the pages, his eyebrows rise. She doubts the soldier has seen anything like this before and watches as he processes the weird signs and symbols that skitter across its pages. He flicks through the beginning, then, satisfied that it is not a bomb, but wary of what it might be, pushes it over to Daphne with an air of repulsion. Out of the side of his mouth, he says, 'Gefreiter Müller, escort this woman to the meeting room,' and another soldier, whom she had not seen before, rises from the darkness of the small room.

Clean-shaven and younger than the other two, he says nothing at first, then gestures. 'Follow me.'

The barrier rises and he walks ahead at a pace, not looking at her, expecting her to keep up. She does.

It is a different world on the other side. A hive of activity, engine oil and the smell of solder permeate the air, and she can see the hot air rippling out of vents along the buildings. Grey hangars stretch ahead. Workers trundle past, pushing carts that are stacked high with metal parts. The crates are stencilled with black eagles. No one meets her eyes. They all look busy. But there is an air of performance about their movements, as if they are keen to show that they are eager and not tired at all.

They pass a greyish water tower and, behind it, a worksite filled with more crates and twisted mechanical parts, scrap:

misshapen fuselage panels, cables overflowing from large metal boxes, a cockpit half-covered in canvas. She tries to take it all in, knowing that the details will be useful intelligence for her superiors if she gets home. *Once* she gets home.

There must be a workshop near, behind the walls, for she can hear pounding, the thump of factory machinery, cogs screeching on metal, wheels bumping over the ground, or possibly on tracks. Up above her, the noise of an engine revving draws her eyes. She catches sight of a Messerschmitt, taxiing towards the runway, and is reminded of an incident last year, when a new model of Spitfire was stolen from an airbase in Farnborough and flown to Germany. And here she is now, on the enemy's side. She wonders for a moment if the Spitfire landed nearby, but then tells herself to concentrate on the matter in hand. This is the priority now.

Ahead, a flat building constructed from red bricks comes into view. It is as utilitarian as the factory offices at home. Though a large eagle crest dominates the lintel, reminding her she is not in Britain. It is at once a shock to see it there and simultaneously not so. The symbolic creature's talons and hooked beak seem sharper than in her briefing notes.

At the entrance, two more guards flank the door. These ones are armed with a rifle each. A grim-faced man in a navy boiler suit with darkened goggles pushed up and over his head exits as they arrive.

The soldiers step aside to let him out. He glances at Daphne then strides off.

The soldiers re-form and block her way.

Her escort nods at one of them and that guard steps aside to allow entry.

The young man stops. Evidently this is as far as he is prepared to go. He turns to her. 'Inside. Second door on the left. Do not speak unless spoken to.'

'Thank you,' she croaks and tries to swallow but there is no saliva in her mouth any more. There are no other women here.

Her escort clicks his heels together and retreats.

Inside, she follows the directions and walks down a long corridor to the room. Trying the handle, she finds the door unlocked, so in she goes. A precise rectangle, its walls are painted a dull green. A long table dominates the centre. Made of oak, scuffed at the edges, ashtrays are spaced along it at regular intervals.

A large map of the Reich hangs along the far wall, bordered by red pins and lengths of string which she presumes trace air routes and supply lines. It is not so different to the Section W HQ at home. Or how it was before the bombs.

Below the map, a sideboard holds a jug of water, a stack of glasses and a large black telephone. There are windows on one side that look over the hangar.

She pulls out one of the high-backed chairs dotted around the table and sits down. Only then does she notice, by the wall she came through, a portrait of Hitler watching her. He wears a Nazi Party uniform, which she thought was meant to be brown, but in the light from the windows looks more yellow. The colour of cowardice, she thinks, and feels minutely less afraid. A swastika armband on his left arm looks more like a mourning band. Although his posture is upright, his hand is on his hip, in a slightly foppish style. The notion makes her smile. And this in turn decreases the tension in her body. She waits. Though whenever she fidgets and moves, Hitler's eyes are upon her. Even though she leans back to shift his gaze, they continue to follow her around.

Several times she hears footsteps outside, in the corridor, but they traipse on down the passage.

After twenty minutes she begins to worry. Surely Herr Hess should have been alerted to her arrival by now. Has something gone wrong? No, he is probably busy. He is an important man.

Minutes pass. She hears the main door slam shut and two men walking towards the room. 'Reserve tanks,' one says.

'Both of them,' says the other, 'To hold seven hundred litres.'

'But how?' says the first.

'Built into the wings.'

'On the ME 110?'

The door to the meeting room opens and they enter: an older man in his forties with white, wiry hair wearing a navy business suit, and another perhaps ten years younger, with a brown workcoat over a shirt and trousers.

'That's correct,' says the older man. 'For a long-distance flight of the utmost—'

The younger sights Daphne, frowns and jerks his head at her, the older spins round. His eyes are pronounced under a very high forehead and prominent nose. He does not look like an engineer but is more academic in his bearing.

'Hello?' he says, quite kindly, as if he has found a puppy. 'And who are you?'

She gets to her feet, suddenly unsure if she should shake hands or bow or something else. 'Dora de Vigne,' she tells him. 'I have something for the Deputy Führer.'

'Ah,' says the older. 'Well, I'm afraid you have missed him. He has gone into the city. He is speaking to the NS-Frauenschaft.'

Her eyes widen. She has heard the name before, a twist on the Women's Institute. 'Oh.'

'He's at the Golden Ballroom,' says the younger man, looking at her. 'I'm going that way. If you give me half an hour, I can drop you there.' He glances at the man in the suit. Ambitious, she thinks, eager to please his boss – and also the Deputy Führer.

'There you go,' says the older one to her. 'Perfect solution.'

Daphne tips her head and smiles, 'Thank you so much. I'd

appreciate that,' and she makes as if to sit down, but the younger says, 'No not here. We must clear up some work. I will have you taken to my car,' and he indicates she should follow him.

She bobs at the older man. It is almost a curtsey, and she tells herself off. But he only seems amused, not suspicious, and she follows the younger to the main doors. He speaks to one of the guards there. The soldier nods and beckons to her.

'Won't take long,' says the younger man and she is led off back the way she came.

CHAPTER TEN

Why can't anything be straightforward?

Although the current deviation still means she is on track to deliver the book.

And this way she gets a lift back into town.

Though with a stranger.

Her stomach emits a rumbling sound. She's not hungry. It is churning.

Her back is slick despite the fact that outside the temperature is cooling to fifty degrees Fahrenheit.

She sits in the passenger seat of the car. The door had been open. Why would it be locked in a place like this? The security is robust.

Pulling her satchel onto her lap, she checks the grimoire. It better be worth it.

Flicking through the pages, she turns to the prophecy at the back. It is the key to the whole mission.

'Here, affirmation sought by the winged man.' Not all of it has been forged. The most convincing fakes never are entirely. The best blend authenticity, half-truths and suggestion, using the individual's expectations against them. These words have been enhanced by the Section W experts. She knows the new lines by heart now.

'Whose iron wings shall open and span,
To Angel Isle, pact of lion and eagle forged by dew.
Though stars align to draw such fated two,
White flower drowns, then to be raised,

Mars declines, Saturn shall blaze.
Winged glory to the lion and king
And quiet where once warbirds did sting.'

Parts of it are indeed as original as the grimoire. Other lines have been doctored by the specialists to encourage a particular response in the reader. The 'winged man', she first heard named back in Iceland, in a séance room, uttered from the lips of a choking clairvoyant.

And it has brought her all this way to a car in a compound in the heart of Nazi Germany.

She eyes the aircraft hangar. The Deputy Führer has a keen interest in aviation, the Messerschmitt factory and its production. She wonders if he will identify himself as the winged man foreseen by the ancient scryer.

His name has been on lists and information sheets alongside such words as astrology, cosmobiology, parapsychology, clairvoyance, psychokinesis, magnetism, fortune-telling, astral travel, occultism. His keen fascination in the seer Nostradamus has commanded the attention of the British Security Service chiefs. Not because they are interested in such phenomena necessarily, but because they view his belief to offer an opportunity, a crack to exploit.

She takes her handkerchief and moves it over her forehead, knocks the felt fabric of her hat, remembers it is fastened there by a dagger disguised as a hat pin, smiles to herself and fingers it.

She spies the young man approaching the car park and sends him the most glorious of smiles. One which, in fact, almost stops him in his tracks. He puts a hand to his neck and gives his tie a little twist, then expands his shoulders and sends her one back.

Opening the rear door he slides a briefcase along the back seats, then gets in the front and turns to her, hand extended. 'I haven't introduced myself. Dr Hans-Georg Neumann.'

'Pleased to meet you,' she shakes it. 'A doctor?'

'Of engineering, naturally. I work with Messerschmitt.'

Goodness. Was that who was with him in the meeting room? Professor Messerschmitt? She tries to revisit an image of the man: mid-forties, perhaps a little younger, about five foot nine, medium build, slightly stooped. Light-brown hair, thinning on top, brushed very neatly. Pale eyes, grey or blue, it was hard to tell, the meeting was so brief. Bavarian accent, educated. Not a military man, but seemed entirely sure of himself, like military men often are.

Like her driver is.

She glances at him. Some kind of executive assistant or manager. He hasn't said. Younger than his boss, mid-thirties perhaps. Slightly taller than Messerschmitt, average build. Dark hair, well-kept, parted and slicked back. Complexion pale, clean-shaven. Darker eyes, hazel. Alert but tired. She knows very well it is possible to be both at the same time.

He turns the vehicle in the car park, and she assesses the distance between the gate and the brick-built HQ, the hangar, the sounds, the clues. Tries to commit them to memory, too.

Though she only has seconds before they pass through the barrier and turn into the road. She pretends to look at the sky by angling her face forward and up, but scans the road, 'I hope we won't get rain,' she says to make conversation.

Neumann crouches over the wheel and also looks upwards. 'Nein. The clouds do not look full. They will give good cover.'

And she realises he is talking about the Allies and their bombs. Or perhaps it is the other way round – the Messerschmitts will go out tonight with their bellies fully loaded, ready to pummel London and its occupants, many of whom she knows.

Her stomach tightens. She wants to clench her fists but cannot show evidence of anything but serenity, gratitude for the lift, so smiles widely once more, pressing down the back of her teeth, hoping her jaw can take the tension and her bulging cheeks hide it. She is staring straight ahead: he can only see her profile. And, really, he should keep his eyes on the road because the trees are giving way to the city and the buildings are growing more dense. They pass a square, Adolf Hitler Platz. She knows from her briefing documents that it was renamed by the city council eight years ago to demonstrate loyalty to the new Nazi regime. It is a wonder that someone like Greta lives here. To be discovered and found to be a traitor to the motherland would result in a punishment most severe. That there are *any* German citizens willing to help the British is really a miracle, testament to the spirit of resistance and justice.

They navigate across the platz. The landmark helps her work out where she is. They move on, deeper into the centre. Neumann tuts at a driver up ahead who has swerved slightly. No deviations are acceptable here, she thinks. Conformity is everything.

He motors right up to the back of the Rathaus and beckons over a guard. Recognising the driver instantly, the soldier comes to his door and opens it. Another scoots into the road to open Daphne's door. If only they knew.

She doesn't thank him but nods curtly as if she deserves such deference and follows Neumann to a side door. The lower windows are fortified by a mesh of iron, the entrance heavily guarded. Neumann is clearly a familiar face and once more the soldiers step aside to give them access to the interior.

And then they are admitted into a huge lobby. Footsteps echo into the high-vaulted ceilings. Women bustle past, clipboards clutched to their breasts, heels click-clacking across the stone floor. In a room above, someone is tuning a cello. As she raises her eyes instinctively to try and locate the sound, she sees red-and-black banners. So many of them. It is a special occasion evidently.

Neuman appears utterly at home among the hectic glut of people. But Daphne cannot help feeling her vulnerability. Part of her cannot believe this is happening. The audacity of it! That she, of all people, is being led calmly, by a civilian official, through the marbled corridors of this Nazi stronghold, not as a prisoner, but as a guest. The absurdity threatens to tense the muscles around her shoulders. But she straightens them and smiles, for another portion of her psyche has defaulted back to her theatrical training. She is playing a role: it is what comes naturally and makes her half-believe this is all a great performance, a game. Certainly, it will be one of the most important in her life. Yet, things have moved so quickly that it also feels very unreal, like a dream, or a play in which she is improvising. It will, she thinks, be her final act. Her finale. She must take great care.

A woman with silver hair, on a chair by an arched doorway, adjusts the drape of her navy jacket while yelling orders to two girls no older than Daphne's niece, Luciana, still at school somewhere in the North of England.

She glances to her left and sees her reflection in the glass doors of a display cabinet – a woman in a suit carrying a satchel. Perfectly posed, one of the many women ferrying things around the place. She looks the part.

Neumann stops, extends his arm to a stone staircase. He is being courteous, directing her up, so she starts to climb.

When she reaches the landing, she pauses. Giant embellished doors open onto a vast ballroom with veined marble flooring. Through them she sees women are practising the waltz in pairs. The cello she heard a moment ago accompanies their dance. It is a strange sight and adds to her sense of having crossed into, what can she call it? An unreality? A surreality?

She moves forward thinking that they are going to enter the ballroom, but Neuman taps her arm. As she turns, he shakes his head. He is holding one elbow, watching her, his hand covering his chin, almost concealing an amused smile.

Another door at the side of the landing is guarded by two soldiers. Neuman speaks to them, but they shake their heads. This time his familiar face and charm have not worked. 'Wait here,' he tells Daphne.

Clearly security on this level is not local. He takes out his papers and shows them. After close inspection, they admit him. But not her. Again, she is told to wait.

Making an effort to appear unbothered by this, she loiters, affects a listless pose, and gradually inches closer to look at the ballroom. It really is extravagant in there, lined with pilasters. Huge windows at each end would let in all the light of day, if they were not blacked out. Instead, to provide light, candelabras have been placed around the perimeter: their bobbing flames reflect on the shining floor. But it is the ceiling, soaring above the women, which is the most striking. Gold leaf adorns the plasterwork – so opulent – and framed paintings: Greek pastorals from the look of it. For a moment she forgets where she is and stands in marvel, hypnotised by the twisting patterns.

Then a group of brown-uniformed figures march past her, and she is snapped back into the present.

She keeps her gaze down and pretends to check her fingernails are clean, saunters away, stands by a wall with her back to the ballroom.

The side doors open and Neumann emerges. He sights her and beckons her over. 'The Deputy Führer is busy. You must wait in here.' But one of the guards puts his hand up – halt. She stops immediately and cannot suppress a frown. Has she betrayed herself?

He points down, indicates her bag.

Of course, a security check.

She opens it for him. 'This,' she says of the package, 'is what the Deputy Führer is expecting.'

'Show.'

Her hands have a tremble now, which is visible to the men watching her, but she takes it out and shows them the book, leafs through the pages.

At last, he nods and permits her entry.

Neumann escorts her across the threshold, past the men, into an antechamber furnished with chairs lined up against one wall.

Unaware of her agitation, he whispers as if in confidence, 'I had hoped to discuss something with Herr Hess but it will have to keep. So now I must leave you.' He executes a shallow bow.

'Thank you,' she says, summoning breath to calm her voice and deepen it. 'You have been most kind.'

He smiles, 'My pleasure, Fräulein.'

For a moment, as she watches him leave, her anxiety escalates, creeping up her neck, tightening her jaw.

The guard throws a sour glance at her before closing the door.

Now she really is all on her own.

CHAPTER ELEVEN

Minutes tick by. Do the hours fly too?

She cannot tell how long she sits there. Her watch was taken from her before she left England.

The window has been blacked out, but she has a feeling night has come down. And she still has not completed her mission.

Yet there is nothing else for it but to wait.

Adrenaline continues to discharge through her veins.

She has rewrapped the book, carefully tied the cord back around it. It lies on her lap, throbbing. Though it is the blood in her veins beating against its weight, fraught with anticipation: what the hell is now to come?

To distract herself, immerse her senses in the 'now', she reverts to the mundane and counts the wooden panels on the wall: four on two walls, three on one, two interrupted by the window. The door through which she came is on her left, the door to the room where she anticipates the Reichsminister is working is on her right. She expands the images of what she has seen on her way here – the side entrance, the corridor, the lobby, the stairs, the ballroom – and flattens them into a floorplan. Next, she does the same with the factory; tries to remember the direction and length of time it took to reach the administration block and then back again with Neuman. Attempts to summon the details of the car, the speedometer, how long it took to drive there and back. The knowledge will be priceless. As long as she lives to relay it.

She is mentally inspecting the images of the meeting room, calculating the length of it, the width, location in the complex when the door on her right, the inner door, springs open. A man is silhouetted in the doorway. He barks an order, 'Get up. Come now. Quick.'

She scrambles to her feet, a spasm of fear going off in her stomach, and enters the room.

It is larger than the antechamber, panelled with the same wood; windows are covered by dark-green velvet curtains. Immediately she becomes aware once more that she is the only woman here.

It contains several tables, around which crowd men in Luftwaffe uniforms. As she passes them there is a moment when she attracts a few inquisitive glances, but the men return to their business immediately, not wishing to be interrupted by a trifle of a woman.

The soldier who admitted her pushes her shoulder, quite roughly, she thinks, and she sees the corner where a delicate chinois screen has been erected to separate that part of the room.

She glances back and he gestures that she should walk round it.

Behind the screen is a desk; shifted against the exterior wall, a bookshelf. They have been positioned to give the occupant of this little nook some privacy.

And there he is – the occupant.

It is a shock to see him in the flesh, no longer flat and monochrome but three dimensional. Though she instantly recognises the low, dense brow and square forehead from photographs in the papers. But there is something else about this man that is not captured by photographs. It is as if he is partially clouded, cloaked in dark matter, so that his edges appear fuzzy. She blinks, looks again, but her gaze slides off.

Only his face seems real – focused but also distracted. In this room but also elsewhere, flickering in and out of the edges of reality. She cannot gauge him at all.

Aware of her presence, he takes his eyes off a document that has been spread out over the desktop and sits up straight. His uniform is impeccable, with straight, exact creases and a high collar. When his gaze lands on her, she feels it, like all the bright beams of the Lindau lighthouse have been gathered into one single, intense blast. For a moment she feels entirely exposed.

'Fräulein de Vigne,' he says. His eyes are energetic, dancing, slightly frenetic, as if he is trying to place her on a chart, or in a memory, trying to map her.

Breathe.

'I can't spare much time.' His words are clipped, hard on the consonants. Unexpectedly, though, his voice is soft and civil. But then she has only seen him on Pathé newsreels and in films, ranting like a lunatic. Yet, in this quiet room it carries authority. The power of his status is like a force-field that buzzes and radiates from him: everyone, whether they have their eyes on him or not, is aware of his every move.

She smooths down her hair, half-fearing it has picked up electrical static from his energy.

He doesn't extend a hand and remains seated, expecting her to come to him.

She complies, though her feet are reluctant to propel her any closer.

But the stakes are high and she must play this part well.

'Guten Abend, Reichsminister,' she replies with accurate pronunciation. Every nerve in every tiny part of her body is jangling under the scrutiny of the second-in-command of this enemy land.

She takes a deep, raggedy breath and swallows, though she hadn't intended to. He notices but does not appear fazed. No doubt he is used to having this effect on the plebiscite.

'Please,' he says, beckoning her, though it is an order. He has his back to the bookshelf. The screen blocks him from the eyes of the officers mulling around in the room.

As Daphne moves to the desk she realises she is now hidden from their eyes too.

There is no further dialogue. He knows why she is here, and it is unnecessary for her to explain, so she opens her satchel and removes the package, in its paper wrappings, bound with cord. With both hands, as if she were holding a baby, she lifts it up and places it on the desk between them.

For a moment she worries that the gesture is too highfalutin, too dramatic, too showy, too *showgirl*.

But, in the next, her worries disappear: his eyes are upon it instantly, then his fingers. He undoes the cord quickly without hesitation.

The paper falls away revealing the grimoire.

He opens it and turns the first page, then the second, the next and several after that. There is no finesse. His movements aren't delicate, as the fragile pages require, but quick and careless. He rifles through them to the section at the end, then draws in a breath.

It is almost imperceptible, but Daphne hears it.

He has reached the Nostradamus papers.

She tries hard to look casual again, though she is observing him, taking in every muscle movement on his face.

'And it *is* authentic?' he asks, leaning forward, lowering the volume of his speech.

'Herr Keller has inserted the certificate within the first two pages.'

He moves forward another inch. 'I'm not asking him. I'm asking you.'

The question, direct as it is, does not destabilise her. 'It was found in north Iceland in the possession of a native family. They have been sorcerers for centuries.'

A smile begins on one side of his mouth. 'So this is *it*, then. I had a message from Reykjavík many months ago . . . was alerted to its existence . . .' he pauses and looks down again, a fingertip tracing the arc of a rune on the page.

Her mind darts back to the Icelandic clairvoyant Sindri Karlsson, whom she investigated for evidence of collaboration with the Nazis. This, then, is confirmation from the very top. When she returns to England, the news will carry some weight. Karlsson is still working out there, though under the control of the British. Now she knows for sure that there is a network of sympathisers carrying messages directly to Germany. They can be fed false information.

Despite this quick rotation of thoughts, she says, in a low whisper, 'The prophecies were once thought lost to us, but these were discovered in this ancient tome. It is, indeed, an *extraordinary* find.'

'You have done well, Fräulein de Vigne,' he says, then drops his gaze, hunches over the book, as if shielding it from view, and, to her astonishment, begins to rip out the pages.

A small pang of disgust at the wanton vandalism threatens to twist her lips. She quiets it. It is clear what matters to him: the arcane knowledge of the seiðr – the tradition of Norse magic and shamanism almost wiped out – means nothing. She would be consumed by rage if she wasn't already strung so tight.

He looks to his left, into the room, ensuring he has not been watched, tucks the prophecies in his top pocket and pushes the grimoire back to her. 'You can have the book back,' he says more loudly. 'It is not what I expected. Perhaps sell it on, for your efforts. There is great interest in this literature at the moment. I doubt you would have trouble finding another buyer.'

A man, an advisor presumably, who has, for the past minute, been loitering the other side of the screen, waiting for an opportunity to interrupt, coughs for attention and steps round to her side.

Hess eyes him, annoyance crossing his face, raises three fingers and bends them – 'All right then, come over if you must.' And the man complies, manoeuvring round the desk. Bowing his head he bends to the Reichsminister's shoulder.

'Sir,' he says in a whisper that Daphne is able to hear, 'you may not wish to keep the grimoire, however, Reichsführer-SS would no doubt want to see it. Very much, I'd imagine. The Ahnenerbe commissioned an expedition only three years ago,' he says with meaning.

Daphne has heard fragments about this 'Ahnenerbe' department. It is, according to one of the operatives in Section W, focused on archaeology, anthropology and historical research into the Aryan race and the Germanic people's origins. 'Some sort of crackpot outfit Himmler's set up to prove the Germans came out of Atlantis,' was how Cyril had described it. In fact, before she had set off for the plane, he'd pulled her aside and instructed she take note of any references to runic studies, prehistoric skulls or sacred landscapes. 'Himmler has his pet scholars burrowing about in strange corners of Europe. Everything, anything, may be of use.'

Of course, she had agreed. But her target was not Himmler. It had not even been the Reichsminister, sitting before her. All she had been required to do was deliver the grimoire for certification. But, she thinks again, here she is.

Attuning her ears to the conversation she becomes aware of the advisor's gaze on her.

In response, she lowers her eyes, the picture of feminine obsequiousness, and simpers, 'It would be my pleasure if I could help further and give the grimoire—'

Interrupting her, Hess grunts. The thick, slightly Neanderthal brow lowers, displeasure queers his features.

The advisor freezes.

For one prickly moment a silence invades the room. Behind the screen, all movement, shuffling, voices in conversation have stopped. Everyone within the four wood-panelled walls is so very attentive to the mood of the Deputy Führer, Daphne imagines they are all holding their breath. The air around him waits.

Then he breathes out through his mouth and places his hand flat on the grimoire, laying claim to it.

'No.' He nudges it further towards her. 'If he wants it, he can get it himself.'

Daphne resists the impulse to step back.

He does not dismiss her but stands up, stretches.

The action, his movement, breaks the tension in the room. Men return to their conversations, the advisor clasps his hands together over his chest and nods rapidly, the soldiers breathe again.

She sees Hess's fingers begin to move to this pocket where the sage's visions are hidden. He wants to touch them, she thinks. But he restrains himself, drops his hand, puts the other in his pocket and saunters over to a tall door. A soldier there opens it and he disappears into the golden ballroom. Half a dozen uniformed officers follow him through. A round of applause breaks out inside.

The advisor glares at her, as if it was she who refused his suggestion.

A sudden overwhelming compulsion comes over her: *take it*. It is almost like an order in her head.

She steps forward, gathers up the grimoire and walks as quickly as she can out of the room.

CHAPTER TWELVE

God be praised. She has done it! Completed the objective! She can breathe again.

Glory!

Back on the streets, the grimoire still weighs heavy at her side, but her body feels lighter, almost buoyant.

She is amazed by herself, by the feat she has just pulled off.

The Deputy Führer is in possession of the forged prophecy, and he believes it to be genuine!

Certainly, the rest of them are real. Or as real as the experts have managed to calculate in terms of probability.

It is remarkable.

And she allows herself a moment of self-congratulation – she must be quite remarkable too, surely. For what are the chances that she could assume a German identity and pass herself off quite successfully. No – *so* successfully that she has met the second most powerful man in the Axis force.

And not been challenged!

Not once.

A euphoria floods her.

She is *good* at this game.

Hugh Devereaux could see it, even Septimus observed it in the end. And now she has justified their faith in her.

Someone up above is looking after her.

Her mind skitters against an image of her grandfather Günter. He said he would keep watch over her. Perhaps it is he? Or is it Rafn, who might have been her lover if the fates had not been so cruel, whose life was the price of this damned book she carries now? God, she thinks and looks at her satchel. Will she never be rid of the thing?

She has forgotten that pride comes before a fall.

As she turns the corner and into the street which will take her away from the Rathaus, she realises, suddenly, that night has come down like the stage curtain at the end of the show. She has no idea what time it is. Blackout has turned off the streetlamps, boarded the windows, shuttered doorways, sucked all the light out of the air. And tonight, there is a cold drizzle, no moon. Darkness presses down from above.

The weather has emptied all the streets.

Though she knows her way and continues down the road. A door opens briefly and a rectangle of amber light falls across the pavement, wafting with it voices, the clink of glass, someone laughing. For a moment she wants to drop everything, go in and get herself a celebratory drink.

How ridiculous, she thinks, how reckless to even think it.

Must be the exhilaration deluging her brain, mixed with a surfeit of adrenaline. Of course she cannot do such a thing. Her guard cannot be lowered. All of that can wait till she gets home. Whenever that may be. Hopefully in a few days. Perhaps she can persuade Jack to go to a jazz club with her. Until then she must hold herself together, keep her information stored in her brain, until the debrief. There is such a great deal now to pass on. The confirmation about Karlsson is priceless. Hugh, her commanding officer will be so proud. He always had confidence in her, even when she was unsure about her own strengths.

She has done it!

So wrapped up in her subtle triumph and taste of victory is she that when she rounds the corner towards the Fuggerei, she marches straight to the iron gates without checking the road. The grimoire, which she hazards can be brought home and potentially used again, the forged prophecy in Hess's pocket, the image of Hugh's delighted smile, all crowd her mind. She does not notice the gates are locked until she reaches them.

Though that is no problem. There is a night watchman. But as she calls out for him, she sees his door is open and his post empty.

She taps the gate again. 'Hello?'

Nothing.

It's all right, she thinks. *I can wait. I've spent most of the day in limbo*.

But she has not noticed a solitary soldier sheltering from the rain in a doorway at the side of the road, his face illuminated by the glow of his cigarette tip.

'Fräulein,' he says, now at her shoulder.

And she starts and spins on her heels. Momentarily her face betrays surprise: eyes flashing wide, jaw tightening. Then she rolls down her stage smile, though she's not sure he can see it.

'Do you live here?' he asks and breathes smoke out over her. 'Where is your key?'

'No, I, I,' she stammers. Come on Daphne, quick! She has been told not to mention Greta if challenged by the Wehrmacht. Her contact is far too valuable to be given up. *Take the truth and expand it*. 'I unexpectedly find myself in possession of a rare book. My intended customer did not want it. But another, who lives here, might be interested.' She taps her satchel.

He tilts his head, studying her with a frown. 'So late?'

'You're right,' she says. 'It *is* probably too late. Though I thought I could deliver it tonight as I have such a busy day tomorrow. But I'll return home now. It can wait.'

There is a layer of judgement in his voice as he replies, 'So I shall escort you home then. It is not safe for Fräuleins to be out in the blackout on their own.'

Her stomach twists. *No. No, no, no.* She cannot let him walk her anywhere. Least of all to an address she does not have.

'That's very kind,' she says quickly, trying for lightness, though her voice is a little too high. 'But really, there is no need. It is not far.'

He doesn't move. His expression does not change, but he pauses, and she senses his scrutiny.

'Where is it, then?' he asks and throws the stub of his cigarette into the road.

He could ask to see her papers, her certificate of residence, but so far, he has held off. Possibly because it is too dark.

Her mind swivels. She shrugs, tries a faint laugh. 'A few streets away. A bookshop just up here,' and she points and then remembers she has a cigarette case in her jacket pocket, on the left side. She reaches into it and unclasps the catch. 'May I offer you a cigarette for your trouble, Herr Offizier?'

'Danke,' he takes one.

'Take another.'

He does, asking, 'You not having one?'

'Not now,' she says. 'It keeps me up if I smoke at this time.'

She sees the shadows on his face fill out as he smiles. Replacing the tin back in her pocket, she insists, 'Really, I can take it from here.'

'I will at least walk you to the end of the street.'

And so there is nothing else for it. They set off soon enough, reaching the junction. She turns down into a narrow alley, hoping he will leave, maybe watch her from the corner. But he doesn't.

Oh lord, where now?

She becomes stiff under her jacket.

It is too risky to go to Keller's. They will be asleep by now and, if woken, surely surprised. In addition, Hedwig did not warm to her and is unlikely to play along. Especially if Daphne turns up with a soldier.

She forces her lips to lift cheerfully, something much warmer than her last, though her mouth feels strange, as mechanical as an automaton's.

She gestures vaguely towards the alley ahead. 'I can see myself from here. Really, you don't need to—'

A low, startling sound begins to reach through the drizzle. Faint – at first she thinks it is a car horn. But it becomes something louder and more consistent: the scream of an air raid siren.

The soldier stops mid-step. She halts too.

He turns his head towards the sound.

'Verdammt,' he mutters, then narrows his eyes at the patchy sky. Daphne follows, blinking as raindrops fall across her face. Briefly she thinks of Neumann peering through the windscreen: *The clouds . . . they will give good cover*. But there are no visible plane lights, no slim crucifix-shaped shadows crossing the skies above.

'Is it real?' Daphne asks. Whatever country you are in, whether soldier or civilian, bombs do not discriminate. They flatten, burn, destroy. How ironic it would be to die, the night of her success, on enemy soil, at the hands of the Allies.

He checks his watch, frowns. 'Maybe. They've been jumpy this week. False alarms. And now Hamburg has been hit.'

'No!' she says, feigning patriotic outrage.

'We'll need to clear the street.' His eyes scan the road, up and down. 'You should find shelter just in case. There's a Luftschutzkeller beneath the church on Barfüßerstraße.'

'Of course,' Daphne says quickly. 'I'll go straight there.'

He hesitates, eyes leaping from her face to the satchel at her side. She presses her fingers to the flap as if to reassure him it's harmless, nothing more than a book. Just a book. If only.

At last, he nods. 'Good night, Fräulein.'

'And to you.'

She strides off, doesn't look back.

Now it will be impossible to get into the Fuggerei: she cannot risk being seen by him again.

There is only one place left, though it is just as fraught with danger.

But for reasons she could never guess.

CHAPTER THIRTEEN

By the time she has reached the green door of Jack's boarding house the siren has wound down. Thank goodness. The streets have settled back into their hush.

She stands hunched beneath the eaves of a shuttered café opposite. Hopefully he is in the designated room: first floor, second from the right. Please God he is still up.

As she examines the window, she makes out a sliver of yellow through a gap in the blackout curtains. A quick glance up and down the street, then she bends, finds a loose bit of brick near the gutter. The first piece she hurls taps the windowpane and bounces off, at an angle, hardly making any sound. The second cracks against it.

Light moves behind the curtain. A shadow darts across the gap.

She waits. Nothing happens.

Where is he?

Hopefully not allotted a different room.

She finds a small pebble and chucks it.

It clips the wood of the frame.

Finally, the curtain tugs back an inch. A face appears in the gap. The shape and short hair suggest a male, so she takes a breath and steps out of the shadows, lifting her hand, palm up. She does not wave but holds it there as a signal, hoping he can see her in the darkness.

The curtain falls back.

There is nothing for her to do but stand at the door. If it is not him then she must come up with an excuse – the package may yet prove useful.

The front door creaks open, she takes the pin from her hat and holds it in her hand, ready to attack if necessary.

To her relief it is indeed Jack there in the unlit hallway. 'Were you followed?'

Only halfway, she thinks. There is no point telling him all the details. 'No.'

'You're late,' he whispers, pulling braces up and over his shoulders. 'Extremely.'

Daphne searches his expression for any sign of warmth or affection. She suddenly needs it. But there's none. Where the Deputy Führer's edges were loose and fuzzy, Jack's seem to have sharpened in her absence.

Without another word, he nods. 'Come in, then. Quickly.'

For the first time in days she feels the muscles in her shoulders loosen very slightly. He leads her up the stairs to his room.

It is small and functional with a desk and a chair and a single bed, which he gestures for her to sit on.

She sinks down with a groan. The bed springs squeak and jangle. Up until this point, the constant flow of tension and her accelerated heartbeat have kept her from feeling tired, but now she has reached shelter, everything seems to be catching up with her.

'Shh,' says Jack. 'We can't wake the landlady. If she finds us both here . . .'

Daphne nods – she gets it. A single man and single woman in a bedroom in the middle of the night would be scandalous. She removes her hat.

When she moves forward to rest her hands on her knees, he says, 'No suitcase?' then scowls. 'You're not finished, are you?'

'Yes and no,' Daphne replies. 'The main objective has been achieved. Although I still have the grimoire.' She taps her satchel, which she has thrown to the floor by her feet. 'But that is fine. However, there are a couple of things I need to organise tomorrow.' Collect her belongings from Greta at the Fuggerei. 'I'm sure we can leave by seven.'

'You look as though you could do with some kip,' he says. 'But travelling when the Augsburger are going to work will carry risks.'

She knows this too. 'I have been taken for a native, it seems. Your German is passable, your French excellent. I can do most of the talking in this country. You can lean on me. We'll get by.' The words come out more confidently than she expected.

Jack nods, but it seems to her that his eyes lack conviction. 'All right then, but we should leave earlier – perhaps six? I'll wake you up. Best to clear out of the city while it's still dark. Look, you get some sleep. I'll nap downstairs on the couch in the dining room. Better slide a note under the landlady's door, explaining that you're here.'

Daphne's hand reaches into her satchel to offer him her gold pen. It's a beauty, perfect for writing and desirable enough to be converted into ready cash, should one need it suddenly. 'I have paper too.'

'No, it's fine,' he says. 'There's stationery downstairs.'

Her hand drops. 'Say I had problems with the key to my lodgings.' It's true-ish.

'Right, yes.'

She wants him to come over and touch her. No necking or anything of that sort, just a physical reassurance – maybe a hand on the shoulder or a stroke of her arm – that might comfort, set her right, restore her inner balance. But he doesn't. Simply inches towards the door and then out.

The stairs creak under his weight as he pads down and she hears a door opening and then a deep thud as it shuts, like that of a front door but, of course, it must be the dining room. These houses are old, with thick walls, solid doors and chunky iron fittings.

She tucks the pen away in a slim pocket hidden under the arm of her jacket.

Then there is nothing but the quiet of the siren-less night.

Exhaustion nets her and she falls back, kicking her shoes off, not even pulling the blanket over, and slips into unconsciousness as soon as her head touches the pillow.

Sleep well, Daphne. The conjunctions are already sliding into place, prophecies becoming real.

CHAPTER FOURTEEN

3rd May

Jack is shaking her shoulder.

She has been in a deep sleep and dreaming, she thinks, of Rafn. For when she acknowledges Jack's face, she feels a transference of the affection she felt for the other.

Jack with his eyes of blue and peony lips. Such symmetrical features. It is not hard to see why she was besotted last summer. Though nothing had really come of it. Plans, friendships, courtships cannot often withstand the contortions of war. One is no longer an individual but works for the good of the whole country. And that is, for sure, a love affair which must take priority over any other. It has certainly taken over theirs. Although it has been nearly seven months since Rafn's death, yet in some ways it is almost like yesterday. Certain memories she can recall in detail – their kiss under the aurora borealis, talking on the boat, feelings of connection, of understanding without words. Rafn's clear hazel eyes regarding her from his seat by the stove, in a house carved from a hillside, while the storm raged outside. His words, spoken as a statement, which almost made her laugh: 'You look attractive in this light.' As if she looked terrible in all others. She has permitted herself to go over these memories again and again so they have become ingrained, part of the landscape of her mind. But they are also a source of pain, like a scar inside her which opens every now and then. Often, she thinks she should not let her mind drift there. Though at other times it makes her happy to imagine what might have been. Really, she should move on. Really, she must only think of the now.

So, she shakes off the night and reads the expression on Jack's face.

It alarms her.

His jaw is rigid and clenched, eyes pinched, wrinkling the skin around them. There seems to be a crick in his neck. As he straightens up, he does so with difficulty, as if his body is straining.

It is not like him to lack suppleness. His grace and confidence are two of the qualities she continues to admire. But both have presently deserted him. He seems older, crooked.

Is it morning? she wonders briefly, glancing at the window. The bulk of Jack's body blocks the view, but a pale light enters the room. Not the watery glow that comes after the stars have vanished, but the full reach of morning, when the sky is the colour of chalky Dover cliffs.

'You didn't wake me,' she says to Jack with reproach. 'I thought you said we should be up by six.'

He grimaces and scratches his nose, a gesture he defaults to under pressure. 'Change of plan.'

'Oh, right,' she says, wondering what has happened to stress him so.

He takes a step back.

Only then is she able to view the wider room.

It takes a moment for her to realise they are not alone.

When she does, her chest instantly constricts, squeezing the air out of her lungs in an audible wheeze. Adrenaline discharges through her veins.

My God.

All her nightmares set upon her like a murder of crows.

There, blocking the only exit, are two soldiers of the SS.

CHAPTER FIFTEEN

Attempting to steady herself, she composes a relaxed, vacant expression that will counter any other trying to twist her face.

Stay calm. Panic will only clutter your mind and give you away.

But her body is reacting ahead of her brain's instructions: a cold, sickly sweat has broken out over her skin – every single inch of it. She's not sure she has ever experienced such a reaction before – chill and fever at the same time. For her cheeks are flushing, the blood in her veins boiling, funnelling up her chest and neck to her sticky forehead.

Though she can see them, she still does not really believe her eyes: the SS!

One is stocky, a light moustache over his downturned lips and golden skin. The other ruddy with a wide, flat face. Less tense than Jack but still taut, he steps forward, 'You must come with us.'

In the perplexing onslaught of emotions and thoughts that tumble blindly about her, she sees a hand move forward – Jack's – takes it. Such a gentlemanly gesture, which she is grateful for in this moment of crisis. 'Thank you.'

Setting her on her feet, he hands her a tumbler. 'Water. Drink it.' And she complies. Her mind is gaining speed, turning over possibilities, reasons why the soldiers may be there. An unexpected check of the boarding house? A search of the occupants' papers?

Then Jack reaches down to her satchel, at the side of the bed, and lifts out the grimoire. 'This is the book,' he says to the older SS man.

What is he doing?

He does not hand it over but holds it tightly to his chest. *Possessively.*

Something cold begins to uncoil inside her stomach.

A notion so terrible she wants to crush it before it can become real.

'Do you want it?' Jack asks the soldier.

No, no, no, no, no.

'Or shall I take it to the Reichsführer myself?' he says.

The words knock out her breath.

She clasps her hands together and squeezes, instinct urging her body to brace itself.

The younger one with the butterscotch skin shakes his head. 'Our instructions are to arrest her.'

Now she gasps. She cannot help it. There is no air in the room. She tries to gulp it down, drags her gaze to Jack. Who nods.

Not at her – but at the soldier.

He *nods!*

At *them*.

For a moment, her world dips. Darkens. Slides into a place where nothing makes sense.

What is he doing? *Why* is he nodding? *How* does he know these men?

Her mouth opens and closes like a fish on dry land.

'All right,' he says.

And with those words monstrous meaning breaks through at last.

He is *colluding!*

With *them*.

'She can translate the contents,' Jack continues. 'Bear that in mind.'

The young soldier drops his head – message understood. The other steps forward and seizes Daphne's arm.

She pushes her feet into her shoes, her body moving without her, and looks at Jack, as stunned as if she has been whacked on the head.

'Her Ausweis,' he says and hands over her identity papers. 'Forged.'

He locks on to her gaze then, trying to beam something into her eyes, but she is too staggered to interpret his meaning.

Then he raises his hands in a small gesture of surrender and shrugs.

'I'm sorry,' he says.

As the younger soldier begins pushing her to the door, Jack turns his back on the scene and looks towards the curtained window.

Now panic rises, sending her heart thumping. Flutters of acid in her stomach make her feel like she is going to be sick.

Try as she might, she can't think straight as she is marched out of the room and down the stairs. Her actions are slow, uncoordinated, her mind sluggish from the enormity of what is happening, which makes the soldiers rough, impatient with her pace. On the landing, the younger shoves her and she bashes her face on the wall, knocks off a picture hanging there. Though a numbness is starting to overtake her.

At the bottom, in a doorway, an old woman wrapped in a grey shawl stands.

She tuts at Daphne, then spits.

It hits her cheek. She wipes it away with her sleeve. But the crude act has shocked her, cut through the fog: her senses return, her mind zips into focus.

'There must be some mistake,' she says to the soldiers. 'It is imperative I return to Cologne. I am a bookseller.' They ignore her, continuing on.

Out the door onto the narrow pavement, she is manhandled down to the corner, into the larger road. Eyes are on her.

Pedestrians have stopped walking to stare, others shuffle past, look away and keep their heads down.

She is elbowed and prodded across the street, looks back briefly, glimpses Jack standing at the corner. He is still holding the grimoire tightly, watching her, biting his lip.

Somehow, she seems to have cut hers and can taste blood in her mouth. She spits it out in his direction. The traitor.

How ironic, she thinks, after all she has survived – the high security factory, the inner sanctum of Nazi high command, it is not the enemy who has undone her now. But the one she trusted most.

CHAPTER SIXTEEN

6th May

She no longer knows what day it is.

The light in the cell keeps changing. Sometimes the single light bulb is off, and she is kept in darkness. More oftentimes it is on. Blinking constantly. Buzzing. Is there a German factory somewhere that makes them like that?

She tries to measure time but there is not much to mark it by. Sometimes the guards wake her, banging on the door with something hard and metallic – a baton, she suspects. For the sudden racket is terrifying, jerking her from sleep as the soldiers shout her name. Other times they leave her so long in silence she begins to wonder if they've forgotten she's here. That's almost worse. She thinks of those cruel vertical shafts that were built into medieval castles into which prisoners were dropped and left. Oubliettes. Then she scrubs the thought from her mind. It won't help.

Cold climbs up through the stone floor into her feet. Her breath is visible, despite the temperature outside on the city streets.

They haven't beaten her. She had expected that might happen. Perhaps they are saving it for later.

They have allowed her some water but no food. However, she has gone without meals for long stretches of time before. One of her last stops, prior to leaving England, was an old country mansion on a beautiful estate in the Midlands. She and three men were often dropped off at some remote place in the countryside and told to make their own way back, avoiding villages. It regularly took hours and when they finally reached HQ, they were told the cook was ill and there was no dinner. Then the next day there would be a five-mile march and no breakfast. Often, they weren't fed for thirty-six hours because of some reason or another. It was, of course, all done with purpose, to prepare them for instances such as this.

She had experienced sleep deprivation then too – woken up at different times during the night for various drills, pulled out of bed, shouted at. Of course it outraged her, bewildered her, fatigued her, left her nerves jangling. But it didn't *frighten* her. Not really. The training there was theoretical. They all knew they were safe, even if they got caught up in the alarm of the moment. But this – she touches the mould on the wall and winces – this is real and she knows she is not safe. Not at all.

She has paced the room looking for anything that might help her get out. Once she managed to escape the clutches of German spies. But then, her prison was opportunist: a tumble-down barn in the New Forest. This new confinement could not be more different. Where the dilapidated farm building was spacious, this cell is barely six feet wide, ten feet in length. She has measured it in paces. Something to keep her occupied, though now, she has been here so long she has started to see things in the damp that stains the walls with a mildewy tideline. By the steel door, dark lines of it trail upwards from the floor. At first, she thought of them as veins, then they changed to the spidery outline of tree branches and leaves against fog, similar in shape to a picture that Viktor, the last owner of the grimoire, had once shown her: the *Yggdrasill*, the World Tree. For it was green and white towards the top, dirty black near the root. The *Yggdrasill*, he told her, connected existence and the universe. The thought has entered her mind that because this mould-tree resembles the sacred ash, it is trying to connect with her, trying to speak to her.

Tempting as it is to believe, she understands also that it is a clue, a symptom of her mind beginning to fray at the edges.

Rubbing her eyes, she tries to dispel the pattern of the tree. Opens them widely, looks from side to side, blinks three times. It works: the symbol disappears. Spreading itself across the wall is nothing more than a fusty blur, a fungus that likes to feast on damp.

Still, once you see something in the creeping mess, it's always there, waiting to emerge again. She knows, as a former stage magician's girl, the human eye, the *mind*, will always reach for meaning in chaos.

She decides to retire to the bare bed, wrought from iron and bolted to the floor. The thin straw mattress is covered in terrible brown stains. She averts her eyes to the ceiling bulb, though they swivel to the corner where a dented toilet-bucket sits. It does not have a lid and the smell emanating from it is atrocious. Beside it, a small iron washbasin with a rusted tap that runs cold only, of course. No other furniture.

She has entertained ideas of lifting the bucket and hitting the guard over the head with it when he brings in her water. But even if she were to disorientate him and get out, she noted, on her march in, that there are soldiers guarding each corridor. This section is a basement and guarded by two at the entrance. Then there are stairs, which only go up, to another level of cells. These are secured by another set of guards. Beyond them is the courtyard, overseen by offices that surround it. This gives on to the only entrance and exit, stationed with another sentry point and three soldiers.

Though there must be a way to get out of here.

The light goes out as she is turning over and rejecting ideas.

There is a tiny, barred window, no more than twelve inches high and eighteen wide, positioned just below ceiling level, which now lets in a tiny slat of grey light. Though she can reach the bottom of the frame by standing on the bed, which is strictly forbidden, the bars are rock solid. She has tried picking at the flaking plaster. Though they have taken her shoes and belt away, she has found one slim blade sewn into the lapel of her jacket. It's not much, but it may yet offer her a way out, a final kind of freedom. But in the meantime she is using it on the plaster around the window frame. Depressingly, the iron bars are deeply embedded. The wall itself is two feet thick and hewn from stone.

She has tried pulling on them and, when that failed, used them to do further exercise. Last year at the Oriental, Loretta, the trapeze girl from the high-wire act, fell and fractured a bone in her toe. Daphne trained with Sebastian, Loretta's partner in the act, and managed to fill in for a month till her replacement was able to start. As a result, she knows the basic principles, a few poses and balances on the bar and ropes, how to swing to generate momentum, time her release and fall safely. She spent ages pulling herself up and down on the ropes to improve her upper-body strength. The bars on the window are better than nothing, and if she breaks them, which she doubts, she may be able to escape. After all she has succeeded before. Though her former prison was makeshift and made of wood and stone, guarded by two poorly trained German agents, who mostly slept. This is a purpose-built detention centre, patrolled by Gestapo and the SS. Even Houdini would have trouble.

The thought of her confinement in the New Forest draws her mind back to last summer when she had worked alongside Jack.

Was he a traitor then? Would she have noticed? Probably not, for she was too in love with his beauty to think critically about him.

The first time she saw his face she had felt an instant attraction that was so intense it almost winded her. She couldn't understand how the others at the pub weren't gasping, sighing or collapsing into chairs at the glorious sight of the man.

Her adoration must have been obvious. She moans and bites a fingernail. *How easy was it for him to manipulate her?*

A memory returns: the land undulating like an ocean, waves of purple heather, yellow gorse, green, green grass, bracken. So lovely, so verdant, so full of life. She and Jack sitting in a car on a cliff top, looking out at the forest.

He had spoken in wistful tones about a time after the war, when he intended to get away from everything. And everyone. *Start afresh*, he had said, with a curious emphasis, and even expressed a desire for a new name. Everyone talked of beginning again once war was over, but she could not think of anyone else who meant to shed their name as well. She had found it odd at the time.

Now she sees it for what it was: a slip.

Of course he would need a new name. If he was a double agent and Britain was to win, he would have to disappear. Or be shot. For treason.

The signs had been there in his words. She had simply refused to hear them.

Or see them, she thinks as her mind snags on another scene later that day. They had gone for a drink. So caught up in conversation were they, Jack had lost track of time and rushed off, leaving his watch on the table. She had picked it up and gone after him, following him into the woods. Her thoughtfulness was her undoing.

A narrow path had taken her into a dense thicket.

The blow had come from behind – a cosh to the head, then nothing.

But just before a twig had cracked somewhere behind her, she had sighted something in the trees up ahead that was far more compelling: a flash of colour. A glimpse of blue among the trunks.

Jack had been wearing blue that day.

What a fool I have been, she thinks and clenches her hands.

But he had been assessed by the authorities too – all of them had been vetted. And he had been popular, liked by all. Then she remembers her boss, Jonty, who always had good instincts, had never really taken a shine to him. Though, despite his visionary on-stage personae, she doubts The Grand Mystique could have foreseen this.

That she had almost fallen for Jack is becoming horrifying to her. Had *anything* between them been real?

How long had he been playing her, playing both sides?

The questions send her spinning, her mind a whirlpool. She knows they will weary her mentally, and she should turn her inner gaze away from such black machinations, but she can't help but give in to them. Perhaps it will be a type of exorcism.

There are scrapes coming from the other side of the door. She braces herself for the violent sounds – the guards and their batons.

Instead, light from the corridor slants into the cell. She blinks, raises a hand against it.

Footsteps. Soldiers' boots.

The bulb comes back on.

She lowers her hand and squints around the cell.

A clunk, and the heavy door opens again.

Instead of the guard, two uniformed soldiers enter the cell.

'You,' says one. 'Now!'

'Where are you taking me?' she asks, not moving. 'A POW camp?'

'Hah!' she gets a sneer back. 'You are not a soldier and will not be treated like one.'

What does that mean? she thinks, as he grabs her shoulder and pushes it towards the door.

As she steps into the corridor, the light overhead crackles then goes out.

For a moment it occurs to her to make a dash for it, but then she remembers the levels, the guards on each floor. As she takes her first tentative steps into the darkness, she has no idea that she will encounter so much more.

II

I wandered deep where shadows fall,
Where birches lean and thrushes call,
And saw beneath a shroud of green
A forest mere, both still and keen.
There, rising slow from waters drear,
Yon castle olde did reappear;
Its turrets crowned with ivy sere,
As though I dreamt of yesteryear.
No banners flew, no voices stirred,
The seldom hush of leaf and bird;
Yet something in that haunted light
Promised thus the world would turn to night.

Dreamleye Grey in Greenwood

after Freiligrath

CHAPTER SEVENTEEN

She had been loaded into the back of a truck which had only tarpaulin across the sides. Her hands had been cuffed again which had made it difficult to stay upright the whole time and there had been lots of sharp turns and corners as they had driven out of Augsburg city centre. They become less frequent as they move into the countryside. Though the provincial roads are either gravelly or made of mud, they have fewer corners. She guesses the terrain is not mountainous, but hilly. None of this gives her a clue as to her destination.

Her mood is grim.

She has worked out what the SS man meant: only soldiers have rights in war. Spies don't become prisoners. They are finished off.

But who knows what she will go through before they snuff her out?

They will want names. Dates. Contacts. They will take them slowly, bit by bit, breaking her down till she cannot take any more.

The only certainties left are the pill in her hem, or the slim blade back in her lapel.

At least she has them. To be used as a last resort.

But she is not at that point just yet. And while she lives, she will try to learn, soak up details that may be of use, even if she does not manage to relay them.

Several times she has tried to peek through the canvas flaps when they have come into villages. The last time though, the guard who sat next to her on the wooden bench noticed. Not the skinny one with the thin moustache, silent and smoking, but the older, grizzled soldier with a smear of something oily, maybe paint, on his thumb. He had leant forward while her attention was on the back of the truck and then flicked the side of her head with two fingers. It wasn't hard, but it had made her jump. Just enough to remind her she was being watched and who had the power. Though she has rubbed the skin there, she feels contaminated by the touch.

'You're going to a place without windows,' he said, answering her unspoken question.

After that she kept her head down and tried not to think about his words. But all that crowds her mind now are things without windows, like coffins. For a moment she experiences a fleeting image – of being helped into one and nailed in. Alive. A strange image: she seemed compliant in it. Not afraid, only cautious.

Her mind is giving her hope.

Is that a bad thing, she wonders as she stares at the metal floor? Or should she resign herself now, pop the pill?

The truck is shifting into a lower gear and she lifts her eyes, looks to the back with expectation. The two guards have noticed the change in speed too.

The skinny blond unslings his rifle and holds it in front of him. The older one moves up the bench and opens the rear flap.

The truck is slowing on a country road, pulling into a crossing point.

Why would they be doing that? she wonders.

'Execution' flashes across her mind.

No, she tells herself, if they wanted to kill me, they could have done that miles ago. But then again, they would have witnesses in the town. Her hand reaches to the hem of her skirt. She can't feel anything there.

'Toilet pause,' says the older guard. But not to her.

'I must visit the WC,' Daphne says, perhaps she can examine her skirt, find the pill, take it.

He laughs. 'None here.'

But the skinny one, who has looked at her sadly a couple of times, whispers something to him. The other grunts, 'I'll see.'

When they finally stop, he gets out. The truck shakes and rattles as soldiers disembark from the cab up front. She hears voices. The old one is asking about her. He takes a step closer to the frame or turns her way because his words become clearer. 'I don't want the stink of it in the back,' he says. 'If she bursts.'

Skinny, still in the back with her, cringes apologetically.

She breathes; he's talking about her request. *They are not going to kill her.*

A moment later and both canvas flaps are pulled back. 'Schmidt!' the old guard barks. 'Take her into the woods.'

She worries again that she has misheard, that he must do the other's dirty work.

He is gentler than the others and does not touch or push as he escorts her into the pines. In fact, he uncuffs her hands and allows her to walk a couple of paces ahead, alone, into ferny bracken. 'Enough!' he shouts when she ducks behind the plants. 'Stop there.' That's as far as his compassion extends: he doesn't turn round when she begins to urinate but keeps his eyes on her head.

Her fingers run around the circumference of her skirt. It is flat. Damn and blast! She finds a hole at the seam. The pill must have fallen out. Perhaps it is on the floor of the truck.

She contemplates running off into the woods, but the odds have to be against her. These men have guns. Her own weapon is in a suitcase in Greta's house in the Fuggerei or has been disposed of discreetly, along with the rest of her belongings when she failed to return. If Daphne were to make a dash for it, she has no doubt she would be shot in the back instantly. Even if she managed to dodge the bullets and get away from her captors, she has no idea where she is, who to contact, where to go. Though she would sincerely prefer to take her chances, she must be sensible. But it would be a quick death. Now the pill has disappeared, all that can confer autonomy on her fate is the final blade in her lapel. Bleeding out will take time. And be painful.

Skinny raises his eyes as she tucks herself back in.

It is getting dark. Above the trees the sky is tones of grey and mauve. The temperature is falling and she detects dampness in the air.

When she returns to him, he points to a small stream she had not seen trickling through the woods. Quite clear and fresh-looking; she washes herself and cups a hand to drink some of the water. It tastes so clean, and the joy of it on her tongue momentarily lifts her spirits. She sips a little more until the soldier pokes her with his rifle, not so gentlemanly this time, and slides an iron cuff over her wrist, then another. He points her back in the direction of the truck and gives her another prod.

As they both stumble and trip across the mossy ground, she sees the other occupants of the truck standing outside it, deep in conversation: the old guard, the driver (another SS soldier in field-grey) and a third, a navigator maybe. Leaning over a map, it is the third man, the navigator, who is pointing.

She tries to keep her step light as they approach, so she can listen in.

'Well, it's not up to you, is it?' the driver is saying to the old guard, whose face has become much more ruddy.

'There,' says the navigator and taps the paper. The pair stop arguing and look down.

'But that will take us out of our way,' says the guard.

'It's what they radioed. Not for us to question orders,' the navigator nods. 'We don't know what else is going on.'

'Don't need to know,' adds the driver.

The old guard grunts again.

The navigator's eyes land on Daphne and the young guard approaching. 'Quick,' he says, 'Get her in. We need to go.'

Skinny helps her back up the step, but as she bends to step over the frame of the truck, a sudden blow lands hard across her buttocks. A rifle butt, she realises, just as she's pitched forward. Without her hands free she sprawls onto the truck's floor, chin hitting against the edge of the wooden bench. Now she has pain at both ends. But she will not show it.

'What's the point of that?' It is Skinny, hooking his hands under her collar. The older guard merely shrugs and gets in.

The young one hauls her first by the collar, which rips, then takes her arm in his free hand and guides her onto the bench. It hurts to sit down, but as she does, the lapel of her jacket, with the final blade, comes off in his hand. Without a second thought he throws it out of the back of the truck onto the road, then takes up a place next to Daphne.

That's it now – she has nothing to work with – her belt, shoes, pill and blades are all gone. She masks her dismay and glances at his face. He rolls his eyes fractionally and she gets the idea that he might voice regret for his colleague's barbaric behaviour if he were alone.

But he's not.

Both of them hang their heads.

It is a few hours later that they stop again.

There is a clock or a church tower nearby, for she thinks she can hear the toll of a bell, though doesn't manage to count how many chimes there are. A lot. Maybe ten or eleven.

This, then, means two things – first that there is some kind of building with people in or around it. And, secondly, that it is late. They set off in the light when the sun was just past its zenith, now the truck has come to a halt in the dark. They drove quickly at about forty miles an hour, though with stops and starts and lots of bends to slow down for. She calculates that they have driven over a hundred miles north and has a feeling that their original orders have been replaced by fresh ones received when she was in the woods. Though, of course, she cannot be certain.

The old guard jumps down first, landing heavily, spits, hauls back the canvas flap and waits. Skinny sends Daphne a nod – move. She slides carefully towards the edge. Despite her youth and agility her limbs have been stiffened with the cold and hours of rattling and swerving through the back roads. Her rear is still sore and aching. In fact, as she climbs out of the truck, her feet meet the ground awkwardly, causing her knees to almost give way. That is not like her at all. She manages to steady herself and remembers she must keep her strength, try to do her exercises to remain supple.

As long as she has the energy: they do not feed her regularly. When they do the provisions are grey, lumpy and seriously devoid of vitamins.

But they have not starved her, for which she must be grateful. She knows, despite her enemy status, she is getting more nourishment than the occupants of Kaufbeuren-Irsee.

They have stopped in some sort of courtyard. She is not sure if it is the memory of her contact in the Catholic Fuggerei that is colouring her perception, but it seems to her that, architecturally, there is an element of a convent or religious building in the wooden arches that front each wall.

Before her looms a formal entrance to the inner complex. Its stone walls have been built high and inserted with narrow shuttered windows. Steps lead up to a large wooden tower with a clock at the top. Ah, she thinks and reads the hour – just gone nine. She commits it to her mental file.

Above the entrance, in a niche, she spies a statue of St Augustine. His face is worn by the elements, eyes so eroded that he is blind. Perhaps that is just as well.

So it's a monastery, she thinks, an Augustine monastery and, for a moment, a flare of hope begins to burn. Perhaps there are holy men here? Might they help her?

'This way.' It is the navigator who is taking the lead now.

She expects to be pushed up the steps to the main entrance, but he goes left across mossy flagstones. Mossy – she thinks. Unusual. Holy orders, in her limited experience, are very structured, the monks disciplined, compelled to maintain their buildings and work their lands to maximum efficiency. The courtyard, she notices now, is overgrown; the paving stones strewn with weeds. Her heart begins to sink as she concludes the Augustines have either been moved on or are not allowed access to this place. She cannot think they would let it fall into such disrepair.

She breathes out through her nose and commits the scene to memory: they have come through an arch and a gatehouse, which comprises one side of the yard. Two more are sheltered by a wooden porch which wraps around them about ten foot high. Only one, she sees, is crumbling, pockmarked and stained. Then she squints her eyes and realises the marks are bullet-holes, the stains a deep russet.

It is awful to see the holy place turned into a gallows.

Dear God, is this where the monks disappeared?

And then it hits her – is this where she finishes too?

Do they intend to line her up and get out their guns?

She hadn't realised she had stopped moving, but she is staggered. Fear is smouldering in her stomach. Though she knows she should look away. *Move on Daphne*, she urges herself. But despite the clamour of her internal voice she finds she cannot help but stare at the wall. Never before has she seen a place of such grotesque finality. Every single brick is soaked with blood and violence. *Oh dear God, will mine be added to the mix?*

She stumbles. Her feet are bare and the cobbles cold. The men are moving towards a side door. Sitting on blocks outside it, two soldiers are lounging.

The navigator speaks to one, shows him a set of papers. He nods and gestures through the door. The other glances up at her, expressionless, uninterested, takes a drag on his cigarette and throws it onto the flagstones near her bare feet.

But she is called on through a door which opens onto a cloister. At least she is moving away from the execution site. She breathes in, conscious of her heartbeat.

Halfway down it, she is told to stop outside a heavy iron-banded wooden door. The navigator knocks and is admitted along with the driver and the old guard. She waits outside with Skinny. There are no monks to be seen anywhere: this place has been commandeered and repurposed. Unless the military are sharing it with the monks? In her early training, the castle, where she was stationed, was shared with the bishop and his staff. Though they tended to keep out of each other's way.

Maybe there are a couple of clerics left.

She tries to crane her neck and look through into the room as the navigator emerges with a key in his hand. He instructs her to continue down the corridor. Skinny hasn't been asked but he follows.

They pass a chapel. The door is padlocked. A crucifix above it hangs at a crooked angle. No one has straightened it for months. Cobwebs grow between Christ's downturned chin and the lance in his side.

Glassless windows in the corridor open onto another courtyard. In the middle, a dry fountain. Weeds crawl up from its base, sending feelers into the cracks, exploiting vulnerabilities and pulling it apart. It is a visual metaphor, she thinks briefly: the Reich are the weeds. Pestilent, fast and utterly relentless, destroying everything they reach for.

She looks away sadly and sees there is a staircase ahead. The navigator points to the ground, and they descend a stone flight into a narrow hallway. As she passes through, she sees the doors here have windows in them: they are storerooms with foodstuffs inside.

The navigator stops and fits his key into one with a 'V' painted over the door. It opens and she is thrust inside.

'Try not to freeze,' Skinny says, lifting his gaze but not meeting her eyes.

The navigator unfastens her cuffs and nudges her towards the wall. 'I'll see if they can get you something to eat.'

She nods, aware this is a change of attitude. Though still unpleasant, there is a subtle hint of care.

It emboldens her enough to ask, 'Where are we? What is going to happen?'

What a surprise it is to see him open his mouth to speak. She had expected silence or a cruel dismissal.

But he says, 'Tomorrow,' then steps back out.

The door slams shut behind him and the key turns in the lock.

Low-ceilinged with bare white walls, some sacks on the floor, no mattress, it is better than her previous prison. Another bucket in the corner stands as testament to the fact that this has housed another detainee previously. It does not smell male in here. Somehow, she knows another woman has been imprisoned in this place.

Some light comes through the lower metal window from the functional bulbs in the corridor. There are, she sees now, marks on the wall. It looks like someone has tried to keep a tally of their time. Underneath, a name has been scratched into the whitewash, 'Judith S.'

She counts forty-six marks in total, the final scratches heart-breakingly faint.

Daphne stands in the half-dark, throat dry, body aching, exhaustion fraying her nerves.

Then she sits down on the sacks and begins to cry.

CHAPTER EIGHTEEN

7th May

Back against the wall, knees drawn up, Daphne listens. The monastery is quiet now and so is she.

Although she has been primed, warned even, about the importance of keeping ones spirits up in captivity, it is so so hard. And sometimes she cannot be that strong. It is as if her feelings just need to be *felt* and that fighting them will not help. This is not a stoic admission, she's aware. Officer Atkins constantly drilled it into the girls in training that they should keep themselves calm and composed, exert 'an iron-like grip' over their emotions, 'endure' inwardly, display resilience externally.

No one has seen her moment of weakness, she is sure. And despite all the officer's cautions, Daphne feels like her tears have been a conduit through which fear and frustration have been flushed out of her.

Once emptied, she had finally fallen asleep. She does not know for how long.

Though she could not possibly be described as 'better', she feels less weighed down. Of course, she would be a damn fool not to realise the gravity of her situation. But now she has got rid of a surfeit of emotion and grabbed a bit of kip, her mind is clearer, functioning.

Though no food has been forthcoming, the mere mention of it, she realises, has implications: they want to keep her alive. For the moment anyway. Unless it was the navigator's spiteful joke. She wouldn't put it past him. Past any of them. Even Skinny, who seemed less hardened than his mates.

Try not to freeze, she thinks and remembers his eyes. He wasn't looking at her but up at the ceiling. When she glances there, she sees that empty sacks have been fastened over the top windows, to give the occupant privacy. Though they can be used for warmth. She pulls them down and lays them over her legs and body as makeshift blankets. So one of them is human, at least.

Oh, how stiff are her limbs! She rubs them, teeth chattering. Her blouse and hair are now dampish. As she passes her fingers through her tresses, she becomes aware of a rigid boning in her jacket. It is not part of the design. When she slips her hands into her jacket, she is amazed to find what has been digging into her ribs. The gold pen has been caught in the lining. Everything else is gone. But she has this! The pen! Given to her to be sold, if she needs money. At first she thinks it is useless in this situation. But then she turns it over in her hands and examines the nib.

Rising slowly from the floor, she moves to the door. It is ancient, fashioned from thick wood, evidently locked from the outside. Her fingers trail along the edges of the doorframe, testing for a weakness or flaw, then the walls. One stone near the floor shifts slightly beneath her touch. It's not completely loose. But it could be, and this thought galvanises her. Removing the cap from the pen she uses the nib to pick at it. Carefully.

She works at it until the nib gets caught in a crack. She tries to pull it out, but it is stuck.

Footsteps.

Oh no.

She stops. They are faint but getting louder. A guard must be making his rounds. She kicks the pen, so the nib snaps off, picks up the rest of it and inserts it into the lining of her jacket. Next, she shoves the stone into place with the heel of her shoe and folds herself back into the corner.

The key rattles in the lock.

The door opens.

Torchlight leaks across the floor. A man enters the frame, pauses.

Is he just checking on her?

He doesn't step in but says, 'Up, now.'

She obeys, pretends to be sluggish, as if she had just woken up.

He pulls her out of the cell into the corridor.

'Where am I going?' she asks and waits for the handcuffs to go on.

But he merely says, 'Up,' and shoves her down the passage.

The nib will have to stay. Maybe the next occupant will have more luck. Her small acts of defiance here and in the Gestapo cell lend her a bleak optimism. If nothing else, at least she has sown the seeds to help others.

They retrace their steps up to the courtyard. Where it is warmer. Heat is building, the yard is filling gradually with grey light coming from the east. Just after dawn, she supposes. Dew has amassed on the cobblestones in spots, turning them into giant grey-and-white ladybirds, or statues of ladybirds. As she processes that last thought she realises it is not normal: she must be dehydrated. She has not had any water since that mouthful in the woods. No wonder her thoughts are drifting. She does not feel extraordinarily thirsty, just regularly so. But that is probably a bad sign.

So she takes a deep, deep breath in and floods herself with air, with oxygen.

It helps. Her eyes roam over the yard, the wooden porch, and then linger on the bullet-ridden firing wall. Oh God, she thinks, they have brought me here.

Where there are no witnesses.

And it's dawn.

First light.

The time when executions are carried out.

She breathes in again, more deeply this time, hears Atkins' voice: *Calm yourself.*

Breathes out, and this time she moves her head, surveys the yard, measures the distance to the arched exit.

A black car is there.

There are witnesses after all. Or have they come to see the deed done?

The engine purrs, the exhaust sending streams of smoke into the air: spectres of the dead waiting for her.

Stop, she thinks, refusing to give in to hysteria.

Better to meet one's end with a clear head.

But it is not to the wall she is led but the waiting car.

Interrogators?

Two soldiers stand beside it. Not the same as yesterday's squad. One is picking at his fingernails, the other stands as still as a statue, eyes hidden in the shadow beneath the brim of his cap.

Nobody speaks as she is guided round to the side of the car.

The rear door is open.

The soldier to her left nudges her forward. 'In.'

She hesitates only a moment, then ducks her head and climbs into the car.

As she reaches the leather seat, she looks up. All the air that she soaked into her body leaves her in one sharp exhalation.

There is someone there. In a black suit and tie, with his legs crossed, eyes down.

Beside him his overcoat has been folded precisely. A trilby sits on top. He is clean and shaved and neat. There's a faint smell of perfume or cologne, something citrusy around him. It amplifies his composed appearance and momentarily she wonders just how unhygienic she smells.

He turns. 'Hello, Daphne.'

A click behind her: the door shuts, the lock engages.

Above them the bell begins to toll.

CHAPTER NINETEEN

'Jack,' she says. It is an observation, not a greeting. Her voice is creaky, unused.

He leans over, slides back a screen that separates the rear section from the driver's.

The chauffeur there turns.

'Get out,' Jack tells him.

He obeys instantly and closes the door behind him.

Now they are on their own.

Jack slides back the screen and turns to her.

His face, she thinks, is paler, somehow. His suit amplifies the hard angles of his body.

She looks at him – this man who had rescued her when she was under attack in Iceland, whom she had kissed in a Soho alley. This man who has turned her over to the enemy.

There are so many words waiting, but none of them are coming to her.

He taps his lap and says, 'I'm surprised you haven't asked me why? I always thought, when I pictured it, that would be the first thing you'd want to know.' He folds his arms. 'Now is your opportunity.'

She doesn't care why. She just cares that he has done it. But something is going on here. As she doesn't know what and isn't sure how to behave, she shuts up, purses her lips.

'Which leads me to conclude,' he says, 'that you already understand the *why*, the reason I have pledged allegiance to the Reich.'

How repulsively archaic and melodramatic, she thinks, like a knight from tales of old, swearing an oath of loyalty to his king. And he thinks he knows her! The arrogance! But she gives none of this away and nods. It encourages him.

'You can see that we're building something here,' he continues, gesturing without irony at the decaying monastery. 'A future without sickness, without weakness. Look around you. Here there is strength and cohesion. In Britain the streets are littered with beggars, soldiers with stumps and sticks . . .'

'But that's from the last war!' she says without thinking. She has repressed her next sentence – 'Which the Germans started too.' Now, she wonders how he will react.

He is, however, on a roll, puffed up with zeal. 'A society must not waste itself on the broken. It is inhibiting. Sacrifices have to be made for the good of all.'

'You see,' he says, inching towards her, thoroughly enthused by his own words. 'Every so many years the human race takes a great leap forward and evolves. Did you know that, Daphne? It's something they don't tell you at school.'

She shakes her head.

'Here the Germans are establishing the right conditions for that to happen. They wish to create a world where the strong will thrive and will beget children who are even stronger. Imagine – no illness, no mental weakness, no disease. A race of humans who are genetically superior. Think of the potential that can be unlocked.' His eyes glitter and whirr, brows up high. 'Daphne, *you* are strong. I've seen you in action, heard people speak about your work, what you have achieved, the challenges you have risen to.'

He waits for her to say something, but she merely crunches her brow.

'Look,' he says. 'I am not like the other men; I don't underestimate you. You have told me of your German heritage, which means you may be permitted to become part of this too. If you play your hand right.'

Bile rises in her throat.

She is not sure what to say.

Of course, the idea is absolutely repulsive – how could she ever . . .? No, it is not worth contemplating. How can he even think that . . .?

He turns his body fully towards her. 'I *know* you understand the appeal of this.'

Flatter him, she thinks, and broadens the smile so that there is an ounce of coquette in her features. 'You never were easily deceived, Jack,' she lies.

'I knew it.' He smiles again, satisfied. 'Look, you have something to barter with that others do not. Your Aryan descent, yes. But also, your knowledge of the grimoire.'

She frowns now, genuinely surprised. 'That book?' Then she pauses: could it be the damn thing might offer a way out?

He laughs at her expression. 'Indeed, while of no interest to the Gestapo, there are those *with power* sufficiently intrigued to be persuaded that your life is of value.'

Her ears prick.

'You don't have to fall on your sword, Daphne,' he says, more softly.

'No,' she answers. 'I prefer to swallow it.'

His lips curve upwards, but only slightly.

Her mind becomes suddenly cluttered with possibilities.

'I've risked a lot by pleading your case,' he is saying. 'It seems your actions in Augsburg have come to nothing. There has been little to no impact. Which is unlucky for your paymasters but fortuitous for you.' That half smile again. 'If you take this offer, you will have to play your part well. Be compliant, co-operative, share your expertise.'

'My part?'

'You're the only one in the country who knows what the Icelandic grimoire means. Your translations may save you yet.'

My God, she thinks, can this be true? Then, as quickly as the thought expresses itself, another pops up: if she grasps at this, then does she not become as damned as the grimoire? Can she do it? Will her soul allow her to fall so low? No, there must be other ways . . .

'Or what?' she asks.

'Or . . .' his eyes swivel to the execution site. 'You can add your signature to the wall.'

She breathes in, horrified. So it is as stark as that.

'It's your choice,' he says. 'You can get it over now. Or else, live and make yourself useful.'

She will not ever submit to Nazi rule – it is not in her. She simply can't do it. But, she reasons, she can *appear* to. Until she finds another way out.

Bending towards him she whispers, 'Jack, dear one, I'm in.'

When he grins, she sees that there is victory in it.

Despite the poison that has dripped from his lips, she widens her eyes and sends him an expression full of gratitude, hinting at warmth and the promise of something more sensual.

He has played all of them at Section W.

But there is time for her own manoeuvres yet.

CHAPTER TWENTY

He has been courteous and had even packed a flask of tea and ham sandwiches, which she guzzled down as slowly and politely as she could manage while he averted his eyes.

When they stopped at a garrison for a break, he had slipped her a package of brown paper. At first she had thought it was the grimoire, but it was too floppy and light. She was escorted to a private room with a bathroom miraculously connected to it, and although under guard with the door ajar, she was permitted to use the facilities. When she unwrapped the package she found a fresh blouse, new underwear and half a bottle of Eau de Cologne – 4711. It must have been his own – the fragrance she had smelled in the car. The sight of the little bottle had almost made her cry. The label with its rich turquoises and golds decorated with scrolling rococo flourishes had seemed impossibly luxurious. What a joy to wash, get out of her soiled clothes and dab some perfume behind her ears. The stink of her had become savage. Perhaps that's why Jack had added the bottle.

Returning, after an hour, she is desperate to speak to him.

'Where are we going?' she asks. 'Will you tell me?'

'To the north,' he says. But that's it and then he opens the screen and speaks to the chauffeur. His German is impeccable.

She had no idea he knew the language so well. It must have been so hard for him to swallow his pride and pretend he understood only a smattering of phrases throughout the course in London. But he has faked so much. She must adjust to this new person.

Outwardly, there are small changes that can be detected. The way he holds himself is composed. She had always thought him confident but there is something more in the way he interacts with the soldiers – a stillness, an absolute surety, as if his frame has grown bigger. As if he exudes more presence now that he is back in his 'natural place'. There is certainly more authority evident. The soldiers defer to him. He has more status than a mere double agent. Could he be the recruiter, the spy maker, the one who turns operatives against their own? So many questions she cannot ask.

As the afternoon progresses, the car becomes stifling. She keeps widening her eyes to fight off sleep. The atmosphere has taken on more moisture and become clammy and humid. Outside, the sun has sunk below the hills and the sky has taken on a shade of lavender. Clouds blot out the afternoon light. Low on the horizon, more are threaded with heavy grey streams on their undersides. And they are pulling together. Rain, she thinks, conscious that her throat is dry.

This road has been cut through pine woods that seem, in the muted light, to be closing in like strange grey armies. It could be her own mood that is reflected back, but it seems that the darkness between each tree is shimmering. As if something shapeless and malevolent waits there. A cursive S, a grinning serpent wraps itself around the trunks, sinking its fangs into the bark, mixing its venom with the sap.

She jolts upright, gasping, unable to control her breathing.

'All right?' asks Jack and hands over a bottle of water. 'You nodded off.'

She takes it and drinks, trying to force air deep down into her lungs around the gulps. When her breathing becomes more regular, she returns the bottle with a 'Thank you.'

Wind begins to stir and rustle the leaves. The air is heavy and pregnant. She feels headachy and touches her hand to her temple.

All the windows in the car have been opened, and she can hear the sounds coming from the forest that borders the road: birds returning to the nest, crickets quietening. The animals are preparing. In the distance, there is a low growl of thunder.

As they clear the trees the landscape opens up around them. Fields with crops are bordered by hedges, streams. In the distance, hills are decked with grey spraying clouds. Ahead, the road is darkening. The headlights have been turned up to two blackout slits.

The car slows, struggling as the land starts to incline. She can see that they are turning now. She has not seen any signs of civilisation since they passed a farmstead just before she fell asleep. But that was hours ago.

They drive over two low bridges – a black river running quickly and then a stream – and she shudders like someone is walking over her grave.

Leaning forward she angles her face to see out through the windscreen. This place does not feel right.

The dark slope of a hill is unfolding, with buildings at either side. On the top, sticking out from a huddle of trees, is a white castle.

The hair on the back of her neck prickles. An omen. And she is possessed by the feeling that something terrible is going to happen here, that perhaps she should have taken her chances in the wood or faced the wall.

Her hand strays to the handle of the door, though she knows already it is locked.

Death is here, Daphne. Death is here.

'Yes,' says Jack, though she has asked no question. 'You have sensed correctly,' he adds. 'Our destination. We're nearly there.'

She forces her eyes from the castle and turns to him. 'What is it?'

He smiles, horribly, like the serpent. 'The spiritual centre of the Schutzstaffel.'

As if he had timed it just to frighten her, a sheet of lightning flashes across the hill, lighting up the landscape, filling it with an intense white that reddens like blood on the edges and at the sides of her vision.

'What's that?' she asks him as a crack of thunder ricochets from above to the hill ahead, like bullets flying over their heads.

The driver inhales audibly and slows. The first great drop of rain plops onto the windscreen.

'A castle. Very old and very strongly constructed,' he says. 'But it is so much more than that. The headquarters and a Reichsführer school for the SS.'

The words cause Daphne to flinch. My God, can she really be on her way there? Into the nest of vipers?

Above them the rain breaks and a hammering starts up on the metal roof.

'Hail stones,' says the driver. As he speaks, the windscreen is attacked by white objects the size of a shilling, which hit the surface repeatedly and bounce. There are so many the windscreen wipers barely clear their view.

Could nature be attempting to halt their progress?

If only it were that simple.

With a loud crack the glass in the corner fractures.

The silent soldier in the passenger seat exclaims, 'Was zum Teufel!'

What the hell?

They slow to a crawl. The gearbox crunches as they change into first and creep round beneath the castle's grassy ramparts.

A small village opens up.

She is surprised to spy a young man, a teenager in farm

clothes, scurrying home from work in the fields. For a moment she had thought no human beings would live here – only Nosferatu's brides, wolves and bloodsucking ghouls. And in a way, this is true. But the boy looks real enough, holding a sack over his head for protection against the hail.

As they drive past, he sights them. When she turns to look, he meets her gaze. A flash of panic passes over his features then, quickly, he drops his eyes and turns his face away.

The engine splutters. They change gear. The houses grow denser.

It is so dark in the storm that lights are coming on inside most of them. Is it her imagination or are the villagers drawing the curtains against them as they pass? Like peasants in an old tale, shuttering their homes against the damned.

In the half-light, she sees a church at the top of the hill cowering in the storm. It is shadowy and does not look Christian, not benign at all.

A man in black is coming out of it, opening his brolly. He turns and shakes the umbrella at them like a shield, wincing as it goes up over his head. For a moment more he watches the car. Then, as they turn right, he shakes his head, looks down at his shoes and rushes off.

Her imagination may well be fuelled by the adrenaline coursing through her veins, but she cannot stop the thought: this village has a terrible secret. And she is being driven into the heart of it.

The car turns right again and the view opens onto a high wall. Beyond that is the castle.

'Wewelsburg,' Jack almost sighs out the name.

She knows immediately that he has been here before.

Castle Wewelsburg rises up ahead of them like no other place she has clapped eyes on before. For an instant, lightning illuminates it, imprinting its shape onto the horizon: triangular with three towers. The two closest to them even have pewter-grey roofs like the caps of the SS soldiers. Have they built it to embody, to *personify*, those within? She shivers; no, it is too old. It must predate this new political movement, though no doubt it has been chosen because of its peculiar geometry. Three is a magic number, full of echoes: three wyrd sisters of Macbeth, the three knocks at midnight that foretell calamity, the number of Fates, the Moirai . . .

And then, snap, as she is thinking this, the light is gone, and the shape diminishes into shadow, hiding itself in the blackness.

It is almost as if it is sentient, aware of her arrival.

No, that's a wild thought without substance, she thinks.

But for all our erudition and rationality, under the skin we are still animals with well-founded instincts for danger.

Daphne's heartbeat grows frenetic: it *knows* what is to come.

CHAPTER TWENTY-ONE

The gates set into the high wall around the castle are firmly shut. At either side of them two sentries stand. Water courses down from the wall onto one, who does not flinch one bit, but stays motionless and resigned. The other approaches the car and bends to speak to their driver.

Daphne darts a glance at Jack. His lips are set in a firm line that tapers up at its corners. 'Have you been here before?' she asks, though she already knows the answer.

'A few times,' he says. 'It's a privilege to be back.'

She marvels at his treachery. A *few* times. A 'privilege'. How long has he been in thrall to the Germans? Was he ever fighting on her side? When did he change?

The SS soldier sends a signal and the gates slide open. The car rolls through the castle's walls into the dark mouth of the fortress, a great mass of stone and unyielding grimness.

They come into an inner courtyard, where the driver parks.

The gates close behind them and Daphne is suddenly overcome by a feeling of claustrophobia, like someone has pulled a bag over her head. She cannot stop the fluttering panic rising within her, needs to get more air into her lungs. For it feels to her that this place has always been waiting for her, as if she has seen it in her dreams.

'Stay,' Jack orders her, while he gets out, calls to another sentry stationed at the head of the bridge that arches over the moat to the castle's main entrance. The soldier nods and takes three paces forward, keeping his eyes on Daphne.

Hyperaware now, taking in everything, she sees that he wears no rain-covering but pulls down the peak of his cap with its motif of an eagle clutching a swastika, the Totenkopf skull-and-crossbones emblem, centred on the black cap-band.

Daphne has seen the symbol before of course, on documents, in whispered intelligence briefings, but now she understands it signifies the purpose of these men for whom death is routine, institutional and authorised. For a moment she has the irrational certainty that the skull is meant for her: somewhere nearby her own ending lies, patient as the river's dark yawn of water below the bridge.

The soldiers jump down and, with Jack, duck through the rain into a large guardhouse.

There are SS men running into it.

This *is* their centre.

About that Jack was telling the truth.

She thinks at first it is strange that they have left her in the car on her own. But then realises there is nowhere to run. She is contained on all sides: her fate is sealed within these walls.

Her hands are shaking. She folds them onto her lap. Looks ahead, tries to muster some dignity in this, the most terrible of situations.

There are lights on the bridge that stretch to the large, gated entrance. Some of it illuminates the moat below. If she moves forward, she can peer into it.

It looks like there is movement down there.

Despite the raging storm, there seem to be people still working. People in striped pyjamas. Why have they not been brought inside? Why would they continue to work in this weather and in bedwear too? It cannot be efficient in such conditions.

She sits back in the car. Her stomach begins to twist.

* * *

After ten minutes, perhaps more, Jack and the soldiers return to the car. She is told to get out and is marched over the bridge.

Though the hail is diminishing, the wind is still up and whips her hair around her.

'What am I to do here?' she asks Jack, trying to make her voice strong.

But he doesn't speak. Not until they reach another checkpoint underneath the old arch of the main doors. Then he whispers, 'For all intents and purposes you are an expert. Try to emanate it. Cooperate.'

Unnerved as she is, she still has the wherewithal to square her shoulders and walk steadily, holding her chin up.

Following Jack through, she steps into a three-sided castle courtyard. Two wings of the building converge in a large, castellated tower. The walls are engraved with Nazi insignia, the sight of which cannot stop a pronounced shiver which crawls over her shoulders and judders her chin. The darkness in here is so intense.

She feels a tap in the small of her back and keeps walking over the wet flagstones till a woman steps forward.

It is a surprise to see a female in this military stronghold of hard stone and men. The woman does not have a uniform, but wears a dark wool skirt, stockings, sturdy shoes and a work blouse. Under her apron is a smock. Silently she beckons Daphne to her.

A soldier follows. She looks around for Jack, but he is no longer there.

The maid opens an arched portal into a corridor with dim lamplight. 'This way.'

Daphne follows her along the passage until they reach a stone staircase. Stairs go up, stairs go down. Daphne expects she will be taken down, aware that most cells and prisons are subterranean.

This time it is not down, but up that they go.

Two steps, three steps, four.

The staircase curves round.

Are they in one of the towers?

She can't tell. But climbs obediently, listening to the maid's exertions and the grunts of the guard behind her.

At the top, another corridor. The maid stops outside a heavy oak door.

'Here,' she says, causing Daphne to stop. She takes out a key and unlocks it, goes in.

Daphne follows her into a narrow chamber.

It is not what she was expecting at all. Modest, yet domestic, there is a carved bed with a wooden headboard, a washstand with porcelain basin and jug. Beside them she sees two tortoise-shell hair combs. The floor is made of parquet and polished so it gleams.

The maid closes the door softly and speaks, her voice steady, 'Dinner will be at eight.'

'Dinner?' Daphne is thrown off balance.

Jack's promise is real.

She must take it and play her part as instructed. 'Please – what time is it?'

'You have forty-five minutes. Make sure you wash thoroughly. From head to toe,' she pauses by the washstand and picks up half a brick of soap, fixes her eyes on Daphne. 'Impurity repels them.'

Daphne notes the use of 'them' not 'us'. Pushes further. 'Who?'

But the woman hunches over and scurries out the room.

The key turns in the door.

She hears the soldier outside say something and shuffle around then stop.

He has evidently been told to take up position there. Is that to stop her coming out or others coming in?

She doesn't know the answer to any of the questions pinging around her head.

Surveying the room, she sees that the window shutters are half open.

Through the gap she can see, in the distance, the rectangular guardhouse, behind it the bridge over which she entered the castle.

The moat beneath is no longer visible: the air full of mist and vapour as if she and the castle were floating on a ghostly cloud.

Perhaps she is, she thinks. It is so unreal, she feels, for a moment, she is dead. As if she has refused Jack's offer and taken a bullet at the monastery, now found herself in some kind of purgatorial limbo.

No, she thinks and pulls the shutters to, she is hungry. Physical sensation would cease if she were dead or dreaming: the stress of everything is taking a toll.

She must keep her wits about her.

Though the castle is so odd, like something out of a fairy tale or a nightmare, and her circumstances so strange that she can understand how her mind reaches for wayward explanations. It will take a while for her to acclimatise.

She will revisit the view tomorrow when the air has cleared, check her bearings, try to work out what part of the country she is in, calculate the number of soldiers on duty, explore the system.

For, she decides now, she has been given this chance to survive.

And she will take it.

She will live.

As she turns back towards the room, her eyes skim over the bed. She hadn't noticed before but there is a dress draped across it. Drawn by curiosity, she sees it is fashioned from pure white silk, cut elegantly on the bias, beaded across the bodice.

Can things get any odder?

She picks the dress up and holds it against her.

The fabric is so fine it weighs hardly anything and glimmers in her hands. The proportions, she marvels, are just right: it will fit like a glove.

How did they know?

It is this, she presumes, that she must wear for dinner.

The dress carries with it a message – put me on. It is an order, unspoken, but imperative.

And she thinks again about the words of her trainers: *You're worth more to us alive than dead.*

Laying the dress on the bed she runs her fingers over the delicate pattern stitched down the front panel. This is not new, it has been worn once or twice before. There are imperfections in a curl of the beading, though it has been corrected – the replacement beads are slightly whiter than the rest. She wonders who it used to belong to? How it came to be lain here on this bed.

Wearing it will signify surrender. She will yield to an enemy who is cruel and heartless. But it is a means to an end, and can buy her more time.

She holds it to her frame.

With a little cunning, she can amplify her looks, heighten her desirability. Though she has never particularly rated it as such, when you have nothing left – no blades, no pills, no network, beauty can become its own weapon. She must wield it now.

CHAPTER TWENTY-TWO

7th May

She is ready, waiting by the bed, when someone knocks on the door. It is very different to the loud yelling thrash of the Gestapo cell. This is, by contrast, polite. Even formal.

She looks up and meets herself in the full-length mirror behind the door. The image unsettles her. Despite everything she has endured, the woman staring back looks assured, almost radiant – competent, polished and strangely glamorous.

She has used every trick available to her to accentuate her natural assets.

Her hair has been brushed with the tortoiseshell combs until it shone. Then slicked with a light application of water so her curls are smoothed. Once tamed she has fastened them into an elegant chignon which skims her neck and highlights her shoulder blades – she has always been active and kept herself trim and knows the effect a well-defined female back can have on some men. Her breasts she has bathed in cold water to make them pert: the cut of the dress dips down to expose just enough cleavage. Alluring but not cheap.

Her face has also been washed in cold water to tighten her skin and make it glow. She has pinched her cheeks to bring up the natural colour. Her lips have been bitten for a temporary flush, her eyes massaged to get rid of the heavy bags underneath.

She stands for the briefest of moments admiring her work before the door opens and the maid enters again. She glances at Daphne and sniffs with approval then brushes past, lays a nightdress on the bed and a pair of shoes on the floor. 'Try these,' she says. 'Hopefully not too small. Too big, you can deal with.' Then she crosses the room and pulls the shutters closed and slips down the fastening. 'Don't open till morning. Or you will forfeit your privileges and be consigned to . . .' she drops the last few words on the floor so Daphne can't hear them. Though the threat is clear.

'Fine,' says Daphne.

In response, the maid steps toward her, so she is very, very close – their noses perhaps only eight inches apart. Surprising, almost impertinent for a domestic. Although there is something in the maid's demeanour, her movements, which exude a lithe kind of grace that suggests she may have studied ballet. Daphne is sure she is not of village stock. There is more refinement in the way she carries herself, finishing her movements with twists and curves. Her dark eyes roam over Daphne's face.

Without warning she spits.

Daphne, taken aback, steps away. But the servant has caught the saliva in her hand.

'Here,' she says, commanding Daphne even closer. 'You have missed a spot.' And she dabs at Daphne's forehead. 'Better.'

Releasing Daphne and stepping back, she looks around. 'Where are your dirty clothes? I am to clean them.'

'It's quite all right,' says Daphne and stands across the bed, where she flung them down only half hour ago. She is thinking that there is weaponry concealed within them, but of course it has all been taken now. Though she continues, 'If you refresh the water and leave soap, I can do that myself.'

But the maid spots them on the bed. 'My orders are to wash them,' and she gathers them up into her arms.

'Time for dinner.'

As she passes through the doorway, Daphne can tell this woman does not like the soldier, though her face stays down on the flagstone floor. Perhaps she does not like soldiers at all.

She gestures for Daphne to follow.

The guard grunts, gives the woman a smack on the shoulder with the heel of his palm and points her down the corridor. Clearly there is no love lost between the two, but the casual brutality appalls Daphne. These SS men are callous to their core, like a different breed of human.

Following, Daphne trails down a hallway with windows that look onto the triangular courtyard.

On her right a fleet of doors. All shut. At the end another set of stairs. She steps down the narrow, spiralling stone steps. Though her room was furnished with an electric lamp, here she notes flaming torches have been lit to illuminate the way. They are presumably to deepen the sense of history and legend. Certainly they imbue the place with a mediaeval feel. The light they cast dances over the walls with menace as she descends.

With each turn she can feel the air cool.

There is a strange smell coming up from the lower floor and, for the briefest of instants, she has the notion that she is sinking into the belly of something that is dead and rotting.

The maid leaves the staircase on the ground floor and indicates Daphne should follow to another corridor.

This place is like a maze. She cannot tell which way is north or south.

They come into a large hall, which despite its height and vaulted ceiling is not well lit but intensely gloomy. In the centre stands a large, round table with leather upholstered chairs. These, she sees, are each decorated with a double sig rune: lightning bolts impressed into the backrest. This place is like a ghoulish Camelot.

The maid slows in front of a set of large double doors.

Someone coughs and rises.

'That will be all, thank you, Annaliese.'

Jack has been waiting for her. Lurking, always lurking.

The maid curtseys and retreats, shutting the door behind her so that they are alone in the strange and ghastly room.

He leans forward and offers her a cigarette. She hesitates – he hadn't smoked before – but then accepts. He lights a match and holds it, illuminating his face, his facade, then hers.

In the brief flare of light, she sees his eyes are roving all over her body.

'You look beautiful,' he says, sucking down smoke.

Compliments have always struck her as a kind of verdict, like she has been approved of, come up to scratch. Knowing, however, that her fate rests with this man, she answers more effusively than she feels.

'Thank you, Jack.' She grits her teeth, widens her smile and opens her lips. 'The gown is beautiful too.' Probably requisitioned, she thinks with guilt.

As if she had uttered the thought, he taps the end of his cigarette and says, 'It's very reductive to think of us as all brutes, you know. Inside these doors, you'll find good, fine brains. And sophistication.'

She looks at the doors as though they were windows.

'You are the not the first to turn sides,' he says, taps his cigarette again, grins. 'Only the latest in the line. To avoid prejudice, I have given the impression you have always been working for us.'

There is a suggestion in his tone that she should thank him for this, but she cannot bear to do so.

'Though they probably won't ask. All right?' he blows out smoke.

She forces back a confirmation. 'Yes. I can do that.'

He nods, and pauses, as if waiting for more.

She cannot afford to lose him now and will have to pander. 'I can't tell you how grateful I am,' she begins.

He steps forward.

The movement confuses her, but she continues, 'You have always been . . .' she trails off as he stoops towards her. 'So—'

He stops her words with a kiss.

His lips are fleshy, like a woman's, and stink of nicotine and boiled cabbage.

Do it, says a voice within.

So she accepts it and pushes back with her lips, feeling a part of her wither.

He breaks off quickly to puff on the cigarette. 'When we're through this, we can be a team again,' he says, cupping her chin with his hand. 'You'd agree – we work well.'

There is nothing further from the truth, but she says, 'Oh, to be back in the field. And with you – I couldn't wish for anything more.'

'It could work,' he says, holding her gaze.

Slowly he runs a finger down the side of her cheek, then nods to himself, releases her and takes a step back. Then his smile disappears and he broadens his shoulders as if getting down to business.

'Look,' he says. 'The Ahnenerbe has dispatched several archaeological expeditions to Iceland. The last in '38. They sought out ancient sites of Norse worship, where pre-Christian Germanic rituals took place. Though success was . . . limited. But Reichsführer-SS Himmler believes Iceland's *Eddas* and sagas preserve traces of our ancient Aryan religion. So this is where you come in.'

He beckons her towards him and holds out his arm.

Feeling thoroughly traitorous and sick, she slides into it.

She baulks at the thought that the Führer's right-hand man has been apprised of her existence. However, really it is no surprise. 'Is he inside?' she asks.

'No,' he laughs. 'No, my dear. He has many responsibilities, though visits from time to time to check on progress. This grimoire with its runic secrets and practices of the seiðr, well . . . it is quite a thing to find. Especially now, when Iceland is cut off to us, under British occupation,' Jack laments. 'I have outlined to him that which is contained within its pages, the spells that you told me of. As a consequence, the Reichsführer-SS believes this book will bind the strands together, potentially connect the dots where the expedition failed. And I have apprised him, Daphne, that you hold the key to it. As you explained, women were the primary practitioners of the seiðr tradition, this confers upon you an extra dimension and value that no other possesses.'

She had been beginning to lean this way with her thoughts, following the thread of logic as Jack speaks. But his last words astonish her. Yes, she knows about the book and some of the secrets it contains but, 'He can't think I'm a völva, Jack!'

'A seeress? A weaver of fates?' Now his eyes gleam. 'I'd say you come close. I've seen you work, remember. In the New Forest. I've heard the rumours.'

They are at the huge double doors now. Slowly, he pauses and turns to face her. 'Daphne, your knowledge is currency here. Right here, in this castle. Himmler envisions Wewelsburg becoming the centre of the SS, as you know, but then the whole world.' His voice is rising with passion and she notices a slight shaking of the arm she holds. 'It will be a place of power, ritual and renewal for his men. Something so much more than stone and blood.'

Blood? She wonders at Jack's description. The allusion to stone is of course understandable – she is surrounded by it. But blood? He must be speaking metaphorically.

'A spiritual home for his new order, the heart of a reborn Germanic race.' His face is flushed. 'Your knowledge – the grimoire – will strengthen that vision, endow it with force and *reality*,' He is truly lost, she thinks. 'Using the magic and power of our ancestral line – those Icelandic Aryans.' He finishes with a flourish of his hand, dips his head, as if bowing to the words and then turns once more to the door.

She swallows. How ironic, she thinks, that those very dark pursuits exploited for Section W may now work for her, might actually save her life.

'Smile,' he says and pats her arm. Then he knocks on the double doors.

With a click, they are opened by two liveried young men, pale and thin. They do not make eye contact with Daphne but bow their heads as she and Jack pass into the room.

The sight inside momentarily overwhelms her. The grand formal dining hall is illuminated by black candelabras, for the long windows are shuttered tight against the night. Heavy tapestries line the walls, not with scenes of hunting or court life, but embroidered with the stark insignia of the SS: the hooked cross, the Totenkopf grinning down from a funerary wreath of oak leaves.

A dining table is laid with a white tablecloth, silver cutlery and crystal glasses. At the far end, four men sit, each in black SS uniform. Another woman smoking a cigarette wears an evening dress not unlike Daphne's. The chatter dies as they notice the newcomers.

'Daphne,' Jack says. 'Please.' And he points to the empty chair next to a man with rimmed glasses at the head of the table.

To the rest of the diners, he adds, 'Daphne Devine, a guest of the SS,' as she sits down. He nods to his audience and indicates the man with the glasses. 'Dr Hennecke, custodian of the castle library, who is particularly keen to talk to you about the Icelandic grimoire, learn your translations.'

Hennecke raises his goblet to her, which is also engraved with the SS insignia, takes a sip. 'Exceedingly keen,' he says, 'but it can wait. Let's not sully our leisure time with work.'

He is younger than she would suppose a head librarian to be, possibly mid- to late-thirties, with dark hair and darker eyes. She bows her head.

Opposite, Jack introduces, 'The scholar, Herr Rudolf Jourdamaine,' and bows slightly to indicate a man with lighter hair wearing round spectacles. He has a weak double chin, which makes his face appear slightly feminine.

She hears Dr Hennecke scoff lightly at his title. Jack speeds on, raising his voice over the sound. 'Director of the Department of Geology and Prehistory. Also interested in the authentication of the grimoire and the runic alphabet within.'

At this, Jourdamaine, who is also smoking, lifts both his hands. 'Guilty as charged.' He sends her a smile that is lewd.

She notes that his uniform has silver piping at the collars, indicating a man of rank, and understands that she is surrounded by them, even if she cannot translate every insignia. Obergruppenführer, she thinks, lieutenant generals and higher, men accustomed to deference. Though she feels as if her blood is curdling, she nods, curves her lips, widens her eyes and flutters the lashes very subtly.

Closest to Jack sits a round-faced man. His hair is oiled, the eyes drooping slightly but he still seems alert. 'Sturmbannführer Vogel,' Jack says, as if it were an afterthought. 'Genealogist of the Reichsführer-SS.'

Vogel inclines his head and sniffs like a dinosaur scenting prey.

'His lovely wife Frau Vogel,' Jack indicates the other woman there, who drops her eyes and stubs out her cigarette, ignoring Daphne.

'Rudi darling,' she calls to her husband. 'Fetch a Burgundy. I'm sure there's a Côte de Beaune '34. I think Gaynor said it was duck tonight.'

Despite herself, Daphne's mouth waters at the mention of the meat. It has been so long since she has eaten well. Years, perhaps. Could rationing not be observed here? Surely it must be.

'And by no means least, SS-Obbersturmführer Hast,' says Jack, indicating a pudgy middle-aged man, with a moustache the same as his leader, 'commandant of our Wewelsburg Concentration Camp.'

A camp, thinks Daphne. She has heard of these places of imprisonment, where inmates are mistreated and forced to labour for Nazi projects. 'Where is it?' she asks and hopes she does not seem impudent. 'Near?'

Hast leans forward. The light cast by the candles illuminates a scar that drags across his cheek and into his nose and deforms the symmetry of his face. His voice is rough, guttural. 'Close enough.'

'Many men?' she asks.

He picks up a glass and raises it to his lips before answering. It's a show of power. 'Not enough,' he says, taking another moment to smell the wine. He nods with approval then returns to her, as if bored by her question. 'There is such and such to be done here, for the remodelling of the castle. The men break stone for us, haul timber, dig until their hands split, if necessary, but still progress is too slow.'

'Yes, I agree,' Vogel says, 'Talking of which – where is Bartels? I supposed he'd be here tonight.'

Hast grunts. 'Greedy-guts has probably dined earlier. You know how partial he is to duck.'

The rest of them snort in agreement. Though Jourdamaine breaks off to raise his voice, 'Well, he can't have all the rabble. Not tomorrow. I need a selection, strong enough to continue the excavation at Externsteine. It is of high priority. The Reichsführer-SS is personally committed to overseeing the project and will be down to see it soon.'

'Yes,' says Hennecke, 'there's something I wish to talk about with him.'

Daphne keeps half her attention on the conversation as it glides though the discussion of an acquisition Hennecke wishes to procure for the library or museum. The other half is spinning with questions: where does Jack fit into all of this? Is he purely the courier who has brought them a new toy? And will she be able to fake it enough for them to accept what he has said about her?

The meal begins. Vogel pours the wine and announces he is intrigued to hear about her 'studies'. She offers fragments of truth – magic and runes, 'dark arts' and mysterious 'cabinets'. Only does not mention she used the latter on stage and omits to detail the false bottom it was equipped with. When his questions veer too close for comfort, she defaults to the tools of her theatrical trade: misdirection and diversion. Eyebrows raised, face open, she requests more information on his 'fascinating' genealogical pursuits. Like most of the high-ranking military men she's met, he is more than willing to speak about himself.

At such great length, in fact, that when the plates are cleared by the two liveried staff, he still has half his meal on it. It doesn't seem to bother him. They are clearly used to being fed well and regularly here. She eyes the wasted food with disdain and hopes the servants will be able to salvage some of it. They look far too thin.

Cigarettes and cigars are lit. Everyone has one or the other in their hand, so smoke fills the room.

As others break out into side conversations, the commandant leans across the table towards her. He is flushed, sweating from his armpits and forehead, and fat with a bellyful of duck, potatoes, gravy. His paunch presses against the tablecloth. 'And what is it you are here to teach?'

Before she can answer, Jack cuts in: 'The Icelandic grimoire. Daphne holds the key, as I've told you.'

'I don't believe it,' blurts Hast suddenly, and Daphne's own stomach lurches. She can feel the blood draining from her face but feigns delighted surprise. His eyes fix on her and glint. 'A woman like that, in this hall.' He laughs. 'No sir, she must prove to me she is not simply a pretty distraction. And prove it damn hard.' He drains his glass, slams it down and sends her a wink.

She feels sick but laughs, then presses her hand to her face, disguising it as a smile, though it transforms itself into a yawn. *Please God,* she prays, *let the gesture not offend him.*

Lightning quick, Jack takes the cue and springs to his feet. 'Gentlemen, let us not interrogate our guest at dinner. You will forgive the commandant, Daphne. Your journey has been long and, I can see, has tired you. Please allow me to escort you to your quarters.'

To the others seated at the table he delivers a short and shallow bow. 'Excuse us.'

Hast mouths, 'Spoilsport,' to Daphne, rolls his eyes in Jack's direction and raises his glass to her in farewell.

She lets go a little laugh, nods to everyone and meets Jack by the door.

Outside the dining room there are now two guards. Jack dismisses one with a wave of his hand, but the man ignores the order and shadows them through the hall. The other remains by the door.

It is only when they reach the spiral stairway, that the man falls back.

'You did well,' Jack says, when he has gone. 'I think they liked you. But . . .' his voice lowers, 'it would be remiss of me not to mention that such good treatment will not last if you fail to deliver.'

Though his tone is not unkind, as she climbs the steps, she

gasps, covers it up as the exertion from climbing. A cold, horrible chill has come down over her.

He turns his head slightly. 'I should warn you that others here have less patience. I am opposed to torture, Daphne. My view is more modern, that people invent under such conditions. In my experience, prisoners will say anything once they reach the point of proper distress. In such a state words are not to be relied upon. Most of what comes out their mouths is nonsense. Their memory collapses, I've seen it. Fabrication fills the gaps. They'll say whatever they think will end the pain. You don't get truth that way.'

Has he just admitted to torture? Who *is* this man? How could she have got him so wrong? She can feel the pores of her body tingle all over as a fearful sweat begins.

He turns and looks down at her as he ascends. 'Some of those who you have met tonight hold to the old ways – which is not surprising when you remember their studies. But they entertain the idea that when the body is pushed *hard* enough, it develops a truthful voice. Daft, in my opinion, but there you go.'

Pausing on the upper landing, he waits for her to reach him.

On his lips he wears a faint smile. A smile! How can he possibly, when he talks of these things? She tries to focus on walking, ignoring the bile that rises in her throat.

The guard outside her room stands to attention as he hears them approach.

Jack's voice softens. 'Of course, I'd rather spare you all that. But it is important that you know who is watching.'

Is this just a warning? she wonders, as the guard steps aside, allowing access to the door.

No, she concludes. She's still a prisoner here, not an equal. For all his professed affection and respect, Jack's words are clearly a threat.

She grips the doorhandle for support.

Jack inclines his head and for a moment she thinks, dreadfully, he is bowing to kiss her again.

But the peony lips do not pucker; he lowers his mouth to her ear, so only the two of them can hear his words. 'So work as best as you can with Hennecke, yes? He'll send for you when he's ready.'

She nods, unable to muster any words.

Jack takes a step back, returning to his courtier mode once more, bows.

'Good, then.' He takes three strides away, then turns. 'Of course, as a gesture of faith, proof that you are now committed – you'll have to give us all your contacts. Including your host in Augsburg.'

CHAPTER TWENTY-THREE

11th May

Mystery Crash Near Eaglesham

Last night, in the early hours, local residents near Eaglesham reported the sudden appearance of a low-flying aircraft, which seemed to be in distress. Witnesses described the plane as a twin-engine aircraft, which vanished behind Eaglesham Moor woods before a loud crash was heard.

Authorities were quickly alerted, and Home Guard personnel along with local police arrived on the scene shortly thereafter.

Early reports indicate that the plane came down in a remote field. The pilot was taken into custody by local authorities. No casualties among the residents have been reported.

- *The Glasgow Sentinel*, 11th May 1941

CHAPTER TWENTY-FOUR

They have left her to stew, she supposes, the possibility of torture dangling over her head like the sword of Damocles. No one has knocked at her door. For two days she has been contained in this room.

Though the absence of activity, of people, is a relief in some ways, the idea of what may come is its own kind of torment.

She cannot possibly give up Greta. It is obscene. Already she has put her mind to different formulations she can deliver to them: a blending of fiction and fact that will not be easy to verify. It will take them some time to check what she says, and that might allow Greta to get away if she hasn't already. The news of her own arrest must have spread: the soldiers and Gestapo made no attempt to hide it. Surely Greta would have gone to ground?

Though the possibility that she has not must also be considered.

There is nothing else for it, Daphne has decided, she *must* get out of here.

So a great deal of her time has been spent looking out the high, mullioned window across the land, assessing the possibility of escape.

The conclusions she has drawn are thoroughly depressing.

Opposite her window, across the moat, there is a surge of trees. Through their leaves she can see the roofs of the houses in Wewelsburg village. Near, but so far.

To her left is the curve of the massive tower that anchors the triangle's tip. It dominates the rest of the castle. Sometimes the shape of it brings to mind the trapped Rapunzel, though Daphne's hair reaches only down to her shoulders, and she doubts there are any passing knights or princes who might come to her aid.

Even if she were to smash the window, climb out and jump, she would be unlikely to survive the fall. Her room is too high up, on the third floor. If she did make it, she would undoubtedly be injured and left to die there. In agony.

The castle is heavily fortified. Its walls are thick, far too firm and sturdy for her to breach by force. The fabric of it will not yield easily. If at all. The only weakness, she concludes, is human: the people that patrol it, work in it. Not all of them can be brainwashed, can they? There must be a human heart in one of them. She has to find it, connect to it and ignite the compassion within. This, she deduces, is her only way out.

But then what? She is a stranger on enemy soil. And does not even know where she is.

Not entirely.

The progress of the sun has helped her to orientate the castle a little: she has determined that the tower is positioned at the northernmost point, which makes sense, given the geometry. It is the narrowest part of the isosceles triangle, at the front, like the prow of a ship, cutting through the trees that froth around the first floor like it is creating a green wake.

It is the centre of building activity. All day long she has heard the rap of chisels and hammers on stone and footsteps pacing to and fro across the scaffolding that crisscrosses its walls. When the wind picks up, canvas and ropes on the wooden poles and boards flap free in the wind, reminding Daphne of a patient in bandages. Or Frankenstein's monster caught, in the moment between ruin and resurrection. As she soon will be. Its process of metamorphosis, she knows, is being determined by a creator as mad as Dr Frankenstein: Himmler's obsessions are guiding its way. It is not restoration as such, but preparation for something so dark and malevolent, it makes her want to scream.

What the hell are they turning it into?

She can't look at it, turns her eyes away, trying to latch on to something real, something that will make her feel safe.

But there is nothing.

The window is locked but she has found that if she moves the desk a foot over and stands on it then presses the side of her head into the frame she can get a better view. Though that too is just as frightening. Beneath her, the poor men are working the moat. They don't look well: arms brittle, faces unshaven, grey, and wasted so much their faces look like skulls. Many of them stagger under the weight of baskets of earth and rock. The rags they are forced to wear are more like the prison clothes of criminals.

Yesterday she sighted a buzzard circling and watched to see what it was waiting for.

Every time an officer walked across the bridge to the castle's entrance the SS soldiers overseeing the workers started to bark out orders and swing their batons. For show. When one of the prisoners, clearly scared, stumbled and dropped his load, he was struck across the back of the head. The crack carried up to her. She couldn't help but cry out as the man fell headfirst into the mud and then lay still. Another prisoner, the nearest to the injured man, darted forward and dragged the limp body aside. His speed and efficiency indicated he had done it before. Leaving the unconscious man, he returned to the abandoned basket, righting it and lifting the load onto his own shoulders, then continuing the work.

No one paid the injured prisoner any attention, though he clearly needed some.

It was, she realised then, exactly as Jack had described: this place was being built of stone – and blood.

It was too awful a thought to contemplate and she turned her face away, so did not see the buzzard dive. Nor did she notice that, just one moment before, it turned its eye on her. For, just then, there was movement at the door and the stony-faced maid entered the room.

Immediately, she let her eyes fall to Daphne's suit which was draped over her arm and did not mention the desk that was sticking out, in a different position to before.

In the midst of such barbarity, this act – or rather non-act – presented itself as an opening.

Which ought to be capitalised upon.

'Good afternoon,' said Daphne and beamed a wide smile.

But the maid did not reply, only refreshed her water and asked for the dress.

However, Daphne was not prepared to let her go without speaking; she needed to establish a relationship, even if that of prisoner and prison warden. She had to start somewhere.

She pointed down to the moat and asked, 'What do the triangles mean?'

The maid's hands stopped folding the gown for a moment.

'The violet badges on their uniforms?' Daphne continued.

She wasn't expecting a reply, but the maid turned her body to the window. 'The prisoners are mainly Jehovah's Witnesses. Bibelforscher. They are identified as such by the purple triangle.'

'The Jehovah's Witnesses?' That confused her. 'But they are a peace-loving faith? What crimes have they committed? To be treated so?'

Avoiding eye contact, the woman replied, 'Their religious beliefs conflict with those of the state.'

Goodness, Daphne marvelled, does she mean thought-crime? 'So they haven't actually *done* anything wrong?'

'Bibelforscher have the opportunity to be released' – the maid's voice was flat and unexpressive – 'if they sign a declaration renouncing their faith and pledging loyalty to the Reich. These men have refused.' She shrugged and turned back to Daphne with a sigh, dropping her head again. 'It is therefore their wish.'

'To be treated like animals?' Daphne exclaimed, her voice rising. 'Sorry,' she added, and rubbed her hands together in an effort to conceal a deep inward breath. 'It's just . . .'

For a moment Daphne thought she might have lost her, with her undisguised outrage. But the woman spoke. 'The officials here believe these men serve history with their labour. They compare their work to that of the pyramids or Stonehenge. Were they not also built on *sacrifice*?' she finished, emphasising the word.

She wasn't sure if the domestic expected a response. Was it her imagination or had she drawn her attention to that word on purpose?

Sacrifice.

Was she trying to communicate something?

But before she could ask more, the maid rapped on the door and disappeared outside.

Though she had left Daphne with some uncomfortable thoughts.

It would do no good to let them overcome her so she tried to banish them from her mind with physical activity; drinking water, then bathing, washing the window so she could keep it transparent.

With all those chores completed she finally gave her attention to her fresh clothes. They smelled so much better, pressed too. Changing into the skirt, she picked up the jacket from the bed. Where the lapel had been ripped away, the tear had been mended: the fraying fabric tucked into the seam and sewn over with tiny, regulated stiches in a thread that matched the pink of the pattern. The other side had been fixed to mirror the new edging so that the jacket was now smart and symmetrical. It was good work. She smoothed it down with her hand and noticed her fingers ran over a bump: there was something hard, under the twill, on the front. On the left side, beneath the facing of the V-shaped panel, she was astonished to discover her gold pen. It had been unscrewed into its component parts, then flattened and sewn into the breast pocket. Absolutely remarkable! It was almost as if whoever had done it knew why the pen was there. Not as a writing implement but something that could be converted into cash when required. Could it possibly have been the maid? But she was so sullen. Her words about the prisoners had come across as heartless. Though were they?

She turned her mind over her interactions with the domestic as she washed herself and dressed for dinner. But again, no one came to fetch her. Resolving to ask her when she next visited the room, she waited. But there were no more knocks that day.

Dehydrated, she was forced to drink some of her washing water.

To combat hunger, she went to bed while the sun was still up.

Though sleep was evasive, when it finally embraced her, she was touched by a dream. The men in stripes look up from a pit and marvel at her. For she is like a witch, and flies over their heads. To where? she does not know. Only, in that strange, warped logic of dreams, she experiences a moment of connectivity, of them willing her on, of understanding that they *want* her to fly.

When she wakes, she is seized by a desire to fling open the shutters and leap from the window, to test the possibility of flight.

But immediately quells the thought.

That way certain death lies. There is no point doing the job for them – she will not hasten her end.

No one collects her today either. She sits on her bed staring at the ceiling, listening to the castle, trying to pay no attention to the thoughts in her head or her empty belly.

But, of course, her mind cannot relax.

How could it? When she is here, a prisoner?

Although she has made peace with the issue of 'cooperation' in so far as translating the grimoire's spells, she has begun to wonder what will happen once she has told all that she knows. When she has given up her value?

She returns to the window and inspects the thick trees across the moat, which she now sees grow *beyond* the castle wall. One way out would be via their branches. If only she could get out to them.

But how?

In the evening, the maid arrives with a tray bearing a pitcher of fresh water and a bowl of stew. It smells delicious.

'I'm sorry,' the maid says, though omits what for. 'The castle has had an important visitor. Everyone has been running around making preparations.'

'Oh, who is that?' Daphne asks.

But she merely puts the bowl on the chest of drawers with a spoon and pours Daphne a glass of water.

'Thank you,' says Daphne as it is handed over and she straightens her jacket with meaning. 'And thank you for washing and mending my clothes. I appreciate you taking such care with my pen.'

The woman's face sours and Daphne wonders if she has blown it, if someone else oversaw the cleaning process.

But then she shrugs and meets Daphne's gaze. 'Neither of us wishes to be here. We must make the best of it till we can leave.'

It confirms something that Daphne has suspected. The men that toil at the excavation, below her in the moat, those who serve the castle staff at dinner – all of them are captives. The maid is no different.

'What did you do wrong, then?' Daphne asks. 'To be here?'

But she drops her shoulders and leaves the room. Someone outside locks the door.

It is not till the following evening that they resume their conversation.

Daphne has spent another day in solitude, though this time water, bread and soup have been delivered. Time has slowed and stretched. She has had nothing to read, nothing to do. However, she has tried to keep active with exercises: press-ups, running on the spot, handstands against the wall. And she has spent more time at the window, studying the contours of the land, working out the ratio of the incline around the wall. It is steep, she thinks. Beyond the tower, the land drops away sharply from the castle's promontory into the curve of a valley. Some way ahead it meets a river, which cuts through meadows and fields. She glimpses hedgerows and narrow lanes, all good for hiding.

'Is the guest still here?' she asks the maid when she brings her supper on a tray.

'He'll leave tomorrow, then another will come. I have heard that this one wishes to see you. You may be called for breakfast. So be dressed and ready early.'

'Thank you for the tip,' Daphne smiles at her.

The maid refreshes the washing bowl with clean water. 'I'm not,' she says as she pours.

Daphne, confused by this, shrugs.

'Not a prisoner as such,' she says. 'Not like you.'

'Oh, I thought that you . . . with the pen . . . that—'

'No.' She makes a clicking noise with her tongue. 'It's yours.

But if you don't hide it someone else will take it. That's what it's like here. I don't like it, but I am absolving my "year of service". It is compulsory.'

'Oh,' says Daphne. 'For all young women?'

'For those like me who are racially "irreproachable".' She spits out the words as though they are maggots in her mouth. 'Though I would rather be at home, teaching.'

'Why can't you do that?' In England teaching is considered a 'reserved occupation'. So far none have been called up.

'My parents frown upon my friendship with another teacher. They pulled some strings and had me sent here, on the off-chance my head will be turned while I am surrounded by the strong, strapping men of the SS.' Her last words are lengthened with contempt.

'Oh,' says Daphne. 'I'm sorry. I hope you are still able to keep in touch? With your friend?'

The maid nods. 'So far, I do not think they have censored the post. And Helga, my friend, writes regularly.'

Ah, now Daphne understands her parents' concern. For six years, homosexuality has been a crime in Germany. Men have been arrested, dispatched to concentration camps. At every level of society, there are these 'snares' and 'thought traps'. It seems so many traits can brand one as 'deviant' or 'asozial'. The prisons must be overflowing.

Although still taboo at home, she has always thought hostility towards homosexuals and lesbians absurd and unrealistic. Like trying to stop a stream with a strong word. Men loved men long before Plato wrote of it in his *Symposium* and women loved women long before Sappho gave them voice. She knows, of course, that her theatrical world is far more permissive than most, and does not reflect society at large, but she prefers it that way. The trapeze artist, Loretta, had lived very openly with Sunny-Mae from the Wild West

Rodeo show. Nobody cared about it. But she is no longer backstage at the Oriental Theatre. And the maid isn't teaching at her old school.

'Anneliese,' she says suddenly by way of introduction.

'Daphne,' she returns.

'I know,' says Anneliese and very nearly smiles.

'Well, thank you for the—' she smooths her fingers over the jacket and is about to say 'diligent laundering', when Annaliese holds up her hand and points at the door then at her ear.

Of course, the guard will be listening.

'Thank you for the fresh laundry,' says Daphne.

Annaliese nods, whispers. 'I do not like the way they treat their prisoners here.' Daphne quiets the breath she takes as Annaliese continues, 'They grind them down until nothing is left.' Her eyes rest longer on Daphne's face. 'Fodder only,' she says very, very quietly. 'Not human any more.'

It haunts her through the night. Not Annaliese's words, but the look on the maid's face as if she was trying to broadcast another message with her eyes. In a place like this her words would certainly be construed as seditious, an admission of dissent, a flaw in her patriotism. Tomorrow Daphne will try to find out more, tell her that this government are also killing their most frail in places like Kaufbeuren-Irsee.

When she dreams, she sees herself swinging from one trapeze to the next, then flying again through the air. Perhaps it was the thought of Loretta from the Oriental that prompted such a fancy, but she takes something from it and exercises her limbs and practises stretching when she wakes.

Remembering Annaliese's warning about breakfast she dresses herself in her clean suit and a fresh blouse. As she is tucking it into the waist, there is a knock on the door. Someone is here to take her downstairs.

As she leaves, an impulse causes her to turn for one last glance: the narrow bed, the desk pressed against the window, the pitcher and bowl beside it. She does not yet know it, but she will never see it again.

CHAPTER TWENTY-FIVE

11th May

They are all there again at breakfast. Though this time there are several more tables in the room. Officers are at different stages of dining.

Jack is waiting for her at the door and leads her over to a table where Jourdamaine is buttering toast.

'Ah,' he says. 'A sight for sore eyes.'

Pulling out a chair, Jack helps her sit before taking his place beside her. 'Our esteemed director here,' he nods at Jourdamaine who inclines his head and half shuts his eyes in appreciation, 'has found the time to show you round the castle museum before you see Hennecke about the grimoire.'

As if cracking a joke, Jourdamaine says, 'Perhaps you will be able to tell me something about the exhibits? Your understanding of pagan practice is appreciated here.'

'Thank you. That sounds very exciting,' says Daphne. It doesn't. These men are inebriated by their own obsessions, building an utterly deranged new world order on foundations as insubstantial as sand. Still, she must play along.

Pouring a fresh cup of coffee – bliss – her eyes drift across the dining table. The silver knives stamped with the SS insignia, crockery to match, butter dish, cups – it's all staged, so desperate to impress. Or depress. She adds sugar and takes a sip, smiling sweetly at Jourdamaine.

'You must be quick,' he says, impatient to show her around.

Despite her hunger, she is only able to consume a piece of toast with jam before Jourdamaine summons a footman to open a door; not the one they entered through, but another in the far corner. 'Quick,' he says, almost snapping his fingers. 'Through here.'

She has barely time to brush the crumbs from her skirt before passing through a low, narrow arch into a short corridor. Opposite stands a heavy oak door, its brass handle and key are ornate. Above the keyhole is a small carved design of a goblet, but Jourdamaine's hand quickly comes down on it, obscuring her view. Still puzzling over its meaning, it swings open.

'Goodness,' she mutters, her breath catching.

She stalls at the threshold of a circular chamber of stone and marble. The air within is heavy and charged, like the theatre at home before the climax of a show.

The north tower. So this is what it looks like from the inside.

She guesses, from the view through the windows, that this is the first floor. The room, no – it is more like a hall or a chapel – is so unusually shaped. She quickly counts twelve sides, twelve niches. Eight of them have a window. A walkway runs around the central circular floor, its path broken at regular intervals by twelve columns that form interlocking arches. They are strangely coloured, hewn from – what is it? sandstone? – no, they have a sickly green glow. Limestone then? She shrugs internally. It doesn't matter, it is not the main thing. The main thing is the effect, which is one of high drama. Her eyes lift to the flat stuccoed ceiling and she sees that there is a hole waiting for a light fitting. Or perhaps for something else. A chimney?

As she walks over the polished floor towards Jourdamaine, she notices a man, an artisan, in a smock. He is finishing some sort of mosaic in very dark green, almost black, marble or stone: a wheel made of runes. No, not runes – swastikas – lots of them. Probably twelve, she thinks. There are twelve of everything here. The pattern is like a wheel radiating from the centre of the floor, or a fantastical spider growing.

'What is it?' she asks the artisan, who raises his body and rests back on his haunches.

But Jourdamaine shakes his head. 'Don't interrupt him. He must finish soon, before . . .' his head twitches. 'No matter.'

'It's so . . .' she can't help the words falling from her lips, but can't finish them either. The acoustics and grandiloquent architecture suggest something like a church. But of course, aware of Himmler's proclivities she knows this is no church. At least not one dedicated to God or Christ.

'Sacred architecture,' says Jourdamaine. 'The hall . . .' he pauses and clasps his hands loosely behind his back, lowering his voice, 'and the one below. The crypt . . . no,' he shakes his head again, more or less at himself. At least this is what Daphne thinks he is doing. 'You won't see that.' His fingers have found his chin and cup it until he looks up again more brightly and nods at Daphne. 'This is the Obergruppenführersaal.'

Quite a mouthful she thinks, but doesn't say, as Jourdamaine's tone is almost reverent. 'It is the Reichsführer's ambition that this will become the centre of the world, you know.'

'Jack said,' she murmurs and looks down at the mosaic artist who has returned to filing a piece of black marble.

'The castle, you will have noticed, is a triangle, like an arrowhead or the tip of a spear,' Jourdamaine is saying, walking anticlockwise around the hall. 'The Reichsführer intends to make the spear shaft into a main street, a magnificent avenue which will connect the castle to special gateways. And these will protect the citadel that this will become.'

'A citadel?' She wonders if she has heard right? 'You mean a city? Here?'

'Indeed. The village will be developed into a city which will be enclosed in a circle with eighteen towers sealing off the area.

All the village buildings will be solely for use by the SS Reichsleadership. Every element is to be constructed under Himmler's direction.'

Daphne steps forward despite herself and draws the mosaicist's attention. His face is grim. Does he see it too – the grotesquerie of this place – one man building a monument to himself? To evil? It is incongruous and yet not so. In many ways she can see a consistency in the egomania that dominates this country. Though it is depraved that the whole world is in upheaval, good, decent men shooting each other, because of the whims of these powerful lunatics.

The artisan quickly looks away. It is probably wise to mind one's own business here. Who knew what could happen if you said the wrong thing, looked the wrong way, thought out of turn?

Jourdamaine's eyes fix on her shoes. Or is he looking at the patterned centre. 'It will be,' he says, 'no, it already *is* the heart of the Order. A symbol of might, of power. And continuity: the past, we revere, drawn into the present, so that this new era might guide the future. Himmler has given us this place as a centre of gravity, upon which we intend to build his titanic vision.'

He has his hands open, palms up, eyes half closed. Daphne lowers her eyes. The image of him makes her cringe. Why do they all talk like this? So overblown and full of hyperbole, like they are trying to convince themselves or are worried that the walls can hear them and report back. She gives him what he wants and tries to look impressed. 'And the museum?' she asks.

'Ah yes.' Jourdamaine gestures towards a narrow archway across the floor. '*My* museum is down a level. This way, if you please.'

She follows him, eager to leave the space, wondering what the crypt looks like, pleased that she won't see it.

When she exits the hall, she follows the director down into the basement, along the corridor, where the air is damper and a touch musty. Though she keeps getting whiffs of a horrible foulness. Something necrotic. Perhaps the rubbish is stored nearby.

Jourdamaine picks up a lantern and lights it, despite the fact dim electric ones hum along the walls. Everything here is for show.

They pass a reading room and then come out into another, which is surprisingly light and airy for one on such a level. There are windows on one side, looking out into the moat.

'Here,' says Jourdamaine, 'I am king of all I survey!'

She is not sure what to make of that – delusions of grandeur seem commonplace, but then he laughs and she realises he is trying to be amusing.

'Let me show you some of my most treasured finds,' he says and leads her into the room, long and narrow. It is lined with glass cabinets, their contents laid out with reverence. 'Here is the true heart of Wewelsburg,' he says with pride.

Daphne folds her arms, eyes darting over the displays, unsure of what is required.

He stops before a narrow case. Inside she sees a single flint scraper, crude, its surface scratched.

'An age-old tool,' Jourdamaine explains. 'Discovered at Ringelstein Forest. Proof that our forebears spread wide, carrying their knowledge across borders. The inscription reveals contact between the ancient Aryan people and those of the East. It is evidence of migration.'

Daphne bends closer. To her, the markings are just little scratches. It's all so manufactured – the conclusions they draw from these artefacts. Like cramming an ill-fitting jigsaw together and insisting the picture is perfect.

He moves on, gesturing to a tray where three coins, small and tarnished, are laid out side by side.

'Polish,' he says. 'Symbols of a people who once stood at the edge of civilisation. Yet even here, Aryan traces endure. Look at the designs, the geometry – unmistakable.'

Further along, another cabinet glitters under the lights. Stone Age flints, neatly arranged in rows, their blades sharp despite the passing of centuries.

'These,' Jourdamaine intones, 'are the tools of our ancestors. Their survival is no accident. They prove the endurance of a people chosen to persist. Himmler understands this. That is why the Reich not only builds for the present, but to reclaim and preserve what was always ours.'

He sounds as if he is parroting a speech he has delivered many times before, justifying the insanity of it all. She nods, bringing her hands together, and lets her gaze drift from case to case. Stones, coins, fragments – mundane objects imbued with a new, spurious, meaning.

'Of course, I am also interested,' Jourdamaine continues. 'In your experience of Iceland . . .'

'As am I,' says another voice, from the door.

They both turn and see Dr Hennecke approaching. 'I'm afraid, I must steal Fräulein Devine away from you.' He pushes his rimmed glasses up his nose. 'Dr Müller will be here in a couple of hours, and,' he smiles at Daphne, 'he will definitely wish to see you. So I must take my chance and spirit you to the library while I can.'

A small flare of panic goes off in Daphne's stomach. Why would this Doctor Müller wish to see her?

She looks back at the museum director to catch his reaction. His nose has been put out of joint, she thinks. Although he says, 'Dear Bruno. I heard he wasn't arriving until this evening.'

'Mmm,' says Hennecke and beckons Daphne over. 'His car has been seen passing through the Straßensperre in Warburg.'

'Oh?' says Jourdamaine, trying to assert some authority. 'The terrain around that checkpoint is hilly, roads very circular and winding. Not a straightforward route at all. He'll be another hour and a half. Perhaps even two? Mark my words.'

But Hennecke shakes his head, 'Apparently, he is keen to get here. An air of urgency has been noted in his entourage.'

Jourdamaine shrugs. 'Urgency can easily be confused with self-importance. You know how the world revolves around Bruno . . .'

Dr Henneke throws his hands up and turns to the door. 'However, I *am* going to steal our expert, Bernard. This way,' he says to Daphne and holds the door for her.

She bids goodbye to Jourdamaine. His eyes trail down her and she knows they will be on her behind as she walks away from him.

'Who is Bruno Müller?' she asks Dr Hennecke as they walk over the cold flagstones. 'Why does he want to see me?' She wonders if she should have phrased that more subtly, but it is out now.

Anyway, Hennecke doesn't seem to have detected any anxiety. He leads her down the darkened corridor. 'Oh, Dr Müller travelled to Iceland in the mid-1930s. For the Ahnenerbe. His task was to collect folk tales, sagas, songs and linguistic material, relevant to our Germanic culture. The sagas, of course, are direct windows into our Aryan past. You must be familiar with them yourself, Fräulein Devine?'

She has heard of them but would not describe herself as well acquainted with the texts. 'What was Müller's role exactly?' she asks to dodge an answer.

'Well,' he says and pauses to flick on a switch. As it comes on, she spots in the corner of the room a spiral staircase carved out of wood, that she had not noticed. *If* she has come this way before.

He ascends the stairs before her. 'He was to document language and traditions and to recruit Icelandic scholars and gain access to manuscript collections. Though that was not met with enthusiasm. Some scholars saw his work as intrusive, rather bizarrely, and there were suspicions about his true intentions. Then the press published some wild stories a couple of years ago, claiming his planned expedition was based on false ideas about Icelandic heritage and that he sought old church records which did not exist.'

'Oh dear,' says Daphne automatically. She is trying to work out where she is, though quite disoriented.

'The Reichsführer was not happy about that,' he says and pauses. At the top of the stairs, there is a heavy door, which he pushes open. 'Though Dr Müller nevertheless continued with his preparations. But then the English, in May last year, as I'm sure you know, they invaded the island . . .' he shrugs and goes through.

Daphne follows him and steps into the library. And goodness, a further architectural peculiarity. With curving walls, it is another circular chamber. Lined from floor to ceiling with bookshelves, the air reminds her of the Kellers' bookshop. Though this is larger.

While Hennecke gathers his breath, she moves to the nearest shelf. So many different volumes – folktales, obscure Germanic texts, treatises on runes, and odd, leather-bound manuscripts on the histories of Europe.

In the centre of the room, a low circular table bears a few open volumes. She notices the neatness of the arrangement. Beside it is a higher table with two seats. In its centre, the grimoire has been laid out, ready for inspection. Despite her misgivings about the book, she is strangely pleased to see it. For now it does not represent death, but hope.

Hennecke's voice is firm as he speaks. 'This is where our officers study. So they can understand that our ideology is rooted in history, *true* history, the history of our people.'

He is an intelligent man, she thinks, to have achieved the

academic rank of 'doctor'; can he not hear the blinkered fanaticism in his voice?

'Please,' he says and draws out a chair, 'take a seat.'

She forces herself to relax her shoulders so she appears not so tense, looks collaborative, eager to start.

'I am sorry I have been unable to see you sooner, but I understand you have been busy with your own studies. The work of the scholar never ends, does it? One's whole life becomes a quest for knowledge with no separation.'

'Well put,' says Daphne. Perhaps this is the way into his heart. 'I could not agree more Dr Hennecke.'

'So,' he says, drawing up a chair. 'To say I am intrigued to find out what the grimoire contains is something of an understatement. The runes are unlike any I have come across before. At least, many of them are entirely different. I can understand some of it, but not enough to perceive any sort of coherence. So it is with bated breath I await your wisdom.'

She will give him enough to keep him enticed and keep herself alive.

'This one,' she says and flicks through the grimoire's pages. 'This is the one I learned first.' And as Hennecke leans to her, she points to the runes. When she first was taught how to execute this charm she had thought of the whole of Germany, but now she finds it is the traitorous Jack who springs to mind.

'What is it for?' asks Hennecke ardently.

'Something most powerful,' she says, her voice shaking, not with fear or trepidation, but because she has been waiting to say it for a long, long time. 'This spell,' she says, 'is for vengeance.'

CHAPTER TWENTY-SIX

They are discussing the vagaries of corpse-wrestling when it happens.

Both she and the librarian had become immersed in their conversation, connecting across ideology by way of fascination, Henneke becoming mesmerised by her descriptions of Iceland, full of black mountains, surrounded by mists and high waves. The way the land had changed as she had journeyed out of Reykjavík, from green, to amber, to black, white and red. An arctic flower, she explained, growing on elevations, which changed color in response to environmental conditions and temperature. And Henneke, who it transpired was also a keen botanist, brought in pencils and paper for her to sketch out its shape.

The 'ling spell' for wind that she witnessed on a boat journey during her 'expedition', had intrigued him. At his request she had also drawn the fish head and pointed him to the matching spell in the grimoire, decoding the sigils and staves, the Icelandic alphabet. She has told him that to be found in possession of magical staves or grimoires was a terrible crime in the 16th and 17th centuries: a third of those persecuted for witchcraft were found with these books, so many were destroyed. 'Which is why this is of such value.'

And he had nodded. 'The secular and spiritual authorities at that time wished to erase magic?'

She bowed her head and spoke with respect. 'But they couldn't. It lives in the veins of the people still. You can tell.

When you meet them. Some of them . . .' she says, thinking of one in particular, 'you can see it in their character.'

And he'd asked about that. How was it so?

The sun had passed over the top of the castle and was starting to slip down to the west, allowing shadows to crawl into the library, though they had been so absorbed in conversation neither of them had noticed or thought to turn on a lamp.

'We have our own scholars who are working for the Hexenkartothek, indexing witch hunts,' said Hennecke. 'The Catholic Church and its inquisition purposefully targeted Aryan women. Female deities and spirits were erased. They wished to suppress Germanic traditions and wipe out magical literacy. They tortured them so they would confess their secrets.' His lips curved into a strange smile, 'The Strappado, the thumbscrew, hot irons, torches. We've some instruments here, in fact. They say you could hear the bones crack, the hair burn, skin bubble, the fat underneath sizzle . . .'

But she did not want to see these implements in the library. Instead, she said, 'Because some magic is too powerful for women to be trusted with?'

'Indeed,' he answered with gravity. 'Are you thinking of some? Powerful magic?'

She wasn't, but cast her mind back to Iceland once more. To a hut high on a mountain pass, to a fight, to a sorcerer and then to a strange creature she heard but did not see. 'There are spells,' she said, 'far stranger than the wind charms or fish staves.' Her voice drew him ever closer. 'In here,' she taps the book again, 'is one which can summon the dead. And not just that – you can enchant it, to enact the sorcerer's will.'

Hennecke had shivered. 'The notion of a body, of a soul, forced to submit to human will is both repulsive and exquisite.'

'And I've seen it,' said Daphne. 'Well, the shredded mess that it made of a man. So much blood,' she said, her mind still on it.

'A blood sacrifice?' he asked, without shame or embarrassment as if he was merely asking if she took sugar with her tea.

'I suppose you could look at it that way,' she said, reflecting nonchalance back to him.

'Mm,' he murmured. 'Blood has always been considered a vehicle of the spirit. A sacred substance that contains more than just the physical life of each person. Very important here . . . Where is the spell?'

And so she bent to the grimoire again and searched for it.

Now, as she reaches the page with the resurrection spell, she says, 'This one,' and sees he has bent right over the desk, pushed up his spectacles so he can scrutinise the inscription.

'You must prick your thumb, just here.' She points to the fleshy pad. 'Not here,' she adds, trying to make it seem more exact and lets her finger circle the edge of her thumb. 'But here,' and touches the middle of the whorl of her thumbprint, 'the very centre. It must be precise to work. There are those that have tried it a hundred times but failed to master the spirit.' This is not what she was told by the sorcerer on the long journey from Iceland to Scotland. However, as her currency is wisdom, she understands that she must amplify her experience. 'Draw blood. Just a prick of it, like a small bead on a dress. No bigger than a paillette.'

Raising a finger, Hennecke halts her. 'A what?'

Internally Daphne smiles, she has netted him. His eyebrows have risen high into his wrinkled forehead. He is hanging on her every word.

'Oh yes. It's, I suppose, a female term,' she nods, raises her eyes to the ceiling as if creating a mental note. 'I will show you later. There are some on my dress. The size is important, because too little and it will not work. Too much and—' she stops, becoming aware of a disturbance outside the door. The sound of marching and shouts. Hennecke looks up, they both do.

The door bursts open. Three uniformed men rush into the room.

'Dr Müller,' says Hennecke, getting to his feet. 'Bruno.' He offers his hand to the one in the officer's cap.

But Müller rejects the greeting and bats his hand away. Instead points to Daphne. 'Seize her.'

Hennecke is wrong-footed by this, looking from Daphne to the fuming Doctor Müller. 'But we are discussing Iceland. You would be fascinated, Bruno. We have much to learn. Fräulein Devine is a guest here. An expert.'

'Oh Reinhard, she's not,' Dr Müller tuts. 'You've been deceived. She's English.'

'Yes, but she's working for us.'

'Well, she's damn well delivered something to Hess. Something bad.'

'Is this true?' Henneke asks her, as the two soldiers grab her arms.

She jostles against them, though it is pointless to fight. They are so much stronger. 'Yes, I delivered this grimoire,' she says. 'The Deputy Führer was my buyer. But he didn't want it. That's why I was able to bring it here.'

'No, it was something else, wasn't it?' Müller returns, walking up to Daphne and gripping her face so hard she can feel the edges of his fingernails compress her flesh.

'Careful now,' says Hennecke, alarmed by this sudden and disorienting turn.

Müller lets go of her jaw with a push that makes her neck click.

'Shut up Henneke!' He shouts at the librarian. 'You'll get yourself into trouble. Whatever she did, she's fucked everything. Perhaps it was a spell, I don't know, but something got to him and now,' he pauses and wipes his forehead with his arm, shakes his head and sighs. 'Now the damn fool has flown to Scotland.'

'Doctor Müller! Bruno!' Hennecke raises his voice with indignation. 'Language. You are talking about our nation's deputy leader!'

'Not any more, he's not. The Führer has just got word of his capture and arrest.'

'What?' says Hennecke, incredulous. 'Captured? Where was his squadron?'

'We have learned it was a solo flight.' He turns back to Daphne. 'From the Messerschmitt factory in Augsburg.'

Daphne feels her left knee begin to tremble, as if operating of its own accord. She tries to regulate her breathing and assimilate the new information. So, the winged man has taken to the skies. It is what she was sent for. It is what her bosses intended. She would be pleased if she weren't so scared.

'Oh my,' says Hennecke aghast. As if he has received a physical blow, he rests his hand on his desk to regain his strength.

'We're to find out what happened.' Müller faces her, hands clenching.

'Quite,' says Hennecke, recovering, then to the guards, 'I'm shocked. I had thought that . . .' he shrugs. 'Can't quite believe it. You'd better take her down to the dungeon.'

'Dr Hennecke,' she cries out. 'I can explain.'

'The Hexenkeller,' he says, avoiding her eye. 'We've just been discussing some of its functions. Appropriate now, but for a different kind of witch.'

Panic flares briefly into anger, and she throws her weight about, trying to shake them off, twisting, squirming, then forcing her body to be a dead weight as they drag it over to the door. She kicks out, getting her heels into their shins. A hand slaps her. Fingers claw at her collar. She jerks her head sideways and sinks her teeth hard into knuckle and flesh. A shout from the soldier and his grip slackens. For a heartbeat she thinks she might break free. Then something hard cracks against her skull, and the world becomes black.

CHAPTER TWENTY-SEVEN

12th May

It is the senses that come back first, before the brain can square what is happening.

She feels cold rock beneath her.

The ground is uneven, sloping slightly, coarse and hard, the air fetid and close.

Her head aches so badly.

A bruise is swelling the skin on her forehead, she can feel it, and something else – a thick stain – liquid that has leaked from the swelling, dried as she has lain prone, and matted into her hair, making it crunchy.

She opens one eye, listens. It doesn't sound like anyone is near – no breathing nor rustling.

Opening the other eye she finds herself in darkness. Can't see anything.

Both eyes close.

She doesn't want to open them again.

A feeling of dread is growing.

She needs to see where she is but she doesn't want to see where she is. She wants to rest and do nothing. Except, it is becoming obvious that this position is not comfortable.

All right then, she thinks, *I must face it*, and forces both eyes open.

After a minute, perhaps five – she can't tell – shapes begin to emerge as her vision adjusts. There is some light, though it is thin. And the smell of sulphur – it must be coming from one of the flaming torches that they are so stupidly fond of here.

Although the light is stationary, steady – no one is holding it. It must be fixed to a bracket far off.

Her hair, she can feel, is also damp from sweat. The feral reek of it is rising from her clothes, more pungent and musky than her regular odour. Fear, she thinks. This is what she smells of.

She sends her hand out to pat the ground. Where she is lying is lumpy and cold and dusty. Edges she detects underneath her finger pads suggest stones that are uneven and irregular. What is this place? A cave?

Pushing down on her hand she tries to lift her upper body into a sitting position, but her vision starts to spin. She touches her swollen temple and winces as pain discharges throughout her head.

Once that has passed, she looks around and surveys her new prison: the walls are curved, though not regular and smooth like the rooms in the towers. Here the ceiling is very low, the building materials that make up the wall are stones jutting out at odd angles. Over in the corner there is an opening to the outside – a hole or a window – though tiny and too high to reach.

There is a wooden door at the other end on iron hinges. Yes, she's in a cell. A dungeon, in fact. Somewhere in the bowels of the castle, the old foundations upon which it was built. Ugh, the smell is rancid: sweat, human excrement, vomit, vegetation, wood and mould. Are people rotting down here too?

She tries to put her other hand down and gain purchase to stand, but it is not working as it should. Heavier than expected it clanks as it hits the ground. A chain runs from an iron ring screwed onto her wrist to another heavy round ring on the wall. While unconscious, she has been manacled. She pulls it hard but there is no give.

A sound starts up. Low, bestial but also very human, it dissolves into a groan. One that is loaded with utter desperation.

Someone is there. Someone who can help her. Surely? Not in this cell but possibly on the other side of the wall to her.

Daphne tries once more to turn her head, though every effort, every pull on the muscles in her neck, the sinews in her back, even the slightest quiver of the flesh on her head – sends shocks of pain through her. *No matter*, she thinks, *I have been in more dire situations*. Though she cannot presently think of one. But she is, has always been, determined to survive. *I am a fighter not a weeper,* she tells herself and, slowly, she turns towards the sound, and though her throat is dry she calls, 'Hello? Who's there? I'm Daphne.' The effort of speaking feels like it is making her skull swell.

She lies still for a moment, listening out for more sounds. Decay permeates the air. It tells her people have died down here. And this makes her inch to the wall that separates her from the other occupant of the dungeon.

'What's your name?' she whispers to the crack in the door where the wood is not flush against the wall.

The sobbing peters out. Then a rusty voice creaks, 'Shut up. Sh.'

At first Daphne is startled by this harsh response but then she hears something else: footsteps approaching.

She finds herself stiffening despite the objections of her muscles. Fear can do that – overwhelm the senses, paralyse the neurons so that the transmitters don't work or don't receive. She knows this, she has felt fear before. And despite her aching body, she quickly attempts to clear her mind. It is so difficult – chained as she is, with the imminent arrival of what she knows will be an adversary. But she reaches into the blackness of her mind and calls for her muscles, her skin, her tendons to give up their tensions. Breathes in and fills out her body with air, relaxes herself into a state of pliant flexibility.

The latch clanks. She opens her eyes, sees light under the gap beneath the old door.

A soldier enters, his uniform obscure in the torchlight. But his insignia glints – the runic shape like the fangs of a vampire.

He points at her. 'You! Get up.'

She moves onto her knees obediently. He steps towards her and nudges her ribs with his boot once, then offers something that is more of a kick. She yowls then shuts her mouth. Despite the fact his jaw is clean shaven, he has a swarthy look about him and greasy lips. He takes out a key and unscrews the lock on her wrist manacle.

She experiences a brief pang of gratitude to be released, then quenches it, gets to her feet and rubs the skin underneath where it has chafed. While she is inspecting her bruised flesh the soldier hits her hard in the small of her back, 'Off.'

'What?'

'Take your jacket off or I will.'

She daren't look at him, daren't think about why he wants her clothes off. But she complies, slips it onto the floor by the manacles and chain.

'Onwards.' He knocks her shoulders with the flat palm of his hand.

It is like he hates her. There is no clearer indication that her guest status has expired. There will be no more fine dining, no silken robes, no visits to the library.

That game is well and truly over.

Innately she understands the worst moments of her life are about to begin.

CHAPTER TWENTY-EIGHT

The soldier pushes her on.

'Out!'

Daphne limps forward, passing through a narrow stone corridor that leads into a larger room. The air in here is even worse: fire, bad sweat, unwashed bodies, smoke. The latter is coming from flaming torches wedged into iron rings on the wall. They make it feel horribly archaic. No doubt just what the doctors ordered.

Someone clears their throat and coughs. The sound comes from above, so she looks up; the ceiling must be at least twenty-five feet high. There is a viewing platform built into the wall about fifteen feet up. Why? she wonders, then sees Dr Müller standing there, talking in low murmurs with Dr Hennecke.

When she catches sight of chains hanging from the walls she stops in shock.

The soldier yanks a rope and something overhead creaks. She follows the rope up to a pulley, which is fastened into the ceiling. Coiled chains and waiting hooks dangle from it. She has seen this before in her history books. A hideous invention. Used by the inquisitors of old – the strappado that Hennecke mentioned is a machine for hanging, for stretching, for breaking. For torture.

Sweat breaks through every pore of her body.

She eyes the chamber for an escape route. There are steep stone stairs on the right, another door beside them. At the top, the stairs curve round, presumably to an entrance. Presumably guarded. The other door, though, the one at the bottom? Might that lead out into the moat?

They halt in front of a low wooden platform. Upon it are strewn leather straps, handcuffs, manacles.

Oh God.

Another soldier, thinner, leans against the wall behind it, watching Daphne's expression. The first man, the hefty one, drags her forward.

She stands for a moment looking at him as he smiles, then he tries to push her up onto the platform.

No, she thinks. *No cooperation. No more. If this is to be hard for me, I will make it hard for them.*

As he shoves her, she wrenches her arm free, lashes out with it and kicks his shin.

He grunts, hops, clutches his leg while the second soldier laughs at both of them and pushes off the wall. She flings her arm out at him too, connects with filled-out fabric – his chest?

But he catches her hand. 'Now, now, Fräulein,' he says, still laughing as if she is here to entertain him, grabs her other arm and wrenches both of them behind her back, clipping them together with one deft movement, arranging her effortlessly, as if she were a doll.

The first soldier bends down and pins her legs. The second kneels, rope in his hands, and binds her wrists and ankles, then loops her knees together. Daphne screams as each knot pulls at her skin. But she has been bound before and now she puts her mind to filling out the space, resisting as the ropes sting and tighten.

She half-roars, half-groans at them, 'Get off me.'

A damp cloth is forced between her teeth to shut her up.

The second soldier steps back and looks her over, admiring the handiwork of his knots, how constricting they are, nods and looks up.

She follows his eyes. Dangling, the hooks catch the torchlight.

What are they waiting for, she wonders? She twists round to see if she can catch a glimpse of the sobbing woman in the next cell. But the angle is all wrong, she can't see through the passageway.

The second soldier approaches with more rope and ties a final knot around her chest.

With a deep, deep inhalation of breath, she reminds herself that she is no stranger to pain and has overcome it before.

She summons the words of the Tibetan troupe who appeared at the Oriental Theatre. Billed as monks, though they may well not have been, they had told her a secret – that the key to endurance in difficult situations was the ability to shift focus away from the body. Like most skills, the more one practised, the easier it became, and she sat in with them during their exercises almost every day for the duration of their contract at the Oriental. Six weeks. She hadn't known why she had felt compelled to join in, but now she thinks it must have been some kind of foreshadowing, as if part of herself understood that it would become useful to know how to tolerate pain, that there would come a time when she would need the skill.

She works now to 'watch' the sensation arise. Though it is not just one but several: her shoulders are prickling, as if pre-empting the ordeal on its way; her skin smarts under the rope as her heart is bang-bang-banging, pulsing in her chest like it will explode. *This will pass*, she tells herself. *It is temporary*. And she feels it diminish minutely. Her instructors back at Section W had told her to summon a happy childhood memory to distract herself.

Will she have the presence of mind to do any of this? She must.

The clank of a distant door echoes into the chamber. Voices. Orders.

The soldier with the rope steps back, satisfied. The first jerks his head towards the strappado.

'Up.'

She thought they might have waited for someone senior but no, she is lifted onto the platform and turned round. Her arms wrench upward behind her back as she is hooked into the mechanism.

Although she can feel her muscles stretch across her shoulders, there is not too much pain. Not yet. But she cries out, anyway, as it is what they want. The sound is muffled by the rag in her mouth. It puffs in and out as her breathing accelerates.

Above, the pulley creaks as the rope tightens.

One of the soldiers – she cannot see which from this angle – tugs upon it.

As her arms and hands are tugged up, her back goes forwards, her head down.

Oh my God.

Her shoulders instantly begin to burn. She gasps into the gag. Her spine is stretching, stretching, stretching.

Another pull.

Her body lifts, toes scraping against the wooden platform but still able to support her weight on the very tips.

The soldiers step back and move in front of her so she can see them.

One is sneering. Can it really be cruel delight in her discomfort that she sees on his lips?

One more pull and she will come off her feet. The full weight of her body will transfer to her wrists and shoulders.

Her lungs are hurting now too.

Everything is taut, pulled, strained.

Her breathing has become shallow. Difficult.

She summons to mind her father. Sitting in his lap. He is singing. 'Row row row the boat . . .'

One of them moves to the winch, puts his hand on the handle.

A door slams shut.

The soldier in front of her looks up and to the stairs. The other has paused.

Heavy, measured footsteps thud down the stone steps. The grin on the second man evaporates. Both of them stand to attention.

Dr Bruno Müller enters.

She is breathing through her nose and can smell horse hair.

Tall and imposing, well filled out, he carries a notebook beneath one arm. His hands are gloved and a riding crop taps lightly against his thigh. He pauses. Though it pains her to keep her head up, she watches his eyes trace over her body, taking in the strain of her shoulders, the flush across her face. His expression is clinical, like a scientist studying a specimen.

For a moment he appreciates the view, then with a sigh says, 'Get her down!'

The soldier with the greasy lips looks appalled and as if he is about to protest, but the other she hears stepping onto the platform, obeying his superior immediately.

Müller lets out a light snort. 'Doctor Hennecke wants her to demonstrate something. She'll need the use of her hands.'

Nodding, the greasy one replies, 'We've barely started.' There is disappointment in his voice.

'I know,' says Müller and shakes his head. 'Don't ask me.'

The crank whines as it goes round and she feels the rope begin to slacken, her hands lowering with every turn of the wheel.

Her feet flatten. She spreads her weight across them and is able to stand up.

One of them frees her hands from the hook.

Briefly, she experiences relief. A reprieve.

The soldiers glance at one another, awaiting orders. Müller sets the notebook on a table and turns to them. 'You are to report to your section head immediately for reassignment. The Führer has ordered a dispatch to the east.'

She hears all of this. Why is he telling them in front of her? Then the relief she experienced just a moment before converts instantly into fear as it comes to her – she is nothing to them. Müller does not see her as a threat or potential leak because he knows she will not survive her stay in the castle. Her death will be imminent. Either that or that she will be kept here forever. Both scenarios appal.

'Plans are changing,' he continues.

'But der Osten?' says one.

'Enough.' Müller snaps. 'Questioning orders?'

The greasy-lipped man takes a step back and drops his head. 'Apologies, sir.'

'Now!' he barks.

They shuffle off towards the door, leaving her alone with Müller.

The east? Why would troops be sent there? All their efforts are concentrated in the west. Germany already holds half of Poland. The rest of it has been occupied by Russia. Despite her state of high anxiety, she understands this intelligence will be of prime importance to her officers at home. Though there is no time to dwell on it as Müller's gaze locks on to her face. His head is angular, with sharp pronounced cheekbones and a severe jawline, skin tanned from exposure to sun. 'I'm not going to pretend we don't know who you are, and you shouldn't masquerade either. It really is of little point, and we are where we are.'

He circles her slowly. The crop flicks against his boot.

When he comes back to his position in front of her, he tugs the gag free. Her lips burn. She breathes through her mouth, then – spits. It lands on the floor between them.

Müller raises an eyebrow then lifts her chin with the end of his crop. 'Tell me what you gave to Hess.'

'Grimoire,' she says, recovering her breath. 'I told you. He didn't want it.'

'But there was something *in* the grimoire,' he says.

How does he know that? Only a handful of people are aware of the extra pages.

The crop taps twice against his glove. 'Something Hess took. Or read. What was it?'

She clenches her teeth, tasting blood.

'I don't know,' she rasps.

'Just need to know what it was,' he murmurs. 'A code?'

Ah, she thinks, he's guessing.

He leans in close, so she can see sweat on his temple.

'Hess does nothing without purpose. He would not fly to Scotland on a whim. He carried with him something forbidden. You will tell me what it was.'

The crop flicks against her shoulder. It does not carry much force yet, but stings under the fabric and her eyes begin to water.

Müller tilts his head, studying her face for clues. 'Better,' he says, with satisfaction. 'Pain encourages truth. Now again: what did Hess take from the grimoire?'

'All right,' she says. The deed is done. Hess cannot fly back. But she can make it easier for herself. 'A prophecy! Nostradamus. Found in the grimoire.'

Dr Müller lets out a 'Gah!' Then mutters more or less to himself, 'The man is obsessed. What whimsy. A great character flaw. There will be hell to pay for this.' Then he raises the crop to her face again.

She flinches. Involuntarily her eyes begin to blink.

'So who arranged the facilitation of the book to the Deputy Führer?'

She is fast turning over her options. It is better now to drop some breadcrumbs. 'The Kellers,' she says. 'But they knew nothing of my identity. Only that I was a book dealer from Cologne.'

He nods – good. 'You stayed in Augsburg. Where?'

But this time she hesitates. She will *not* give Greta up.

Crack! The crop hits her across the cheek, cutting through the skin, leaving a welt on her cheek that will stay there for the rest of her short life, and flicks her eye. Pain shoots through her face.

'A name.'

The bruising starts immediately, her eye waters and her lid begins to expand.

A muscle starts to spasm in her unharmed eyelid and doesn't stop.

'Hotel,' she blurts. 'Hotel Augsburg.'

Out of her good eye she sees Müller pull out a pen and write in his book. Back to her he calls, 'But who facilitated it? Name!'

'We don't do names,' she says. 'You know that.' It must be the same for the German operatives overseas.

And, she thinks that at last, he must admit this because he sighs.

But he pushes back his shoulders. Then, without warning, he administers a quick punch to her stomach.

Hands and legs bound, she cannot do anything to break her fall and goes over backwards, off the platform.

With a splintering crunch, her head hits the stone floor.

News Bulletin, 8 p.m. – Berliner Reichswelle

It is hereby formally announced that party member Rudolf Hess, who for several years has suffered from a chronic illness and was expressly prohibited from undertaking further flights, nonetheless obtained control of an aircraft. On the morning of Saturday, 10 May, around 4 a.m., he departed from Augsburg on a flight from which he has not yet returned and may have ended his life by jumping from the aircraft.

A letter found among his possessions bears evidence of a disturbed state of mind and suggests he may have been subject to hallucinations.

The Führer has immediately ordered the detention of adjutants of party member Hess, who alone had cognisance of these flights and did not, contrary to the Führer's orders, of which they were fully aware, either prevent or report the flight.

CHAPTER TWENTY-NINE

14th May

She tries to move, but her body responds with moans. Pain floods the space behind her eyes. Her head is pulsing. Both cheeks are hot against the stone floor. The taste of blood lingers on her tongue.

Her limbs throb.

Only one eye will open, but through it she can see she is back in the dungeon.

She cannot tell if it is day or night but doesn't care.

Pain is everywhere.

Light from the window-hole slants across the dungeon.

Memory returns in bits and pieces.

She sighs loudly with despondence. Her mouth is dry, so very dry, tongue furred and lips cracked. Moving her head very gently, to minimise the discomfort, she sees to her immense astonishment that there is a bowl a few feet away. Beside it a stoup. Perhaps it has water in.

With great effort she wriggles.

The water there is like a gift from the gods. Cool, mineral, wet. She drinks down greedily, then twists so she can lean her body up against the wall and catch her breath.

It takes two, maybe three minutes before she realises that somewhere in the gloom someone else is breathing.

'Who is it there?' Her voice sounds like that of an old woman, fluctuating and weak.

A figure stirs and moves out of the shadows. She stiffens, but that causes more pain.

There is a man. In uniform, of course. Young, she thinks. Straight hair. Must be blond, as the light catches it.

He squats, watching her. Instinctively she tries to close her legs. What is he doing in her cell?

He moves forward a couple of inches. 'Here,' he says and pushes a flat wooden plate over the stones on the floor.

It looks like bread and some cheese and . . . are they? Grapes? Can it be?

She reaches for it, but finds her arm is heavy and drops to the floor.

To her amazement he leans over and pushes it further so she can reach. The action undoes her momentarily and she feels a pain in her heart for this scrap of decency. But takes the plate and brings it onto her lap.

Now she has it, she cannot stop herself tearing at the bread, grabbing at the cheese, shoving it into her mouth.

She takes two grapes and pops them in. As her teeth bite into the flesh the juice squirts across her tongue.

Gradually she becomes aware that the soldier is still watching her.

He has not quite retreated into the shadows, and a little light falls across his face. Under the straw-coloured hair his eyes are anxious. He is frowning. 'Jude?' he asks.

She shakes her head.

'Bibelforscher?'

She remembers the term. The maid, Annaliese, had used it – Jehovah's Witnesses. 'No.'

He moves across slowly so as not to alarm her, then lays her jacket on her knees.

She realises now she has not been manacled to the wall and, with care not to move her head too quickly, slides the jacket on.

'Then why are you in here?' asks the soldier.

'I gave something to the Deputy Führer.'

'Oh dear,' he says, retreating back to the door. 'Before he flew?'

The jacket, though ripped and tatty now, provides some warmth. 'Yes.' She rips another piece of bread off and nods. 'Thank you. They think I had something to do with it. With his flight.'

'And did you?'

'I gave him a book that he wanted.'

'And that was it?' he asks. His eyes are large in his face and dark.

She nods. 'Yes.'

He sits back on his heels. 'Tell them that.'

'I have.'

'They don't believe you?' he asks, strangely curious.

'I don't know.' She shrugs. The bread is doughy with a crisp crust. She wants to savour it. It may be the last meal of the condemned.

After a while the guard says, 'Your accent. It is not entirely Germanic?'

'My mother is Italian,' she says.

He smiles. 'Yes. There is something familiar in it. We used to holiday in the Dolomites. Skiing. Italy is our ally.'

She nods, surprised she is having this conversation. Amazed that he isn't taunting her or kicking her. So she pushes her luck, 'How do I get out of here?'

But he shrugs.

A door clangs and he stands up quickly. 'There is no point holding out,' he says. 'They get what they want.'

Then he leaves the cell, locking the door behind him.

She calls, 'Hello?' to the cell next door, but there is no answer. Instinctively she understands there is nobody there. Or that there is a body, but no soul in it any more.

CHAPTER THIRTY

15th May

A different man enters the dungeon. This one is huge, a giant. Not only does he fill out his uniform, stretching the seams round his chest and stomach, he must stoop to enter through the door. From this short distance she can see his whole face is shining and can smell his sweat. It is tinged with hops or something yeasty. He has been drinking.

Not good.

Her head is still aching, but the pain has much diminished since yesterday. Unsteadily, she stumbles to her feet.

The guard slurs his words as he commands her out, nods for her to follow him.

Entering the Hexenkeller, the giant stops her with his hand on her shoulder. 'You were not at Hotel Augsburg. It has been checked.'

Already? she thinks. Did they really or is he just saying that? Looking around she sees Müller is not present today. Undoubtedly, he has left instructions.

Pushing her on, the guard starts: 'Where did you stay? Who with? Tell us or endure.'

His eyes are glassy, bright yet unfocused.

Though she doesn't say anything, the fat guard takes her silence for a refusal.

'The man that you stayed with. He has been taken in.'

She thinks back over her route. A man? Well, yes there was one. She summons to mind the one called 'Twenty-Four'. Could this be true? Or are they playing her? But then she remembers Jack is likely to have laid out what he knows. The thought makes her weak with guilt.

The soldier looks up intentionally at the pulley. Is it just a threat or has Hennecke given up on her and decided her arms may be ripped off?

But the giant doesn't stop there and leads her across the cellar. It seems they have other plans for her today.

'Let's see if some company will make you talk?' He propels her on to the door at the bottom of the stairs built into the wall. And she perks up a bit. Does this lead to the moat? Can she, at least, make a dash for freedom? Perhaps it is better, she thinks, to be shot in the back than to die by torture or on the strappado.

The giant taps on the door three times.

When it opens, she observes steps going down into a deeper darkness within. Her heart sinks – if it is subterranean then it goes only further into the ground.

Another two guards line the corridor. Both are blank and silent.

A dull light is coming in from somewhere.

'Steck sie rein!' the soldier holding her says.

She sees a flicker of confusion cross the nearest guard's face. 'Sie?' he asks, doubtful.

'Ja, sie. Los jetzt,' he retorts – yes, get on with it.

The other guard shoves her forward, down the stone steps. She rights herself just in time for them to pick her up and propel her towards another door.

She can hear the guard behind her breathe in deeply before the other unlocks it and holds his nose. It swings open abruptly, and with one hard shove she is inside.

The door shuts behind her. A key turns in its lock.

Inside, the air is absolutely rank, sour with sweat and other terrible smells: acidic urine, the filthy ammoniac and charred reek of human waste.

The stench presses against her mouth like an airborne contaminant that wants to invade her body. It is so powerful. She recognises it – this is what pervades the lower reaches of the castle.

She doesn't want to breathe in. Doesn't want to see into the dark.

For one suffocating moment, her eyes register nothing but pitch black.

Then, as her vision adjusts, she begins to perceive forms in the dark.

Light peeps round the edges of the door, the tiny gaps between the wall and the frame.

Slowly it begins to illuminate.

At first she thinks it was some kind of storage room or larder. With meat propped against the sides.

She looks down at the dim light spreading across the floor and sees it touches toes. Human feet.

She blinks, looks up.

And makes out the shapes.

It is not meat, but *men* stacked here.

Thin and haggard, with skin that stretches tight over each one's ribs: men that are not dead.

But who are barely alive.

She paddles back, the ache in her head forgotten as her mind is drenched absolutely with horror.

Fear, disgust, repulsion, pity – all fight for supremacy in her mind.

She cannot really believe what she is seeing.

But this is real.

They are here – naked, in the shadows, huddling together.

In fact, they are on both sides, swaying where they stand, with large hands out of proportion to their skeletal bodies.

The breath comes out of her.

Some turn their heads to the sound, slowly, so slowly, fixing her with hollow eyes.

One raises a hand. Then more mouths begin to twitch and move.

Faint, jumbled whispers start.

'Help me,' she hears but can't tell from whom. The darkness amplifies every sound.

A chain rattles on the floor: one of them is moving.

She wants to step back, to flee, yet she is paralysed, cannot look away.

Who *are* these men?

The camps' prisoners?

My God, how can the SS do this? Keep them here like this, packed into a black cellar, suspended in endless darkness?

She almost buckles with the enormity, the inhumanity of the act, puts out a hand to steady herself, touches cold flesh, then realises she is completely surrounded by them.

Scores of them in this tiny space.

She pulls her hands over her body protectively.

Waits for the first touch.

Girds herself.

But they do not move towards her.

They do not speak.

They do not do anything.

Just stand. And sway.

Don't even moan.

She frees her voice from horror's grip. 'What's happening. Why are you here?'

But there comes only the murmur of inconsolable voices.

A low sob.

Then one voice comes through louder, though it is so rusty and broken, as if a long time since it has been used. 'They take us out,' it says, then pauses for breath. It is such an effort. 'One by one. Those that go, they never come back.'

'Where?' she asks. 'Where do they take you?'

But there is no response.

It is like a larder, she thinks. Where they keep meat for purposes unknown.

Her breath comes in with a jagged noise like it is tearing her throat, like she is choking on their suffering.

The place is unbearable.

But she has been put here.

Left here!

For a moment her mind stutters.

Then terror explodes.

No, no, no.

She can't stay here, the thought is too dreadful and releases a surge of adrenaline; she turns round and bangs on the door. 'Let me out.'

She can hear them, in the corridor, talking and laughing. How can they? How can they be so disconnected from the misery in here that they can *laugh*?

'Please!'

Her fist is hurting but terror explodes. 'Help!'

She begins to scream.

A chorus of cries, 'Help, help,' goes up in the cellar.

Then there is light.

She blinks.

A rough hand grips her arm.

And she is dragged back into the corridor.

The guards thud down the narrow stone passage as they come towards her. Though she slides against the wall, feeling like she is about to faint, the giant brute hoists her over his back and carries her into the Hexenkeller again. This time he pushes her up against the wall, where the ropes to the pulley are fastened on a hook.

Her mind is unloosed, wrenched from its moorings . . .

A paw around her neck keeps her pinned there. 'Contact one – Augsburg,' he barks, 'please,' then tightens his grip on her larynx so she can barely swallow.

She hears herself before her mind even processes it. 'Helen.'

He smiles slowly; he has succeeded where the Doctor has not. 'Patronymic?'

'Keller,' she says.

The giant oaf calls out to the other guard, 'Bauer! Write it down – Augsburg – Helen Keller.'

The young soldier who gave her the bread, is sitting on a stool by the table. He hesitates, his eyes dart at her, but he obeys and opens the notebook lying there, glances at them one last time before writing it down with a frown.

The giant thinks he has got her on a roll. 'Who told you Herr Hess wanted the grimoire?' he asks.

She cannot draw in enough breath to speak and gestures to his hand. He relaxes his grip minutely. She gasps, wheezes, gulps down air.

Now he starts to squeeze again. 'Hess? Who told you?'

'Don't know,' she shrieks as if it is an insult. 'Instructions in code. I only had to deliver it. Courier. Courier.' Her eyes are full of water. 'Look at me,' she says in desperation. 'I am only a girl.'

And he does look at her. For a very long time, as liquid brims over her lids and slides down her cheeks to her chin.

At last, he makes some inner decision, removes his hand.

Daphne slides to the floor, lets her fingers fly to her bruising neck and rub the tender flesh. She breathes in more freely. A fragment of command returns and she attempts to rein herself in, bring her senses under control. The Germans think they are a different race and so they are. So they are. Something has gone wrong with them. They have become monstrous. 'Bauer!' shouts the giant again. 'Fetch the dagger, then help me take her to the crypt.'

The young man's face drops.

'What?' Daphne grabs at the giant's trouser leg.

'If you can't make yourself useful, then we will find other ways you can contribute.' And he raps on the entrance to the corridor again.

'No, no,' she says again. 'Not there, please.'

This time when the door opens, she screeches.

It is the sound of a banshee foretelling death.

CHAPTER THIRTY-ONE

Each of them has slipped a shoulder under her armpit. She makes no effort to move her body, so it flops around, is difficult to carry. But they are so much stronger and her mass is slight, the weight easy to transport between the two of them.

Her brain is not working properly. She is in shock but does not understand this, thinks she is dying.

Half holding, half dragging, they haul her over the flagstones. Her feet trail across the stone, toenails catching on the hard jutting edges. It doesn't matter, she doesn't care. Pain, pain – she knows where it leads to, what its end is. Perhaps it is better to give in to it, let it carry her away to oblivion.

Down.

The corridor goes on and on.

They pass the larder.

At least, there is that.

The floor begins to incline.

But she knows, she has come to the end of the line.

They pass torches and more doors as they advance up the slope.

Despite her misery, a tiny reptile part of her brain, the one reserved for survival, is still working.

Damp stone becomes sharper-edged, fresher.

The stench of the men's cell is overwritten by a new brace of smells: earth, wood dust and burning solder.

Ahead, an archway.

Her body is lifted up over a step onto a landing, then without waiting, they turn her round, prop her up, push.

Three more steps down and then another door. Arched. Not a dungeon. Something grander.

Crossing the threshold, she feels all the dread she has ever felt before rise up, flow through her body along her arms and legs to the tips of her fingers and toes. Her jaw starts to judder, for she has passed into . . . what? A room, no – a hall? A sepulchre?

It is large, domed and circular. Above, in the centre of the roof, two swastikas are set into the stone.

As she looks around, she sees niches and plinths.

On one is a figure of Lucifer, the Fallen. Tatty wings spread wide, he looks up to the swastikas with a sly smile. On another plinth is that goblet again. But it is not any chalice. There is a cross carved into its side – a grail.

Like the decorations on the handle in the room above.

And she understands that the crypt is sacred to them. Some kind of a ritual chamber.

In the middle, under the blackened swastikas, she can see an open pit in the floor. In it, pipes or drains.

Just when she thought she had nothing left inside, a primeval scream fills the rooms, the sound of a cornered animal.

Though when her lungs empty, her body draws in air.

Pressure is building behind her eyes, but she is now aware of it.

Unable to twist her eyes away, she sees beneath that deep, deep pit, an unnatural blackness which sucks all the light in.

Around it, the stones glimmer darkly as if wet.

It is all stifling.

'Pit,' instructs the giant soldier.

The word causes the beat of her heart to spike.

Could it be one of those 'forgetting places'? An oubliette?

'Pit,' she thinks, and her mind reaches for others – the Black Hole of Calcutta, Poe's bottomless abyss, Dante's Inferno.

They congest her mind, begin to spin with the flood of adrenaline, like a crazy carousel going off its wheel.

It is, at last, too much for her. She sends her gaze away, up and over and around the curved walls, and as she does, a memory fleetingly presents itself to her, then pivots upon itself. A dream from last summer. A glimpse into the past – twelve acolytes surrounding a man, a spear or knife, the ritual slaying, a spume of blood.

Twelve she had seen. There are twelve plinths here. Twelve walls too.

Yes, she has seen this place in her dreams.

In her nightmares.

This, she realises, is a shrine to violence, a chamber of horrors.

And now she finally comprehends what is about to take place, why the dagger is needed.

'Noooo,' she tries to struggle out of their grip. Her cry echoes around the wall and returns to her ears. She turns to look at them. Her vision continues to revolve after her head has stopped moving. Or are the walls themselves starting to rotate?

The soldiers don't blink, don't stop, only grip more tightly and yank her to the hollow gaping at the centre, the circle cut into stone, black as sin, no bottom visible.

The pit.

'Oh God,' she says and at the sound of her blasphemous words it feels as if the ground shifts: something down there cracks and opens, releasing an old and putrid thing into the air. Darkness expands out of it, moves up and around like a vast cloud of mosquitoes.

And it is humming.

Bluebottles! She thinks, blow flies, a swarm of them.

And they are hauling her to it.

She is too terrified to question if what she is seeing is real. Only knows that if she is taken there, she will die.

Her heels catch against the rough stone. Pushing them desperately against the slabs, hoping to slow them down, all she does is split the skin.

'Ugh,' she lets go of a squeezed, strangulated sound as full of despair as the groan from the woman in the next cell, the men in the larder, and closes her eyes, shakes her head. 'No, no, no.'

One of the guards swears, pulls her forward by the hair.

When she opens her eyes again it seems as if the chamber is alive and awake. Or as if some *thing* within it is – an entity that is of the chamber, but also of the world. Some *thing* that is gathering strength from the brutality it is witness to.

She stumbles down the three steps to the pit, nearly falling. Only the soldiers' grip keeps her upright.

Her senses grow sharper, whirl out of her, higher and higher, so she is looking down on herself. She cannot see the presence, only feel it.

It is close, getting nearer. Eating up her fear, no not eating – nurtured by it. Waiting, as if it were used to being fed such dark offerings, such perverse devotions.

Daphne's mind roams back and forth through time. The men in the cellar, she thinks, they are not just prisoners – they are stock. To be used, to be spent, sacrifices to this darkness.

Sacrifices. Annaliese had tried to warn her.

That this is what she is, will become!

'There,' one of the soldiers says. She doesn't know which one now – they have both become distortions. Against the whirling chamber they are one with the faceless demonic swarm, eyes glowing black like marbles, not human any more.

One of them forces her arms back, gripping both her wrists

in his fist, taking her to the edge of the circle, forcing her face down the pit.

She is both above and below, in her body yet out of it.

The other steps in front, radiating foul energy, a vibration, a pitch that is amplified then reflected back by walls designed precisely for this purpose.

Breath coming fast, sour and acrid, he pulls the dagger out and brandishes it high.

'Stop. Please, no more.' She can hear the scream of some poor soul at the end of despair and terror and has no idea that it is herself. Fear is overwhelming her nervous system and as much as she is trying to hold on to her rational self, the sensory overload has allowed disassociation to slip in.

The giant with black eyes and greenish skin points to the dagger and smiles like a silent movie villain.

He presses the blade to her throat and the physicality of pain, localised there – under her chin, pinches her back into reality again. She feels her other self descend into her body. The two halves snap back together.

'Who gave the instructions about Hess?' he asks. 'Tell me now. Or I'll cut you open and let it run.'

The blade has pierced the skin but not gone far.

A trickle from the fresh wound runs down her neck.

'Come on,' he says. 'The pit is thirsty. If you refuse, I will happily let it drink your blood.'

This must be it then, this is her moment – she must claw back autonomy, push herself onto the blade, finish the job herself. 'I am sorry,' she whispers to her unseen parents – Carabella would not approve. It is a sin to take one's own life – but what is left to her now?

And then
the world
slows.

The men's movements grow sluggish, as if they are automatons winding down. The air buckles and warps. The darkness that she saw floating out of the pit has become static and finite like mist on a window.

She tries to move forward but it seems she, too, is fixed.

Then – a noise at the doorway and the spell is broken.

The giant hears it, snaps back into movement, lifts his head, lets the knife fall away slightly, distracted. She can feel the other's hands loosen on her shoulders.

Boom – a shot.

The sound ricochets round the dome.

One minute she is watching a frown come down over the giant's forehead, the next it is no longer there: no frown, no forehead and she is blinking against a scarlet spray.

His mouth opens in an expression of shock, then the giant falls forward, arms out and slack.

The other soldier, the young one, lets go of her completely, and she realises she is resting on the wall around the pit, panting, wiping her eyes free of brain matter.

She can hear the young one's voice near her ear. 'No, please,' he is saying. 'We were only scaring her.'

Someone else grabs her arm, and she screams again – so much screaming – but as she turns, she sees it is Jack.

He has her in one hand, in the other a gun.

He kicks the body of the fat soldier.

It rolls into the pit.

A low roar.

'Come here,' he says to the young man, who obediently draws close. With one neat crack on the temple that guard, too, goes down.

She is confused – what is Jack doing? He is *in league* with these men.

'I couldn't let you . . .' he begins, but her brain is too stunned to coalesce the rest of his words into any meaningful interpretation. '. . . think me a traitor,' he is saying, 'but there are some things that I cannot countenance . . .'

She can't focus, only gawp at the prone form of the young soldier.

'Not . . . for . . . you. I didn't think . . . I . . .' Breathless now, Jack touches her neck and says, 'Thank God, it's superficial. Can you walk?'

But all she says is, 'Jack the giant-slayer. I knew you'd come.'

Though she didn't.

Then he is pulling her out of the chamber and up the stairs, opening a door. She is not sure if she wants to go, but he kicks it open anyway and finds there is someone there, blocking their way, silhouetted in the light, carrying a tray. Someone who opens her mouth and gasps with shock at the sight of him, and of Daphne covered in blood.

'Oh it's Annaliese. Hello,' says Daphne, as if she is greeting the maid on a fine morning.

The woman looks from Jack to Daphne then back again and nods, 'Go. I'll lock the door.' And then she closes it once more.

Then Daphne is tugged and dragged quickly to the left and then through another, thicker door.

And suddenly they are out, blinking into sunshine.

She puts her arm up to cover her eyes.

Jack scans the yard, jumps onto the scaffolding that encases the North Tower.

He opens his hand to Daphne. 'Quick. Jump on. Got to get out of here before the alarm goes up.'

The men below them in the moat are still wearing their pyjamas. Some of them have stopped working to watch.

'Daphne!'

She looks up, grabs his hand and he pulls her onto the wooden boards.

'This way,' he says and they climb up a ladder to the next level.

The gangway is caked with dust; with ropes, chains and pulleys for stone; equipment dangling down from the higher levels above them.

For a moment she hesitates: he is the enemy. What is he doing? Is this another trap? No, he has killed one of his own.

'Come!' he commands her when he sees her faltering. 'I'm trying to help you.'

'But where?'

'Out of here! Quickly now, Daphne. We can't walk out through the gate. It's all patrolled. Hurry. They'll kill us if they find us.'

'But . . .' she says, aware of a clamour starting up inside the castle walls: guards, shouts, voices raised in alarm. 'Why now? I haven't changed.'

'Events have overtaken us,' he says, and when he sees she hasn't moved, 'I couldn't leave you there. Not like that. Daphne, you . . . look I'll explain when we get out of here. You need to *move!*' He barks the last word, making her jump. But she manages some momentum. As he turns his back on her and begins to make off again, her feet find purchase on the floor and she hobbles after him.

As she breaks into a painful canter she experiences another moment of déjà vu. This too has been in her dreams. She was flying. That is all she knows. And then it comes to her that this is what she must do – fly again. And somehow the thought of it clarifies and brings her back to the present.

Good lord, she thinks, I am out!

Free.

Another voice inside her says, 'No, not yet. You must *get* free.'

Hang on then, where *is* she?

Looking around, to her right she sees the moat, ahead the thick forestation that has grown over the old ramparts.

'There,' she says to Jack, quite amazed now that there is no wall to the north. At least none she can see. She points ahead to the trees. 'We must get into them.'

'How?' he says.

And she can't quite believe why he is asking because, full of nerves and anaesthetised by adrenaline, it seems so very clear now. 'Follow me.'

And just like that, with a nod to him – Jack the traitor, the hero – she dips her hands into the air, raises a leg like a show-girl, jumps, then puts her head down. Next, Daphne Devine runs down the gangplank until she reaches the end, pushes down upon the planks with the soles of her feet then launches up into the air catching a rope that is hanging down. *I will either plummet to the ground,* she thinks, *or I will be back on the trapeze.*

And the Gods must be watching and cheering her on, for it is the latter wish that is granted.

The weight of her body propels her forward and swings the rope across the moat like a pendulum. Beneath, she glimpses the prisoners staring and knows they are willing her on.

As she swivels into the trees she lets go, opens her arms, reaches for a branch, any branch.

There is a moment of panic when her fingers close on nothing.

But as she begins the arc of descent, her feet connect with a branch. Though they slip, her fall has been broken. Her hands flail, find a hold, grip hard onto the branch. She uses the thrust of her dip to direct her body over to the next branch, on the neighbouring tree. One that is slightly lower. In her head she can feel the warmth of the spotlight on her, hear the applause, see the bright appreciative faces of the audience at the Oriental.

She smiles at them and blows a kiss. Leaps to another branch, then another. She is a monkey gliding effortlessly.

Then – crack! The next one breaks. She is thrown to the floor. Though it is only a yard or so.

Her body is caught by thick bush and bracken.

She bounces on them a moment then leaps off.

Her feet plant down onto the forest floor.

She can feel no pain at all.

Am I dead? she wonders. It won't be the last time that crosses her mind. But she cannot stop to think, for all her senses have woken again, her mind shakes free of shock – she is in danger, but she is *alive*.

Though so near to the castle grounds: she is still in peril and must get away.

Denser growth lies ahead to the north. To her left the hill drops sharply.

She chooses the left route and rushes down, gravity speeding her faster than her body can keep pace with, feet skidding over shrubs, hands grabbing at fallen trunks, calves stung by thorns and nettles.

Down, down, down – half slipping, half sliding – until she reaches the last part of the bank. Arms flung wide for balance, her feet adjust to the gradient – a steep dash to flat ground. She runs the final stretch, bursting out of the trees and into the open at the foot of the great hill.

There is a lane. They must have taken this when she arrived here. It curls down from the castle and village, then forks. The left hand runs along the bottom of the hill, the right goes west over a bridge and a stream.

She runs across the bridge. Before her, another bridge, a wider stream. She hears a grunt behind. Pauses to look back. It is Jack, charging out of the trees, clothes ripped, one lip bloodied, but nonetheless intact.

'Go on,' he shouts, indicating she should turn, continue to run. 'Across the river.'

She begins to race towards the next bridge, but hears him yell, 'No, *cross* the river.' Though she is almost upon the curved bridge as he bellows, '*In* the water. Hurry. They've let out the dogs.'

And she realises what he's saying: the hounds will follow their scent. If they have any hope of surviving, they must lose them. She changes direction, runs instead into the meadow, rushes on, splashes into the stream. No, not a stream, a river.

The water is a shock – so icy. Soon it comes up to her thighs, The current is very strong, recent rain has swollen it. It flows north in a torrent which hinders her progress as she pushes her legs in. For a moment she worries that it will be too deep in the middle: she's not swum for ages, three years it must be, but she wades ahead anyway. There is no other option.

Rapid sloshing out of sight suggests Jack has encountered the first stream. Good. He is not too far behind: there is a chance, now, isn't there? That they may get out alive?

She reaches the middle, water up to her waist, rushing against her bruised ribs.

Then a shout, far off but unmistakable. Not Jack. Soldiers.

A sudden crack follows, then a deeper bang. Something whines through the air. Bark splinters from a tree on the far bank; one branch breaks loose and crashes down, striking the water.

She ducks, pauses, keeping her head low.

'Don't stop. Swim, Daphne! Then run as fast as you can!' she hears him yell across the meadow. But there's a tearing strain in his voice that makes her take one more step – then turn.

And oh God, she wishes she hadn't.

Behind Jack, barely twenty yards away, are two SS soldiers. One is advancing at a steady run; the other has stopped to take aim.

'Jack, she shrieks. 'Gun.'

'Yes,' he pants, running for his life, arms up at his sides, punching air, legs motoring hard, knees lifting as he barrels forward. Then – another bang, the soldier's gun discharges.

'Quick!' he says, but she sees his eyes widen in shocked disbelief. His mouth is open as if he is about to say something else, command her to do something else, but there is only half of it there – a raggedy patch of skin and flesh, a couple of teeth. Part of his head seems to have detached and burst, bits of it going in different directions. She can see the trees where his right eye should be, and realises, with a terrible reality, that the beautiful face has been blown apart. Some of it lands on her own, warm and moist.

He sways once, the knees buckle, give way, then he plunges half-headfirst, into the river.

'Jack!' she cries and takes a step forward, holds her arms out, realises in an instant – no, there is nothing she can do – begins to turn as another shot rings out.

And she is not surprised by the parting air, already expecting the bullet's whistle.

What does surprise her is the searing pain in her chest – the way it scalds and twists, spinning her body round.

Then her face hits the water, and her form collapses into it, limp and weightless. She floats.

The blackness at the edges of her vision pitches forward and overwhelms all light.

Under the water her lungs exhale her breath into bubbles.

When she inhales, unconsciously, the water follows in through her nose, mouth into her phalanx.

Her chest heaves. She spasms. And gives out her final breath, allowing more river to swim into her windpipe.

Like the seamen she has dreamed of, torpedoed in the Atlantic, like Uncle Guiseppe's unfortunate fellow passengers, like so many who have gone before her.

Her last fleeting thought that of her father, holding her hands, on his lap:

Row row row the boat gently down the stream . . .

Three lives,
Two lives,
one life gone.
Life is but a dream.

III

From: Reichsführer-SS, Reinhard Heydrich

To all Commanders of the Sicherheitspolizei and Heads of SD:

Recent events have alerted the authorities to the danger posed by individuals and organisations who trade in superstitions, cartomancy, divination, occult systems etc. Such practices threaten the Reich, spread disquiet among the populace, and may impact upon the loyalties of those entrusted with positions of responsibility.

Effective immediately:

1. All lodges, societies and private groups dedicated to astrology, occultism, mysticism or other esoteric teachings must be dissolved without delay. Records of membership, correspondence and all prior publications are to be seized immediately and forwarded to SD headquarters for inspection.
2. Individuals engaged in these practices, or consulted for guidance, are to be arrested and interrogated. Detention is to be prescribed in cases where loyalty to the Führer is in question or where influence over others is evident.
3. Publications containing astrological or occult content, including prophecies, almanacs, journals

and pamphlets, are strictly prohibited. Confiscated materials must be submitted for review; distribution in any form will be met with immediate legal action.

4. Reports of compliance, including the identification of resistant individuals or organisations, are to be submitted to SD headquarters within thirty days.

The Reich will not tolerate deviation. Those who insist on continuing such practices risk not only their freedom but the full weight of the law. Every official is tc enforce this directive with vigilance, rigour and without hesitation.

By Order of the Reichsführer-SS,
Reinhard Heydrich

CHAPTER THIRTY-TWO

The seventh son of a seventh son, Josef Baumann, had suffered his fair share of digs and jibes over the years. Even when a seven-year-old boy, he remembered his grandmother pulling him aside and muttering into his ear, 'Have you seen them yet, Little Josef?'

'Who Grandmother Baumann?' he had asked. He was quite afraid of her and the curly strands that grew from her chin and scratched his cheeks like pony hairs. 'Seen who?'

'Why the dead of course, Josef.'

Thankfully his mother had overheard and snatched him away before Grandmother Baumann could do any more damage.

'You are lucky, the gift is yours,' his grandmother called after him.

But he had never felt lucky. The legacy he was, allegedly, due to inherit followed him around school, behind hands where whispers were traded from child to child and fingers pointed at the weird one, the seventh son.

His brothers told him to ignore the other children, that it was nothing but a stupid saying. But that was easy enough if you were the fourth son or even the fifth. Half the village knew who the Baumann's firstborn was. Approximately a quarter knew the name of the second and third, but everyone knew Josef and his position in the line.

His grandmother was never rewarded by a positive response, though she often asked.

Twelve years after her first question, when his brother had died by his side on a battlefield at the Somme, he might have reported that he saw his dead features on the face of every soldier he bayonetted. By the time the war ended, and he found his way home, his grandmother had already beaten his brothers to the grave.

Only two of them came out of that war. He, with a bullet in his leg that had left him with a limp, and his older brother Heinrich. With Kristian, the idiot son who could not fight because of his malady, there were only three surviving children out of the eight born to the Baumanns. It was a loss so bitter they all turned inwards and uttered curses upon the enemy victors, then their own defeated leaders and then finally themselves.

His mother, once so opposed to all the superstition that surrounded her seventh child, started to look at Josef with yearning.

'Have you seen them?' she asked him one night, when they were alone and his father had gone to bed to rest his broken heart.

'You have seen your brothers? Are they at peace?'

When he replied that he hadn't, she had stared at him with a gaze so intense, he could not read what she was feeling. Pity? Betrayal? Anger? Disgust? He settled on the latter and, as if she could read his mind and was appalled by her unmaternal sentiment, she had started to weep again and gone into the yard to be alone. But he heard her sobs and felt his deficiency keenly. What was the point of him? He could not help his brothers in battle; now limping, he could not help his father on the farm, and could not help his mother with comfort.

That night a great rage descended upon him and entered his flesh. The world, he saw, was empty of magic. There was to be no inheritance of mystery or foresight and no god who watched from the heavens. The Bible was a book of deceits. Christianity a clever ruse devised centuries ago so that men might answer the unanswerable and seem wise. The meek, they said, would inherit the earth – but only in death. The oldest trick in the book. The whole idea of divination, or any kind of gift, was wrong. A swindle. Superstition. And from that moment he stood firmly against it, meeting every pious or mystical word with scorn.

Which made the stories coming out of Wewelsburg even more despicable. Here they were again with another war, another set of warlords. Didn't people learn anything? And up at that castle – the things they were doing. Some said it was an ancient religion, others that it was new. What was the point of either when all the gods were deaf?

Or dead.

Though, he lamented to himself when he went into the village to run errands from time to time, without divine bindings it seemed that the conscience of men had become untethered.

He had witnessed the guards marching the prisoners through the lanes up there. Had seen them become thinner, paler, bones held together with tendons and ligaments. Last month Heinrich had passed a piece of bread to one. The look of joy on the prisoner's face, Heinrich said, had made him go home to his wife and weep. None of the villagers spoke of it openly but they are, all of them, aware that more and more people go into that camp, go to work at that castle – but they never come out again.

How had it come to this? That they could not do anything when brought before such perversity?

Though, he had to say, he was impressed by the strength of the Führer. Josef understood the man's drive to make Germany great again. A noble cause. A *good* cause. They had suffered disproportionately under the Weimar Republic. Everyone knew that. Yes, he had a lot of time for Herr Hitler. It was the corruption of the elite members of the Nazi party that really got his goat. That Göring continued to hunt and hold lavish banquets while the rest of the people worked hard for low wages. And as for the one at the castle . . . that dough-faced, chinless oddity with thick specs, nothing like the sharp young soldiers he liked to keep around him – well, his ideas were twisted into shapes of sheer strangeness. Depraved, from what he'd heard. There was talk of the Devil there. Though that held no fear for Josef. He knew Satan was just as dead as God.

In sum, Josef's nature was honourable but conflicted. Which is why perhaps, on that day, he did not run from but *to* the sound of the gunshots. It would be hard to explain later when he was questioned by his wife, and in five years' time it would stand as a credential of sorts – chalked up to integrity, to a rejection of ideology. He was never entirely sure if that was true, but he had no hesitation in claiming the glory.

What he did recall was that it was on his mind to take the cows in first. The morning had been wet, and the drizzle had soaked through his clothes. His leg had been playing up again, around the site where the bullet had pierced his flesh. It always did when the weather was like this. But the day had brightened and dried, so he had left the cows until mid-afternoon.

He was on his way there, crossing the stone bridge, when he first heard voices. Shouts. The yapping of dogs. Then the shots rang out. One, two, then a pause, finally a third. It wasn't unusual to hear them over at the castle. But these were closer by.

His instinct was to take cover and squat down behind the wall of the bridge.

After a few minutes he crouch-walked to the bank. The voices, two male, were becoming more indistinct. Whatever had happened out there was now over.

He was looking through the trees over the field in the direction of the gunshots when he became aware of something floating down the river. A quick glance and his first thought was that the soldiers had chucked a sack into the water and now it was being carried along by the current. As he turned back, intending to make his way to the paddock, his mind processed the image and the scarlet water that clung to the bag. He snapped his gaze back. The thing had gone under the bridge.

Keeping to the ground, he stumbled round to the other side and saw that the bundle had snagged on a rock under the arch.

It was the hair, a rich chestnut, waving in the water like a curtain, that made him stride into the wet. More out of curiosity than anything else. Though he had become a bit of a scavenger of late, picking over found objects, trying to find things to sell. Times were hard, the war had raised prices but none of it came back to the farmers. And this lot at the castle took what they wanted anyway.

When he came within three or four feet of it, he realised it was human. Another step and he saw it was a woman. She was face down in the water, arms spread out either side. He spied a ripped skirt and jacket. Instinct kicked in again: he reached out, grabbed her collar, turned her over and was met with the most beautiful face. Like an angel, he would describe her in years to come. And so young. She weighed hardly anything as he picked her up in his arms and staggered to the bank.

Needing his hands for purchase, he tried to lay her down on the grass, but his shoe slipped on a rock and somehow he lost his grip. Her body slipped out of his arms and dropped onto the bank.

But then, and this was the interesting thing for a man who professed little or no faith, it was, as he would recount to crowds at parties, 'as if a miracle happened. For as she hit the ground, her mouth opened and water flew out of it.' She gasped, lungs working hard, contracting, squeezing, expelling the river from them, sucking down air.

Trying to help, he pushed onto her chest, the way he had when the foal had fallen into the Alme last spring in the storm. And she vomited out the river once more. Josef hit her back and pushed it until he thought she might die.

But she didn't, she coughed and spluttered and the water came out. So he turned her round and saw her eyes had closed.

Bending his head to her chest he listened. She was breathing. Though blood from her chest was soaking through her clothes. He found the wound, nothing much, took a smooth pebble from the river, placed it over the top and tied it on with his belt.

Then, he picked up Daphne Devine, threw her over his shoulder and quickly carried her home.

CHAPTER THIRTY-THREE

19th May

When she opens her eyes, it is black as pitch, though less dark than where she has been. She is dull, confused.

Am I dead? she wonders. Then is more bewildered by the déjà vu of the thought.

Have I gone to Hell?

The idea sends her right hand on its way to touch her forehead, heart in the sign of the cross. But it does not reach her head. It is stopped by something hard and rough. She opens her hand, trails her fingers over it: wood.

I am in a coffin, she thinks. *About to be buried.*

But no, it is not straight and level – it is angled. She follows the wood until she becomes aware of pain, shooting down her arm from her chest, and her arm drops. She folds it back. Slowly she becomes aware of her body: her arms ache, shoulders are stretched and sore, her cheek burns and her ribs protest when she breathes in and out. One eye is swollen too. But despite this, or maybe because of this, she realises she must be alive. If she were dead, she would surely feel nothing?

She tries to sit up: easing her elbows onto the floor, raising her poor shoulders. But her breathing is laboured and clogging, her throat so dry it also hurts. Her lungs are crackling. She coughs. It's painful and is too much effort. Exhausted, she lies back but with her eyes open.

As they adapt, she begins to make out a ceiling. There is no light, but she can feel a breeze on her cheeks, across the blouse. Her fingers feel the fabric – no, this isn't hers. The garment she wears is made of rough cotton and comes all the way down to her knees. Eh?

Carefully she reaches her hand to the side and onto whatever she is lying on – some kind of thin mattress, stuffed with straw. Then flatness, a wooden floor, slightly dusty and grainy. She brushes against something solid and heavy. A cold clay mug? She moves her fingers around the rim, then dips over the side into wetness. A drink?

She tries to grip the vessel. Though it hurts to squeeze her fingers shut she persists and brings it to her lips.

Water!

Spilling some down her chin onto her chest, she gulps it urgently. If her throat is sore, her chest feels as if it has been compressed in a clamp. But the water brings a little relief.

It is hot in here. Wherever 'here' is.

Her mind is still fuggy, her memories flitting just outside the edges of recall. She remembers the theatre, up high on the trapeze and wonders where Jonty is. He will be annoyed she did that by herself. He likes to be the centre of attention. She will make it up to him.

Replacing the cup, Daphne reclines again, overcome rather rapidly by fatigue. The effort has depleted her, emptied her of all energy, so her head falls onto the pillow and she sinks back into a long, dreamless sleep.

Outside, the stars burn brighter and the moon tilts across the velvety sky, silvering the meadows. The night mists settle over rivers and sink into valleys, then reach into the thick forests and become a pale haze. In the west, Orion bows his head behind the low ridges of the Sauerland, and in the east, the sun rises once more. The heavens turn on their ancient axis, unaware of the myriad human dramas beneath them.

* * *

Down below, a woman's consciousness rises.

Daphne's eyes snap open.

Another day has passed.

Above her she sees not those starry constellations but a wooden roof with gaps between the planks through which light is streaming in. Not much, but enough to inform her that she is in some kind of attic.

There are noises by the wall in front. She sits up. Her arms and legs are beginning to heal, though her torso feels all wrong. But she is distracted by the space around her, which is triangular and tiny. Two sides meet only inches above her head.

Someone has dressed her in not a blouse but a white nightdress. She reaches to examine it more closely, but before she has the opportunity, the wall opposite creaks and then slides back. From the darkness beyond, a man emerges, crawling on all fours.

She feels her body tense. What is this?

The man snaps his head up. 'Oh,' he says when he meets her gaze and sees her expression. 'Wait.'

Beads of sweat pop across her brow; her heart accelerates.

To her relief the man retreats, creeping back the way he came in. Outside, he kneels and speaks to someone else, who is obscured by a wall of hay bales.

She is not in the theatre. No. Though has a memory of staging, a sense of dark malignance . . . and then a shadow of the castle returns. My God – somehow, she has made it out of that place of evil.

Though she does not want to allow herself the luxury, it is hard for her not to feel a glimmer of hope.

Out there it is lighter than where she lies, though still dim. Still inside.

A silhouette steps into the doorframe: Daphne can tell from the shape of the skirt it is a female. Not as tall as the man, the newcomer only needs to stoop to enter through the tiny door in the wall.

She steps inside and Daphne feels the space contract.

At the end of the mattress the woman stops.

'You are awake,' she says. Her German is heavily accented with the tones of the region, so it takes a moment for Daphne to understand.

When she does, she replies. 'Where am I?'

The woman moves forward and light coming in through a crack in the wall reveals a girl, perhaps only eleven or twelve years old. She doesn't answer Daphne's question but instead asks another. 'How are you feeling?'

There are still some parts of Daphne's brain that need repair and are not functioning at speed, but she is beginning to make some sense of the situation.

'Well,' she says to the girl, though she is not, but seems better than she was. Thirsty, she reaches for the cup only to find it has gone. How?

'You have been asleep,' says the girl, answering her surprised expression. 'For a long time.' She is blonde and slim, wearing an apron over a smock.

'For how long?' Daphne asks.

'My uncle found you. In the Alme,' she says.

'The Alme?' Daphne repeats the words to herself. They do not carry meaning.

'The river,' says the girl.

A sensation of being water-logged returns, bringing with it an uncomfortable image: shivering, a cold hard table. Her head on it, without a pillow. Two faces – a man and a woman, leaning over her while she vomits brown liquid into a tin pail. Then it fades again.

'We think you came from the castle,' the girl says slowly, regarding Daphne with wary eyes.

Yes, she thinks but doesn't say. That awful, awful room – the ritual chamber, crypt. She shudders as the flash of a knife tip penetrating her flesh races across her inner landscape. In response she lifts a hand to her neck. There is a scab covering the wound. It had been so damn frightening and wicked. She had honestly thought she had come to the end, that her blood would flow into the hollow. But then, everything had slowed, then everything changed – there was a noise and over by the doorway she saw . . . 'Jack!' she says out loud. And her hand flies from her neck to her mouth, covering it. Her memory of his words, when he came to her in the crypt, are stifled and impregnable now. Though she has a sense that what the soldiers were doing to her, where they had taken her, she shudders, was a step too far.

Even for him.

Somehow news of her ordeal must have reached him. He was a traitor, yes, but one that still had some morality left. Had it been that that had stirred him, spurred him into an action that would put him at odds with the regime he had become enamoured of?

Or was it their link, their intimacy? The days they had spent together, the summer in a forest in England? A genuine connection that had reached down into his soul and brought out a response that may have even surprised him?

She will never, know, she thinks. Though, one day, it may come to her.

'He is your friend?' the girl asks. 'Jack? You were calling for him in your fevers.'

She sees his peony mouth, then his beautiful face which detonates, sending fragments of skull and scarlet tissue over her. A tremble starts in her stomach and spreads through her entire upper body. It is too much. She does not want to remember him like that.

Closing her eyes for a moment she tells the girl, 'He is dead.'

'I am sorry . . .' she begins.

But Daphne does not want to hear apologies. She must regain herself, her power. All will be lost if she is dragged down by grief. Though is that what she feels – grief? she asks herself. There is something there, for sure. For all his treachery, he did save her in the end.

Sighing, she shakes her head. All efforts, all mental energy must be brought to focus on the now, for she is sure she cannot yet be out of danger. 'How long have I been here?' She taps the roof.

'Four days on our farm. Before, at Uncle Josef's. He moved you in the night.'

'Where is this place?' she looks around. 'How close is the castle?' A charge goes off in her heart. She begins to move onto her knees, readying to fight or flee. But her ribs are still injured, the movement excruciating, and she puts out a hand. The girl takes it and helps her to sit down again.

'Not as near to the castle as the house of Uncle Josef. You have suffered much. Rest,' she says with compassion. 'But – no,' the girl continues. 'We are ten kilometres from Wewelsburg. Though you must go soon. We fear searches. They did have the dogs out.'

She needs to think, and orders her intelligence: her present position is on a farm, potentially in a hayrick, ten kilometres from the castle. Safe enough now, but what if the castle widens its search? And where exactly is she?

There is a silk map somewhere in the lining of her jacket. It was useless to her before, but now she can show it to the girl.

She looks around her, sure she was wearing her jacket when, when they took her to the crypt. She must have been – the young soldier had put it on her lap and she had pulled it on and not taken it off. But it is nowhere to be seen. 'My clothes? Where are they?'

'A very bad state they were,' she looks away, embarrassed. 'But better now. I have washed them. Mended. Would you like?'

'Yes please,' she says. Her stomach rumbles loudly. She covers it with her hand.

The girl hears it and grins. 'That is good – you are hungry. Healing. I will get you some milk and bread.'

'Thank you,' says Daphne.

'And, outside, there is a pail of water, for you to wash. But . . .' she says as she crawls back through the door. She is able to stand fully upright outside, 'do not go down. It is unsafe for you to be seen.' She pauses, 'If you came from the castle.'

'I did.' Daphne senses the girl's discomfort with the place. 'And now I *must* get away.'

For a moment a scowl tugs at the girl's mouth. She's disappointed, thinks Daphne. It is like I'm her pet. 'To where?'

'I'll tell you when you are back.' Daphne waits a moment, then crawls out the way the girl went.

Once through the door, she finds that she is on a platform surrounded by hay bales piled high to the roof. The nook in which she has been sleeping is just a tiny part of it. Two rectangular bundles of straw have been stacked in front. Two more bales at the side must have previously concealed the door through which the man and the girl came. It is a clever hiding place.

Shuffling and mooing float up from below. She inches closer to the edge and spies a ladder running from the platform down to the ground, which is perhaps fifteen feet below.

Two cows down there are sniffing the ground. Though she guesses this is home to many more, judging from the smell of manure. One of the barn doors must be open because daylight is flooding the interior.

The rest of the herd must have gone out to pasture.

For a moment she wonders if she might just slip down the ladder and run away. But then she remembers what the girl said about the search dogs. Too risky. Her captors have clothes she has worn, which no doubt still retain her scent. And she would rather die than be returned to Castle Wewelsburg.

So instead, she turns to the pail and dips her fingers in it. The temperature of the chill water shocks and returns the same memory to her: Jack's fragmenting head. But then it enlarges, and she recalls her own pain – intense, searing, sudden – localised in her chest.

She was shot! She's sure of it. As she lifts the shift and examines herself, she finds an ugly sight. The flesh is purple and bruised. But there is no wound.

Everything is so confusing. She sits down on a hay bale and tries to take her mind back to that moment, but it is unwilling to be sent back. Only a murky blackness lies there. This, she concludes eventually, is another item to stow in the fortress at the back of her head for further inspection once she is safely back home.

Home – the thought of it, of seeing her parents, laughing with Jonty, raises her somewhat. The possibility is becoming real again. And, she has intelligence she must deliver. Troops are being deployed to the east. That must be of some importance.

She must, she thinks, start looking lively, plotting, get herself shipshape, to ensure her escape is not a short-lived victory.

While she washes herself with a lump of cream-coloured soap she turns over options in her head. Though nothing can really be done until she finds out where she is.

But then what? Where must she go next?

Return to Twenty-Four is impossible. As much as she is conflicted by Jack's final act of heroism, it does not erase his betrayal of the agent and possibly the entire network.

There will be nothing for her in Augsburg either. Greta must have got out by now.

Hopefully the Catholic community will join ranks to protect their own. Then her mind stalls on a word – Catholics. An itch begins in the back of her mind. Greta had said something about them, when she had told her about the awful things the doctors were doing to the infirm at Kaufbeuren-Irsee. That's right: her local clergy were ignoring the killings but there was a man in the north who was paying attention to the issue. A holy man in defiance of the Reich. Defiance meant resistance, opposition.

'My enemy's enemies are my friends,' she says to herself, beginning to formulate a plan. It isn't much, but it is better than nothing. She has no network, no radio, no contacts, no way of getting out of Germany. There is only this one person, who *might* not have been caught by the Reich's ideology. Who *might* be in a position to help. What did Greta say his name was? A bishop of somewhere . . . She tries to delve deeper into the memory: Greta's tiny kitchen in the Fuggerei, the sink, smell of chamomile as she washed her hair . . .

The ladder rattles against the platform and she hears the huffs and puffs of the girl as she climbs up.

When her face appears at the top of the ladder, Daphne asks immediately, 'How far is Münster?'

The girl reaches the top and swings over onto the platform. On her back she is wearing a string bag, the arms of it are looped over her neck and shoulders. She tugs over a haybale then slides the bag off and lays it across the straw, so it is like a table. 'About 100k.'

'Can I get there? Can you help me? Can your father?'

The girl sits down and shrugs.

'Will you ask him?'

She pulls the bag open with a nod, which dislodges a lock of hair from behind her ears. Frowning she brushes it back carelessly. The gesture is so unselfconscious and innocent that Daphne is reminded that she is really just a child.

'Perhaps I should speak to your father about that. Will you ask him to come up?'

The girl nods.

'Thank you—' Daphne suddenly realises she doesn't know her name, so asks.

'Roswita,' she tells her. 'Yours?'

Should she reveal her name she wonders, but then thinks so much has been done already there is no point in subterfuge. However, children being children can forget rules and speak out of turn. So she says, 'Dorothea.'

Roswita nods again. 'Before I speak to papa, I must give you these.' She opens the bag and takes out Daphne's clothes.

Curiously, she is surprised by how pleased she is to see them. Like her, the garments are survivors.

And Roswita is right, she *has* done a good job of washing and fixing them. The blood has been cleaned up, only a light brown stain remains, which is barely noticeable – only at its edges. And it could be spilled tea. The jacket is less smart, and tatty, though still gives off an aura of formality.

'I had to take the pocket off,' says Roswita and hands over the jacket. 'It was too damaged with the hole and the burn. That is where the bullet went in. And there was something else there. Wait a moment,' she whips the jacket back before Daphne can stop her. 'This,' she says, and reaches into the remaining pocket on the front. She slips out two raggedy metal pieces. 'Here. These have saved you.'

When Daphne sees them, she understands immediately what has happened. Thank God for Annaliese. The woman could not have known how prescient her actions with the pen had been, but they must have surely saved Daphne's life.

Roswita drops the two battered pieces of gold into Daphne's outstretched palm. In the thicker of the strips a bullet is embedded. A crescent scars the metal; grey smears surround it like a bruise. The bullet must have come in at a glancing angle, skimmed across the metal and then embedded itself there. Thank God the gold was there. It is so soft though, the fact it has stopped it is a miracle. It must have been a defective weapon or bullet. Or else someone was watching over her. And for the first time in a long while she thinks of Rafn, the man she lost, and smiles sadly for him.

Then she takes back the jacket and spreads it out on the floor with the skirt. Her armour. So flimsy and feminine. She puts her hands into the lining of the jacket and feels around. No map. She is not really very surprised. Both she and the jacket have been through a great deal.

'I have this,' says Roswita. It is a plain blouse, patched under the armpits. 'The other – too soiled. I think with your . . .' she gestures to her own neck and Daphne remembers the knife in the crypt. 'Dripping down. Very difficult to scrub out.'

'Ah yes,' says Daphne. 'I must have bled quite a bit. Thank you Roswita for looking after me. I will always remember your kindness.'

The girl is pleased by these words and glows. 'I will find father for you.'

CHAPTER THIRTY-FOUR

21st May

It makes her think of Sweet Brenda Fay and her music hall routine. 'It won't be a stylish marriage, I can't afford a carriage.'

And she still can't. But a horse and cart will do just as well in this situation. She would like to sing the lines out to Roswita. The girl would appreciate them, she thinks. But she can't. The family think she is German, possibly from the south, and a Jehovah's witness, like the men put to work at the castle. Daphne has done nothing to dispel these notions. However, she keeps her interaction with Heinrich to a minimum. The farmer is more likely to notice holes in her story than his young daughter.

He is a good sort. 'A decent chap,' as Jonty would say. Not a natural dissident, she thinks, but as a father of five daughters (Roswita is the eldest of the three who still live at home) he is deeply outraged by the way Daphne has been treated. 'Your father would do the same for my daughters, I expect,' he has said mournfully to her. And she has agreed, he would.

One portion of the battered gold pen has been offered to repay the family for the generosity of the past few days and the other put down as payment for the next two during which Daphne will be secreted under the wooden bed of a cart. There are four removable panels that leave a space of approximately twenty-odd inches for her to lie in. On top of the boards, around her hiding place, the family are loading sacks of hay, potatoes, grain, a tureen of milk and firewood.

Clasping Roswita in her arms, Daphne tells her little friend that she is sorry she has nothing to give, but will remedy that when she reaches safety. Roswita, however, has something for her. It is a small child's wristwatch. These are precious today, and she shakes her head. 'No, I can't.'

But Roswita says, 'It's not a gift, it's a 'borrow'. Send it back when you are home.'

Daphne is so touched by the child's unselfish gesture, her eyes begin to fill. So funny she thinks, she has not cried over her ordeal in the castle or Jack's death, but this little girl's generosity nearly undoes her. She nods and waves the watch. 'I will do that Roswita, though it may take a while.'

Then a wave goodbye to Heinrich's wife as her husband climbs onto the cart and beckons Daphne up.

It is such a tight squeeze. Some sacks and a sprinkle of hay are the only padding between her and the hard boards. But at least these will soften the bumps, muffle the sounds of her movements.

Before she pulls a sack over, Heinrich hands her a bottle of water and a handkerchief with a small loaf and wedge of cheese. These are valuable items and she is touched.

'I don't know how long till I will be able to feed you again,' he says. 'Ration it.'

She has been hungry before, she will be so again. It is no price to pay for this extraction: Operation Hope.

Nodding to him she smiles, 'I know,' and curls up on her side. He slides the panels into place and everything is thrown into darkness. There are knocks and bumps as Heinrich moves the hay, sacks and wood over the top. Then she hears his footsteps tramp over her as he returns to the carriage.

Cracks in the wood let in some light, though she cannot at present see anything through them. This is reassuring – if she can see out, it means those outside can see in. She is content to swap light for safety, though not aware she is living on borrowed time. Daphne has used up all her lives.

Heinrich has discussed with her the situation at Wewelsburg. Joseph, his brother, put his ear to the ground, listened to the noise and rumours coming out of the castle, and spoke with the villagers living close to it. Some sort of scandal has embarrassed the SS positioned there. Heads must roll. Traitors in their midst are dead now. One body has been recovered. However, after bitter recriminations and severe sanctions the soldiers who dispatched the second conspirator have been commissioned to retrieve her body. It can't have gone far.

'Are you a traitor?' Heinrich has asked.

'Anyone who challenges or escapes the brutality of the Reich is such,' she had responded and he had nodded. She didn't have to say any more.

Local people, he told her, knew too much about the castle to disagree. Some kept quiet because they believed sacrifices had to be made to reclaim Germany's power and position in the world, to win this war. Some of them did not like their complicity. But they liked their families being alive.

Heinrich's act of defiance will have grave consequences, should he be discovered. The stakes are high – there is a team on the lookout for her. It's only a matter of time before they realise that either someone is hiding her body (for who knows what reason?) or – the more likely deduction – that she is alive.

And then what?

She shivers inside her hiding place and gives thanks that the farmer is a man of his word. He has promised to get her to Münster. After that she is on her own.

Again.

The cart lurches and they set off.

As they leave the farmyard's mud-hardened drive and bump onto the open road, the wheels drop into a deep rut. Daphne flinches at the jolt but reminds herself this is to be expected. The road ahead will be rough and punishing. But that, to her mind, is far better than waiting like a sitting duck.

They have not been going very long when the cart stops. The judder of the wheels sends sparks of pain flying along her ribs. Her hands are folded tightly against her chest, her face scratched by straw, eyes blinking against the cracks of light. She tries to bring the watch up, to see how long it's been and work out where they might be, but the confines of the space will not allow it. Outside she can hear the horses snort and stamp. They are tense and restless.

Heinrich mutters something she can't make out.

Someone has clearly stopped the cart.

She lies extremely still knowing even breathing could betray her presence if keen-eared soldiers or neighbours are nearby.

Then a tapping starts up along the cart's side. As it comes closer she realises someone is prodding the side of the wain with a stick. They must be at a checkpoint.

The muscles in her legs lock. But no way can she shift position.

A thud. The cart rocks. Someone has got on. Knock, rustle, swish, thunk. The sound has changed: metal on wood. Are they using a bayonet?

She is tightly wound, swallows hard. A strand of hay begins to tickle her nose. Swish, clack, clack. *Please don't let him see the false bottom.*

She hears Heinrich speak in a low voice which is surprisingly steady. 'Nur ein paar Kartoffeln.' Only a few potatoes.

The soldier grunts, knocks on the side, listens. A pause.

Daphne stops breathing.

Then the cart heaves, becomes lighter: the soldier has jumped down.

They jerk forward again, and Daphne exhales in a long, silent sigh. Her body is cramped, her limbs cold and almost numb, but relief saturates her chest.

She dares a tiny glance through a crack. And sees, yes, soldiers. Thank God, she didn't look before. But they are already watching another wagon.

The cart rolls on.

The horses' hooves pat out a rhythm on the road – thud, thud, thud, clip clop clip – echoing the words she hears in her head: not too long, not too long.

CHAPTER THIRTY-FIVE

23rd May

Though it is not quite evening, already the streets of Münster are dark and full of rain. Her shoes slip on the cobbles, but at least she has some. Abandoned by one of Heinrich's older daughters and requisitioned for her use, they are scuffed and worn. Daphne is impossibly grateful for them. They cushion her soles from the hard stone underneath, and she would be easily spotted, let's face it, if she was barefoot in the city.

The place is medieval. Citizens flit around her like tall, spindly moths stopping in doorways or fluttering past shops. They have an anxious, flighty look to them as if they can't settle, or are trying not to be seen.

The city's crooked streets have tall, pointy buildings which remind her of gingerbread houses and make her feel like she's stepped into a fairy tale. But not the sugared versions her mother would tell. The dusky light, which does not reach to the pavements of those gabled terraces, conveys something that is more essentially Grimm. It is not difficult for her to imagine witches peering from behind curtains, ogres watching from Münster's towers, ready to swoop and attack any enemy they spy.

And there are many towers here.

The Lambertikirche rises before her. Heinrich has done well with his description, told her she should not mistake it for the cathedral, though it is almost as grand. Also sinister, with grim gargoyles perching on the roof. Its blackened spire bears three cages that look like gibbets. Why would a church set them up there? Is everything in this country contaminated by death and decay?

No, not everything, she reminds herself. Heinrich has been true to his word and dropped her inside the city, in the yard of an old coaching house. Münster's high walls and warren of streets mean there are shadows and alleys everywhere. They made good use of them. The farmer brushed her down, shook her hand and unexpectedly pressed a couple of coins into her palm, almost furtively – the man was embarrassed by his own generosity. And she had taken that calloused hand and held it for a moment, knowing the sacrifice involved which he could not afford. The family had done so much for her already.

Then he mounted the cart and was gone, leaving her with instructions on how to get to the cathedral. Sankt Paulus-Dom was what he called it: St Paul's Cathedral. Though very unlike the one at home. No dome.

Instead, the cathedral has two spires, and these have helped guide her in, past the Rathaus, past the Lambertikirche and on to the Domplatz, the square on which it is sited. She hopes the bishop is there. He has to be. All her plans rely on it.

There are many people buzzing around the cathedral. The rain is stopping now but they are packing away stalls and cleaning up. There has been a market. As she crosses the square, an apple rolls off a nearby cart into the gutter. Though she longs for the taste of it, her mouth already salivating, she will not pick it up for fear of drawing attention to herself and keeps her head down.

There is a door round the back and up the side, which she chooses over the main entrance. Though she has no idea if it is locked, she walks with purpose, as if she is meeting someone behind it, knowing she is less likely to be stopped this way.

It *is* open, thank goodness.

Inside, a corridor with high vaulted ceilings and ornate windows looks onto a cloistered square with large rectangular stones laid across it. The cathedral complex is huge and, for a moment, she worries she may get lost. Or worse, be found.

She hesitates, wondering which direction to take. Then the strains of an organ start up. The sound is coming from the huge wooden door at the end of the corridor. She follows it into the main body of the cathedral.

Despite her urgency she is awed by the huge scale of the building. Yet, rather than making her feel insignificant, as large churches have done in the past, this time her experience is different. Voices join together in hymn as the great organ hefts out its chords.

Above the nave, the walls rise from arches into a stone canopy. As she gazes up inside, the heavens briefly part and sunshine pours through the stained-glass windows picking out different colours.

Sapphire, ruby and amber hues appear across the flagstones, changing as the clouds' fluffy fringes pass across the sky.

She stops in a yellow pool and, head tilted back, inhales the light and, for one unexpected moment, is possessed by the conviction that it is washing the darkness of the castle out of her soul.

I need this, she thinks, *please cleanse me.*

Just as the thought completes itself, another ray of sunshine, freed from a cloud, hits the high altar. The gold there becomes luminous, shining and radiating light.

Aware of the flames above the votive candles, the smoky fragrance of incense, the congregation's voices, she senses her mother's faith, the warmth of it, as if Carabella's prayers are travelling across the miles, the ocean, over the guns and tanks, to her. And she follows a memory, sees an image of herself, as a child, kneeling beside her mother at Mass, with this same smell and these candles, Carabella whispering prayers, her finger drawing a wet cross on her forehead.

Mother.

When she opens her eyes, she realises a cleric has been watching. He frowns, either puzzled, curious or disapproving.

It is not good to be seen; she should not draw attention to herself like this. Turning, she looks for somewhere more discreet to wait.

At the rear, a few steps lower than the cathedral floor, is a small chapel. She steps down into it.

Inside stands a statue of Mary, serene and sorrowful. This is who she needs right now – a female deity. One who embodies compassion, charity, humility and mercy, a gentle antidote to everything she has suffered at the hands of men who despise such qualities.

Daphne kneels and bows her head. Her hair falls forward, almost touching the sculpted hem of Mary's robes. *Holy Mother of mothers.*

The prayer wells up within. *Oh Mary, please – hear me. Help me.*

She closes her eyes again, brings her palms together and moves her lips in the same prayer she remembered Carabella reciting: *Hail Mary, full of grace, the Lord is with thee. Blessed art thou amongst women . . .* and for a moment it feels as if something *is* there in the chapel, a presence, as if the god form might be listening.

'Guten Abend,' says a voice nearby.

She jumps. Scrambles to her feet.

It is the cleric – a canon – who has come to find her. 'Are you waiting for someone?'

She tries to relax herself. She must be careful, *so* careful, about how she approaches him. Her request must sound natural not desperate. 'Yes. I was praying. But, perhaps you have answered it. I need, I mean, I would like to see the bishop please. It is fairly urgent.'

A frown tenses his forehead. 'I'm sorry,' he says, pushing his hands together and now bowing his head. 'Herr Bishop is away visiting a parish.'

'Oh,' she says. Not what she was expecting.

It is a blow, and in order to take it, she sits down on the chair. Without meaning to, she lets out a loud, frustrated sigh. 'When is he back?'

'I'm afraid I am unable to tell you that for certain. Perhaps tomorrow or the day after? That is the usual length of time.'

Tomorrow! How could she possibly wait until then, or worse, for two entire days? Where would she sleep? A woman is far more at risk in the city than anywhere else. The countryside might be exposed, but at least she could build some kind of shelter there and hide in the hedgerows and woods. Here, there are many more people and many more dangers and, most significantly, the Gestapo have a headquarters in every city. There will no doubt be one in Münster.

'Right,' she says. 'Fine. I'll wait.'

He nods, clearly expecting her to move but she doesn't. Then he gets her meaning. 'I'm afraid you can't stay here,' he says.

She folds her arms, doesn't move. 'I'll be fine.'

Under the long black robe she can tell he is shifting his weight, hesitating. 'Is there something that I can help you with, Fräulein?'

Can he help her, she wonders? If, as Greta told her that night in the Fuggerei, Bishop von Galen shares her outrage over the treatment and forced euthanasia of the vulnerable, it does not mean those who serve him feel the same. Her strategy, if it can be called that, is to inform the bishop about what's happening in the hospital Greta named: Kaufbeuren-Irsee. Then she will ask for his help to leave the country. A trade, of sorts.

Though that cheapens what she's doing: the mentally ill and the sick are not the enemy. They deserve protection, no matter which side of the war they stand on. She feels that deeply.

But in this hostile land, she must grab at every chance.

Or she will be dead in a matter of days. The bishop does not need to know how she got the information nor that she is not a German citizen – she has passed so far. Nor does he need to know where she wishes to return to. The whole thing is a dangerous gamble: he may not be willing, or even able, to help her. Listening to her story will be perfectly Christian. To act on it, however, may be considered treachery. So much is in this strange, upside-down land.

And this tall man before her is not even a bishop but a canon. How much power does he have? And where does *his* loyalty lie? To the Reich or to the Pope or to God?

She knows from Greta that some of the church clerics have turned a blind eye to what is going on, buried their heads in the sand. How does it happen that good can turn so bad, she wonders, feeling the coldness of the stone around her.

As she is thinking about this the canon bends so his face is level with hers.

'Mmm . . .' he hovers there, looking into her. She returns his gaze, searching his face for a sign, something that might indicate where this man lies on the moral spectrum.

He is not unattractive for a holy man. Short dark hair speckled with grey, blue eyes and dark lashes that would look pretty on a girl. There is something wholesome about his face and clean in his eyes. But, she knows all too well now that appearances can be deceiving, and briefly she pictures Jack in the pub where they first met and remembers how struck by his beauty she was.

The canon nods to himself as if he has been able to make a decision. He straightens up. 'Come with me.'

And he turns and walks out, up the steps, cassock swishing.

Right, she thinks, there is no choice but to follow. So she

scampers after him, turns back through the door she came and into the cloistered corridor, half open to the garden outside that contains not square slabs, she sees now, but tombstones.

At the end there is a chapel with low iron gates.

They pass it, through a sacristy.

The canon turns, beckons, says nothing, crosses to another door at the far end. Daphne glances around at the ornate cupboards. The room smells very masculine.

It makes her worry about where he is taking her.

Opening a second door he stands aside to let her in first. Beyond is a smaller room, almost a cell. She hesitates, can't see another door in there. 'After you,' she says.

He raises an eyebrow but walks through and she sees there *is* another door in a niche at the end. This takes them outside into a courtyard edged by outhouses. They must be beyond the cathedral complex: for the atmosphere is very different. She can hear the buzz of traffic in the city's streets.

Though the rain has stopped and the sky cleared, there are puddles on the cobbles. The canon doesn't lift his skirts but splashes through them. Daphne is more cautious – there are holes in her shoes. Water has already got in. She steps around them.

The cleric is heading for a large house, more of a mansion really.

While she has been inside, the sun has sunk down behind the towers. Dusk is on its way. Night will soon follow: she needs to be off the streets and out of sight by then. The canon stops, briefly looks behind him and to either side before he leads her round not to the front but a small back door.

Again, he uses a key from his pocket to open it and then lock it after they have entered. Another corridor. Finally, he stops in front of a small door. Opening it, he bends to go in. She comes into a small sitting room with a desk and two wooden chairs.

An armchair sits in front of a fireplace. On the wall there is a crucifix. Papers are stacked on a desk with a lamp which the canon turns on.

'Make yourself comfortable,' he says. And so she chooses the armchair.

Outside, the cathedral clock chimes, the bells carrying across the courtyard: seven o'clock. Oh, it is indeed getting late.

He brings the wooden chair to the fireplace so he is sitting opposite her.

'So,' he says. 'How can I help you?'

There is something in his eyes now which suggests he is more guarded here, in his room, perhaps worried, uncomfortable even. But his feelings can't be spared. Right now, she has run out of options; he is her only hope.

'I am a bookseller from Cologne,' she says, aware of her shabbiness. She probably has hay from the journey in her hair.

His eyes roll over her, assessing, though his features remain fixed.

So she begins, 'While on business in Bavaria, I came into some information, which was extremely distressing.'

He nods, does not betray any scepticism. 'Go on.'

'There is a place. An institution not far from Augsburg. Some Catholic sisters work there with medical staff. It is a hospital.' She pauses. 'They are taking in the infirm and those who have psychiatric problems and . . .' she takes a breath and watches him. It is almost as if he knows what is coming, ' . . . they are killing them.'

His face remains impassive apart from an eyebrow, which twitches.

The lack of reaction disconcerts her. Perhaps he does not believe her.

She leans forward, 'It sounds like it is systematic. Following the "racial hygiene" policies . . .' she was going to say 'here' but realises, in the nick of time, that it makes her sound foreign – as if she is not from 'here'. So quickly she adds, 'that the government are . . .' she doesn't know how to say it neutrally, changes tack. 'Lethal injections. They are overdosing them with barbiturates. And also, it is awful to say, but they are starving them too – the patients. Putting them on special diets with no vitamins. Children also. "Mercy Killings" they call them.'

'How do you know this?' he asks.

'The person I spoke to has a cousin who works there, or has worked there. It's the institute at Kaufbeuren-Irsee.'

He reaches into the folds of his cassock and brings out a notebook and pencil. She watches as he writes something down.

'This is why I had to see the bishop,' she continues, aware her voice has been rising. 'Because we have heard that he is collating information.'

He snaps his notebook shut and looks at her sharply. 'From where? Who did you hear this from?'

'Me? From the person in Augsburg.'

'Name?'

She shuts her mouth, then says simply, 'No.'

He nods his head very slightly, acknowledging, she thinks, her loyalty, but then sighs. And it carries the same emotion as a very deep and painful groan. She has no doubt that what she has said has hurt the canon – it is terrible news to break. Grimacing, he says, 'It is happening in this diocese too.'

He believes her.

A feeling of guilt-ridden relief takes hold.

'*Can* you give me the name of the person who informed you? So we can investigate and authenticate?'

The word *'inform'* is a startling choice, she thinks, so heavy with menace under this present government. Has it slipped from his mind to his tongue because that is exactly what he is thinking of: informing on her?

She shakes her head again. 'I can't, no.'

He looks at her for so long, she knows he is inspecting her soul. It is not free of stains. But she maintains eye contact, doesn't break off. 'I see,' he says at last.

Now is the time that she must strike and ask for help in return. How should she frame it, she wonders. But she must act now. She has to get away. 'And there is another thing I must ask you for?'

'Yes?'

'Sanctuary.'

He says nothing. This time his eyebrows rise. 'Sanctuary?'

'Yes,' she swallows. 'The SS are looking for me and I am in fear for my life.'

This appears to totally bewilder him.

'I have to get out of the country.'

'I see,' he says. 'I see.' He rubs his forehead, composure quite gone now with no attempt to hide the fact.

'Please,' she says. 'I am throwing myself on your mercy. I know that you cannot have embraced the current ideology. Not if you are researching places like Kaufbeuren-Irsee. It means that you are still good. That you have not yet been corrupted.'

He glances at the door then leans forward. 'We must be careful here,' he says, as if reciting something by rote. 'Investigate as unobtrusively as possible. Acquire witness statements.'

'Well, now you have more to add to your file. Will you help *me*?' she slides off the chair and onto her knees, hands clasped together in front of him. 'I call upon you as a vessel for the Lord Jesus Christ, to show compassion.' She doesn't know where that has come from, but it feels right.

He looks down at her for a moment and then his lips move silently as if he is talking to himself.

She has no idea if her actions are moving him, and bows her head so it is closer, so she may hear his words, vaguely aware her pose is one of devout supplication.

'Withhold not good from those who are due it,' he is whispering to himself. 'When it is in thy power to give.'

She has heard that, seen it before, where? Then she remembers Greta's kitchen, her embroidered sampler, and she meets his gaze and smiles. 'Proverbs, chapter three, verse twenty-seven.'

His eyes widen for a moment, then he makes the sign of the cross. Pinching the bridge of his nose, he briefly raises his eyes to the heavens, mouths 'Amen', then drops his gaze on her once more. 'It seems you leave me no choice.'

Thank the Lord, she thinks, if he is there.

'There is a convent,' he says, 'In Belgium. I know the Sister Superior there.'

'I have no identity papers,' Daphne adds.

He laughs this time, but it is a sound born out of despair. 'I see,' he says for possibly the fifth time. 'Right, let me think,' he says, then, 'How attached are you to your hair?'

CHAPTER THIRTY-SIX

24th May

Head shorn and dressed in a cassock, Daphne sits up front, in the passenger seat next to the canon, who she now knows as Ludwig Verholt.

Their plan is to cross the border into the Netherlands, which they are nearing now, and then make their way to Belgium. There has been no time to find or fake identity papers, so Ludwig will do the talking if they are stopped, which is why they are travelling at night in one of the few cathedral cars that have not been requisitioned by the army. It has taken longer through the back roads and country lanes but so far, they have not been stopped. Is luck at last back by her side?

Although she is not out of danger, she has come further than she expected. Her latest sacrifice, though willingly given, was not so easily received.

Ludwig had raised the scissors but then faltered, unable to bring himself to cut her hair. She wondered if, as a priest, the act of touching her was a sin or transgression. Whatever, he had gone to seek help and a matronly house servant named Frau Hartz, who seemed very fond of him, had brought a sharper pair of scissors. She made a better job of it than Daphne suspected the canon was likely to have done, and asked no questions.

Frau Hartz had also thought to bring a mirror. Which Daphne was grateful for until she had looked into it. It was the first time that she had seen herself since the castle and she was dismayed by her reflection. There were lines under her eyes that had not been there before and a little scar on her cheek she could not remember getting. And she was so much thinner. Her suit hung off her shoulder blades and flapped around her waist.

Once the deed was done, perhaps noticing the grim expression on her face, the housekeeper took pity on Daphne and, being a woman with a keener nose, announced she would run a bath for her. Hopefully now she has washed the odour of livestock away.

With her new crop cut, freshly scrubbed face and the cassock, she can pass for a young priest, but her voice is distinctly female. They have decided that if asked, she is observing a vow of silence. However, in order for Ludwig not to lie, she has had to take such a vow, with one condition – that she may speak if they are alone. And he will refer to her as Father Johann Fischer, if necessary. Apparently, she vaguely resembles the man of that name, who Ludwig once met at the Vatican, so he could be mistaken when he calls her that.

She has long since given up justifying lies – she needs them, they have become a way of life.

Without conversation and with nothing to see but the cars' spotlights on the road, she has drifted off to sleep several times. This carriage is more comfortable than the cart.

It is only now, as the sky behind them is brightening from black to navy and the lane widens into a road, that she rubs her eyes and sits up. In the distance, on the other side of the road, she can see a German army convoy approaching. Trucks, at least four of them, are crammed full of men and supplies. On one a small tank is fastened by ropes and chains.

'That's not the first I've seen,' says Ludwig. 'Half the army seems to be on the move.'

'Yes,' Daphne agrees. Lots of troop movements, the transportation of tanks, suggest something significant is about to happen in the east. Though what, she has no idea. At the very least it might mean a reprieve for England, a chance to rearm, train more soldiers, to think more clearly about strategy rather than just fighting off the enemy constantly. 'Will they stop us?'

He shakes his head but says, 'I don't know.'

They are so close now, Daphne can see the faces of the soldiers in the front cabs. They produce an involuntary shudder. Though she is very aware that she must try to control herself.

'*All* going that way?' she says trying to sound vague.

'Frau Hast's son says it is do with the Bolsheviks,' says the priest, steering to the outside of the road, creating more space for the convoy to pass. '

What? thinks Daphne. Why? And she phrases her next words carefully. 'The communists? But we have signed a pact with Stalin?'

'I don't know,' Ludwig shrugs. 'It is my job to find peace where I can, not explain this war.'

Though this has got her mind ticking over. Treaties mean very little to Hitler. They are not morally binding but disposable, tools to get what he wants. Germany has invaded Czechoslovakia and Poland after sealing similar agreements. If the Führer intends to break the Molotov–Ribbentrop Pact, then is he looking to wage war on the USSR? Their army is huge, the population greater than this country's. At least twice the size.

'But they all look eastwards.'

'East,' Daphne repeats to herself, remembering words chanted in a forest in England in the dark of midnight. 'Look east, turn east: we take this power and we turn it against you . . .'

'Good.'

The canon squints at her, brows crunched.

Of course, she must remember that she is still a patriot of some kind. 'I mean, if there is so much movement then hopefully the soldiers will be flooding the checkpoints. Takes the pressure off us. We may be waved through.'

He nods, yet she catches a flicker of scepticism behind his eyes. Undoubtedly, he already has an idea it is no ordinary German citizen who sits next to him. Though he knows she must flee and appears committed to their mission. She has no doubts about that.

But this nugget of information, albeit rumour, might well be decisive. If it reaches British ears in time, it could change everything. She won't be going home empty-handed. She will be returning with news that might ignite hope. As well as all the intelligence she has gathered along the way. Her foot twitches on an imaginary accelerator.

The trucks pass without incident. She follows their progress in the side mirror.

They continue on to the horizon which has become violet now, with streaks of salmony pink.

Feeling safer, she looks through the windscreen: the Low Countries stretch out in front: flat fields, grey and empty.

As if chastising her for relaxing Ludwig says sharply, 'Up ahead, look. There is a checkpoint. Not far. Remember your vow.'

She nods and clutches her hands together with 'piety'.

The car trundles along, then they turn into the border road. She takes a deep breath, oxygenates her blood.

On her lap, her knuckles whiten. She fidgets and checks her cassock is straight.

The concrete blocks of the sentry point come into view; a barrier arm is down across the road.

Dawn is breaking, exposing the car, revealing her features. It is astonishing, she thinks, how quickly the world changes from dark to light. And how, she reflects, her fortune has changed too. No longer just fleeing, she feels charged with the urgency of a messenger.

Up ahead, she is aware, anything could happen.

Ludwig changes gear and begins to break as they arrive.

A single German soldier paces up and down the road. She notices the rifle hanging at his side – they all have them. Unconsciously, her hand goes to her chest, beside her breast, where the bullet's bruise has changed from purple to a yellow-brown. Then she remembers she is a man now. Putting back her shoulders, she lowers her brow, sets her jaw as she thinks men do.

Ludwig winds the window down, smiles at the soldier. 'Keep still,' he murmurs to her out of the side of his mouth. 'Let me speak.'

The soldier raises a hand. 'Halt! Papiere.'

Here we go, thinks Daphne and clenches.

On her left side, the canon offers his documents. She chances a quick look at his face. His expression is, thankfully, composed. She looks away at the road ahead.

'Pater Ludwig Verholt,' he announces. 'I travel to Maastricht on church business.' He thumbs a briefcase on the backseat. 'Delivering the holy sacrament.'

The soldier glances in the back then looks through the papers. He peers into the car, gaze landing on Daphne. 'And him?' he asks. 'His papers?'

There is no hesitation 'This young priest, Father Johann, has taken a vow of silence,' he says. 'He is under my supervision.'

The soldier's eyes narrow. 'That is not what I asked.'

Daphne hears her pulse, loud at her temple, keeps her lips pressed together.

Ludwig shakes his head, 'And I'm afraid, he has left his papers at the Bishop's Hof. I have only just now discovered the omission. These acts of consecration are not without their difficulties.'

The soldier leans closer to the window, examining her face in the half-light. 'A vow of silence,' he repeats.

'An ancient devotion,' Ludwig replies. Daphne is surprised at how even his voice is. 'You may phone the diocese in Münster if you wish to verify it. But I doubt they will appreciate being woken at dawn.'

For a long moment, the soldier says nothing. Daphne hears the titter of a young bird waking with the daylight, then another's sharp cries pricking the air. The birds have cautioned her before, but she has not heeded their warnings. Now however, she hears them loud and clear: danger, Daphne, predators are near.

She cannot help swallowing and hopes it is not too obvious. The hairs on her arms prickle to attention under the black robe. She prays to God, any god who might be listening, that the soldier will not notice her body betraying her fear.

From inside the hut a tinny rattle erupts. The soldier rolls his eyes and frowns at a field telephone hanging on the wall.

He looks at Ludwig, folds the papers. 'Go,' he says, manner curt, and hands them back. 'Next time, make sure your companion carries identification.' Then he marches to the hut as quick as he can.

Ludwig shifts the car into gear, drives forward with the ghost of a smile on his lips.

Only when they are twenty yards past checkpoint does Daphne blow out her breath.

'You see?' Ludwig murmurs, eyes still on the road. 'He answered you, didn't he? Faith can move mountains and sometimes also the border guards.'

Daphne manages a nod, though her fingers are hot, itching and tight. And lies, she thinks but doesn't say, are not holy but so too can save lives.

CHAPTER THIRTY-SEVEN

25th May

Saint-Hubert is surrounded by forest. The Ardennes Forest to be precise. According to Ludwig, the town is named after the patron saint of hunters.

'Hubert was a nobleman,' he says as they drive through the thick pines. There is no other vehicle on the road, hasn't been for some time, and the tension in the car has finally unwound.

'He was stealing through the forest when he sighted a magnificent stag.'

Daphne gazes into the leaves, as if trying to catch a glimpse of the long-dead saint.

'He gave chase,' Ludwig continues as she makes out oaks and beeches alongside the omnipresent pines. The trees are close and their branches tangle together. Though the speed of the car affects her perception and blurs them into something like a green-and-brown mosaic. Occasionally shafts of light slant through them like ethereal spears.

'As he neared, the animal suddenly turned, and there, between its antlers, to Hubert's astonishment, he beheld a shining crucifix.'

Hearing the passion in his voice Daphne turns her gaze. His eyes are bright, his face animated.

'And suddenly a voice spoke to him. 'Hubert,' it said. 'Unless thou turnest to the Lord, and leadest a holy life, thou shalt quickly go down into Hell.' They both sway as the car goes over a dip. 'Struck by awe and repentance, Hubert fell to his knees and renounced his former life. And so became known for converting the pagans of Ardennes, founding churches and reforming the clergy. The people here,' he tells her, 'still speak his name before entering the woods, as if the trees remember.'

Daphne thinks about this for a moment. The window is down and she can smell moss, earth and pine needles. There is a lot to contemplate in this story in order to supply a reaction that will seem genuine and appreciative. 'So,' she says at last, 'faith was born out of the pursuit of death. And Christ, if he was the voice, stopped the hunter.' She perches her arm on the window ledge. 'That must be a good omen. Has to be,' she says.

Ludwig studies her face. 'You are thinking of your own hunters.'

She inclines her head – yes. In these rare moments of calm, her mind wanders back to Wewelsburg. The talk of St Hubert has made her think of dogs on her scent. She dreads to think what the SS will be doing now her body has not turned up?

How far will they go to find her?

Jack had handed over her Ausweis to the SS soldiers in Augsburg. It had a small black-and-white photo. Not the best quality but good enough to be reproduced on pamphlets and memos issued to Gestapo agents in all corners of the country. If she is caught, she knows that this time they won't consider imprisonment. A shot straight to the head is the most likely outcome.

She must have groaned aloud as Ludwig glances over. 'You must put your faith in the Lord and ask Him to deliver you.'

That's easy to say, she thinks. She's not sure she has much faith and knows it can be corrupted. Does he have any idea, she wonders, about what they do at the castle – the rites, the old gods they turn to now? What would Ludwig say if he knew that the Antichrist had become a role model? And why, if his God is so just, does He allow that?

She shakes her head, which Ludwig mistakes for a rebuttal.

'But look how far we have come. And you without papers, too. It is nothing short of a miracle.'

She nods again, though her smile doesn't surface. Fear, her companion for the past four weeks, has soaked through her pores, and though she feels more at ease here in the car with no one around, in the middle of a huge forest, there is so much further to go.

Outside, the trees are thinning. Many of them, she sees, have been cut down. They were doing that last year in the New Forest. The Lumberjills were felling them for timber as there was a shortage.

The forest begins to give way to fields. The light changes. No longer green and dappled but bright. Unconsciously she shrinks in the passenger seat, as if trying to hide.

Ludwig slows the car as they leave the shadow of the forest. The road ahead is narrow and stony, climbing towards the town that crowns a hill in the distance. She notes a shrine at the roadside – a little stone niche with a wooden roof over the top and the figure of a saint behind glass, his eyes lifted heavenwards. Someone has left a bundle of flowers there, tied with a faded blue ribbon, but they are dead now. She must not frame it as another omen.

They pass a large farmhouse, then a terrace of cottages, a stream. In the distance above the treetops she sights a spire, then two more.

The buildings grow closer together as they meet the outskirts of the town and its façades of brick and stone, windows with shutters open catching the light. Some are large and imposing. Perhaps that signifies officials are stationed here.

There is no respite, she thinks. *Every step of this journey will be fraught with danger. There is Gestapo in every city and every town.*

Her only solace is that her hair is shorn. And, she hopes, they won't be searching for a young priest. 'Is it a big town?' she asks.

He misses the point. 'There is a very fine basilica. Definitely worth a trip,' he says. She doubts that will happen. 'Almost there,' he says.

The road becomes cobbled, the houses older, with crooked beams and flaking plaster on their exterior walls.

They climb higher up another hill to the church and then turn into the main square. There is a café in one corner. A soldier sits on a bench. Daphne's muscles contract. However, his eyes are on a woman sitting beside him, who is fussing over a baby in a pram. She had hoped there might not be any military here, but that is obviously wishful thinking. They are as prolific as pigeons, a cluster of which takes off as they approach and fly west, away from the basilica. In the centre of the square there is an ornamental fountain. Behind it, the basilica rises, a square tower on either side.

Ludwig brakes and they slow to a putter. He crosses himself as they pass the square, then turn right, down a small road. At the bottom she can see another church. Much smaller than the basilica.

'Yes,' he says, catching her gaze. 'The convent is there.'

She's assuming it will open its arms in the Christian tradition. But what if it has a different allegiance now?

CHAPTER THIRTY-EIGHT

25th May

Steering into the gravel courtyard, Ludwig pulls up and parks. He gets out and begins to move towards her door, to open it for her, then stops and shakes his head, rubs his forehead: she is meant to be a young man not a woman. Daphne registers the mistake with a grin and an 'Uh oh.' Then gets out herself and joins him.

They walk together back onto the road and up to the main door. It's heavy and bolted, an effective barrier to the outside world.

Ludwig raps on it and turns to her, sends her a smile which she thinks is meant to be reassuring, though already she is feeling restless again. Fear is back, as it always is with every new situation, threatening to strike and fetch its sister, panic. She is starting to see it like a shadow that follows her around. Although it keeps her in a state of discomfort, she knows it has its function: many of her responses have become shaped by it. She is more vigilant; aware of windows, doorways, curtains, footsteps, cars, checking for exits constantly. While they wait, she has already subconsciously registered the traffic on the street, scanned the pavement for signs of the soldier, his wife and child, and identified two potential hiding places in the churchyard opposite.

Though it is exhausting. And after their long trip, her eyes are becoming gritty and heavy. In other situations, she would try for a nap to top up her energy. But that is a luxury reserved for peacetime.

She is alerted to a screeching noise and a small, square grille in the door slides open. Behind the criss-crossed iron net, the round face of a young nun appears.

'Oui? Who is it?' She asks in French. Her eyes skim from Ludwig to Daphne and then back again.

'We request admission,' Ludwig says. 'I am Canon Ludwig from St Paulus-Dom, in Münster.'

Daphne is inspected again.

'And Father Johann. We wish to see the Sister Superior. We have brought the sacrament she requested for the feast.' He raises his briefcase and points at it.

The nun frowns. 'Je vois.' But she does not open the door.

Under her scrutiny Daphne bows her head and brings her hands together in a prayerlike pose. It feels ridiculous but she's a magician's assistant, not a cleric, and is clutching at straws – she doesn't know how she's meant to behave. They didn't discuss it in the car. Which now, she regards as an error.

The nun eyes them for a moment longer, her expression suggesting doubt. But finally, she nods. 'Je vois,' she says again.

The grille closes. There is a fumbling around at the lock, then the door opens.

She and Ludwig cross over the threshold and the door is locked behind them, which makes Daphne feel more secure.

Inside, the convent is much quieter. Just like the Fuggerei, these walls must be thick and soak up the noise of the outside world.

The nun beckons them across a hallway with a stone floor. Wooden benches line the walls. A pair of nuns glide silently past them, keeping their eyes on the ground, signalling they do not wish to engage with the outsiders. For a moment Daphne worries that all of them have taken a vow of silence. It worked briefly in the car, but she doesn't think she would last long if she had to stay quiet for days. Then she remembers that the nun ahead spoke when they were admitted.

The convent is nothing like the Augustine monastery where the soldiers stopped en route to Wewelsburg, thank goodness. It is quite refreshing to be somewhere meticulously clean and thoroughly female. The floors are polished and she also catches the fragrance of roses and the stronger scent of lavender nearby. The walls are devoid of marks or scratches, and freshly white-washed. Hanging on one she is pleased to see a painting of the Virgin Mary and feels a pang of homesickness, a sudden yearning for her mother. I will see her soon enough, she tells herself. In among the many crucifixes she sights a pair of stag's horns. For the town's saint no doubt.

'This way.' The nun leads them down another corridor, across a courtyard through an arched doorway then waits for them outside a small, arched door. Pointing to two benches inside, she says, 'You may wait there.'

They move down and take their seats. When Daphne looks up again the nun has disappeared.

'I haven't asked you before,' she says. 'Do you know this place? I can't remember you saying. Have you visited it?'

'A few times,' says Ludwig but then closes his eyes. 'I am known to the Sister Superior.'

She wants to ask more but realises that he is resting for a moment.

It has been a long, tense night and an anxious day. Now she is watching him, she feels her own fatigue returning. Hopefully it won't be long until they can rest.

'Hello?'

She must have drifted off. Glancing at the canon she sees that he too is asleep, snoring softly. The young nun has returned.

'The Sister Superior will see you now. Can you rouse Canon Ludwig?'

Oh yes, she thinks. They are probably not meant to touch men. She goes to shake him by the arm but hesitates and wonders if he is allowed to be touched by a woman? She stops and clears her throat loudly. It makes no difference, so she prods him. He snuffles then opens his eyes and jerks up.

'Apologies,' he says. 'I must have . . .' He rubs his eyes and yawns.

'It's been quite a journey,' she explains to the nun, noticing her eyes on them. Possibly it is Daphne's voice, which is higher than most males', even the young ones.

Ludwig struggles to his feet and they are escorted up the hallway and into an office.

It is exactly how she imagined a holy woman's parlour to be: thick ledgers and hefty, religious tomes line the shelves; a crucifix hangs on the wall. There is a desk, with paperwork in a tray at one end. A small brass bell and another cross are also there. Behind it sits a woman of middle years, wrinkles under her eyes and thread veins on her cheeks. However, with her hands folded calmly before her she radiates composure.

The Sister Superior studies them. Her gaze stays on Daphne, dropping to her waist over her chest and lingering on her eyes, then returns to Ludwig. One eyebrow is hoisted. 'It is good to see you, Canon Ludwig.'

He nods, taps his chin with one finger repeatedly then rubs his forehead. 'We have brought the sacrament that you requested for the feast,' he says at last and holds up his briefcase again, aware that the young nun who brought them is still in the room.

For a very tiny moment Daphne sees the sharp grey eyes of the Sister Superior widen.

'Of course,' she says. 'You may sit,' and she gestures to the chairs before the desk. Then nods at the nun waiting by the wall. 'Merci, Sœur Madeline.'

The young nun steps back and closes the door behind her.

'So,' the Sister Superior leans forward. 'Which feast is this, Canon Ludwig?' She angles her chin down, an amused smile curving her lips.

'In four days' time, I believe it will be the feast day of St

Bernard of Montjoux,' he says and lifts the briefcase onto his lap. 'Here . . .' he removes a small gold box and lays it on the desk, then plucks out a receptacle with liquid in it and passes it over to the sister. 'Most apt,' he gives Daphne a quick stare then fixes his gaze on the old nun, 'that Saint Bernard gives safe passage and refuge to travellers and pilgrims in peril.'

'Thank you, Canon,' she says, picking up the small bottle. 'I see,' she says, then breaks off to regard Daphne once again.

It is as if she is directing a searchlight over her. This nun, thinks Daphne, is far shrewder than any soldier she has encountered thus far.

'And your young priest?' she asks Ludwig.

For a moment the canon says nothing. Is he finding a way to speak without uttering any lies, she wonders?

The minutes roll out. The office becomes silent and stifled.

After a minute, which seems a very long time to Daphne, the Sister Superior says, 'We are quite alone here, father.'

He nods, rubs his forehead again, then exhales noisily and says, 'Father Daphne is seeking her own St Bernard.'

She is startled to hear her real name mentioned and waits to see how the sister will react.

But there is hardly any movement of the features. A brief narrowing of the eyes, followed by a polite, well-practised half-smile. She focuses her eyes on Daphne, 'Belgique?'

'Non.' She hesitates. Can she trust this woman? She glances at Ludwig. He clearly does. So she returns to the sister and says, 'Anglaise.'

Next to her, she hears Ludwig inhale. He didn't know. He has abetted an enemy. How does that lie upon his conscience? She can't bear to look at him.

'Ah,' says the sister. 'You wish to become one of us? We have English speakers here.'

Daphne shakes her head. 'I wish to get back to my home country.'

'I understand.' She turns to the canon. 'Father, you must be tired. Can I provide you with a meal and a room for the night?'

Daphne dares to look at him, at last. Grey shadows have accumulated underneath the eyes and his lids are drooping. Events of the last twenty-four hours have taken it out of him. 'A meal would be appreciated,' he says, 'but I have already been away too long. I must set off tonight. There is a monastery I can visit on the return journey. The abbot there is a friend of mine. He will ask no questions.'

'As you wish.'

The sister rings the bell on the table. 'I will call for Sister Rosalind,' she tells them.

CHAPTER THIRTY-NINE

Before she leaves with the nun, Sister Rosalind, she gets up and stands before the canon.

Moving too fast however, her arm knocks against her chest. She winces. The wound is healing but the skin there is still fragile and tender. She tries to ignore it. 'I cannot thank you enough,' she says with absolute sincerity. He must be relieved to have discharged his duties, though his face is not readable. 'If you hadn't taken pity on me then . . .' she doesn't want to say it, doesn't want to tempt fate. 'I don't know where I would be now. You have saved me, Canon. Ludwig.'

He seems discomfited, drops his eyes, clasps his hands on his lap. But she means all of this and wants him to know.

The Sister Superior whispers something to Sister Rosalind, which Daphne doesn't catch.

Then he looks up, returns his gaze to her. His hand moves and she wonders for a moment if he is going to reach for her. But it hangs in front of his face for a moment, then drops back into his lap. 'It's all right,' he says.

Unsure if he means her deception or is simply acknowledging her gratitude. However, she nods and says, 'Germany may be at war with my country, and its rulers may be merciless, yet there remains goodness among its people. I will remember your act of mercy always.'

He accepts this with a small smile. 'You owe the favour to someone else now,' he says. 'Be merciful, Daphne.'

'I will,' she promises and bends down and quickly kisses his cheek.

The Sister Superior coughs and Daphne looks back at her. Sister Rosalind puts her hands into her sleeves and waits in the doorway.

Daphne sends a final glance to Canon Ludwig who has his hand pressed to the place where her lips touched. Though his lips are starting to curl up. The sister comes forward, touches her arm and then she is outside in the corridor and escorted away.

'You have hurt yourself?' the nun asks. 'The Sister Superior reports that you are injured.'

Daphne stops and turns to Sister Rosalind, mouth open in shock. But it is not the Sister Superior's sharp-eyed assessment of her aching body that gives her pause, though that of course is extremely astute. More staggering yet is Sister Rosalind's accent. 'You are Canadian? Here in occupied territory? I can't believe it.'

'I am,' she says. 'The Sister Superior has a way of talking to the authorities and can be very persuasive.' She smiles.

'But, how, how are *you* here?'

'I have been in Belgium for over two years,' she says. 'Initially I was in Our Lady of Namur, but the motherhouse was lost in the invasion and I was posted here. To teach. We have a school for girls.'

'Do the Germans allow you to remain? You are a hostile?'

Rosalind beckons her on. 'We report to the Kommandantur twice a month. They are satisfied by that, as long as our behaviour is impeccable.'

'Which of course it is,' Daphne adds. 'You're a nun, after all.'

'That is correct.' She stops outside another door and opens it. 'Though,' she says, 'the standards of the Lord and the standards of the Reich are very different.' And she sends Daphne a meaningful stare.

'Is it possible,' Daphne asks, 'for me to use a telephone?' There are people at HQ who must be waiting to hear from her, who may have assumed she was dead. If she can access a phone, then she can get a message out. And she will, of course, take care – perhaps speaking in German, phoning the Swiss exchange first and routing the call that way.

But Sister Rosalind shakes her head. 'No. Too dangerous. You will have to wait until you are no longer in the country. You are still behind enemy lines.'

Daphne had supposed it might have been something like that.

'Please,' says Sister Rosalind holding her hand out and gesturing around the room.

Daphne had hardly been aware of the place they have entered, a storeroom without windows, and full of cupboards.

'We will have your size somewhere,' says Sister Rosalind, indicating two large wardrobes in the room. 'Find something that fits.'

The cupboards are full of habits. Of course, she must give up her priestly vestments if she is to remain here.

Rosalind instructs her to disrobe, then collects her cassock and cap and takes it to the Sister Superior. Another nun will accompany Ludwig out of the convent in his car and will wear the priest's garb, just in case the canon and young priest were seen entering together. Then the nun will change into her habit at a farm the convent runs and return promptly. 'In our habits, one sister looks very much like any other,' Rosalind tells her with a wink.

Hiding in plain sight, thinks Daphne. It is brave and it is clever.

Over the next few days she becomes attuned to the rhythm of the convent.

Mornings are early. The nuns rise before dawn for Matins and Lauds. Daphne memorises some of the prayers. 'Deus, in adjutorium meum intende' has become a favourite – 'O God, come to my assistance'.

She has learned to enter the chapel in silence, bow to the altar and take her place without speaking.

Prime, a short office, marks the beginning of the day with a reading and a blessing. After this they go to the refectory for breakfast. It is simple: often just bread, but the convent's farm has an orchard. There, the girls they teach are inducted in agricultural practice. Nothing goes to waste; every single piece of produce has as long a life as they can stretch to and the nuns are lucky enough to have jam on the table regularly. They praise the Lord a LOT about this.

She works until noon. Though they have not asked about the specifics of her injuries, the nuns are aware that she is still recovering from some 'bad thing', so she undertakes light chores. Simple ones: darning socks, mending habits, repairing gloves for the coming winter. Silence is observed, which she is not used to, though she is enjoying the novelty of tranquility, at least within the walls of the convent. It is so utterly and unusually female, which is restorative, after all she has endured at the hands of men. The convent is the very opposite, in so many ways, to the castle. And this, at times, lulls her into feeling a measure of security. Which she must quash as soon as she becomes conscious of tension leaving her body. She cannot afford to relax.

Though she hasn't ventured out of the convent, some of the day girls come in. She hopes they haven't noticed the new novice. Any childish remark, no matter how innocent, might set adult tongues wagging.

So she blends in, follows Rosalind's instructions. Prayers are offered at Sext, followed by lunch, which is eaten while one sister reads aloud from a devotional text or saint's life. There is then a brief hour when speech is allowed and sometimes Sister Rosalind takes her for a walk in the cloistered garden. When the other sisters go to work, schooling the girls, working the farm or cleaning the convent, Rosalind teaches Daphne how to be a nun.

While she has been used to slapping on her fixed stage grin when she needs cover, Sister Rosalind instructs her that it is not appropriate and demonstrates what she calls 'prayer face', which she thinks makes her 'inscrutable'. It is a mode of being whereby she is alert and aware, but communicates no emotional facial clues. The head is tilted slightly forward, slightly down, the mouth held in a neutral line, eyes lowered and the brow kept smooth and unlined. It takes her a while, but she gets it and after a few days is able to slide it on at will whenever Sister Rosalind calls 'Prayer face' to her.

There is training in how to tread lightly too. *The same as dancing,* she had thought, but no it is a slow, deliberate pace that means she is almost unheard as she walks the convent. 'An erect posture expresses calmness and serenity,' says Rosalind as she shows her how to glide over the polished floors. 'The custom of inserting hands in the sleeves of the tunic,' she confides, 'eliminates nervous and unnecessary hand movements. Or at least keeps them out of sight.'

When she had first tried on the habit, she had been surprised by the long and deep pockets sewn into it. 'Are these for crosses and rosaries?' she had asked Rosalind.

Who had laughed.

'No, of course not.'

Daphne didn't know why she found it so funny until the Canadian added, 'They are to transport documents, or radio parts. We are,' she explained to her mentee's arched eyebrows, 'to become useful. To cooperate with the resistance when it serves the cause of mercy. The Mother General, the head of our order and convents, has instructed us to resist the Nazi regime. She thinks it is evil. And it is advancing.'

Daphne does not disagree.

'We are bound by the rule that forbids us from taking part in any act that might lead to bloodshed. Still, the Mother General has learned of the persecution of the Jews. So cruel. She has already helped two Jewish girls to safety beyond our borders. The occupation grows harsher by the day: more arrests, more searches, more fear. Passive defiance is no longer sufficient. Our orders are to stand against the Nazis and aid the resistance wherever possible.'

She has been impressed by the courage in those words.

If Sister Rosalind is needed, another nun, Sister Beatrice, who is Belgian-born but speaks excellent English, teaches her specific prayers and responses; The Angelus, The Rosary, The Litany of the Saints, the recitation of Psalm 91: 'Qui habitat in adjutorio Altissimi'. These will all be necessary should she be tested and asked to recite her order's holy rites.

After Vespers and supper, the nuns are permitted to listen to the BBC 'News from Belgium' even though the radio station is forbidden by the occupying force. Some of them read the underground newspaper, *La Libre Belgique*, and report back to the others. The news in its pages is often very different to what they hear from official media. But that is the paper's function Rosalind tells her, 'to counter the German propaganda. And to boost the morale of resisters.'

As the summer days lengthen and the evenings remain hot, the windows of the convent are propped open. Other neighbours have the same idea and often music drifts out on the breeze to the convent. Jazz mostly. They listen to it and smile. An elderly nun called Sister Joan has told Daphne that the Germans classify it as 'Negermusik' and as it emanates from the 'racially inferior', they have outlawed the form. In the towns and cities under occupation this is a red flag to a bull. And, as such, Belgians play it as much as they can, as loudly as they can, as often as they can. 'I like it,' Sister Joan is fond of saying as she waves her knitting to the beat, 'the sound of this music.'

The final office, when the candles burn low, is late. The women sing 'Salve Regina' to the Virgin, invoking protection through the night. Daphne, though she does not share a dormitory, still ends each day with the prayer, 'In manus tuas, Domine, commendo spiritum meum.' Into your hands, O Lord, I commend my spirit. She is still unsure if God exists, though has found solace in the idea that Mary is watching over. Religion, she has begun to see, is not just worship of a deity, though of course that lends focus to the collective and ritualised acts of devotion. It is also, perhaps more importantly, a complex moral arbiter. It is not Jesus Christ who is laying down the rules but the Christian masses who are saying, 'This is how we live our lives. We believe you must love; you must forgive, you must be humble. You must not lie, not hate, not raise your hand in cruelty.' It is a way of being, a code of conduct that keeps the soul clean even when the rest of occupied Europe is contaminated by evil. And she would much rather be confined to these four walls than those of Lucifer's court in Wewelsburg.

She cannot of course be free of its memories, though they are unclear and blurred around the edges now. And she is troubled by the blood on her hands, the sights she saw. Every night she wakes up screaming.

Sister Rosalind has urged her to confess her sins, assuming it will relieve the burden she is carrying. But Daphne has declined. She wouldn't know where to begin and believes that if she were honest, really honest, then the sisters might change their mind about helping her. For she has sinned too greatly to ever tell all. She never will in fact. And some of what she has done will continue to haunt her till her dying day.

Jack appears to her at night, sitting in the corner of her room, talking as he once did in a forest in England about what he will do after the war, and the peace he will experience, while he feels around his empty socket and tries to put his eye back in.

She feels guilty about his death while also understanding it was not her fault. It was not her who pulled the trigger. Though there is a spiteful part of herself – a voice in her head that sounds like her – which wants her to hurt, and which needles her about the vengeance spell she taught the librarian, Hennecke. How she recited it from the grimoire's pages (that damn book). And how, while she was pronouncing the words, translating the sigils, casting the runes, it was the Canadian whom she pictured.

But it is a coincidence. Surely.

In the mornings, Sister Rosalind tries to soothe her, though Daphne does not speak of what makes her scream at night. Rosalind insists that sometimes 'one must embrace suffering without surrendering to it.' And that makes some kind of sense to her.

It has become evident that there are other sanctuary-seekers in the convent. Six people live in the cellar. In fact, it is not the cellar but a room that has been carved out of it, accessible only by a trapdoor in the refectory. A Jewish couple occupy a corner of the attic and there is a man with one arm in a hideout behind the main stairwell.

When she asks Sister Rosalind where they are all going, she tells Daphne, 'Nowhere. They will stay here till the war is over. They are too old.'

But Rosalind must be referring to the Jewish couple because over the next few days the six in the cellar become four, then two. And on that all the nuns are silent.

Although she has been told that the Sister Superior is making subtle enquiries, formulating a plan, nothing has been communicated to Daphne. Burying her impatience, she emanates the nuns' silence. But before dawn on the thirteenth morning, Sister Rosalind wakes her, and they travel out of the convent for the first time, through the deserted streets.

Daphne is surprised how wonderful it feels to be out in the world. The air of the summer morning has that yellow freshness to it and is perfumed with the smell of grass and the watery freshness of dew – everything around her is alive. *I am alive too,* she thinks, *my heart is pumping. There is blood in my veins. I am part of this world. Come what may, I have lived.* And the sense of this extraordinary achievement carries with her into the back kitchen of a butcher's premises where a man with a camera in a flat cap with a loose collar and tie smokes a cigarette.

When he takes a photograph of her against the white wall, Rosalind chastises the glow in her eyes and says, 'Remember, you are a nun.' And she thinks it ironic, because it is precisely then that she feels most awakened, most attuned to the splendour of creation and, perhaps, to the touch of its Creator.

A few days later, after Prime, she is called in by the Sister Superior who tells her the time has come for her to leave.

At last.

Though, as soon as she understands she means right now – this very moment – she begins to tense again. It is a habitual response, which she soon controls. After all, this is what she wants, what she must do. Her time in the convent has been, she realises now she is about to leave it, a peaceful interlude which has healed her in many ways. So now she is ready for the next stage. 'Thank Rosalind,' Daphne says before she is taken into the kitchen.

It is quite a sight.

A black coffin has been set on the table.

For a moment she defaults back to her 'danger setting' – is this a threat?

Or an ending.

But the Sister Superior hands her a forged identity document which states her nationality, French, and her name (though it is misspelled): 'Daphne Divine'.

'Lost in translation,' says the Sister Superior, 'but perhaps a propitious sign.'

She helps her out of her habit and veil, which they fold and lay down on the base of the wooden coffin to act as a cushion. Then the head nun assists Daphne as she climbs up on the table then gets into it, apologising for the tight space. 'This has been used for someone else smaller than you,' she says.

Daphne wonders for a moment if that occupant was animate or on their way to their final resting place. It is not a pleasant thought, so she blows it out with her lips and transfers her mind to a diplomatic answer. 'It is fine,' she says, grateful for all the help she has received. 'I am used to cramming my body into small spaces.' And actually, she finds that she feels quite secure as the coffin is lightly nailed shut – she has escaped from sturdier contraptions before. And though she does not trust God to keep her safe, she has faith in the integrity of the sisters and that is worth more in these circumstances.

'Goodbye,' says the Sister Superior and taps the coffin. 'May God watch over you now and keep you safe where we cannot.'

And she is borne off into a hearse.

It is a grim rehearsal.

Reichsmusikkammer – Directive for Dance and Light Music

(Anordnungen und Richtlinien für die Tanzmusik)

All public and private musical performances must conform to the cultural and aesthetic standards of the Reich. The following regulations are to be observed by all dance orchestras, light music ensembles and related musical institutions:

1. Proportion of Repertoire
The inclusion of compositions in foxtrot or swing rhythm must not exceed twenty per cent of the total programme performed.

2. Character of Jazz-Influenced Works
Within the allowable portion of jazz-influenced material, preference must be given to works composed in a major key and to texts expressing joy, vigour and affirmation of life rather than Jewish and non-Aryan melancholy.

3. Tempo and Expression
Pace must not exceed a certain degree of allegro, commensurate with the Aryan sense of discipline and moderation, order and restraint. Excessively slow 'blues' tempos and exaggeratedly rapid, improvised passages or so-called 'hot jazz' will not be tolerated.

4. Rhythm and Syncopation
Syncopation shall not exceed approximately ten per cent of the rhythmic content of any composition. The remainder shall exhibit

smooth and continuous movement without abrupt or irregular accentuation.

5. Instrumentation

The use of instruments or sound effects foreign to the German musical spirit (such as cowbells, brushes, flexatones or brass mutes that distort the natural tone) is forbidden.

6. Percussion

Drum breaks or solo passages longer than half a bar in 4/4 time are not permitted, except within the context of military marches.

7. Double Bass

The double bass shall be played exclusively with the bow. Plucking of strings is forbidden; if a pizzicato effect is absolutely necessary, the strings must not be allowed to strike the bridge.

8. Vocal Improvisation

Vocal improvisations, including so-called 'scat singing' are prohibited.

9. Saxophones

The use of saxophones should be limited. Ensembles are encouraged to replace them with approved string or folk instrument (viola, cello or similar) better suited to the German national style.

CHAPTER FORTY

The safe house is a four-storey building in the oldest part of Brussels. It is not at all shabby from what she can see: the furnishings are well made, some expensive.

A net curtain hangs across the window, which is covered in a film of dust, thicker at the bottom where cars have splashed mud and rainwater against the glass. From the street it looks like every other house in the road: quiet, respectable, nondescript. She supposes this is exactly what is required for its function.

The woman who escorted Daphne here from the undertaker's, where she was delivered, did not bat an eyelid when she emerged from the room as a nun, merely nodded and told her to follow. She cannot be the only one who has been trained in the garb and comportment of a holy woman. What brave sisters, what daring resolve.

She tries to remember the name of her city escort, but it has already faded away, just as the woman herself did, with as light a step as the sisters in the convent. Though her words still ping round her head: 'Someone will come for you tonight. Wait here. Don't touch anything. Don't speak to anyone.'

Now Daphne sits in the basement kitchen trying to steady her nerves with a cup of lukewarm tea, which she hopes she is permitted to make. The house is empty, the silence another reminder of the convent, which she is starting to think was safer than this.

Out on the avenues and rues, she has been warned, German soldiers are patrolling. Though the Sister Superior told her she would be safer in a city like Brussels with lots of people coming and going, rather than a country town, she is questioning the wisdom of remaining in her habit. Outside of Saint-Hubert and the convent, it makes her stand out like a sore thumb.

Still, there is nothing to be done about it now. She has no other clothes. She has, in fact, nothing at all. She is like a snake, shedding skins, growing in different ways, becoming, she hopes, older and wiser too, learning to live by her wits alone. And the kindness of others.

She does not know who will be coming for her. She has been given no names, nor descriptions, and the anticipation she feels begins to make her legs and hands feel restless. All she does know is that at some point someone *will* arrive.

In this space, between coming and going, she has time to think.

And her mind roams over all she has seen: the darkest side of humanity, the suffering of prisoners, the torture of others and her own. Something inside her has been changing – slowly, for a long time now – and she thinks, fleetingly, of the naïve young girl who stepped up to Wormwood Scrubs last spring, dressed in a patterned summer frock, her hair gleaming and pinned prettily at the sides. Would she have accepted the challenge if she had known what was to come?

There was, of course, her mother Carabella's status – an Italian, interned on the Isle of Man – but she is inclined to believe that even with full knowledge, she would still have agreed. That courage would not have failed her back then in that room at the gentlemen's club when Hugh Deveraux played his opening gambit. And though her body is not wholly recovered, it is getting better. Inwardly she is stronger.

But altered.

Her thoughts now move through a strange, unfamiliar terrain, marked by something she has never known before: an absence. A numbness. Somewhere at the back of her mind she understands that this is not normal, that what she can feel is only the surface. Beneath it – what she *can't* feel – blacker emotions lie submerged and frozen. She cannot look at them yet. They will surface only when she begins, slowly and willingly, to thaw.

And now is not the time to let that process begin.

She turns her gaze from within to without, fastening her thoughts onto the disjointed reports she caught only when the nuns tuned to the illegal BBC Service. The British are still standing after the bombing. In North Africa the fighting continues and Tobruk has not fallen, despite what the official occupation papers announce. She has heard the voice of the Belgian government in exile speaking of endurance and resistance and of a country that still exists, will exist once it has thrown off German shackles. But there have been reports too about the northern edge of Europe which are more alarming. It is sealed shut against Britain, impregnable. No one can go that way any more. The guns at Calais and along the Hook of Holland are now permanently trained on the Channel, stationed all along the shoreline. Which makes her wonder how she will ever get home.

However, it is important not to think such defeatist thoughts. Believing it is impossible will adversely affect her morale. Where there is a will there is a way, she decides, and takes the cup and saucer to the sink and washes it under the tap with a rag. Then she walks from room to room, careful not to make any noise.

There are trams in Brussels. One rattles past a few streets away. They had them in Augsburg too. That place seems a long way away, not just geographically but in time too.

Something inside the room splutters and she jumps, but then sees on the mantel the candle has burned to its stub. The flame is trembling in a draught. Sizzling, it goes out, leaving a puff of smoke hanging in the air, which makes her think suddenly of her old boss, The Grand Mystique. How is he? Frantic, she expects. She has been unable to communicate with anyone since April. It is now June. Though he knows she is being employed by Section W she imagines he has no idea in what capacity. He himself is designing camouflaged armoury back home in Farnham Castle. Or he was when she left England all those months ago. At least he is safe there. Safer.

A car outside passes slowly. Its headlights cross the wallpaper through the gap in the curtains. She wonders if it will stop outside the house, but it doesn't.

Quiet falls down over her again. Then, so soft she thinks she might have imagined it, there is a sound in the street. A single footstep. Then another.

Approaching, she's sure.

She straightens, alert, ready to fight or flee.

The next sound is unmistakable: three knocks at the door.

She gets to her feet. The knocks continue: three, pause, three again. A voice, low, female, calls from the other side of the door:

'Sister Daphne?'

The creak she makes on the floorboard in the hall sounds so loud, like it will wake up the entire neighbourhood. She stops moving for a moment, but the door opens. A woman stands there, coat buttoned up to her throat, hat low and angled over her forehead. She has keys in her hand.

'We don't have much time,' the woman says without any introduction. She speaks English but her accent is strong, French or Belgian. Daphne's ear is not nearly familiar enough to know the difference.

'Come,' she says, and jabs her hand into the street.

Daphne nods, time to leave.

All this waiting, in this terraced house in Brussels, in the convent of Saint-Hubert, it has been only a prologue.

As the adrenaline begins to shoot round her nervous system once more, accelerating her heart, contracting her forehead with tension and elevating her senses, she realises that despite the risks ahead, this is far more preferable to the passivity she has felt only moments before. This is what she is made for, this is her *real* story – one of action and derring-do. Not lying around waiting for others to take the lead, the magician to carve her up, her bosses to give the order.

As she follows the woman through the dark street she feels that now she is mistress of her own destiny.

Though, just like her stage performances, it is an illusion.

They move quickly. Her contact is focused, each turn she takes onto a new street is careful and, Daphne thinks, well practised.

At the end of a narrow lane, more of an alley really, she sees a parked motorcar. The woman opens the rear passenger door. 'There's a blanket in there. Keep your head down. And cover up.'

Daphne obeys without question and slips in.

The journey south is orderly. The woman clearly has done this before and takes the backstreets and byways. Daphne snoozes, lulled by the heat of the summer night. Sometimes when they hit a rut in the road she wakes up, peeks out from under the blanket and glimpses, out the side window, bridges spanning dark rivers, avenues of trees which are thin, tapering and tall. A waxing moon, a crescent, appears through the window before clouds pass across it and dim the sights. Not optimal conditions for a bombing raid, thank goodness. Perhaps they have nothing to fear from those in the sky. Only those on the ground.

She has kept her veil on and when they stop at a checkpoint, one soldier pulls back the blanket to see who is there. When he sees the habit, he crosses himself and covers her up again, waving them through. Sometimes her uniform has more of an impact than the Wehrmacht's own. She does the same as they return to the open road, that old maternal muscle memory which has been reactivated by exposure to the nuns. She has been quite lucky, she thinks, since she has put this costume on, and fleetingly she wonders if, if, if there might be a divine being up there. *No*, she tells herself. *Not now.* Why does the question keep returning?

If she lives, she will consider it. But not at this moment. She must be sharp, utterly, totally in the now. Her mind must be free of abstracts and hypotheses that require the energy which should be consigned to assessing, checking, monitoring her environment for threats.

Later.

And if she is killed then she'll find out if a deity is in control of everything, won't she? Or else she'll know nothing and won't care.

For a moment, she wonders about asking her driver what she makes of it all, but the woman speaks only when necessary. Not like Ludwig. And perhaps she would not want to think about such questions. Sometimes life is easier if you don't, if you just get on with things. She used to be that way.

Just before dawn, they pull into a sleeping quarter of the French capital.

Once she had thought of Paris as dazzling and decadent, a place of music and laughter. But the light is grey and makes it look drab and disappointing. This is another city whose spirit has been battered by the fist of Nazi occupation.

Her driver stops the car in a cul-de-sac outside a low building, the kind that could easily be found in a backstreet of the East End, Wapping. It has bars on the lower windows and exposed utilitarian brickwork.

The woman guides her inside where the rooms are warm. They go down wooden stairs and into a basement. A single oil lamp turned down low is still on in the corner. Someone has been here and prepared the room for them. For her. There is no window, which makes it more secure but also limits escape.

A low camp bed runs along the width of the wall. The dimensions of the room are pretty similar to the Gestapo prison cell. She pushes the memory firmly out of her mind.

'You will wait here,' the woman tells her. 'No one leaves.'

Daphne nods. 'No one leaves' – what does that mean? Is it a quirk of translation? The woman's eyes meet hers. Then she breaks off her gaze and looks away.

What was that there? Daphne wonders, a nugget of suspicion tightening her chest. A tiny unguarded tell of regret?

She puts her hand out to stay the woman, but her contact makes for the stairs. A moment later the door upstairs is shut.

Daphne sits on the edge of the bed, aware that Paris is waking up. Inside the safe house, time slows once more. Alone again, her mind starts to roam. Safe house, she thinks. Then wonders if anywhere can ever really be free from discovery and danger in occupied territory.

Or did her journey in the coffin presage something else?

CHAPTER FORTY-ONE

A woman is here in her room. No, not a woman, a girl who is scampering around and prodding her arm.

Daphne sits up. In the lamplight, for a moment, she is confused. What is a girl doing here, bending over the bed? Is she dreaming? She stares at the girl's flawless skin, so full of youth and dazzle. At least it is a child and not the Gestapo, she supposes, though doubts they would wake her as gently, more likely shoot her in her sleep.

'Sister Daphne?' the girl speaks English, though just like the woman from last night, her accent is also quite distinct. 'I am Didi,' she says. 'I will take you out of here.'

It seems very odd, thinks Daphne, that they have sent a girl, but she does not comment on that. Not everyone is capable enough or willing to volunteer. The resistance must use who they can.

But, she decides, she ought to find out more now – she has been sent this way and that without question since Münster. As she gets closer to home, her spirit has risen, and she feels like she should be more in command of the situation. 'To Calais?' she asks.

The girl, Didi, exhales loudly. It is almost like a laugh. 'No, no, no,' she says, shaking her head, as if she is older than she seems. 'That way,' she waves her hand, 'all blocked. Too dangerous. The Germans have fortified it. Heavily militarised. No civilians. Controlled by checkpoints. Many curfews, and identity inspections. And up there,' she points to the ceiling, 'your planes and pilots fight and bomb.'

'So, the Hook of Holland?'

'No,' she shakes her head again, this time with more energy. 'There are many people in the Netherlands who believe in the German cause.'

It makes sense – she had heard that at the convent – but simultaneously she is perplexed. 'Then where?'

'We go south,' says Didi. 'Down the west coast – there are fewer patrols in Vichy France – over the mountains and into Spain. It is neutral,' she adds when she registers the shock on Daphne's face.

'That's not really true though,' Daphne counters. 'Franco is ideologically aligned to Hitler.'

'It is fine,' Didi sighs and shrugs. 'I will take you.'

Really? thinks Daphne. Didi can hardly be out of school. She is dark-haired and has a youthful, bright-eyed cheeky smile. Ought I *really* put my trust in this blasé child? Or am I being taken for a fool? Lured into a trap to be exchanged for money, food or someone else? Who knows how people get by here – the war has brought its own horsemen of the apocalypse. In France one of them is Poverty.

But before she can shape any of this into sentences Didi claps her hands. 'We must away at once,' she says with impatience and leaves.

As Daphne is getting out of the camp bed, the girl returns to the door and brings in a pail of water. 'Wash,' she says. 'Look clean. Then upstairs. Two minutes.'

Daphne is no longer offended by blunt instructions. She slaps the water over her face, straightening her habit and adjusting her veil.

When she clambers up to the back room with the door to the yard, she finds Didi is there with two men.

'Charles,' says Didi, without pronouncing the 's'. She nods to the older of the two young men, whose hair is cut into a short back and sides and who sports a matching black moustache. He steps forward and offers his hand.

Daphne takes it and shakes it.

'How do you do,' he says. The accent is clipped and well-enunciated and definitely English.

Didi gestures to the other man. 'And Bob,' which she pronounces as Baab. This one is fair with a slight squint in one eye. 'Good to meet you, Sister Daphne,' he says, and winks as she removes her hand. 'Sorry,' he adds and colours slightly. 'Old habits . . .' Then he winces and apologises again.

But Daphne is more taken with the fact that they are Allied soldiers – here – in the occupied land. 'You're both English,' she stammers.

The first man, Charles, dips his head in acknowledgement but the second flinches as if she had just thrown something wet at him. 'Good lord, nay,' he says and shakes his head, 'Ooops, sorry,' then he shrugs. 'I'm no bleedin' English, I'm a Scotsman, Sister.' Then his shoulders jerk as a blush begins to spread over his cheeks. 'Sorry, sorry,' he says again.

'And I'm not a nun,' says Daphne.

'Thank Christ,' he says, then adds, 'Sorry. No offence.'

'None taken.'

'Look,' says Didi, bemused by the elaborate pantomime of foreign manners. 'We must go *now*. You may perhaps find time to talk about your countries on the train.'

'The train?' Crikey. Out in the open, with two Englishmen? She corrects herself: two Brits. In full view of the German police and Wehrmacht?

'You have false identity cards, no?' Didi asks.

'But they say I'm French. I'm not completely fluent in the damn language.' Even in her state of disharmony she adds the blasphemy to make Bob feel more comfortable. 'Hang on,' she remembers her journey with Ludwig. 'I can be observing a vow of silence.'

'Yes!' says Didi. 'And I am delivering you to a convent in the south where you will be taking your final vows.'

'Sounds good,' says Daphne. 'What about them?' she nods at the two Brits. 'Why would we be in the company of men?'

Didi shrugs, looks at her watch. 'We will work that out at the station. If we don't go now we will miss the train.'

And then she is out of the door.

Daphne follows and the men bring up the rear. Her black habit is soaking up the sun, the pavement beneath her reflecting it up. She is baking.

As they move down the pavement and turn onto a main road, she is suddenly aware that she is to be taken in the opposite direction to that which she should go. To head south will be excruciating. Her destiny lies north. The journey this girl intends them to take is convoluted and preposterous. There will be far more danger, the longer they spend in this occupied country.

They reach a crossroads. Opposite is the entrance to a Metro station. But at this point Daphne is seized by the desire to abandon this group: the child and the servicemen will be a red flag. No, she cannot go along with this plan.

So she musters her French as Didi begins to cross and says, 'Allez-y. Je dois aller chercher autre chose.' You go ahead, I must find something else.

And although Didi's mouth opens with the beginnings of surprise, Daphne turns left instead of crossing. And keeps on walking. She hopes they won't stop.

Now she has no idea where she is. However, it is better this way. She feels freer and looks up as two dogs bark at each other by a tall fountain on the other side of the street.

Though as she is congratulating herself, eyes on the animals, she walks straight into a man's chest. He has stopped by a shop and is perusing the newspapers on a rotating stand outside.

'Pardon,' she mumbles and looks up. The uniform hits her at once. That sour block of greenish-grey.

A German soldier.

She hasn't been so very close to one of them since . . . since . . . her brain starts to spin as it summons a crazily rotating scene – a blade pressed to her throat, a swarming black shape, the despicable crypt.

Of their own accord her hands begin to shake. She thrusts them into the sleeves of her habit and grips them hard, but she can't prevent the blood speeding to the surface of her exposed skin, nor the bile rising from her stomach. For a moment she thinks she is going to vomit. Here, on the pavement, in the middle of Paris.

Why was she not more careful? France is occupied. She *knows* this. Stupid, stupid girl!

A smile begins on the soldier's face as he is joined by his other colleagues, who gather around her.

Lowering her gaze, ensuring that she brings down 'prayer face' across mouth and eyes, she looks at the papers, takes one, then withdraws.

Inside the shop, it comes to her that she has no money to pay. She has no money at all.

With reluctance she puts the paper on a side shelf and turns round.

The soldiers are still staring as she moves past them and heads back the way she came.

Now, as her eyes scour the streets, she sees another uniform directing traffic. There are two perched upon the wall by the fountain. One of them throws a crust at a dog.

What a fool she has been.

For a moment she feels the force of defeat. Of her own making.

Immediately she comprehends the arrogance of her error: to stand any chance of getting out of here, of communicating the news of the troops heading east, she must accept the offer of help extended. She sees that now. Money, knowledge, contacts – she has none of them. However dangerous it may be to throw in her lot with the ragtag trio, it is far less of a risk than going solo.

If she is fast, and Fortune is on her side, she will be able to catch the girl up.

She puts her head down and walks briskly away.

CHAPTER FORTY-TWO

Thank the Lord that Lady Luck has seen fit to create a crowd at the Metro ticket office. It has delayed the group, who are still queuing there.

The disguise of her habit eases the indignation of fellow travellers as Daphne pushes in and announces herself again to Didi. The girl acknowledges her with a nod. That is it, nothing more, no request for explanations.

When they reach the office, Didi purchases tickets for all four.

Their next stop is the train station, which is swarming with military personnel; German soldiers stand in groups, checking papers, questioning travellers.

Didi brandishes their tickets and they pass seamlessly, miraculously, through the station.

All trains, each carriage door, are inspected by the uniforms, every civilian checked.

Their group's lateness, however, proves a blessing. With Didi in the lead pointing at her ticket and then frantically at the train readying to depart, a soldier steps forward and blocks their way. She produces Daphne's forged papers with absolute confidence, and, after a cursory glance, they are allowed to run through the gate without answering further questions. The men, only a few paces behind, have taken the opportunity to duck through after them and pelt down the platform, to the great amusement of the guards and soldiers on patrol.

The hiss of steam and a blow of the whistle makes her lift up her habit and jump on board, though it is not the right carriage. No one stops them this time.

When they find the right seats and sit down with the men, they all take a moment to collect themselves.

Alone in the compartment, over the next couple of hours, the four have time to talk to each other, trade stories, confide.

Though Didi is shortish, slender and appears barely older than a schoolgirl, she is twenty-three – only a year younger than Daphne. She whispers to them in her high childlike voice about the hopes of the Belgian people. They have not succumbed, she tells them, and were always ready to resist, should the Germans invade.

'It has happened before,' she says with a toss of her bobbed hair. 'We were occupied in the last war. We did not like it. When our army faced its last stand in May last year at the Lys River, networks from the previous occupation were re-activated. Or so I am told.'

Bob leans towards them and cups his hand over his mouth, 'This is one? A network?'

'Not yet,' says Didi, 'but it will be.'

Daphne is slightly worried by that. Are they the first she has transported? She opens her mouth to ask but then realises she would rather not know.

'We're very grateful to you, Didi,' says Bob. 'Goodness knows what would have become of me.'

Daphne tilts her head, catching his eye and nodding for more. She would like to know how they met.

'I was stranded when the British Expeditionary Force was pushed back to Dunkirk,' Bob says. 'Can't tell you how many times I thought I'd come a cropper.' And he describes how he had been separated from the rest of his unit. 'The retreat was sheer chaos,' he says looking at the floor, and runs a hand through hair the colour of wet sand. The squint in his left eye becomes more pronounced. There are painful memories there. 'Utter mayhem,' he says. 'No clear front line, no direction, no command. You couldna tell if the man running past you was deserting or regrouping. Didnae know whether to follow him or go in the other direction. Everyone was hungry, filthy, bone-tired and the roads were completely clogged, not just with us, like, but civilians fleeing the Hun's advance. They knew what was coming,' he says. When he raises his face, his eyes look not at Daphne but over her shoulder into the past. 'Carts, bicycles, crammed all the paths, prams piled high with bedding and what have you, chickens in crates, farmers herding their cows. The sky was full of smoke from burning fuel dumps and villages.' He pauses and takes a deep breath, coughs as if there again. 'Fires everywhere.' He grimaces and rubs his chest as if in pain. 'Hell on earth. I just kept thinking – what have we done?'

It's a rhetorical question and nobody is sure quite what he means, so Daphne asks him outright, 'How did you meet Didi?' to try and shift his focus.

'Only today, like you.' Bob answers a question she has not asked. Not that it matters; Daphne is pleased she has yanked him from that mental landscape, though he cannot quite leave it entirely. 'I wandered through ruined towns, the state of them. Whoever wins, it's rotten through and through, what war does, what it leaves. The devastation.' He shakes his head. 'But I managed to dodge patrols, hid in barns and haylofts, living off what I could scavenge until I was found by a German patrol. They had captured a lot of our boys,' he says. 'We were sent on a march to Germany by force. No water, no food, no sleep. Some of the older men didn't make it. I could see where we were heading. Not geographically like, but the terrible conditions they had us in. So, I chanced my arm when the guard wasn't looking. Dived into a ditch and managed to escape.

Eventually a farmer discovered me, drinking milk directly from a cow's udder. Took pity and brought me to a friend's house outside of Brussels. Truck,' he says to Didi. 'False bottom. I think they'd done that before.'

There is a pause when none of them speak. Didi neither confirms nor denies the suggestion and Bob says no more.

He has been here for a long, long time then, Daphne thinks as she contextualises what the Scotsman has said. He may be presumed dead by now. No wonder he is thankful to Didi for her intervention, getting him on the move, offering him a chance to return home.

Underneath them the wheels turn, the carriage chugs, steam comes down in white clouds and flies against the windows. Someone passes along the corridor outside.

Still keeping her volume low, Daphne decides to make up for her ill-thought-out diversion back in Paris. 'We've all been fortunate to meet you, Didi,' she says.

And then the three of them look expectantly at Charles to see what he might add.

'RAF,' he says and points a finger at the ceiling of the compartment. 'Plane brought down over northern France. Three crew killed. Two parachuted out before we crashed. I crawled from the wreckage, half-conscious. Knew the Germans would arrive pretty soonish. Kept waiting and waiting, couldn't do anything else. But they never did come. Can't say I can remember much about the next few days.' He puts his hands up in mock surrender. 'Sorry. Disappointing. I must sound like a fearful bore. My only recountable impression is of spending days in ditches, mud soaking cold through all my clothes. I must have looked a frightful mess.' He shivers at the memory. 'Trying to keep warm was nigh on impossible. And I was bleeding. Lost a lot of the stuff. Rather damn foolish of me,' he laughs. It is halfway between self-deprecating and bitter. 'Must have passed out at some point because the next thing I know it's days later and I'm in a farmhouse outside of Lille.'

'I was made aware of Charles by the father of a neighbour,' says Didi. 'A pharmacist. He has been treating hidden people and giving medicine.'

Charles sends her a nod. 'And you?' he asks Daphne.

But it is Didi who replies. 'Sister Daphne came from the convent in Saint-Hubert,' she says.

'But is not a nun,' Bob adds.

'No.'

'What were you doing there?' asks Charles.

Daphne pauses, tries to think of what to say and keep it succinct. It's too difficult, she gives up. 'It's a long story,' she says.

Bob looks as if he is about to protest and press her for more, but a loud screech goes up from outside. The train brakes. The carriage begins to shake. 'We're stopping,' he says.

Charles gets up and goes to the window, pushing it further down.

Daphne can see a farm nestled into the French countryside out the side windows. No town or village though. The terrain is hilly. They must be further south than she supposed, for there are fields of brightly coloured sunflowers. Above them miles of blue sky.

'Patrol along the track?' asks Bob.

Charles, who has leant out and looked to the front, turns back into the compartment. 'Soldiers at the crossing.'

Leaning close to Daphne, Didi whispers: 'Move to the window. We must be ready. One careless word, and it is over. Vow of silence, remember.'

Daphne pushes her hands into the sleeves of her habit, angles her head down to the floor and assumes 'prayer face' once more.

The two servicemen slide up across the seats so that they are close to the internal door. Bob takes out a copy of *Aujourd'hui*, a Vichy newspaper supplied by Didi and, according to her, 'collaborationist'. Charles pulls his cap down over his eyes and feigns sleep as the train finally lurches to a stop.

A connecting door between the coaches opens with a bashing sound, like it has been thrown back in a rush. Footsteps follow.

Daphne keeps her eyes lowered: *Please don't come in here.*

The steps draw closer – tramp, tramp, tramp – then stop. She can't help herself and looks up. A German uniform fills the doorway of their carriage, the brass of the soldier's belt buckle, with its swastika and eagle, scratches against the glass partition window. *Don't open the door*, she thinks, *stay there – in the corridor.* To her mild astonishment, the soldier pushes down on the glass. The sound of it sliding sharp in the quiet, like a blade, jangles her nerves. He glances inside.

Stay there, Daphne wills. The sound of her heart is so loud now she hopes it won't give them all away.

He makes a show of looking from Charles to Daphne, takes in the habit, looks back again and stares. She is sure he is enjoying the uncomfortable impact this is having on the men.

Bob folds the paper and sets it on his knees. Charles, who had looked up at the soldier, quickly drops his gaze in submission. The soldier lets a smile crease his lips for a moment then moves on, expression reverting to neutral.

In the carriage they almost wilt.

Bob picks the paper up and uses it to fan his face. Charles wipes his forehead with his sleeve. Didi leans towards them. 'I think you two should move,' she murmurs. 'After we set off again. Another compartment, up ahead. Less risk there.'

'But when will we know we are at Bayonne?' asks Charles.

'It's the last stop. Go to the men's lavatories on the platform. There is a door that leads to the other side, so you need not pass through the main gate.' She grins. Daphne is stunned by the good humour and marvellous self-possession Didi demonstrates. A girl, younger than herself and one who has risked so much.

'Operation Water Closet,' she continues. And at this both Bob and Charles smile.

Daphne bursts out laughing and is hushed by the other three. She puts a hand over her mouth to smother the sound. It's not very nun-like.

Returning her attention to the men, Didi continues, 'Much safer. Head to the river, the Adour, not the Nive, turn right before the bridge and go to Café du Château. We will meet you there.'

'Ardour,' says Bob, with a wink at Daphne. 'I'll remember that.' Then he smiles. 'Sorry sister. Forgetting myself.'

'I have yet to take my orders,' she returns and sends him a stage wink. It's gallows humour, she knows, but it breaks the tension and makes her realise her wit is returning. She must be slowly reintegrating the parts of herself that have been fragmented by the last few months.

'No, not for passion,' Didi interrupts, wagging a finger, and spells out the correct name, without the first 'r'.

The train begins to move, jerks and shudders, stops then starts again.

'If . . .' says Didi, with a slight strain in her voice, as the men make ready to stand. 'If we *don't* arrive, ask for Jean.'

And with those word Daphne's lightness evaporates.

She watches as the men exit the compartment, sliding along the narrow corridor. And she is left with Didi. A heaviness weights the air they have left behind.

The train begins to fall into a rhythm as the engine fires up and the wheels turn quickly once more.

'Paris is behind us,' says Didi. 'The Pyrenees and Spain lie ahead. The journey will be hard but worth it, my friend. You will be free once more.' She takes Daphne's hand and squeezes it.

'And let us pray you will too, Didi,' she says.

'You know,' says the girl, and her eyes flare with mischief, 'you are a very convincing nun. Perhaps you have found a new vocation.'

CHAPTER FORTY-THREE

'And if they are captured, then the punishment,' Didi sighs and bites her lip. 'Well,' she says, 'these Nazis, they use the guillotine to execute Belgian agents. In parts of Bavaria, they behead them by axe.'

'No!' says Daphne and gasps. It is disgusting. Like a throwback to the dark ages. Bavaria, though, is where Greta is. Hopefully *was*.

The conversation, like the world outside, has turned dark as they approach Bayonne.

The train hisses, as if it has heard Didi's words.

Daphne wants to say she cannot believe it but her own experience would dictate that it is far from unthinkable. Such treatment of the enemy is savage, a reversal of the direction that civilisation has been moving in, a plumbing to the depraved depths of *inhumanity*. And conversely, rather than bearing down on her, frightening her, it provokes something else: she finds defiance billowing out. They *must* be stopped. The whole of Europe cannot be brought under their control. And this thought makes her bolder. She knows she has and will continue to risk her life for the cause.

Like Didi, evidently. She does not know why this young woman is helping. What has prompted her to take on these lost souls. But she experiences an overwhelming swell of gratitude.

'Bayonne,' Daphne murmurs, trying the word out on her lips and tongue.

The train is coming to its final destination.

Though Bayonne, the town's name, seems suddenly laden with violence – is this the home of the bayonet? Or perhaps it is only their conversation that has made her mind list this way to such destructive weapons. She shivers, though it is not cold, and is thankful for the cover of night.

Lamps along the platform are not alight, so present as tall shadows, which make a 'shushing' sound as they pass them by.

'We're here,' Didi whispers. She sets a cap on her head and hands Daphne her ticket.

They hurry down the corridor.

There are not many people around. Most have got off the train at the stations they have passed. But it is also dark, and just as in Britain, thieves and criminals have found the blackout a useful cover. It is not wholly safe to be at large at night. Especially for two unaccompanied women.

Didi pushes back the outer carriage door. It hits the body of the train and bounces. A breeze comes in over the top of Didi's head and blows over Daphne's face. She detects coal smoke and steam, but beyond those is a dampish note of water and she remembers her guide's instructions to the men – 'head for the river'.

They step down onto the platform, Daphne careful to keep her head bowed, her hands tucked into her sleeves. Now her habit feels like it is soaking up the steam, growing heavier. Hopefully it will slow her gait into dignified comportment.

She is surprised to see a porter carrying a lantern through the gloom and looks up to see that they are under a high roof. Only a handful of the panes are glass. The station's few lights are protected from the Allied spotters in the sky.

Soldiers stand smoking, occasionally laughing, near a bench. After her conversation with Didi their mirth appears contemptible. Do they know what is going on? They must do. It is repugnant. She hears a dog bark in a street nearby and the word 'curs' comes to her. It is fitting she thinks, but then stamps out the thought: she must not give her feelings away and assumes 'prayer face' again. It had come in very handy.

At the gate, a uniformed inspector raises a hand, 'Billets.'

Didi steps forward first, her manner unhurried as they present their tickets. The man's eyes take them in – the nun's veil atop her head, Didi's relaxed poise, arms folded, the tapping of one finger on her sleeve suggesting commonplace impatience rather than anxiety. He hesitates for a moment, then Didi yawns, and his mouth begins to twitch in response, nostrils flaring as he tries to suppress one of his own. He stamps the tickets and waves them through before leaning back, rubbing his neck and opening his mouth wide.

The main hall is half full. She knows people are looking at her. But they don't seem bothered. A nun's a nun, both here and at home: slightly unusual to come across, but not deserving of more attention. They acknowledge her habit then look away.

'Keep walking,' Didi murmurs.

There are three huge arched exits and a commotion by the nearest: someone is on the floor, a couple of shouts, another person is pushed. They ignore the kerfuffle and head to the furthest arch, though there is a soldier checking the identity papers of a man with a flat cap and a ragged jacket. They both glance up at the women for a moment. Daphne holds her nerve and continues to walk past and the men return instantly to the papers.

It is hotter here than it was in Brussels or Paris and the front door is wedged open with a wooden block. They go through and then she is out and into the night.

But they don't stop.

That would be too obvious.

As they walk out into the forecourt, Daphne checks for threats. Like most women, her body knows 'fight' should be avoided and 'flight' embraced.

Ahead of them lies a square, two cars waiting for passengers, engines idling, sending blackish fumes from the exhausts to mingle with the warm air. Opposite, three streets with tall buildings five or six storeys high, their windows shuttered. The wood, she can tell, is painted different colours on each house, though it is too dim to discern exact shades. Two men walk down one street and disappear in a doorway. A searchlight beams up from somewhere down river, drifts across the roof-tops, passes over a cloud . . .

They turn right and slip down another street, through a courtyard surrounded by tall buildings, and come out on a road that Didi tells her runs by the Adour. Only a faint shimmer marks the water's current. Didi has said the river is tidal and strong with an undertow that can be fatal. They need to keep to their original plan and not risk crossing the water here.

'Right,' Didi whispers, guiding her along the quay.

A small café comes into view, on the corner, windows shuttered like the rest. Above the door an unlit glass lantern sways in the breeze coming off the water. Daphne spots the words 'du Château' printed on it.

The door opens and light glances out briefly across the pavement. 'Quick,' Didi says. 'You'd better smile too.'

She fixes one on her face and they go in.

Inside, a few locals sit over glasses, the wireless is playing a jazz tune – of course it is jazz. The tables are lit by candles that have been set into green wine bottles, though there is an electric lamp on the bar with a shade printed with castles. Everyone seems to be smoking; she can taste it in the air. A couple of the men appear surprised to see a nun in their midst, but no one says anything.

At a corner table Bob and Charles are doing their best to look louche and French: their jackets are unbuttoned, caps set down casually, elbows – shock horror – on the table. Bob is finishing a small beer while Charles, whose face is tired and pinched, nurses a wineglass. Though their faces light up when they see the two women, a release of tension lowers Bob's jaw and lifts Charles' lips.

Didi glances at the bar, smiles then heads to the corner. The bartender returns to polishing a glass without looking back at them. Daphne senses that he is 'in on the plan'.

She keeps her nun's veil low, noticing every glance, mind already storing the café's exits.

With a grin, Bob offers them the empty seats as if they are exactly the sort of women who are partial to a late coffee or drop of beer in the blackout.

Didi bends to them and says, 'Might look strange if we joined you, what with Sister Daphne here taking a vow of silence.'

'She's not taken her final vows yet,' Bob snickers. 'There's still time.'

She permits a grin then becomes grave again. 'Go outside once we leave. Turn right. You will pass two roads, coming off this one. Take the third, go up till you find three trees. Remember – third road, three trees. There should be bicycles leaning against them. Cycle back down and then cross the river, turn right and continue. We will wait for you outside of Anglet. If the bridge is guarded, you are two brothers going home after working in the north, shipbuilding. Charles, your French is passable. You do the speaking. Have your papers ready.'

They both nod, the triumph of their journey already gone. It is dawning on the three of them they've merely completed stage one.

'Daphne, fold your train ticket and hand it to Charles as if it is a message. Both you boys look very grateful please.'

They comply.

Daphne nods at them both, noticing a droplet of sweat career down the side of Charles's temple and vanish into the space between his collar and neck.

The conversation lasts barely a minute then they are out the side, past stacked chairs and empty tables.

They turn up the third road and see the trees at the side. 'Here,' says Didi and steps beneath the boughs and is camouflaged by leafy shadows.

Three bicycles lean against a low wall, arranged with care.

'Damn,' says Didi, 'there should be four.' She looks at Daphne. Uncharacteristically, a smattering of lines contract her brow. 'I will have to give you a ride. Let us hope the bridge is unguarded.'

Daphne suddenly understands what she means. The boys will need a bike each to avoid scrutiny. If Didi is escorting the nun, where is her bicycle? Certainly, it could be something that the guards might question.

'Too bad,' says Daphne. It is not worth worrying about till they get there. 'Let us walk. I will take the bicycle. You follow alongside.'

Didi looks uncertain but Daphne is already wheeling it back down to the water.

There are guards on duty of course, as grim as the gargoyles on the Lambertikirche.

Daphne hesitates, passes the bike to Didi, who takes it without a word.

Didi rolls the bicycle by the handlebars. Daphne walks half a step behind, veil even lower. Neither speak. The soldiers are watching.

The nearest one comes out onto the pavement and waits for them.

'Papiere.'

Didi is ready. There is her smile again with their forged documents. She leans her weight on one hip and rests the bike against it, angling her face up to them with the bored air of a girl very accustomed to cycling through Bayonne and being stopped all the time by the Wehrmacht. The soldier studies her picture, then her face, then her bicycle.

Her smile doesn't waver.

She should go on the stage, thinks Daphne.

He stamps her papers and jerks his chin towards the far side. She gives a polite nod and rolls on a few paces, waiting just beyond the unlit lamppost.

Then it is Daphne's turn.

She hands over the prepared papers, pleased that her hands are steady, then sticks them straight back in her huge voluminous sleeves to avoid inspection. She can feel her heartbeat in a vein at the side of her throat and is grateful the habit comes to under her chin. The guard looks her up and down. A nun on foot. A nun out late. A nun alone except for this girl with a bike.

His eyes narrow.

Daphne looks up, widens her eyes in an expression that, she hopes, projects innocence, stands there, patient, silent. She can't tell him that she has taken a vow of silence – why hasn't Didi told them? She lets her gaze drift to the ground as if out of respect, not terror.

She has in her eyesight the soldier's hands and watches his thumb flick the edges of her documents. For too long. While she waits, it suddenly occurs to her she doesn't know the name of 'her' convent.

The lie will have to come quickly. Our Lady of Notre Dame was the name of the Saint-Hubert convent. There are lots of convents dedicated to Mary, perhaps she can use the same name? Then she reminds herself she shouldn't speak.

But, he sniffs and returns the identity card without making eye contact, already turning to resume conversation with the other man.

Daphne waits until she is six paces away before she manages a smile for her companion.

Didi pushes the bicycle on, her movements rigid, while Daphne makes an effort not to listen for footsteps or shouts behind them.

Halfway over, the town on the other side of the bank becomes clearer. More densely populated, it has higher buildings, darker streets, tighter alleys. Daphne keeps her eyes forward and her pace sedate, though every part of her is ready to run for her life. Her gaze wanders into the black waters of the Adour. In this get-up would she be able to take the wall and drop into it? Surely that way death lies? The habit would be drenched and take her down in seconds. Though that wouldn't necessarily be the worst thing. Not when faced with some of the other German methods of execution.

'Not far now,' whispers Didi.

And, as they come down over the abutment, Daphne sees she is right. She wants to yelp with delight or swear for the hell of it. But eyes will be watching them, so she demurely follows Didi over the embankment, across another bridge, unguarded this time, and then down through a quieter road.

After five minutes Didi stops and steps into the porch of a derelict building. 'It will take all night to walk to Anglet and we'll rouse suspicion if we are spotted. Look at us.'

Daphne knows what a strange couple they must make.

'There is no one around,' says Didi. 'Not here.'

It's true – the streets are deserted. It is late.

'Get on the back,' says Didi and taps the saddle. 'I will pedal,' she says. 'It is not unusual to see young girls riding around France on bikes.'

That is not the point, thinks Daphne. 'But – nuns!' she says.

Didi shrugs, 'Then take it off.' She points to the saddlebag. 'Stow ici.'

She has wanted to do this for a while but has not had the right moment. 'Are you sure?' she asks.

'Who will know the difference?' Didi says.

So she pulls off her veil and coif, lets the river air flow through her shorn locks. If Didi is surprised by the state of her hair she doesn't show it. Daphne can feel that it has grown a little more while she has been at the convent, but still, it can't be more than a couple of inches long and boyish in style. Next, she removes her rosary and cross, the scapular. All of these Didi takes and folds into the bicycle bag.

'Now the tunic,' she says and tightens Daphne's belt, pulls some of the fabric of the skirt up over the top so the hem brushes her knees. 'Can't let the material get tangled in the wheels,' she explains.

Daphne finds that it is entirely liberating – much cooler and far less cumbersome. As she gathers her skirts and gets on the saddle, she also feels a lightness that she hasn't known for months, possibly years.

Telling her to rest her feet on the frame Didi begins to pedal. Daphne grips her waist, holding on tight as the outskirts of the city rush past.

A bump in the road throws them closer together and Daphne realises that she completely trusts this woman, who she is holding on to.

Didi leans forward as she stands on the pedals to glide, then pushes them harder whenever they hear a truck purr or backfire. But there are not many and, as they get further from the city traffic, those manmade sounds disappear entirely.

They take turns pedalling, then, as they crest the top of a hill, Didi stops for a breather and points. 'There,' she pants. 'Anglet. Where we will find Villa Voisin and our bed for the night. Or for the day rather. We'll do the next stage tomorrow night.'

'What about the men?' asks Daphne, remembering that Didi had told them she would meet them outside the village of Anglet.

Didi points to a dark patch that Daphne can see are trees. 'We'll wait for them there. So last leg,' she says, and Daphne lifts her feet and they push off down the hill.

There is a familiar, child-like joy in moving fast like this. She sticks her legs out on either side. The movement lifts not only her skirts but her spirits, and she cannot help but let go a chuckle: she is alive again. Her giggle is infectious, for she hears Didi join in.

And for that moment, Daphne knows she is no longer fleeing. She is heading towards home. At last.

CHAPTER FORTY-FOUR

The road from Urrugne has narrowed to a mule-track, and even that is now diminishing beneath their boots.

Not boots, she corrects herself, *espadrilles*, and she looks at them again in awe. Such flimsy things and yet they have proved absolutely perfect for the terrain. Everyone that she has seen on the way from Anglet to Saint Jean de Luz and then on to Urrugne is wearing them. Any other footwear would give her away as an outsider.

Elvire, their host at Villa Voisin, had been so generous – feeding them well. In addition to the espadrilles, she had given Daphne clothes to change into: a long brown skirt, beige blouse and black beret, which will camouflage her somewhat in the mountains.

It is incredible, she thinks, how generous these people are. They are not rich. The villa at Anglet was modest, the flat in Saint Jean de Luz also humble and the last place they rested, a farmhouse in Urrugne, belonged to a poor woman called Francia who had been widowed and left with three young children. Hers was a poor situation indeed and yet as soon as they arrived, she had served them a large tortilla. The other person living there was a tanned, young Basque called Juan, who had fought against the fascists and then deserted. Though, because he often visited his parents in Spanish Hernani, he has become a willing recruit to Didi's evader scheme; his knowledge of the Pyrenees is second to none and he is highly skilled on the mountain paths, and as such, an excellent guide.

Which is just as well, as Elvire had told them yesterday, 'This part of the escape route is now guarded by Austrian soldiers. Chosen because they are used to patrolling alpine landscapes.'

And yet it does not put them off. Not Didi, not Francia, not Elvire.

Daphne had commented on her amazement that so many young women are part of the resistance here. Her proclamation made Didi laugh. 'We are so useful though,' she said. 'Documents and microfiche can be hidden in baby prams, baby clothes, brassieres, hair pins. And rolled up and inserted into bicycle pumps.' She took out the one strapped to the bike. 'From Brussels,' she added.

After leaving Francia's, Didi had paused by a derelict shed on a road. 'One minute,' she told them, then hid the pump under a fallen plank near the door.

A perilous game is being played by the Belgians and French. One word out of place, one compromised recruit and the whole network could go down, putting who knew how many scores of lives in danger. The thought makes her sweat, though that is easy to do – as it is so very humid.

Daphne's nerves are now strung as tight as the muscles on her calves and back. Once again night has come down with its cloak.

At this present moment she feels both fully alive and painfully aware of her own mortality, of the fragility of her hopes.

They have been told not to speak nor smoke but none of them feel like it anyway. They all know this is the most dangerous part of their trek.

The wind has cleared the clouds from the sky and the constellations wink above them. Ahead, the mountains rise like the shoulders of sleeping giants, or trolls, and Daphne thinks once more of the bleak volcanic ones upon which she had once been stranded. But that had been winter and the snow had been just as much an adversary as the black-clad German operatives.

This summer terrain is not icy and freezing but the hazards are just as challenging. Some of the slopes before her seem to rise straight up, so steep she does not know how they will climb them.

Bob and Charles are silent, focused in the way soldiers can be.

'All right,' says Juan and gives the signal, touching two fingers to his forehead: follow me. He leads them off the track in single file then up into the brush.

Daphne plants her feet in the footprints he has left. The slope is muddy in places and gravity keeps tugging her backwards. Who would have thought that the simple act of walking could be such tremendously hard work.

Didi follows, though she makes better pace. She must have done this before, Daphne thinks.

They climb.

After an hour they reach the top. Daphne puts her hands on her hips, wipes her brow, then looks ahead. There is another mountain there, higher than the one on which she stands. It is *so* hard.

Juan has paused, waiting just long enough for them to all catch up.

His voice is barely audible: 'Keep down. No lights, no cigarettes. Do not stop. They can't be allowed to see any silhouettes on the ridge, you understand? Follow the stones: do NOT touch the grass.'

The servicemen bob their heads up and down, bending their frames lower. Charles, the taller, crouches close to the ground.

At first, she doesn't understand why they should take the stone path. But then, as her skirt brushes the grass, she hears it rustling. Hell's teeth! The sound is *so* loud. It carries much further than during the day. She's so clumsy!

Bob glances back at Daphne, a quick, check-in: you all right?

She suppresses a sigh and nods. He winks.

It makes her feel fractionally better.

The air up here is thinner, smells wilder. Mosquitoes buzz in clouds. She keeps walking into them. Some must have bitten her around the ankles because she can feel the skin there itch. But they carry on.

Whenever someone snaps a twig underfoot, everyone jumps. Whenever someone slips, they all stop, don't breathe, don't move, in case the sleeping birds might wake up, scream out and give away their location. She had thought this might be an easier leg than the train, when they were out in the open. But it's not. There is so much to think about. Against the clear starry sky the Pyrenees look like one huge undulating wall.

The hours pass.

Her legs start to shake and tremble, but she keeps climbing.

They crest another mount.

About twenty yards over the other side Juan halts. 'Wait.'

They all drop down behind him. He watches the valley below. What for? Headlights, dogs, patrols?

Daphne has gained her night vision but can't see anything there. Then a light appears in the dark, just a few yards below them on the hillside opposite. A door has opened.

The outline of a man appears. Not German, it looks like he wears a three-pointed hat. He pauses mid-stride, gun held close to his chest, ears straining.

Every single one of them stops still.

After what seems like a very long time the soldier turns and goes back in.

'On,' whispers Juan.

Her feet are like clods of earth, unwilling to move. She forces them down, down, down till he pauses again.

Now, in the hush, she can hear the sound of water and smells a river. It makes their guide's next movements better to understand. For he takes off his trousers and ties them round his neck. The two servicemen do the same, Bob looking askance at Daphne, relieved no doubt that she definitely is not a nun.

Didi tugs at her skirt, 'Off. We must cross the Bidasoa.'

It is hardly decorous, but they have been through enough now to make them feel less self-conscious with each other, so Daphne whips off her skirt and apron and ties them round her neck like Didi has.

They stagger down the valley through the bushes until they come out near the river. Juan wades into it immediately. When he is up to his waist in water, he signals to them to follow.

Charles goes in first. When he reaches Juan, he takes his hand then waits for Bob, who does the same thing and holds his hand out to assist Daphne. But Juan shakes his head and puts a finger on his lips: any more will be too noisy.

The men make it to the other side and get dressed as Daphne and Didi hold hands and tentatively walk in, trying not to splash or make a noise.

The water is cold and black. But at least it has not rained recently and it is not too high. The flow is swift, but the water feels 'thin' and does not hinder their movements too severely.

When they reach the other side, they unwrap their skirts and aprons and put them back on. With the sentry point so near, she feels the pressure inside her head as Juan sets off again. She shivers; her underwear is wet.

They move up, cross into a flat plain, but as they reach the road at its edge, they hear the sound of a truck approaching.

Juan points to a cluster of pines and signals they should run.

Daphne, exhausted now, is too slow, and as the beam of the headlights sweeps across the field, she has to fling herself on the ground.

Face in the dirt, she worries. Have they seen her? Is the game up?

She keeps her eyes shut, scrunching her face tightly as if the effort will force away the enemy, starts counting her heartbeats.

A hand touches her shoulder and she almost yelps but stifles it and then, oh so gratefully, opens her eyes onto Didi.

'Thank God,' she wheezes out.

'Spanish Guarda,' says Didi, 'on the way to the sentry point. We must move before the old shift passes back this way.'

Daphne nods, crawls onto her knees then up, using Didi's arm as a prop. 'Hang on,' she says, '*Spanish* police? Are we in Spain?'

'Yes,' says Didi. 'The river is the border.'

'Thank the Lord Almighty,' she says.

'Not quite time to rejoice,' Didi tells her. 'If they find us, they will take us back to France and hand us over to the Vichy authorities.'

Of course it's not over yet, thinks Daphne. 'How much further?'

'One more hill to the other side of the valley.'

And it is a long slog. Juan passes round a bottle of Spanish brandy, which is somewhat reviving. At least it helps with the wet and the cold.

She doesn't know how many minutes or hours pass till they see a farmhouse on the horizon – forever and a day. But when Juan tells them this is the next safe house, the news motivates and speeds them up.

One final push, a special knock and then the door is opened into a parlour with a fireplace which is soon alight.

A woman with a colourful scarf tied around her head hands Daphne a blanket and pats her hand – well done. Within minutes, she is fast asleep.

CHAPTER FORTY-FIVE

The 6.38 from San Sebastian.

Six chairs with room to stretch aching legs.

Four passengers: two women, two men.

One first class compartment.

None of them matching their upmarket surroundings.

The farmer's wife advised Didi that, with only limited spaces, the party are less likely to experience interruption on their final stage of their journey to Bilbao if they paid more for their tickets. And so far, she has been right: they have had the place to themselves.

The sun ascends over the hills in the east; its rays begin to warm the valleys. Out of the window, the Bay of Biscay sparkles into view, appearing between pine trees and dips in the rocky hills. The sea is so lovely, it makes Daphne's heart ache. Somewhere over the whale-blue waves lies home. Perhaps these waters have even visited the shores of Leigh-on-Sea? It is all part of the same great ocean in the end, she supposes.

As they veer closer to shore though, she realises it looks nothing like the Estuary. White spray bursts against splintery rocks like thick needles, or teeth, and the fishing boats list, pitching and diving. Unseen currents are making it rough and choppy despite the clear day and sunshine.

It is early, not quite eight thirty. The train has been boarded by people heading to market and visibly excited by the prospect. Both men and women carry on empty baskets and bags waiting to be filled with goodies.

Daphne is privately amazed that there are still large markets operating, but then again Spain is not at war, of course – that is the difference – though sympathetic to Hitler.

'Sympathetic to Hitler!' she murmurs to herself. After all she has seen, the words seem not to make any sense and feel toxic on her tongue. How could Spain align itself with such malignancy? It is obscene. She cannot fathom the moral acrobatics required to turn a blind eye to what they are doing over the border. Yet she's aware Spain owes Hitler. Juan has told her that without his aircraft and Mussolini's men, Franco might never have won his civil war. The dictator's gratitude has turned into fealty. The country is exhausted by all the blood it has shed and has no appetite for more war. Or to challenge those monsters next door.

But now, occupied France lies behind her.

And they are so very close to their destination.

She can tell the men have, at last, let hope in. It opens their faces up and pulls at the corners of their mouths. They probably can't believe their good fortune. A fidgety glow has taken hold. Bob almost looks giggly. Charles bites his lip and keeps blowing out his cheeks, staring out the window at the coast, as if barely daring to believe that he is out of danger. From time to time he surveys the hills behind them, making sure that nothing is rising from them to snatch him back. She gets it, she half feels that way too.

The coastline has disappeared and the train is curving inland. Here, the countryside is contoured with steep mountains threaded with woods and glinting rivers. It looks so fertile. She bets the markets will be dazzling.

On the green terraced hillsides, farmhouses perch with red-tiled roofs. Laundry – long johns, skirts and bright blouses – flaps from some of the balconies.

Every now and then, as the route goes through the mountains, not around, tunnels envelop the train and they are plunged into blackness. The air pressure changes and there is a 'thump' which makes them all jolt. Though often Didi speaks in these moments, saying anything. Sometimes, 'All right?' or 'Not long now,' as if she knows that they have each experienced their own trauma in darkness and need the sound of her kind voice to hold on to. When the daylight returns, all the Brits blink and smile, as if they have been silly, and a sheepish sort of laughter froths up. Didi pretends not to notice. She is so good, thinks Daphne. So so so good. A saint.

On the train to Bayonne she had mentioned she trained as a nurse, and Daphne can see it now in every gently supportive word that calms their panic before it has a chance to snare them. There is such great peace about her. Though a steely purpose too. Her courage and grit are infectious.

'This is the last one before Bilbao,' says Didi now as the train pauses at another station.

Basque farm workers, in their flat caps or berets, stand by the train and watch it slow. Some children wave. Others, younger ones, hide behind their mothers' skirts, peering up at the train with big eyes. Men lift crates, baskets and sacks. Women and girls haul goods and bags onto the coach. And then they are off again.

She thought that she might feel brighter the closer she got to Bilbao, but the sight of soldiers and police that she glimpses in the streets on the outskirts reminds her that there is just this little bit further. She must hold on to her 'nerve' with a good and competent grip, and opens and closes her hand, flexing her fingers, like it is something she can physically grasp.

And then, they are there.

The train pulls into Bilbao.

With a nod and one last smile at each other, they collect their scant belongings.

Didi beckons them out.

Daphne steps down. She is here and almost cannot believe it as she looks around at the station. It is grand, and more sophisticated than she expected, with stained-glass windows and a high curved roof full of noise and echoes – hundreds of different voices, luggage trollies, whistles, doors slamming, footsteps, pigeons and in the distance the familiar cry of a seagull. *Home!* she thinks again and permits her heart to rise a tiny, tiny fraction.

Bob and Charles gaze around them, unselfconsciously open-mouthed, staggered by the marvel of having actually arrived. They should not look up, she thinks. With their pale skin, Bob's blue eyes and sandy hair, Charles's downy moustache, it is obvious they are not Spanish. Then again, she thinks, this is the hub of a busy metropolis – strangers come and go all the time.

'This way,' says Didi and keeps them moving.

It is hot and steamy under the glass roof, like a greenhouse. Daphne's peasant blouse clings under her armpits, though she does not look out of place with it.

No one collects their tickets at the gate. There are so few checks here compared to France and Germany. It is amazing – what liberty.

Now they are out, on the streets of Bilbao. Stallholders call out the prices of fresh fish and fruit. The oranges are big and bright and exotic. They look like they are crammed full with juice. The apples too gleam as if they have been sprayed and polished by the farmers. Cheeses ooze from paper wrappings. Daphne's mouth begins to water. It is so different to the last city she was in. Where was that? she wonders. Then remembers – Münster. It had been raining and dour, full of pointed architecture and black spires with cages on them that looked like gibbets. She shudders at the memory – she had been so alone as she trudged through those streets. Bilbao could not be more of a contrast. She is no longer on her own – for a start, she is with, what shall she call them? She decides on 'friends'. Yes, she is with friends and there is movement and energy, chaos, smells and sunshine everywhere: such is the vibrancy of everyday life without war.

They turn a corner and up a hill. Halfway to the top Didi pauses. 'Here.'

It is an old building, set back from the road behind iron gates.

The British consulate.

Daphne and the men slow. She is certain that their bodies are tensing like hers and is not sure if it is anticipation or relief, or both, or neither. It is a reaction that has become second nature when she encounters a new place.

Could it really be that within these walls safety waits?

'Let's not hang around outside,' says Didi, ever watchful, and pushes the gate open.

They follow her through and across a courtyard until they reach the entrance.

Without stopping, Didi pushes open the tall wooden door and they go inside. Bob, the last in, turns and firmly shuts out the world.

They are on British ground.

It even smells British in here, Daphne thinks, sniffing out mothballs, the familiar scent of Earl Grey and another fragrance she hasn't come across for many months – Yardley's lavender water.

Bright morning light filters through high windows, illuminating the meticulous reception area. For the first time in days, Daphne feels the psychological weight of constant vigilance begin to lighten.

A young man appears from a side office, dressed in a dark suit and tie. His hair is neatly parted, his expression polite. He looks at them with curiosity, and she realises, in their peasant clothes, they must seem a very unusual group.

'Hello.' Daphne steps forward first and says, 'We are British and in need of help.'

His eyes round and flick over her and the men before resting on Didi.

'Oh,' says Daphne. 'This is Didi, who has helped us – me,' she thumbs her chest, 'Bob and Charles – to escape from France and Belgium. She wishes to set up a regular escape route with you.'

Bob and Charles nod along.

The young man blinks then steps back with the wide eyes and astonishment of someone who might have stumbled upon a travelling freakshow. He rubs his hand over his chin, evidently unsure if this motley gang can really be 'British'. But then his manners reassert themselves and he says in a cut-glass accent, 'I see. Is that so? You,' he turns to Didi, 'are not a British national?'

Which seems, after all Didi has done for them, hardly fair.

But the impertinence goes over Didi's head. 'No,' she says simply.

'Then may I ask you to take a seat inside my office and wait there. The rest, please, follow me inside.' He gestures towards a quieter corridor that opens up behind the office. The men look at each other: this is it, we've done it. Bob actually puts his hands on his hips, leans over and stares at the ground. Charles sticks out his hand to Didi, who shakes it and smiles.

When they are done, Daphne flings her arms around the slight young girl. 'Didi, I cannot ever, ever thank you enough for what you have done for me, for us all.' And to think she had been intending to go it alone! The thought is almost laughable now. But she doesn't laugh. Instead a shaky, weepy emotion that has been kept back for a very long time is now suddenly clamouring for release.

'It is all right,' says Didi and untangles herself, taking Daphne's hand in both of hers. 'Thank you, the British, for fighting for us.'

'We're all very grateful,' says Bob. He has said it before, but the words now seem inadequate. He slips in between them and folds the pretty Belgian in a bear hug.

The official coughs. 'Well, this way then. All of you.' And he guides them through the door into the office with walls lined with maps and, presumably, diplomatic notices. He points to a chair, which Didi takes. The three of them wave at her, then they are ushered down the corridor.

It is not how Daphne thought they would part ways. But perhaps the anticlimax is better. There is far too much to say: how can she sum it all up concisely? The admiration she has for this tiny woman, who is really a titan in disguise, is ineffable. The men feel it too, she can tell. They will all acknowledge their debts to Didi whenever the chance comes their way. When they are eventually allowed to.

'That woman is phenomenal,' says Charles to the young man. 'You must pay her proper attention.'

'He's right,' says Bob. 'The balls of the lass are undeniable,' he adds and doesn't apologise for his language.

Daphne pipes up, 'Seconded,' because she wants to say something, anything, to amplify the fact that they really must take notice of Didi and repay her for her efforts, but the act of talking, saying more, is becoming too much.

As they reach a sitting room, the young man turns to them. 'You're safe here,' he says. 'You really are. I'll ring for some tea. But first let me just take your names.'

While he makes notes, Bob and Charles give him their names, ranks, regiment, battalion, company. Daphne yawns. Their voices are fading. Exhaustion is on its way to claim her. So she takes out her train ticket and scribbles a message down then lays it out prominently on her lap.

When the young man comes over, he finds Daphne asleep. Though he spies the train ticket, picks it up. His eyebrows wriggle as he reads the words: 'Phone Hugh Deveraux and tell him Snowdrop is back.'

CHAPTER FORTY-SIX

One month later

She doesn't know what she was expecting but nonetheless is surprised.

The sheer formality of it. She had assumed the meeting would just be with Hugh, but the Brigadier is here too, his uniform pressed, shoes polished, ginger moustache trimmed, medals gleaming. She's not sure why she has been summoned, having been fully debriefed at the Patriotic School in Wandsworth. Her information about the German army movements was taken with scepticism at first. But then she was subjected to a thorough grilling. Quite trying. Before she was allowed to talk to other personnel she was kept isolated for days.

Not that she is unused to that.

No one ever said, but she assumes her intelligence was corroborated. It must have been. She witnessed troops going east with her own eyes. However, all agents returning from missions are subjected to rigorous questioning and close observation. How else are the officers to ensure they have not been compromised, broken under enemy pressure or even turned? She knows they missed one before.

They all did.

What a chump, she thinks, and for the first time she is not reflecting on her own behaviour, but Jack's. To go to the dark side and then find again his humanity at the last moment. She could have brought him back. If they had escaped together. But then she catches herself: he might have turned again and betrayed more.

Perhaps it is better he is dead.

She does not really feel this, but makes her mind say the words inside her head.

For now, it has become a full stop on her thought cycle, as heartless as it sounds. Now is not the right time to let her ruminations take hold. Though she is not sure when that will ever be.

She smooths the skirt of her frock, a gesture she also hasn't performed for months. Her fingertips brush down gabardine. It is a tailored navy number which has been borrowed from one of the girls at the Oriental. The instructions said 'smart' and she literally has only two dresses of her own, the rest buried under the rubble of the Thomas's bombed-out house. Neither of her surviving garments would do. This one, however, is cinched at the waist with a slim belt and topped off with a pointed collar. The sort of dress she used to love but now finds rather too frivolous: the belt is thin and flimsy, the sleeves too tight, there are no pockets, hidden or otherwise, and the skirt is far too restricting with no give to run. But then again, she could never climb mountains in these heels either. It's not just clothes that feel different: her whole world, the atmosphere and tone, seems to have shifted. She notices the shadows more, inspects them for lurkers, feels the hair on her neck prickle when she has no more than one exit in sight. Even today, she has positioned herself so she can see both the door and the window. To be here now feels half unreal, when they are still at war, like a scene in a silly comedy or farce.

But here she is, playing her part, unsure as ever what that is.

What can the Brigadier want with her? she wonders again.

Goodness knows how many reports she has written. Everything she has told them – about the troops' movements, the Messerschmidt factory, the Deputy Führer, Wewelsburg, the killings at Kaufbeuren-Irsee and Didi – is in the typed papers that have been distributed far and wide. So much she has seen, so much she has heard, so much she has done. She still carries it with her.

Perhaps, she thinks, turning her mind quickly to the present, they want to hear it all from her firsthand. Although their choice of venue is rather odd: a private room, in a gentleman's club, just off the Mall. It's so very male: dark wood adorns the walls, green velvet curtains restrict the daylight. Though good for blackout, she thinks and almost remembers when she waited in a similar room for Hess. But no, this is different. Now she is on home ground. The place is probably only strange to her. These men are the types that treat these clubs like their second homes. Homes without women. Maybe it is that, she thinks – her presence here as a female – which is making them prickle and fidget like two little boys.

Neither have sat down yet. Instead, the three of them stand around a table covered in white damask, laden with teapots and plates and plates of buns and dainty cakes. How they've got their hands on them is anyone's guess. Looks like the best silver has come out too. She should feel flattered but is slightly piqued by the Brigadier's eyes. They keep darting to the door, as if she on her own is not good enough to talk to. Only, just now, as she has her gaze on him, she sees that they have grown wide – another waiter has appeared, pushing in a fresh fruitcake that looks big enough (and hard enough) to sink a U-boat. Perhaps, she tells herself, he really likes fruitcake.

'I think you may have ordered too much,' Daphne says as the Brigadier takes it off him and positions it in the centre of the table.

Hugh smiles.

The waiter asks, 'Would you like me to slice it, sir?'

'No,' the Brigadier replies firmly. 'That will be all for now.'

And he nods and leaves, shutting the door so it becomes very, very quiet in here.

Daphne clears her throat.

For a moment no one says anything, then Hugh breaks the silence. 'Well, Miss Devine, I have to say your report makes interesting reading.'

'Interesting!' the Brigadier snorts. He balances his saucer on one palm, rocking on his heels as if he's about to launch into a speech for his men. 'That's an understatement. The thing is cracking stuff. An absolute treasure trove. You say the Wehrmacht are on the move. East, too! East! And then there's the woman who got you over the alps . . .'

'Didi,' Daphne prompts him.

'That's the one,' he says.

'And it was the Pyrenees,' she adds.

'Prime intel,' he repeats. 'MI9 are pulling her in. Naturally we have to vet all Belgians,' he says. 'I'm confident you understand. Vital to make sure people are who they say they are and all that.'

'Of course,' she nods, knowing that all too well, and takes a sip of her tea.

Mr Deveraux puts his cup and saucer to the side, next to a plinth with a bust of a man with short curly hair.

'Daphne, you have achieved such a great deal. Not just in your last mission, but in Iceland too.'

'Come a long way from the secretary I met in Wormwood Scrubs,' the Brigadier adds. He takes a gulp of tea and smiles. She nods, remembering the papers he handed her to roneo the first time they met. He has forgotten she never was a secretary. But she doesn't correct him and instead says, 'And here I am now,' hoping this will prompt them to tell her why she has been summoned.

But then her words are parroted.

'And here *I* am now!' A male voice. Older. Refined. Behind her.

She turns to see who has entered.

But then suddenly stops.

Her jaw slackens and her mouth hangs open.

The wind entirely taken out of her sails, she stands agog when she processes exactly what she is seeing, exactly *whom* she is seeing – the man coming towards her . . . could it really be?

For a moment, she is confused, wonders if she is in a dream.

'Can't stop long,' says the King, to an echo of 'Your Majesty.'

She leaps to attention, salutes, remembers he is a king not a commander, curtseys. Remembers he is a commander too, salutes. Bobs down again, stands, wilts slightly, blushes.

'This,' he says, snapping open a case produced from his suit pocket, 'I believe is for you.' He steps towards Daphne. 'In recognition of your service and work.'

Though she is overwhelmed, she stutters out thanks as he pins the medal on her chest.

'Yes. An achievement of significance,' the King says, his voice quiet but simultaneously rousing. 'I understand you placed a document into the hands of the Deputy Führer. Into his very hands. No mean feat. And one that demands great courage. You'll be aware now that the Nostradamus prophecy finally tipped him into action. Convinced him that a peace mission with the Duke of Hamilton had been predicted centuries ago and that he was the man to achieve it. Or some such fantasy.' He allows himself a smile, which the Brigadier and the King share. 'Captured of course. Almost instantaneously. A severe bruise to Hitler's pride. Well done, Miss Devine.' He looks proud, and so paternal, she wonders if he knows exactly what her bravery cost? But she doesn't say anything back – for once she is speechless.

At this moment of impasse, the Brigadier dives in. 'Tea, Your Majesty?'

The smile slips. 'If only time permitted. Duty calls.' Already his coat is being straightened, gloves pulled back on. 'Carry on,' he adds a final but royal benediction.

Then he turns. The door opens from the outside and he disappears.

'Goodness me,' says Daphne and begins to fan herself, her eyes searching the room for a chair, or a stool, anything she can sink into before her knees give way. She sights one by the curtains and is about to fetch it as the door bursts open again and in breezes Jonty, the Grand Mystique, in a haze of after-shave and cigarette smoke. He waves in his hand a magnum of champagne.

'Hello, dear one,' he declares. His eyes twinkle with pride and possibly mischief. 'So good to see you again.' He kisses her cheek, passes the bottle. 'Put this down, would you Daphers, it's heavy. Cost me an arm, a leg and possibly a black-market kidney to acquire, but I gather we have something to celebrate?'

His dear old face is a sight for sore eyes and, as she takes the giant bottle from him, she feels something inside herself begin to thaw out, or maybe, defuse. She's about to answer, but never gets the chance, for he's not the only guest who has entered.

Bridget Harkness, flawless and graceful, salutes her as she enters. 'Too long, Daphne,' she says and gives her a light hug, 'Uncle has told me some of it, on the QT.'

Septimus Strange strides in next, in the grey suit he always wears, accompanied by Cyril Williamson, who sends her a raffish smile.

Then, as she is greeting her Section W comrades, to her utter joy, her parents appear in the doorway.

Her mother, Carabella, begins to cry at the sight of her. Her father adjusts his tie, self-conscious in the expensive men's club. Daphne steps forward and pulls their arms around her.

They stiffen very slightly, startled by their daughter's

unrestrained affection. Somehow she senses they know she has changed. But they close around her and she feels in the strength of their embrace the sudden release of love that has been simmering over the months they have been kept apart. Then, at the same time, they all pull away and laugh.

The champagne pops and glasses are handed round. A toast is proposed. They drink. Bubbles rush straight to her head. Her mood elevates higher and higher yet. Another cork rockets across the room, and the group gives up a cheer. The cake is cut, generous slices disappearing into the Brigadier instantly – he *does* really like fruitcake. Someone produces a bottle of brandy – 'Well it's a party, isn't it?' 'Don't have much to celebrate these days so . . .'

Warmth floods her cheeks and she starts to feel radiant, flushed, ridiculously alive, alive-oh; says the words out loud and no one bats an eyelid.

She is just beginning to notice that the floor seems rather unsteady, that her laugh is getting louder, that she is constantly giggling, that she really might be, just a little bit, well – a touch, ever so slightly squiffy. And that is the moment that Hugh takes her aside.

Oh no, she thinks, has he noticed? And braces herself for reprimand.

But with one of his knowing smiles, he leans in close. She can feel his breath tickling the tiny hairs on her ear.

'Now, Snowdrop,' he says, 'before I forget to ask – you do speak Italian, don't you?'

AUTHOR'S NOTES (WITH SPOILERS)

As with most of my books, there is a blend of both fact and fiction here. I tend to take inspiration from history and fill in the gaps with my imagination.

My readers will be aware that my research is always immersive. The fieldwork for this book proved invaluable, uncovering insights that cannot be accessed through books, films, documentaries or archival sources too numerous to mention, however expansive they may be.

My first trip for this book took me initially to Memmingen, in south Germany. From there I made my way to Lindau, where I was able to get a clear view across Lake Constance to the Swiss and Austrian Alps. Austria was annexed or 'reunified' with Germany on 12 March 1938. Switzerland, however, remained neutral. It became evident, in situ, that Daphne would have to fly into the latter, then could reach Germany by crossing the water to somewhere near Lindau. In 1941, Wehrmacht units were stationed there. Now it is a very pretty town with a small island resort, which I would recommend visiting if you happen to be in the area.

Next I travelled to Augsburg, where I spent a few days researching the events that took place in the city in May 1941, and also came across the Fuggerei. Founded by Jackob Fugger in 1521, it is one of the oldest social housing complexes in the world. Established for Augsburg's Catholic citizens, it took in those in need, such as elderly craftsmen, widows and workers who were respectable and hard-working but poor. It was comprised of fifty-two houses originally. Today it is formed into one hundred and forty flats as well as administration buildings, a well, a fountain, workshops, a café, small museum, restaurant and St Mark's church. Augsburg residents still live here for an annual rent of €0.88 and three prayers a day. Now a quaint little village inside the city, during the war it was partially destroyed by British bombs, but rebuilt in 1950.

Aloisia Kempter, who Greta speaks of, was a real person. There is a memorial stone in front of the house at 49 Ochsengasse commemorating her. She was sent to Kaufbeuren-Irsee.

Bishop von Galen did indeed gather intelligence about Aktion T4, the Nazi euthanasia programme for the mentally ill and disabled. Based in Münster Cathedral, his episcopal seat, he and trusted members of his clergy informally collected reports and testimonies from the brave families and contacts who were prepared to come forward with information about what was going on. Like the Fuggerei, the cathedral suffered badly from allied bombing. In fact, there is a stone from Coventry Cathedral, famously bombed by the Germans, displayed on its wall. Underneath, a plaque reads in both German and English 'Forgiving one another as God in Christ forgave you.'

The Lambertikirche (St Lambert's Church) is but a stone's throw away (and does, incidentally, have gibbet-type cages hanging from its steeple which once held the mutilated, rotting corpses of three revolutionary anabaptists). It was there, in the pulpit of this church, on the 3rd of August in 1941, that Bishop von Galen gave a sermon condemning Aktion T4. He declared it contrary to divine law and a violation of human rights, warning that once the state began killing innocent people, no one would be safe, not even soldiers injured in war. His sermon was distributed illegally across Germany and even reached the BBC, who broadcast passages. Leaflets quoting von Galen were written in German and dropped over the country. As a result,

Hitler instructed Aktion T4 to be suspended on 24 August 1941. However, the killings continued in secret afterwards.

Five days after that sermon, on 8 August 1941, Aloisia, along with one hundred and thirty-two other women, was deported from Kaufbeuren-Irsee to the killing centre at Hartheim Castle near Linz, where she was gassed.

It was the last transport to Hartheim.

The Messerschmitt factory in Augsburg received a direct hit from the Royal Air Force during Operation Double Strike on 17 February 1942 and was later subjected to multiple raids from 1943 until the end of the war. As a result, there is very little left to see. Today, the site is a sports ground, though the surrounding street names still indicate its former purpose. As I walked around, I matched photos and aerial views to the grounds and was gradually able to visualise Rudolf Hess taking off from there on his final flight to Scotland at 5.45 p.m., 10th May 1941.

Why he did so is a question that has baffled many ever since.

Over the years I have kept my ears open to suggestions and, at some point, heard that Cecil Williamson, who founded the Museum of Witchcraft and Magic in Boscastle, had been involved with a plan to place a faked Nostradamus quatrain in the hands of the Deputy Führer. It was one of the little nuggets of information that grew in my mind and then formed the overarching plot of the Section W books, which climaxes in *The Final Act of Daphne Devine*. To do your own deep dive on this, you can access the museum's article here: https://museumofwitchcraftandmagic.co.uk/news/diamond-anniversary-of-a-daring-endeavour/

On my way north, I stopped to view the Nuremberg Trial Memorial. The trial was a feat of organisation and sober rationalism, remarkable if you consider the atrocities that had taken place. On display, at the memorial, is the evidence in the form of film footage which was shown to the jurors. It contains images which, once seen, are never forgotten. And while I think it is important to witness the barbarity, to remember the cruel, unhinged mindset of the persecutors and the consequences of their actions, I am not sure I can recommend viewing this material. Part of me is forever changed. And darkened. It is utterly harrowing and depressing, a reminder of what can go so wrong in human evolution if intolerance and megalomania go unchecked. The phrase, loosely attributed to Edmund Burke, is worth underlining here: *'The only thing necessary for the triumph of evil is for good men to do nothing.'* I write this in April 2026 and it's as relevant now as it was back then.

Back to the trip. Not content with putting myself and my companions, Jools and Steph, through that, my next stop was Wewelsburg, the site of Himmler's notorious SS 'Ordensburg'.

In so many ways, it is a problematic place.

For a start, I was surprised to find the castle so very beautiful. That may jar some readers, but one must bear in mind that there has been a building on this site for over a millennium. The Nazis' association with the castle lasted less than eleven years. Its history does not begin, nor end, with them. Nor should it.

Today, most of the castle's rooms are arranged as a museum, charting the different incarnations of the build: as a hunting lodge, through the Middle Ages when it served the Prince-Bishopric of Paderborn, and the later Romantic period. There are also displays featuring Ice Age artefacts from the region. All of this sits uneasily with the knowledge most visitors bring with them: that Himmler intended this place to become the spiritual centre of a new world.

He rented the castle in 1934, establishing it as a school for the SS elite and an impressive venue for gatherings of senior SS leaders. The North Tower is the only relic of this brief and brutal era. It was reconstructed using the forced labour of inmates from its satellite concentration camp, Niederhagen (known until October 1941 as Wewelsburg Concentration Camp). The prisoners were largely Jehovah's Witnesses, but also included political dissidents, Sinti and Romani people, homosexuals, Jews, prisoners of war, and forced labourers from Poland, Belgium, the Soviet Union, Czechoslovakia, France and the Netherlands. Almost a third did not survive their time there. Official records list 1,285 deaths.

One of them was Jelena Kekacina, born in Siberia. Her mother died when she was five and she grew up in extreme poverty. After her father's death, in 1938, she travelled to Ukraine in the hope of finding a better life, only to be forced into labour. She was sent to work for a company in Paderborn, nine miles north-east of Wewelsburg. There she was sexually assaulted by her German employer. When she resisted him, she was arrested and imprisoned in the concentration camp. On 8 March 1943, she was executed by hanging for 'insubordination'. Her story is one of many that powerfully confronts visitors in the Wewelsburg Memorial Museum's permanent exhibition, *Ideology and Terror of the SS*. You must pass through it to reach the North Tower. It's a clever strategy. Though, once again, the material is difficult to handle and rams home the utter contempt the Nazis held for non-Aryan humanity. You cannot help but feel it weigh you down when you come out into the moat and see the North Tower looming ahead.

The circular building is so dark and, quite frankly – quite *obviously* – sinister. Its rounded spaces are designed to make you feel small and anxious, contained and coerced. Especially the crypt, which Daphne describes. Every single person I saw walk through the arched entrance gasped and stopped when they stepped foot inside that place. It is like a punch to the gut, its air layered with so many different kinds of horror. The atmosphere lingers in your brain, a most unwelcome presence that follows you around long after you leave the castle's grounds. There are no statues, but a series of paintings. These are reconstructions of *Memorial Cycle* by Josef Glahé, which depict the human suffering of war and the holocaust. Hard to look at. But, like the Nuremberg evidence, I felt that I had to.

On the second storey, the Obergruppenführersaal, a mosaiced runic sun wheel dominates the floor. Laid in the early 1940s, the symbol was co-opted in the 1990s by extreme right-wing neo-Nazi groups, who gave it the name the 'Black Sun'. To avoid any 'celebration' or 'romanticising' of the thing, while there you are closely monitored. In fact, all visitors to the North Tower are forbidden to take photographs and prohibited from wearing symbols or clothing associated with far-right groups or racist slogans. Which is absolutely fair enough. The hall now forms part of a youth hostel that runs along the top of the castle (yes, you can stay there). When I visited, neon orange and grey bean bags were scattered across the design, a somewhat incongruous sight. Cognitive dissonance peaked when we took a breather to 'decompress' half an hour later in the café: the castle was hosting a family day, and while we sat in the sunshine, drinking coffee on the terrace of the former SS guardhouse, we could hear birdsong and children laughing. Part of you wonders how this can be, on a site so steeped in blood. But I refer you back to the long history of the place: the German people do not have the capacity to linger on that terrible chapter forever. They have acknowledged it, but move forward, never forgetting, always aware.

A question I'm often asked is did Himmler conduct occult rituals here? The truth is we don't know and probably never will. The tower was never completed and on 31 March 1945, as Allied forces drew close, Himmler ordered the SS to demolish the castle, covering his crimes. They blew up most of the east wing. Locals looted the site and discovered the furniture, tapestries and cutlery, which are displayed in the museum – and some 40,000 bottles of fine wine stored in the cellar of the southwest tower (while the rest of the country was strictly rationed). On 2 April, the U.S. 3rd Armored Division and the U.S. 83rd Infantry Division entered the village and liberated the remaining forty-two prisoners of the camp. They found the castle abandoned and its archives and relevant paperwork destroyed.

With those records gone, huge gaps remain in our understanding of what took place there. Perhaps that is a good thing. Though nature fills a void, as they say, and the absence of hard facts combined with the odd, mythological and theatrical architecture of the place has inevitably given rise to speculation and sensational theories. I'm aware I do not do anything to dispel them in this book, though I wrestled with that decision. But if you visit, you'll see that, despite the projection of fantasies onto the space, the North Tower is essentially a monument to failure, grandiose delusion and the capacity of men to inflict harm.

I returned to Wewelsburg a year later, to check the flow of the River Alme and find out in which direction Daphne's body would have been carried along by the current. Quite a way to go to, essentially, play Pooh sticks, but I also wanted to pace out the Hexenkeller and dungeons and re-examine the strappado there. It felt easier to explain my studies on the Essex witch hunts to the staff, rather than my current work in progress. I've never had that experience before. Very kindly the lady at the ticket desk (thank you) let me in at a reduced rate as I had no wish to revisit the rest of the castle, and definitely not the crypt or the hall. Believe me, you only need to see the latter once.

After Wewelsburg we travelled on, to the former convent of Our Lady of Namur in Saint-Hubert. They did in fact have a Sister Superior, for those wondering. It is now part of a senior school and, as it was the summer holidays, I couldn't gain access. However, much of the information about the part that the sisters played in the Belgian resistance effort I gleaned from the book *What Did You Do in the War Sister? Sisters of the Resistance* by Dennis J. Turner. A+ recommended.

Daphne spends time in this convent and then is transported to Brussels in a coffin. And so I went there too, but in a comfortable hire car – there are some aspects of research that even the most dedicated writer declines to undertake. On a grey June morning in the leafy Ixelles district, full of Art Nouveau architecture and cafés, Olivier d'Olne opened up the headquarters of the Fraternelle des Agents Parachutistes for me. I wanted to discuss Andrée de Jongh, upon whom Didi is based.

I spent over four hours chatting with Olivier, a most generous and erudite gentleman. Much of what Didi tells Daphne is drawn from that conversation – proof if it were ever needed – that some of the best research happens over sustained, thoughtful talk. His contribution is addressed in more detail in the acknowledgements.

Andrée was, indeed, an incredible woman who started what became known as the Comet Line evader route in June 1941. I'm still gobsmacked by the fact that she was only twenty-three years old at the time. A nurse, she was inspired by Edith Cavell, who also lived in Brussels, not far from the Fraternelle HQ.

On her first trip, Andrée took the serviceman Private James Cromar of the 1st Gordon Highlanders, a Scotsman, and two Belgian officers who wanted to fight for the British, Robert Merchiers and Ernest Sterckmans, with her on that epic journey.

My partner Jools and I therefore followed their footsteps. To be honest, I could have filled an entire book about the Comet Line – so daring and exciting – but that was not what I was commissioned to do, so that part of the novel has been condensed.

The evaders did indeed journey down the west coast of France to Bayonne. The station is still there and fairly unchanged since Andrée's day. In fact, the men's toilets are in the same place, so you can get a sense of how 'Operation Water Closet' was executed, though I realise many may not wish to hang about there. Then it was on to Anglet on bicycle. There, we tried to find a memorial to the Comet Line which Olivier had mentioned. Round and round we went in the rain rather fruitlessly, looking quite lost and bedraggled, until a woman called Edith took pity on us and led us to a sculpture and plaque in the centre of Anglet. They commemorate the sacrifice of the local women and men and their various resistance networks. Edith was also able to direct us to Villa Voisin, the home of Elvire de Greef and her husband, Fernand, and their children who hid, sheltered, fed and evacuated the evaders. On its plot now stand flats, but another plaque reads: 'De 1941 à 1944 cette demeure – ex-villa "voisin" – fut le centre vital du reseau Comete Sud.' *From 1941 to 1944 this residence – formerly Villa 'Neighbour' – was the vital centre of the Comet Sud network.*

From the villa the evaders went south to Saint Jean de Luz, then to the farmhouse of Francia Usandizaga in Urrugne, after which they would cross the Pyrenees, wading through the River Bidasoa. I can attest to the fact the water is cold, though when I was there, not terribly fast. But it was summer and hot and global warming has shrunk its berth. However, you could see it had the potential to be treacherous. And, in fact, I later learnt that in 1943 an American pilot, James Burch, and a Belgian Comet leader, Count Antoine de Ursel, were tragically drowned while trying to cross it.

On the first attempt, Andrée's guide deserted them at Guipúzcoa, in Spain. The group were forced to stay in a flea-infested farm hut till a new guide appeared and took them to San Sebastian. We avoided the hut but spent a very pleasant couple of days in that lovely city and on its shell-shaped beach before leaving for Bilbao. When Andrée and her group finally arrived at the British consulate in the busy metropolis, she was indeed treated with scepticism. In fact, after she had delivered the men, she was kept waiting for so many days that, in the end, she left and returned to France.

It was only after her third trip to Bilbao, on the 16th of October with two British servicemen, Robert Conville and Alan Cown, that she was finally taken seriously and met by a British diplomat, Michael Creswell. He decided to reimburse the expenses she incurred, which were many. People had to be paid: the guides who took agents and allies through the Pyrenees had to feed their families and this was very dangerous work. Andrée agreed, but asserted that the money would be paid back after the war.

In February 1942, the Comet Line had to change. The British took Morrocco and Algeria from the French, who did not put up much resistance. By way of reprisal the Germans occupied Vichy France, so it became much harder to move through that area. The route altered and the final destination became Gibraltar.

Andrée was in fact arrested by the Gestapo less than a year later at Francia's farmhouse in Urrugne, together with three British airmen. Francia and Andrée were sent to Ravensbrück concentration camp. Francia died on 12 April 1945, during a beating by a Nazi guard. Andrée was liberated by the Red Cross a few weeks later.

Those who worked on the Comet Line were responsible for returning to England more than eight hundred men. But they paid the price: over 60 per cent of Comet helpers were captured and sent to concentration camps from which they never returned. Many were executed or died due to torture, starvation or were beaten to death.

And what of Andrée? Despite her experiences in Ravensbrück, which led to permanent health problems, after the war and for the rest of her working life, she nursed lepers in the Belgian Congo, Cameroon, Addis Ababa, Ethiopia and finally in Senegal.

This remarkable woman died on the 13th of October 2007, aged 90. This book is dedicated to her and her co-workers.

Andrée de Jongh's name deserves to be remembered and celebrated far more widely in Britain than it is today. If you get the opportunity, please tell people what she did. For her courage and compassion remain an enduring inspiration. No wonder Daphne loved her so.

ACKNOWLEDGEMENTS

When I do my talks (and I do LOTS, with slides and films about my research, so catch me if you can), I'm often asked why I write about the subjects that you read about in my books. After all, the witch hunts, the Nazi's obsession with the occult – they are all so dark, right? Well, part of me, I suppose, is deeply troubled by these moments of historical trauma. I can't understand them, so I bend my gaze to try and untie the knots, work out why, who, how. And then tell other people about my findings so they don't have to go there. But also, more than that, there is an impulse, almost urgent, that compels me. My friend, Paddy Magrane, wrote a very moving article about his travels with his father to honour the experiences of his grandfather, Mick Magrane, an officer in the 1st/6th Battalion of the South Staffordshire Regiment (part of the British Expeditionary Force). He fought in the First World War at the Somme, Loos, Ypres, Neuville St Vaast and Cambrai, lost an eye, damaged his leg and took a bullet to the chest (which was prevented from mortally wounding him by his cigarette case – yes, think of Daphne's gold pen). In his article, Paddy talks about visiting the Menin Gate and the pain-staking recreation of it. 'The rebuilding is a magnificent achievement,' he wrote, 'and seems as much about the restoration of beauty as the importance of history – of remembering.' And I think that says it all. We must not forget the atrocities, nor the sacrifices made for freedom, and commemorate them, in whichever form this takes, so we mark down an X, a 'No', a line in the sand that cannot ever be crossed again. War, as we all know well, is not consigned to the past. Thank you, Paddy, for summing it up so well.

Samuel Pauwels is an archivist for the municipality of Anderlecht, Brussels, and manages the archives of the three municipal museums. His main interest lies with the Museum of Resistance (Musée des Résistances), which was closed for refurbishment when I conducted my research trip. Samuel really went over and above the call of duty (pun intended), pointing me in the direction of the Fraternelle des Agents Parachutistes. In addition, he helped me locate the convent where the resistance activities were carried out by nuns in Saint-Hubert, and he also translated my emails.

It was Samuel who put me in touch with the most generous Olivier d'Olne who welcomed me into the Fraternelle des Agents Parachutistes premises. Established to honour Belgian agents, it was also committed to supporting the families and loved ones of those who made the ultimate sacrifice.

Olivier's link came through his grandfather, Jean Verheyleweghen, who was active in the Belgian Resistance and one of the founders of the Fraternelle. He fought at the Belgian army's last stand on the 25th and 26th of May 1940 at the Lys River in France, which Didi mentions. As history tells us, he, along with his fellow soldiers, were defeated and captured. One of my evaders, Bob, has a story which resembles Jean's. The Germans did indeed march all the captured troops across the land to prisoner-of-war camps by foot. However, in the chaos of people fleeing or trying to return to their homes, Jean took a chance when his guard was looking the other way and rolled into a ditch to escape. He was fluent in French and Flemish, managed to change his clothes and make his way back to Brussels. Working for a Brussels museum, Jean was permitted to travel to and from Paris to look at items of interest for the collection. Under this guise he smuggled microfiche and messages out of Belgium to the British.

Olivier was a passionate speaker. He told me a great deal about the wider Belgian resistance. How the early members helped the British by sending intelligence about strategic bases – where they were sited, square footage, how they were protected, and produced the clandestine newspapers which encouraged defiance in the population (and my nuns). He taught me the difference between military escape routes and civilian, or amateur ones, how most people involved didn't know who their contacts were, how it was safer that way, how they left messages under a stone in a pre-ordained building or wall, how it was easier to hide evaders in cities rather than villages. Later in the war, he explained, resisters did move into sabotage, though it was mostly economic and financial. They tried not to get involved with attacking the military, because the reprisals were so fearsome: for every soldier killed, ten civilians would be executed.

By the end of the war, three hundred and thirty Belgians had used the Comet Line to get out to Britain, where they were trained and then parachuted back into Belgium. Half of them were arrested, tortured and sent to concentration camps. One hundred and twenty were executed by firing squad, by the guillotine or, in parts of Bavaria, beheaded by axe.

Olivier also talked with great respect about the important role of the British. Winston Churchill, he stated while we talked in a large room named after him, embodied the spirit of resistance. 'Without him,' he said, as I my eyes filled, 'we would not have freedom today.'

I found I shared with Olivier a commitment to the important act of remembering. We both agreed that one day soon all those involved in the war will be dead, leaving our memories as the only *living* trace.

To say I am hugely indebted to this excellent human being is an understatement.

I learned so much from the people I met, the sites that I went to and the museums I explored. But of course, there are many books I consulted too. *The Comet Escape Line* by Alexander Stilwell was one of these, as was Airey Neave's *Little Cyclone – The Girl Who Started the Comet Line*. Neave himself was the London contact in MI9 for the Pat O'Leary line, a later evader route. He managed to escape from Stalag XX-A in Poland, a German prisoner-of-war camp, but was found, recaptured and then imprisoned again in Colditz. Miraculously, he was able to escape from that infamous high-security prison too. When he met Andrée he was charmed by her and determined to give her as much help as possible. After the war he wrote his book about her and became an MP. He was assassinated on 30 March 1979 by an IRA car bomb at the House of Commons.

The Last Secret Agent by Pippa Latour is a splendid account of this female agent's life and sheds light on the training and operations of a SOE. I mentioned Pippa to Olivier at the Fraternelle and he knew her! She was a friend of a friend.

In 2025 I delivered a talk for Suffolk Libraries in Ipswich about my research into the first book in this series, *The Grand Illusion*. I also mentioned my trip to Castle Wewelsburg and described the crypt and its strange circular pit, the function of which nobody seemed to know. The museum staff at Wewelsburg had told me it had never been used. Though others I met on that trip asserted it was to burn an eternal flame. A man in the audience, who I was later to find out was Martin Willmott, put his hand up and told me he knew what was there. He and his wife Charlotte had read about it in a Bernie Gunther book. I tracked down that novel, written by Philip Kerr, *Pale Criminal*. In it, Bernie goes to Wewelsburg and enters the ritual chamber where he finds a sacrificial altar. Who knows whether or not this is true. I'm sure Philip Kerr would have researched it, and knowing what I do now about Himmler, about the castle and about the crypt, I wouldn't be surprised if it was.

Without Sandra Sawicka's skilful sleight of hand, Wayne Brookes' canny eye, Francine Brody's efficient copy-editing and the magic the whole crew at Oneworld Publications work, this book would not have seen the light of day. It's not easy out there and I know I'm lucky to have such a proficient team backing me.

I was able to read Nola d'Enis's manuscript of *The Rapture*. A novel about a seventeenth-century witch hysteria, also known as the Loudun possessions. D'Enis's writing is profoundly haunting. Indeed, a single word lodged in my subconscious and manifested in my opening page. My thanks to Nola for such richly evocative language and permitting me to steal a pinch of it.

Propping me up, as I immerse myself in the dark side, are a solid army of cheerleaders: Jools, Riley, Dad, Pauline, Mum, Ernie, Josie, Jon, Samuel, Nat, William, Arthur, Richard, Jess, Obie, Kit, Joanne, Lee, Ronnie, Paris, Harry, Matt, John, Jess, Rye, Isla, Anais, Effie and Margaret. And that's just close family. Friends – you know who you are. Without such wonderful souls, the sun would not rise.

Though Ibiza Steph deserves a special mention as she's on the same level of 'weirdo' as me. This means if I say 'Himmler's nutsville SS occult castle' or 'necropants in North Iceland' she's like 'I'm there. Do you need me to research accommodation or anything?' Oh yes, Steph, I do. Always. Thank you, for doing all that you do. Ironically, despite our communal crazy, you keep me sane, my friend.

And finally, to my readers, so many of whom I have met over the years. I am indebted to your patience, encouragement, likes and for buying the books. You make it all mean something.

To all of you mentioned herein my deep, lasting and sincere gratitude.

Thank you.

© Josie Moore

SYD MOORE is best known for her Essex Witch Museum Mysteries. The series was shortlisted for the Good Reader Holmes and Watson Award in 2018 and 2019. Syd founded the Essex Girls' Liberation Front and successfully got the term 'Essex girl' removed from the Oxford dictionary in 2020. She is a consultant fellow of the Royal Literary Fund and works with them managing 'Reading Rounds' across the country in hospice settings.

She is lucky enough to live in the county of Essex.